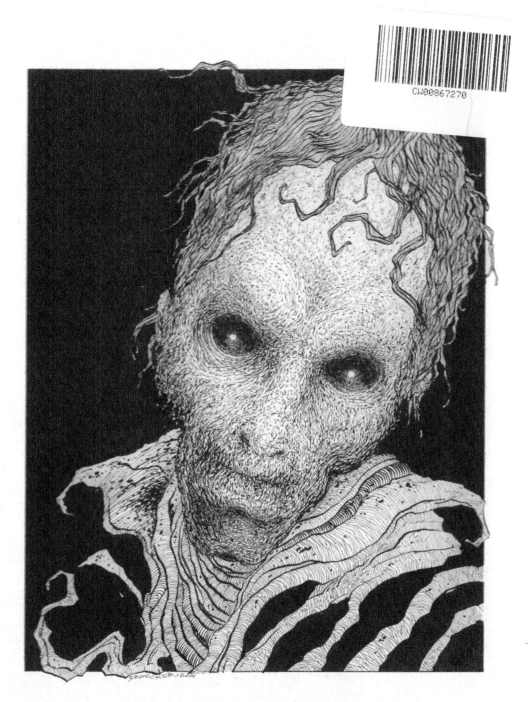

'Can Such Things Be?' by Randy Broecker

ISSUE 22, SPRING 2023

Front cover artwork: 'Vampyre' by Dave Carson

Cover and logo design: Adrian Baldwin, www.adrianbaldwin.info

Interior artwork: Jonny Boyle, Randy Broecker, Dave Carson, Stephen Clarke, Peter Coleborn, Allen Koszowski, Ivan McCann, Reggie Oliver, Jim Pitts, Andrew Smith and "The joey Zone"

Contributors: Leanne Azzabi, Stephen Bacon, Abdul-Qaadir Taariq Bakari-Muhammad, Adrian Baldwin, Tori Borne, William Bove, Dwayne Boyd, David Brilliance, Mike Chinn, Frank Coffman, Con Connolly, Kevin Demant, Lionel Fanthorpe, Patricia Fanthorpe, Kate Farrell, Paul Finch, John Gilbert, Christopher Gray, Noel K. Hannan, Craig Herbertson, Dave Jeffery, Carl R. Jennings, Eugene Johnson, Mark Howard Jones, Marc Damian Lawler, Graham Masterton, Karolina Mogielska, Paul Moore, Paul Mudie, Thana Niveau, Reggie Oliver, Barnaby Page, Evangelia Papanikou, Butch Patrick, Marion Pitman, John Llewellyn Probert, Owen Quinn, David A. Riley, C.M. Saunders, Neal Sayatovich, Helen Scott, Jessica Stevens, Josh Strnad, David A. Sutton, Anna Taborska, David L. Tamarin, Paul Tremblay, Allison Weir, David Williamson, Ciaran Woods and Phil Young

If you would like to contact us at *Phantasmagoria* with feedback or submissions we are available through the following:

Website: www.phantasmagoriamag.co.uk
Email: tkboss@hotmail.com
Facebook: www.facebook.com/PhantasmagoriaMagazine
Twitter: twitter.com/TKBossPhantasm
Instagram: www.instagram.com/tk_pulp_phantasmagoria

***Phantasmagoria* is also featured on the following websites/links**:
www.davejefferyauthor.com/general-4
adrianbaldwin.info/phantasmagoria

Back issues are also available to purchase from
www.phantasmagoriamag.co.uk, Amazon, Forbidden Planet International Belfast, Forbidden Planet Megastore London, Coffee & Heroes (Belfast), **The Secret Bookshelf** (Carrickfergus) and **DMR Books** (dmrbooks.com)

'H.P. Lovecraft's The Outsider' by Jim Pitts

CONTENTS

PHANTASMAGORIA FICTION:

Phantasmagoria

HORROR, FANTASY & SCI-FI

EDITORIAL NOTES

INTRODUCING OUR NEW WEBSITE

AFTER MANY YEARS of planning it but, and on a personal level, never really having the time, or – to be completely honest – the proper technical know-how to create one, we've only gone a set ourselves up with a snazzy – and rather professional-looking – new website, www.PhantasmagoriaMag.co.uk!

A massive thank you and respect to Adrian Baldwin for doing such a super job in designing it for us!

It's still a work in progress but, at time of writing anyway, we should have completed the set-up of the reviews and fiction pages, alongside the Online Store and VIP Lounge. From the Online Store you can order all of our issues and spin-off books directly with certain discounts and special offers available, such as the deal we have for the recent *Fantasy Tales Special*, where if you order a copy from the website you will also receive a complimentary issue of one of the original *Fantasy Tales* editions, signed by Stephen Jones, no less! Go check it out for yourselves today!

I think it's fair to say that social media has now basically taken over the world – for good and bad – as one of the main ways in which people communicate with each other, although I think it is also important to have an online "base" in the form of a website and we most definitely plan to make it a fun and interesting one and very much an extension of the main publication.

Speaking of the "main publication", welcome to our first issue of 2023! We've got another exciting one lined up for you in the form of some fascinating interviews, exclusive fiction from Graham Masterton and Karolina Mogielska (also our headline interview!) and Lionel and Patricia Fanthorpe, a multi-author tribute to the late writer and editor Charles Black, plus the usual fine array of articles, reviews, artwork and more!

Although springtime is already upon us (Where does the time go?!), I'd like to also take the opportunity to wish you all a great 2023 (or at very least what is remaining of it) and thank you for your continued support and friendship – together let's keep bigging up and critically examining our genre at every given opportunity.

So, here's to you, here's to horror (and fantasy and sci-fi) – and here's to the future!

—Trevor Kennedy,
Belfast, Northern Ireland,
March, 2023

'Spawn of Cthulhu' by Dave Carson

Illustration by Andrew Smith

POLISH MYTHS AND LEGENDS WITH GRAHAM MASTERTON AND KAROLINA MOGIELSKA

Interview by Trevor Kennedy

Graham Masterton and Karolina Mogielska

Trevor Kennedy chats with multi-award winning, best-selling author
Graham Masterton** and **Karolina Mogielska
about their latest works . . .

Trevor Kennedy: Graham and Karolina, it's great to be chatting! You have very kindly given us permission to print your brand new story, 'Mr. Nobody'. Could you tell us about this story's genesis please – how did it happen, what is it about exactly?

Graham Masterton: I've been interested in the subject of domestic abuse ever since my days as a junior reporter on the *Crawley Observer*. On my very first day I came across a wife who had been badly bullied by her husband and I saw how she was trapped in her situation and how little sympathy she received from her relatives and how little help she was given by social services.

Over the years I have met so many women who have been abused by their husbands or partners in different ways, varying from gaslighting to out-and-out beating. I had often thought of writing a book about it, but of course I have no professional qualifications and so I thought that it probably would not be taken seriously.

Then, through Facebook, I met Karolina, who turned out to be a qualified psychologist with considerable experience with abused women. Not only is she qualified, her English is immaculate, and so it occurred to me that we could write a book together partly based on her real case histories.

She sent me a number of genuine examples of men who had mistreated the women in their lives, and I saw then that a book would be possible, although it would probably be more acceptable as a novel, rather than a textbook. It could still contain advice and suggestions that would give hope to women who feel that they have no way out.

Both Karolina and I have been monstrously busy over the past year, so we have not been able to devote as much time as we would have liked to the book. I have been completing a new horror novel *What Hides in the Cellar* and Karolina works full-time for several orphanages and a kindergarten. But we decided we did have time for a "practice run" and write a short story together.

'Mr. Nobody' is based on the subject of domestic abuse, and how a wife who has been bullied and treated as a skivvy seeks to get revenge on her drunken husband. Karolina wrote the first draft, and included a powerful Polish goddess as a means by which the wife could get her own back.

TK: 'Mr. Nobody' features Polish folklore and mystical herbalism. Were these aspects of the story something that you had to research much and could give us some more details about them?

Karolina Mogielska: Yes, I cannot hide that those particular elements demanded a great deal of work, especially since I have been a long-lasting enthusiast of Graham's artistic output and I knew quite a lot about his writing style. After I had read his books I used to research on my own some of the matters he wrote about. I can still remember my growing amazement when I was reading the history about Salem based on real events and compared the information I found there with those in Graham's *The Pariah*. It is hard or impossible for many readers to check the information included in any story (even those false ones) or maybe they simply do not have the inclination to do it. However, it does not mean that a good writer should not do the research. To describe it to you in a better way would be that I can still remember the time when I met Graham in person. I was waiting in a medical centre for a vaccination and writing to him. At the time he was writing *The Soul Stealer* and he was reading about what kind of plants were growing in Hollywood, because he wanted to make the story more real, as he always does. I am a Polish woman, but I wrote a diploma paper on Disney's times and life, so I had that knowledge. If Graham had accidentally put into his novel some tree or plant that doesn't actually grow in California, I would have known it at once. It is extraordinarily pleasurable when you encounter some genuine fact in a story about nature or places, dates or people, titles of songs, especially when it is a horror story! They make the stories more real, even when their main elements are not!

The action of 'Mr. Nobody' takes place in Poland, in the lands of Świętokrzyskie Voivodeship, for whose spirit I have a great weakness for many reasons. Not only do I have my roots there, but I am captivated by the everlasting simplicity of many inhabitants and their rich base, not only the legends and history, but also real mysterious events and traditions. I'm sure that every Polish person knows that those lands are famous for the witches from the Bald Mountain. When Graham offered to write our first short story together and sent me a bare outline of the idea to develop it in Polish reality (making it easier for me, as a Polish woman, to animate the characters and their whole background), I knew straight away that I wanted to focus on the lands of Świętokrzyskie. But knowing Graham enough I was aware that I couldn't allow myself simply to focus on the witches.

And so I started to collect the information to find a smart connection between his bare outline with something niche and interesting that belonged to those lands, which I truly hope that I did. The fact that I managed to draw the master of horror's attention is a great honour for me. Fortunately Poland, as a Slavic country, has a rich tradition of herbs and their uses. We used to believe (and some of us still believe) that herbs have their magical attributes, as well as their medical or lethal applications. Thanks to God, I encountered such extracts on magical use of herbs in many books about them. Not mentioning the typical sources about Slavic mythology.

Unfortunately, for the sake of the story length, we had to make our descriptions shorter, but I hope that one day the story will appear in a longer version with all the descriptions of the various herbs and their uses! Not without reason was the length of time we were writing that story. Not only were we both busy during last year, but also the cultural and language differences essentially made the writing process longer. Even though I am an English philologist, it is not an easy task for me to reflect the atmosphere of the places known for me as a Polish woman (the cultural aspect, habits, characteristic objects you can encounter there, smells, way of speaking) to someone who lives in a completely different country. It demands a great deal of knowledge and experience, which, in my opinion, I have not gained enough of yet, but I try and have a fire to achieve that.

TK: I believe you are working on more stories and a collection related to Polish myths and legends. Can you tell us about these upcoming works of yours?

GM: Once we had completed 'Mr. Nobody', Karolina suggested other Polish mythological beings which could inspire short stories. I was very enthusiastic about it, since I have frequently delved into unusual myths and legends from different cultures, right from my first published horror novel *The Manitou*, about American Indian demons. There are so many unusual spirits and demons to be written about, I cannot imagine why so many writers stick in the rut with vampires, ghosts, zombies and werewolves.

KM: We have a plan about writing more stories like 'Mr. Nobody', I mean, such stories that are connected with Polish legends and mythology or history as well as the ones in which the plot is set in Poland. Inspired by Graham's Christmas story 'Anti-Claus' (and as a person who loves Christmas) I wanted to create together with Graham a story that will include the Christmas atmosphere. I must say, that it is not a story connected with Polish legends, but its plot takes place in Poland and, similarly to 'Mr. Nobody', it includes psychological elements. For me, it is also another field to practice myself, not only as a writer, but also as a translator and creator of ideas. Apart from that brand new story which we are writing now, we are going to visit Świętokrzyskie Voivodeship together to feel the spirit of those lands which will let us create more stories which take place there. I have made some contacts with people there who participated in collecting the legends of those lands, so their knowledge on the matter is enormous. Not mentioning the local old-aged inhabitants who are an invaluable source of stories to create, based partially on real events or at least containing some grain of truth. From my point of view, as a Polish woman and someone whose heart belongs there, it is also very essential for future generations to let those memories live forever.

TK: As Graham discussed, 'Mr. Nobody' also concerns domestic abuse, in fact you used to work in this field as a psychologist, Karolina. Obviously this is a very serious and harrowing subject. What was it like to write about it in the context of this story and how important do you feel it is for this subject to spoken about more in varying forms?

KM: That challenge is one of the hardest. Psychology is regarded as the profession of public trust and is one of the fastest ones leading to professional burnout. Of course, whether that phenomenon appears or not and how fast, depends on various factors such as the branch of psychology you deal with, your ability to use the techniques of managing with stress effectively, your ability to be assertive, and so on, including the individual sources of personality you have, your life and professional experiences and the quality of your self-esteem. As for me, I have been working with the victims of violence and with the perpetrators of violence, as well as the victims of other traumatic events such as various illnesses and accidents. I recreated some real case history stories in our story, and that was painful enough, but it helped the story to come alive. From my point of view, I wanted to emphasize the problem of domestic violence to help the victims in knowing that they are not alone and they have to fight with that (although not necessarily in the way that our main character does!) and that there are people around them to bring them the support. It is also the hidden message to those people – a kind of a tribute to them saying: "I remember not only the harm that you suffered, but most of all the dignity with which you bore it."

As a psychologist, I could not always bring help to the victims of domestic violence and I am afraid it is all about the failings of the system of supporting the victims not only in Poland, but also in other countries, including the UK, too. The story written by Graham and I is, in a way, a kind of "sword in the disguise of a pen" – it brings me a memory of the drawings created by *Charlie Hebdo* staff who put the hell of war in the form of "pencils and pens against swords and guns" – I mean that publicising the problem in every way available, is a kind of a guerrilla war against violence all over the world. And, we have to remember that not always can we say about the violence straight away. I can still remember one of the most vivid case studies where an old-aged mother called the police to say that her son was aggressive and constantly overused alcohol. The man fled so that policemen could not do anything practical at that moment. But after some time, the same woman reported that her son was threatening to kill her with an axe. It could have been too late, if we put into our mind the fact that the man was able to go so far in his madness. The woman did right – blowing her son's cover, but the failure of the system to help her the first time plunged her once again into the hell of violence. Of course, she could have run away – as many social workers suggest – but it is not easy to say to someone: "Pack yourself and go to the night-shelter. Your life is more important that all the things you have, including your house." I can also remember another picturesque example – I lent my friend a psychological book on toxic relationships titled *Psychopath Free* and, because of that she had an enormous argument and many problems at home with her husband who encountered the book, whereas it was only a book, nothing more. We are all free people, so we should be able to read what we want. As a human being I can tell that every manifestation of violence should be revealed, but the practical knowledge of the matter taught me that not everything is created in an ideal way and we always should be careful, and "slowly" win that "life-race" of being free and respected again. I mean that we should act, but sometimes in a judicious way.

TK: You mentioned that you guys are additionally also working on a novel together about domestic abuse. When should that be completed by and when can readers expect it?

GM: It should take about nine months to a year for us to finish it, since so much of it will be based on real cases of abuse. So we would estimate that readers will be able to expect it sometime in 2024.

TK: Could you tell us a little about how you write together – how does your collaborative process work and what sort of challenges do you face?

GM: The idea for 'Mr. Nobody' came up after several random conversations between us. Karolina told me she had a friend whose husband treated her like a nobody. I then wrote an outline based on the idea of a woman seeking revenge on her abusive husband. I passed it to Karolina who wrote a first draft of her idea of the story, including the Polish mythology.

KM: Despite the fact that I am an English philologist, in my opinion, I'm not experienced enough so far to be able to "think" in English. As a Polish woman I have never had any problems with the writing process in Polish. On the contrary, as a student I participated in many writing competitions and I even managed to win, but I have never thought that I could do it professionally here in Poland. And then, Graham crossed my life path.

Within just three weeks during our exchanging of very long emails, he offered to write something together that would include something in the psychological field. But it took months to make the final shape of our co-working. To try my skills and teach me some practice, Graham offered to write a short story together. So he made up the bare main idea of the story and sent it to me, asking me to put the plot in Polish. Developing his bare idea in Polish was quite easy for me, if I can say so, because I knew straight away what I wanted to write and how to do it, but after that, I faced the challenge of translating the parts I had written. Of course I could have found a trained translator, but I wanted to try myself to see whether I was able to catch Graham's attention by not only my writing skills, but also the ideas and abilities to animate the written fiction. I bet I have lost some of the the atmosphere I had created in the Polish version, but all that counted at that time was only Graham's feeling about my own writing and translation. And so it was like that – he wrote to me in English, then I translated it and added my part in Polish which next I translated and sent him back, and so on, and so on. It was a great multi-dimensional challenge for me, but I treated it as the equally great adventure and honour which endowed me with energy and thrill of emotion.

TK: Do you have any other future collaborative projects lined up?

GM: Yes, one which is already taking shape.

KM: I don't think Graham will mind if I reveal that our thrilling Christmas story is about the Icelandic creature Gryla, who is living evidence that: "All that glitters is not gold." I think I can also unveil another secret about that – once again, the action takes place in Poland. How and why – we both hope you will find out before long.

TK: You have another connection to Poland, Graham. What exactly is the Graham Masterton Written in Prison Award (Nagroda Grahama Mastertona W Więzieniu Pisane)?

GM: Seven years ago I was taken by Marcin Dymalski who organizes cultural events around the city of Wrocław in southern Poland to give a talk to the inmates of the high-security prison in Wołow. The inmates showed so much interest in books and reading that I suggested to Robert Kuchera the warden that we might run a short-story writing contest for them. It would give them the opportunity not only to be creative but also to express ideas which would be read by people outside the confines of their prison cells, and to some extent this might help with their rehabilitation. Robert was very keen on rehabilitation and so the contest was arranged, not only for Wołow Prison but for every other prison in Poland. We had the support of the Polish Prison Service and many other interested people, including the best-selling crime novelist Joanna Opiat-Bojarska.

We received well over 100 entries, and have done every year. Since I am unable to read Polish, Joanna picks out the twenty best and they are translated for me by Kasia Janusik. I then choose the winner and the nine runners-up. The winner is awarded a brass plaque and the runners-up receive certificates. They all win DVD players, which is about all they are allowed in their cells. I visit Wołow every year to present the prizes and tell Irish jokes to the prisoners.

TK: How did your recent novel, *The Children God Forgot*, come about and what inspired it?

GM: It was inspired more than anything else by the arguments over abortion. Of course every life is valuable, but what would happen if those children who had been aborted for various reasons were somehow able to survive? I know it's a very difficult subject, but I have never shied away from difficult subjects, because I think it is one of the important functions of horror fiction to face up to the unthinkable.

TK: Same question for another recent work of yours, Graham – your haunted house work, *The House of a Hundred Whispers*.

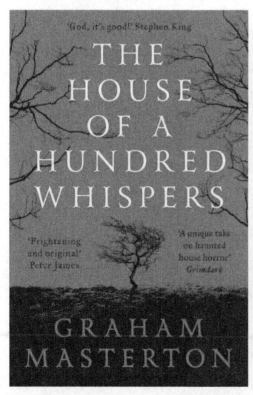 

GM: I was asked by my publishers to write a novel about a haunted house. I have written one ghost novel in the past, *Ghost Music*, about a composer who falls in love with a woman without realizing that she is dead, but I did not want to write about traditional ghosts again. Not the ones who wander about at night under a sheet going "*wooooo!*" So I choose a (real) spooky house, on Dartmoor, where the Hound of the Baskervilles used to roam, and I used the (real) history of priest holes where Catholic priests would hide during the Reformation in order to create a very different kind of spook.

TK: Graham and Karolina, it's been a pleasure to speak with you – thank you very much for taking the time out of your very busy schedule!

You can read Graham and Karolina's 'Mr. Nobody' in the fiction section of this issue, while Trevor Kennedy reviews Graham's brand new novel, The House at Phantom Park *in the reviews section . . .*

'Demon Skull' by Allen Koszowski

THE SANDMAN AND THE ARTFUL ADAPTATION

Tori Borne

Tom Sturridge plays the title role in The Sandman

*Tori Borne examines the recent Netflix adaptation of
Neil Gaiman's* The Sandman, *comparing it to the author's source material.*

"ADAPTATION" HAS BEEN quite the controversial word over the past year – we've been blessed with some incredible adaptations of fantastic works, and some rather . . . poor . . . ones too.

I've always found the art of adaptation rather intriguing. As someone who is into translation, I feel that both translation and adaptation are similar: both require you to make changes that adequately portray the source material whilst maintaining the nuance of the original.

When it comes to adaptation, though, there are many other things to consider – are you going to stay faithful to the source material or "make it your own"? How will you translate the written word (or pages from a comic) into an engaging piece of visual media whilst maintaining a seamless storyline?

It's no easy feat, that is for sure.

You also have to consider that there's no real consensus on what constitutes a "faithful" adaptation – every creative, and every fan, will have different interpretations and expect varying degrees of accuracy.

Personally, for me an adaptation is faithful so long as it embodies the spirit of the original source material. I can totally understand and appreciate when changes are made so long as they serve the story and actually build upon it.

This year we've seen quite a number of authors – and fans – voicing their opinions on adaptations, particularly those of the unfaithful kind.

George R. R. Martin (alongside Neil Gaiman), the author of *A Song of Ice and Fire*, stated during his conversation at the Symphony Space on October 27th, the following (via *Variety*):

"How faithful do you have to be? Some people don't feel that they have to be faithful at all. There's this phrase that goes around: 'I'm going to make it my own.' I hate that phrase. And I think Neil probably hates that phrase, too."

Both Martin and Gaiman made their stances on "illegitimate" changes quite clear, the latter explaining that he "spent 30 years watching people make 'Sandman' their own. And some of those people hadn't even read 'Sandman' to make it their own, they'd just flipped through a few comics or something."

Personally, I have to agree with both of the authors' sentiments. I can't speak as a published writer – my own fiction pieces so far remain for my eyes only – but I have had beloved works of others adapted and felt cheated by the finished product, to the point that I wondered, was there any part of the original in there at all?

A lot of adaptations feel more akin to reimaginings of, or loosely inspired by, the source material.

An example, though a little off-base compared to *The Sandman* and *A Song of Ice And Fire*, would be 2022's adaptation of the Jane Austen classic *Persuasion*. For years I had ached to see Austen's most personal and tentative work brought to the screen.

I longed to see Austen's insight into human nature and social persuasion explored with subtlety and nuance, and instead, was given an anachronism-filled romance comedy that has been described as Bridgerton-meets-Fleabag, but without the finesse or style of either.

A harsh review, I know, but my point is that this "adaptation" totally disregarded so much of the essence of the original work, in an attempt to create something . . . more appealing to a contemporary audience? Yet, the end result was a mess of a film that was so distorted from the original but offered nothing substantial by way of improvement to justify its changes.

Thankfully, on the complete opposite side of the scale, 2022 then blessed us with an absolute masterclass in adaptation, in my opinion, when Netflix's *The Sandman* TV series was released.

For those of you that are unfamiliar, *The Sandman* is a comic series written by Neil Gaiman, and was first serialised in 1989, published by DC Comics' Vertigo imprint.

The story follows the eponymous Sandman, otherwise known as Lord Morpheus, an anthropomorphic personification, and King, of "dreams", as he, to quote the author, "learns that one must change or die, and makes his decision" (Gaiman via Tumblr). Yes, I am being intentionally ambiguous.

I came into contact with *The Sandman* a little later than I care to admit. It wasn't until September 2022, when I got into a conversation with a vendor at Northern Ireland Comic Con, that I decided to pick up the comics.

My friends had been raving about the series since it premiered, but I'd been wanting to check out the comics for a while – but you know what it's like when you have a TBR pile so high that it puts Barad-Dûr to shame. I'd never gotten round to it.

But something changed that day. The lady I was speaking to gave it such a hearty recommendation, going as far as to call it Gaiman's Magnum Opus, his *masterwork*, that I felt I would have to be soulless to do anything less than read it myself.

And so, I bought myself the first collection of the comics, covering issues #1–20, and excitedly began the dream.

I became enthralled with the world that Gaiman had created; a modern mythology that felt so familiar yet new and exciting. I thought to myself that the series had some rather large boots to fill.

I'd seen the word "unadaptable" used to describe the comic series, and after reading it for myself, I can understand why. Immediately, the complexity of the cast of characters struck me. *The Sandman* refuses to clearly define characters as being purely good, or evil, and this fact became more apparent as the series progresses. In the first few issues we do see villains – Burgess, Doctor Destiny, who are for the most part, pretty irredeemable and text-book "evil".

As the series continues, though, this line becomes blurred. Character motivations are not so simple, and a character's nature not so clear cut.

Furthermore, the series also likes to jump around, not quite sticking to a purely linear approach to its storytelling. Whilst these things can – and very much do – work in a comic or literary medium, translating it to a cinematic experience can prove rather challenging (as seen with season 1 of Netflix's *The Witcher*).

And not to be too full of praise, but the comic series is intelligent and delightfully progressive, weaving intricate tales together – some minor and akin to a D&D one-shot, others major and unforgettable – and bound by elevated storytelling. It is, in my opinion, high-literature in graphic novel form. If it's not obvious by now, I really love this comic series, and had high expectations for the adaptation.

And I'm absolutely delighted to say that the series in fact *surpassed* my expectations.

The Sandman series has everything you could ask for, from a powerful cast to effective (and thoughtful) revisions whilst not only respecting the original source material, but actually building on it – minor characters feel fully realized and have more depth than their comic counterparts.

I went in having read the issues that season 1 would cover and was pleasantly surprised to see how attentive to detail the videographers were, with many frames from the comics being stunningly recreated in the series.

I also have to give them a massive commendation for the clever use of camera angles and lighting to recreate Morpheus' twinkling eyes in parts. It was little things like this that truly elevated the series for me.

The Casting and Characters

I was disheartened and a little shocked to see that the casting in the show had faced backlash online – though, I wasn't really *that* surprised given how toxic the internet can be – as I myself thought every single character was expertly cast.

Tom Sturridge brought the dark and dour Morpheus to life with the elevated elegance you would expect from an Endless Being, whilst still acing his, to borrow internet slang, "sad boy" tendencies? I actually saw some criticisms of his portrayal, with people saying he made Morpheus "too emo".

Morpheus. The Being that brought upon the Dreaming a biblical rain storm because his girlfriend left him.

I think Tom did just fine.

I also must say that the rest of the Endless were cast phenomenally too – whilst I don't feel like I've seen enough of Despair to say too much on them just yet, Mason Alexander Park was *made* for the role of Desire and I think they did an outstanding job bringing their antics to the screen.

Furthermore, Kirby Howell-Baptiste brought everyone's favourite goth, Death, to life (pun not intended but acknowledged) with the perfect mix of "older sister who will call you out on your bullshit" and "ethereal being who respects life and understands her purpose to serve it".

Fan-favourite Nightmare The Corinthian, I must say, was pulled from the comic. I don't know what kind of deal the casting directors made and to which entity in order to achieve this, but they nailed the casting of the character. I also thought that introducing him earlier in the story was a great move, especially with the charismatic Boyd Holbrook in the role – I worried he would have been devastatingly under-utilised if they introduced him in line with his comic appearance.

I could genuinely sit here and write about every character and how well they were cast in the series, but then this article would never end. So I'll close this off by saying – fantastic cast, everyone aced the roles, and I am excitedly awaiting to hear who will be the face of sweet Delirium. Please announce it soon, Neil.

Deviation from DC

There are some bigger changes that do stand out from the adaptation, such as the distancing of *The Sandman* universe with the DC Universe – all DC elements are either outright removed or altered enough to go unnoticed.

That meant adapting or outright replacing established characters like John Constantine with Johanna Constantine (played flawlessly by Jenna Coleman) and Doctor Destiny being simplified to "John Dee" (played by David Thewlis) rather than his supervillain alter-ego.

Personally, I think these changes work better for the mythos and the universe of the Sandman. And from reading the comics, so far, I can't see how the distancing from DC will prove detrimental to the series in any way. I read an interview where Neil Gaiman said himself that he feels the Sandman universe they built didn't quite "fit" with the world of superheroes and supervillains, and I would have to agree.

"Its world joined up more and more with our world and became less and less a world in which costumed crime fighters fly around and so on, which meant that by the time 'The Sandman' finished, it had its own aesthetic which really wasn't the DC Universe anymore." (Neil Gaiman to *Variety*.)

I definitely did not dislike these elements in the comics, but let's just say I didn't feel their absence when watching the show.

Jenna Coleman (right) as Johanna Constantine in The Sandman

Plot Changes

I won't sit and pretend that the show is perfect – nothing ever is, and opinions are subjective anyway. Although there are some changes that I did not love – *cough* justice for Gregory the Gargoyle *cough* – as a whole work I feel that this is an outstanding example of artful adaptation.

Changes felt thought-through and in-keeping with the original material, often being used to build upon the strong foundations of the comic to bolster the story for a fluid, cinematic experience with a hell of an emotional impact

This was evident right off-the-bat in episode one. The episode more or less follows the comic, except it expands upon the original and offers characters more depth. Roderick Burgess is humanised more in the show than his comic counterpart in that he wishes to capture Death in order to resurrect his son Randal who died in the war. In the comic, Roderick Burgess is no more than a power-hungry Magus who wants the glory of capturing Death. Whilst that may be true in the show too, he has far more empathic reasons by the introduction of his grief for his lost son. Don't get me wrong though, in both versions, he is a real bastard. The show just offers us a few more reasons as to how.

Burgess' living son, Alex, is also offered more characterisation in the show, with the viewers seeing his strained relationship with his father, who for no confirmed reason, does not seem to consider Alex a legitimate heir.

Furthermore, Alex's own dark intentions are explored more deeply in the series as he makes decisions and takes action in an attempt to win his father's approval – including killing Dream's raven, Jessamy. The biggest surprise comes when Alex, in a moment of frustration and pain, tells his father that he hates him, pushes him, and ultimately kills him.

When you consider how *The Sandman* is always questioning good and evil, intention and accident – the complexity of existence and subjectivity of experience – these changes felt very fitting in the philosophically charged work.

One episode where these ideas are further explored, and of which the comic is one of my favourites, is episode 5 – '24/7'. This episode was a wild ride, and beautifully recreated.

John Dee, harnessing the corrupt power of Dream's Ruby, takes refuge in a small diner, where he watches and studies the local patrons, sizing up their lives, and more importantly, their lies.

As John slowly – so very agonizingly slowly that the tension is palpable – removes the diner guests' ability to lie, harsh truths and dark secrets lead to them indulging in their most animalistic desires, culminating in a sensual bacchanal-like haze of sex. Whilst this unfolds around him, Dee merely watches television with ice-cream, barely interested in the chaos he has unleashed.

And then it gets dark. When confronted by the guests, Dee explains to them that the truth will set them free, but that they seem to prefer suffering. So he gives them suffering.

We witness a budding writer set fire to her most precious piece of work.

We witness characters seeking penance through hammering nails through the flesh of their hands.

We watch as characters mutilate themselves, over and over, all in the name of "truth".

And then they are all dead.

This, if I had to choose one specific episode of the show, is perhaps the episode that I was most impressed by, because it was horrific, utterly devastating, and perfectly encapsulated the brutality – both physical and philosophical – of the comic issue it was adapted from.

When Morpheus confronts Dee, they discuss the concept of lies. Morpheus tells Dee that the "lies" he has freed the diner guests from, are more than falsehoods they tell themselves and others to hide their shame.

Morpheus shows Dee that these lies are dreams, hopes, inspiration – aspects of humanity that are just as important as truth and honesty.

It is philosophically beautiful, and so perfectly executed by Sturridge and Thewlis. It may be sacrilegious to admit it, but I might actually be partial to the show's version of this story due to the complexity of John Dee and his motivations. In the comic, Doctor Destiny inflicts pain, chaos and insanity in order to become a king. In the show, we are treated to a far more dynamic interpretation of the character as he seeks to remove lies from humanity and create an honest world.

I found this revision of his motivations, and the resulting exchange between Dream and Dee, so captivating and loved the direction they took this episode.

I also found Thewlis' portrayal, and the characterisation, of John Dee much more interesting in the show – he was misguided and warped in his ideals of honesty, absolutely, and yes he was cruel.

But he was also passive, and weak, and a hell of a lot more terrifying for it.

If we are to discuss major plot changes, then I think that perhaps the biggest deviation from the comic comes from the adaptation of 'The Doll's House' (comic issues #9–16). This is the storyline that introduces Rose Walker as the vortex, and is the main storyline in which the Corinthian plays a role.

There are many differences in how this story plays out in the comic versus the show, but the outcome, and the impact, remain true.

Rose Walker has inherited the position as the vortex from her (great, in the series) grandmother, Unity Kincaid, whom she travels to England to meet. There are a number of differences in how this story plays out, most notably due to DC Characters such as Hector and Lyta Hall ("Silver Scarab" and "Fury"). Their inclusion in this arc is *a little* different than in the comics.

Hector and Lyta in the comics take up camp in Rose Walker's younger brother, Jed's, dreams, guided by two rogue nightmares that have, much like the Corinthian, fled the Dreaming to pursue their own ambitions.

In the show, however, Lyta is actually a friend of Rose's who has lost her husband, Hector, and mysteriously becomes pregnant with his child due to having a sexual relationship with him in her dreams. Lyta plays a bigger role in the show as she accompanies Rose on her quest to track down her younger brother and meet her mysterious great-grandmother (note: as the show changes the time when Morpheus escapes to "around 2019" instead of 1988, Unity is upgraded to Rose's great-grandmother in the series to facilitate this).

There's also another major change in the motivation behind the nightmare who enters Jed's dreams. In the comic, the two nightmares (named Brute, and Glob, appropriately) were attempting to create a Dreaming of their own to rule over, and Hector and Lyta were mainly tools to that effect in Jed's subconscious. Hector plays the role of the Sandman, and Jed aids him on his adventures against evil.

In the series, the nightmare (named Gault) has a very different reason for entering Jed's dreams. They don't want to be a nightmare and take issue with their existence as one, wanting to inspire dreamers and offer hope and happiness rather than fear and despair. In this adaptation, Gault appears as Jed's deceased mother, and Jed is the Sandman of his own dreams, a superhero in his own right. His dreams offer him a genuine safe-haven from the abuse that he is suffering in his waking hours.

I was, at first, a little puzzled by this change as it didn't immediately seem to have a reason. Changing Lyta's character and actions in the story made sense as they had to essentially introduce her as a totally new character whilst keeping the plot of her pregnancy intact. Changing the Nightmare's motivations to a more positive one, in which they question their own existence and purpose, however, was rather surprising.

But I loved this change. It again felt extremely fitting to the world of the Sandman and the questions the series asks. I also thought it was a clever way to offer Morpheus character growth in tandem with the Corinthian's storyline, as he now had to rethink his whole perception and purpose of nightmares, and even moreso, reconciling creation and function with self-determination and growth.

The heart and soul of the story remains intact, and it is evident that those working with the series have put great care into the crafting of it. I can only imagine the pride that Gaiman feels at seeing one of his most influential works adapted faithfully, as he always imagined it.

So, despite being "unadaptable", *The Sandman* comic now has potentially one of the best first seasons of a fantasy show, with hopefully, many more seasons to come. Aspects of the show that were seen to hinder its cinematic appeal – the kaleidoscope of stories and non-linear narrative, ambiguous characters and refusal to adhere to traditional forms of protagonist and antagonist – have been executed expertly, with very minimal changes needing to be made.

No artistic integrity had to be sacrificed in order to make this series work – all that was needed, it would seem, was for people to have faith, and hope, in the source material. And as Morpheus has shown us in the comic, and in the show, hope always prevails.

I am extremely excited to see that the series has been renewed for a second season, and I wait with bated breath to see how they manage to pull off 'Season of Mists' and 'A Game of You' (whilst also dancing with excitement at the thought of seeing 'A Midsummer Night's Dream'!)

It's going to be awesome.

Comic book covers for The Sandman *(artworks by Dave McKean)*

THE GOGMAGOG CIRCUS

GARRY KILWORTH

LET YOUR HINGED
JAW DO THE
TALKING

Tom Johnstone

Compiled by
STEPHEN JONES

THE ALCHEMY PRESS
BOOK OF THE DEAD 2022

A MISCELLANY OF MONSTERS

THE ALCHEMY PRESS BOOK OF
HORRORS 3
EDITED BY PETER COLEBORN & JAN EDWARDS

alchemypress.co.uk

'Eddie Munster' by Ivan McCann

MUNSTER MASH:
AN INTERVIEW WITH BUTCH PATRICK

Interview by David L. Tamarin

Butch Patrick through the years

BUTCH PATRICK IS a beloved figure in the entertainment industry, playing Eddie Munster on the much-loved 1960s television sitcom The Munsters, *recently released as a film by director Rob Zombie. Butch has also appeared in many other TV shows and films, along with other interesting hobbies such as drag racing and cruising the beach. He was also nice enough to speak to* Phantasmagoria *recently about life,* The Munsters, *and other things.*

—David L. Tamarin

David L. Tamarin: Mr. Patrick, thank you so much for speaking to us. Everyone here at *Phantasmagoria* is delighted and very excited about this interview. Although you began acting at age 7, when did you decide this is what you wanted to do with your life? Was this a conscious decision for you?

Butch Patrick: No, I never made a conscious decision to act. I don't think there are a whole lot of kids aged 7 years old who really know that either, it was just sort of happenstance, the circumstances presented themselves and it just occurred. I don't know too many kids who are tap-dancing their way down to Hollywood at 7.

DLT: That makes sense. So you started at age 7 and by 11 you were a Munster. How did you land the role of Edward Wolfgang Munster?

BP: Basically, they first offered it to Bill Mumy but he turned it down. At the time I was not living in Hollywood and I wasn't involved in the casting process at all. Then they did a pilot with a child actor named Happy Derman and when the networks saw the pilot they didn't like him and they didn't like the mom either, so they recast the kid Eddie, and as Phoebe was the wife's name they changed it to Lilly. My agent got them to fly me out from Illinois to do a screen test which I did with Yvonne (De Carlo) and they hired us both on the spot.

A young Butch Patrick on the set of The Munsters

DLT: After that, you worked for a number of years into your late-teens and then you decided to stop acting for a while. Why was that?

BP: Well, I was an 18-year-old kid and I had been doing it for like 12 years and I'd just finished *Lidsville* in the summer of 1971. I just had other interests so I wanted to surf and drag race and go to the beach and chase girls. It was 1971 so it was a good time to be out in the party scene

DLT: Sounds excellent. Did you get deep into the party scene?

BP: Only for 40 years!

DLT: I read that you have been clean since 2010. That's a lot of time – congratulations on getting clean! That must have been very difficult, it's an amazing accomplishment especially after partying for 40 years!

BP: It was quite a change but a good change. Thank you, I appreciate it very much.

DLT: What was it exactly that made you decide to stop using?

BP: I think everybody with an issue with it knows deep inside that they shouldn't be doing what they are doing, and when it finally surfaces and becomes the elephant in the room, so to speak, then you have to address it, and for me it just happened to take 41 years to address it. I kind of snuck up on it in the last 10 years before I got sober. I started to speak to my friends who had quit using, and asked their opinions, and just sort of tap-danced around but it took almost 10 years to pull the trigger.

DLT: *The Phantom Tollbooth* was one of my favorite books as a kid and it was also made into a movie starring you. How did you get involved in the production?

BP: There is a process – you have an agent, the studio gets the rights to do a project and then sends out a casting breakdown around Hollywood to each agency and it gives them a description of what they are looking for. The agents then go to their files and send over who they feel is the best qualified and the best evaluation for what the casting directors are looking for. Then you get submitted, like I did a lot and it was between me and another kid, Sheldon Collins, another child actor whom I worked with a lot, and who I knew. Chuck Jones ended up picking me and I was really happy to do it and really looking forward to it and to work with Chuck and all the voiceover people I knew he would be bringing into the project.

DLT: You have said that part of the reason you got the role of Eddie Munster was because you have your own fangs. Is that accurate?

BP: Yes.

DLT: How long was the make-up process to turn you into Eddie Munster?

BP: An hour, three days a week

DLT: And how long to remove it?

BP: Five minutes.

DLT: What was shooting like for *The Munsters* and how long did a day's shoot last? I know there are child labor laws that limit how much you can work, although I don't know if they were around at the time of filming *The Munsters*.

BP: Kids' shooting schedules have never wavered. It has always been a 9-hour day. What was different for me was that I lived an hour away so that added on extra time – the coming and going to Hollywood, which has nothing to do with the shoot time but it had to do with the extent of my day. An average day's schedule was an hour of make-up, three hours of school, an hour for lunch, an hour for recreation, and then an hour for filming.

Butch Patrick and Fred Gwynne in The Munsters

DLT: Are you friends with Brandon Cruz?

BP: Yes, he is a good friend of mine.

DLT: Are you a fan of his music at all, the punk band Dr. Know? I know you do music and Brandon is another former child actor just as much known for his punk rock music as his acting.

BP: Yeah, I'm not really into the punk rock scene, that's Brandon's stuff. No, we never performed – we were just a studio band that made a video for MTV. That was the extent of that. Brandon is actually very talented and has toured the world with his acts.

DLT: Tell me about *Lidsville*. I remember seeing it at a young age and what I remember most was how surreal it was.

BP: Same principle. The breakdown went out to my agent and she called me up and said they were looking for someone to play this character. Sid and Marty Krofft just did *H.R. Pufnstuf* and I wasn't that familiar with their work but I went out for the interview and I noticed a picture of Caroline Ellis there and I thought, Caroline Ellis, she's really cute and if I get this job I'll have the chance to meet her! That was a summer shoot of just 11 weeks. I had just finished high school and so I was like, okay, let's do it and I worked with a lot of little people that I was friends with, so that's how that came about.

DLT: Some people say that the *Batman* series was part of the reason *The Munsters* only lasted two years, and that the reason *Batman* was more popular was because it was so wild and colorful, whereas *The Munsters* was filmed in black and white and they could have shot it in color for not much more than it already cost. Did you think that was a mistake to film in black and white?

BP: No. Everything worked out really well for everyone. *Batman* came on and it was the first TV show in color, and yes, we were in black and white, but we wouldn't have done well in color. We were set up as a genre for black and white. Fred and Al were from New York and were ready to go home. It just worked out well for everybody and we wound up doing *Munster, Go Home!* in color. So we left with a feature film and the series to do syndication packaging.

DLT: You have a big following amongst the horror crowd. Are you personally a horror fan?

BP: Not new horror, I like the old classic Universal monsters and the sci-fi atomic 1950s movies. I like suspenseful thriller-type stuff. I'm not a fan of blood and guts and shock value gore.

DLT: Can you tell me more about the band you were in?

BP: Yes, I played bass. I didn't really play bass in the band because my producer was a really good bass player so we let him play it. I wrote the lyrics to 'Whatever Happened to Eddie?'. Our guitar player, who had a much better singing voice than myself, sang, and I just lip-synced it, so I was the original Munster Vanilli!

DLT: I noticed on *IMDB* that you have worked with guitarist John 5 in the past (John 5 is a renowned guitarist who played for Marilyn Manson and now plays for Rob Zombie)?

BP: I did a voice in his video, 'I Am John 5'.

DLT: John 5 is now part of Rob Zombie's band. Is that how you initially met Zombie, director of the new *Munsters* movie?

BP: No, I had met Rob before John 5, oh god, maybe 15 years ago. John and I just met at a convention, he was a big fan obviously and we're friends and Rob has been working on the licensing for the *The Munsters* movie for like the past 20 years. I went up to Rob's house last year with my Munsters Koach and drove him and Sheri around Connecticut and then he told me what was going on with *The Munsters* movie.

DLT: Is it true that *The MTV Basement Tapes* was started because of you and your band?

BP: I believe that was the case. We were the first unsigned act ever to be on MTV and I think they got the idea that, wow, there must be other bands out there that have a video camera and are making videos, wouldn't it be cool to air some of those unknown talent bands that have videos but don't have record deals because of payola? So yes, I do believe *The MTV Basement Tapes* was formed from our video.

DLT: Excellent. You got to hang out for a week with The Monkees and be on their show and I've always wanted to know what it would be like to hang out and act with them.

Butch Patrick and Mike Nesmith in The Monkees

BP: That was a good week! A very popular show, I was a fan of The Monkees and I missed meeting The Beatles a few years earlier when they came to *The Munsters* set, so this was kind of a payback.

DLT: You missed when The Beatles came out to *The Munsters* set?

BP: Yeah, I wasn't working that day. But working with The Monkees was excellent and I became friends with them for life and I saw them occasionally throughout the years and it was always a good thing.

DLT: You've mentioned cars and drag cars – is that your main interest? I know you have a lot of different interests – you have a coffee line for example. Are cars the main thing you are into now?

BP: No, I have my Munster Koach, I have my Dragula and I'm working right now with a place called Indiana Beach which is a medium-sized theme park above Indianapolis in a town called Monticello. I went through there last year for Halloween and really liked the place. It's a 96-year-old park that is geared towards a retro, nostalgia-driven crowd. I have a residency there through the summer and bring a lot of talent with me. They used to have a big ballroom. The Who played there, and Alice Cooper and the Beach Boys. Everybody who was anybody played at the Indiana Beach Ballroom in the 1940s, '50s, '60s and '70s. It's quite a famous place. I'm looking forward to setting up shop there again and doing special events and marketing and promotions for them. It's a 400-acre theme park.

Butch in his Munster Koach

DLT: Wow, that's a huge place. In *The Munsters*, when Beverly Owen left the show to be replaced by Pat Priest for the Marilyn Munster role, was there any friction or did it go smoothly?

BP: No, it went smoothly. The producers weren't happy; they didn't want to just let her go but she was homesick and miserable so Fred and Al told them to let her out of her contract or they would quit and then there wouldn't be a show at all. They went to her defence and they made sure she was allowed to go home and Pat Priest stepped in and did a great job.

DLT: Yeah, she was great. There are two main cars – there is Dragula, and the main Munster Koach. You have a replica of those cars?

BP: Yes, I have one of each and I also have a chopper as well. An Eddie Munster-inspired chopper.

DLT: No way! Really? I don't know if this is true, but I read that you were involved in a tattoo removal place?

BP: (Laughs) No. I gotta tell you, between *Wikipedia* and *IMDB* there is a lot of stuff flying out there. I had a tattoo put on my shoulder from Under My Skin in New Jersey. Tattoo Tony did a comedy/tragedy sobriety date. A friend of mine, Chris 51, had a show, *Epic Ink*, and me and Elvira went up to do an episode and he put another tattoo on me, and his ex-wife did have a company that did tattoo removal. I don't know how my name or association with the place ever came out. I did do some tattoo conventions but was never in the game as far as the business side of things. I had a line of Chris 51 tattoo ink which might have been the connection.

DLT: Is it true you lived in a haunted house?

BP: I bought my grandmother's house in Missouri that I owned for four years and sold two years ago.

DLT: What type of things happened that made you think it was haunted?

BP: We knew it was haunted from the day it was built in 1875. The guy that built the house was murdered and it was common knowledge that the house was built on a vortex and there was a lot of activity going on. I had security cameras switched on at night and they picked up ghosts down in the front door area, and there were noises. The ceiling upstairs collapsed once. I had professionals come in and spend the night and they always left with a bunch of footage for whatever show they were doing. They were happy because they got a lot of activity on their cameras.

DLT: Were you scared living in the house? Did you ever see any ghosts or anything?

BP: No, I never saw anything except on camera and orbs and noises – they kind of left me alone. I was living there only 2 months a year. The people who maintained the house for me were constantly barraged with noises and giggles and things like that.

DLT: Were you pleased with the film *Here Come the Munsters* from the 1990s where you had a cameo appearance?

BP: It was fun. It was nice to see everybody and there was a cameo by Edward Herrmann – he did a pretty good job of Herman Munster, the best yet of anybody.

DLT: I've seen him do it on YouTube – he does a really great job. Thanks for answering my questions. Do you have anything else you want to say to fans?

BP: *(Ed. As per time of interview in 2022)* I'm really excited about Indiana Beach this summer. I'm bringing my Munsters Koach, my Dragula, my chopper, my *Munsters* collection, as well as my friend's *Addams Family* collection and we're going to have a professional, Tom Devlin, who owns the Monster Museum in Boulder City, Nevada, coming in to max out the whole pavilion, so we are going to have a very interesting walk through and people will see what it's like to be on a sound stage of a *Munsters* studio and set in progress. I think they are going to enjoy that. You can go to www.munsters.com which is my website and that will lead you to the social medias like Twitter, Facebook and Instagram. You can also go to my store and see what we have to offer and can check out my schedule.

DLT: Thank you so much for everything!

BP: Thank you buddy, have a good one!

Butch Patrick, then and now

'Our Lady of Death' by Randy Broecker

AUDREY ROSE:
A FORGOTTEN "EVIL CHILD" FILM OF THE 1970s

Barnaby Page

Susan Swift in Audrey Rose *(1977)*

A look at the 1977 Robert Wise film, recently re-released on disc.

NOVELIST FRANK DE Felitta claimed it was his own young son's sudden, inexplicable fluency in piano-playing that led him to write *Audrey Rose*, his 1975 novel of reincarnation which became one of the last films directed by the great Robert Wise and one of the most unusual entries in the 1960s-'70s cycle of "evil child" movies. The son, Raymond, later suggested that his father might have exaggerated the piano incident – but De Felitta was, whatever the truth, clearly smitten by the idea that the human soul might persist after death. Although his previous career in fiction, film-making and TV had not been focused on the occult, with *Audrey Rose* he penned a bestseller and as well as writing the movie's screenplay he took a very active role as producer.

It's no surprise, then, that unlike most of the "evil child" films that had been popular since Roman Polanski's *Rosemary's Baby* (1968), *Audrey Rose* (1977) has the air of a plea for understanding. It's not just playing supernatural what-if to set up some pleasurable scares; the feeling is inescapable that De Felitta (even if not Wise) wants us to *really believe* in reincarnation. Critics at the time were unimpressed, and for good reason: not only do the disquisitions on rebirth sometimes get in the way of the drama, they also fail totally as arguments. *Audrey Rose* never tells us *why* we should accept reincarnation (a fictional tale is hardly persuasive evidence), just that we *should*; the only justification for the idea it produces is that some Asian religions subscribe to it, but again that doesn't even begin to approach proof.

This is not the only way in which *Audrey Rose* differs from the rest of the sub-genre into which it's usually slotted. Indeed, it's not really an "evil child" movie at all – the living girl Ivy may (in a sense) be possessed by the dead girl Audrey Rose, but neither is evil, and both are very much presented as innocent victims. Still, there are times when Wise seems to want to summon up the spirit of films like *The Exorcist* (1973) visually if not thematically, and there are certainly some common concepts too: the idea of the home as well as the child being invaded by something external, for example.

And, after all, there was not (and still isn't) a mainstream "reincarnation" sub-genre into which it could fit; although movies had occasionally explored the subject for decades (as fascinatingly discussed in Lee Gambin's segment on the Blu-ray extras of the film's latest disc release), serious treatments were scarce. *The Reincarnation of Peter Proud* (1975) was a rare recent example but had not been a great success, and light-hearted uses of the premise such as *On a Clear Day You Can See Forever* (1970) or the forthcoming *Heaven Can Wait* (1978) were more common.

Given its sheer oddity and the difficulty in easily classifying it – is it even horror? – perhaps it is inevitable that *Audrey Rose* remains somewhat overlooked today. But Wise, who had started out in the 1930s as an editor, worked on *Citizen Kane* (1941) and then directed 36 movies including *West Side Story* (1961) and *The Sound of Music* (1965) but not much horror, handles the strange script very skilfully, and the film benefits too from strong performances in the four main roles. It has an enduring interest for the philosophical questions it raises, too, bringing them right to the forefront more than most mainstream commercial productions do – even if it does not come close to satisfactorily answering them.

Audrey Rose opens in the mid-1960s with a car crash but soon jumps forward to 1976, where we meet 11-year-old Ivy Templeton (Susan Swift) and her parents Janice (Marsha Mason) and Bill (John Beck), an affluent Manhattan couple whose apparently enviable life is marred by their daughter's nightmares – which seem especially strong around her birthday. The Templetons are put on edge, too, by a strange man who appears to be following them and hanging around Ivy's school. Eventually he contacts them and identifies himself as Elliot Hoover (Anthony Hopkins); his own wife and daughter died some years ago, in what we now realise was the car crash depicted at the beginning, and after a long investigation he has come to the conclusion that Ivy – born at almost exactly the time of his daughter Audrey Rose's death – is her reincarnation.

Naturally, the Templetons are sceptical and even angry, though there are things they can't explain: Hoover seems to have obtained knowledge of their apartment from psychics, and during one of her nightmares, Ivy appears to somehow burn her hands on an ice-cold window. (This is one of relatively few occasions where the inexplicable – and possibly supernatural – is directly shown, rather than merely discussed or suspected, in *Audrey Rose*.) And gradually, despite the Templetons' resistance, Hoover achieves an entrée into their lives, particularly gaining leverage with Janice when he helps calm Ivy down from a particularly bad nightmare.

This, in turn, leads to increasing strain in the marriage ("he was here and you weren't", Janice says to Bill when he protests her having accepted Hoover's help), but the turning point of the movie comes when Hoover goes too far and is arrested. At this point *Audrey Rose* suddenly switches from being a psychological horror story to a courtroom drama, although the most important part of the court case actually takes place in a hospital. The abrupt change of mood does not work well, and the court scenes – in which Hoover's attorney must convince the jury to accept the reality of reincarnation, and thus Hoover's claim to parenthood – verge on the risible. At least to a layperson, nothing about it is legally or procedurally credible; for example a Hindu maharishi, played by the Pakistani actor Aly Wassil, is allowed to philosophise at great length from the witness stand, a transparent excuse for a lecture to the audience.

Marsha Mason and John Beck in Audrey Rose *(1977)*

Audrey Rose does return to its earlier, more unsettling tone toward the end, and indeed the climax in the hospital provides one of its most powerful scenes even if it does avoid explaining some details one might think important. (As at several points in the movie, Wise's editing background must have influenced his masterful direction here, cutting back and forth from character to character before eventually letting the camera rest meaningfully on a floor scattered with broken glass.)

Earlier on, there are genuinely frightening passages during Ivy's nightmares, with her uncontrollable crying and shrieking; and Wise, who despite his limited horror credentials has in recent years been retrospectively acclaimed for his direction of the Shirley Jackson adaptation *The Haunting* (1963), sometimes does craft scenes and individual shots in *Audrey Rose* in a frankly genre way. See, for example, the scene in the upstairs hallway of the Templetons' apartment where Ivy opens a door behind the family lawyer (Stephen Pearlman) and walks toward the oblivious man from her purple-glowing bedroom. It could easily come from any number of "evil child" exercises, as could the gargoyle on the building's exterior, while the sequence where Ivy and her classmates dance around a giant snowman melting in a bonfire has a distinctly *Wicker Man* air and seems rather pagan for a Catholic school.

Occasionally, perhaps, the film falters in striving for effect. In the snowman section, for example, why would Audrey-reincarnated-as-Ivy climb *toward* the fire, if she is reliving her death in the car crash where she tried to *escape* the flames? (And why, for that matter, is the snowman labelled "Sylvester XXIII"? Is it a production error and intended to be a reference to the antipope Sylvester III, or is it a Catholic in-joke that only a tiny fraction of the audience will get?)

But for the most part Wise's direction – unflashy, unhurried, concentrating on what's important – stays away from such gimmicks, and indeed many of the most successful parts of the film are those dealing with the family drama rather than the reincarnation itself. The stairs in the Templetons' apartment are frequently used as handy metaphors, with Janice and Bill walking together upstairs into darkness (the unknown lies ahead), or one standing at the top while the other is at the bottom (they disagree).

Complexity in the characters' relationships is not ignored: in one scene Bill's arm is around his pal the attorney, then he argues with his wife on the stairs, and then he holds *her*; it is clear that he is torn. He doesn't share her point of view on reincarnation or on Hoover, and his instincts push him toward the rational outside world, but he doesn't want to abandon the family either. She, more open-minded in the film's perspective but more gullible in his, has pondered the problem long herself, as illustrated by a shot of her working on a jigsaw puzzle.

Beck portrays Bill as a sensible, sociable, successful, slightly unimaginative man while Mason's Janice is much more openly emotional, but both actors avoid going too far: the mother is not too histrionic or the father too cold, and as a result the way that the relationship is severely shaken but not destroyed is completely plausible. Hopkins as Hoover, his nervous movements contrasting with Bill's comparative immobility, went on to be by far the biggest star of the three and his charismatic dominance of scenes is apparent throughout, although he also gives Hoover a cautious side – the character is well aware that what he is suggesting about the Templetons' daughter will seem outrageous – and indeed his ominous, silent first appearances in the background are every bit as effective as his major speeches.

As Ivy herself, Swift – who did little big-screen work afterwards – captures convincingly a child's mixed reactions to a confusing situation, sometimes accepting adult wisdom, sometimes speaking her own mind directly, and then overtaken by convulsions of fear during her nightmares. We see her looking in the mirror saying "Audrey Rose" over and over again, perhaps enticed by the idea of living forever; but she also tells her mother "I'm my own self and I'm not somebody else", unwittingly highlighting the thorny ontological points that the movie brings up. She has the perfect face for an "evil child", too, an advantage which Wise maximises by dwelling on photos of her.

Among the smaller roles, Ivy Jones as the other driver in the car crash which killed Audrey Rose and *her* mother makes an impactful appearance in the courtroom, while New York locations and Michael Small's uneasy score, with much use of the waterphone, add a great deal to *Audrey Rose*'s atmospheric and at times almost believable narrative.

Perhaps less is gained by the footage of Hindu ceremonies (presumably bought-in material, since the credits mention nothing about shooting in south Asia) or the final quotation from the *Bhagavad Gita*. The film's literal, face-value acceptance of reincarnation is undoubtedly a problem and it certainly comes too quickly. Although individual characters are allowed to doubt, it's as if the *audience* never is; and, lacking all intellectual rigour, *Audrey Rose* doesn't provide the answers that it seems to believe it does. Is the girl Ivy or Audrey Rose? Or somehow both? Are they the *same* girl, or does one "inhabit" the other? What does reincarnation actually *mean*?

Still, there is plenty that is thought-provoking and dramatically rich. Reincarnation itself is a double-edged sword, both reassuring and unsettling: it offers a promise of life after death, but at the expense of a clearly defined self. And it adds an extra element, too, to the inherent emotional impact of any story about the death of a child: it's difficult not to believe that whatever Hoover gains in rediscovering his daughter will be the Templetons' loss and vice-versa, and *Audrey Rose* is less about the offspring and more about the parents than many "evil child" movies.

Plus, of course, any reincarnation story is also a kind of ghost story. To that extent, *Audrey Rose* does have at least one foot in the horror camp, even if its premise is more extraordinary than horrifying. It might not satisfy those looking for rotating-head scares, and it certainly won't satisfy anyone expecting a thoughtful look at the concept of reincarnation, but as an attempt to blend a popular horror sub-genre with the mellower Eastern-influenced spirituality of the 1970s, it is an unforgettably peculiar movie – not least because such an unpromising script is so well directed and acted. There are some exceptionally good extras on the new Blu-ray release, too.

Poster for Audrey Rose *(1977)*

The final part of

DAVE JEFFERY'S

a Quiet Apocalypse Series

HEaR TODaY

"Tribunal is a powerful and emotional ending to a powerful series that explores all aspects of human nature during a catastrophe, from the best to the worst. I can't praise Tribunal enough."

– Sarah Deeming, review editor, The British Fantasy Society

"Supremely dark, intelligent and thought provoking."

– GBHBL Reviews

Paperback & Kindle

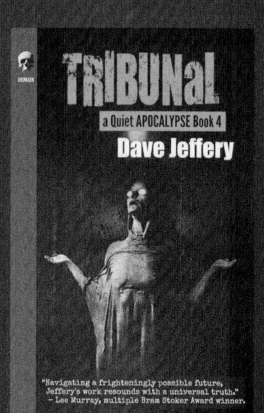

TRIBUNaL

a Quiet APOCALYPSE Book 4

Dave Jeffery

"Navigating a frighteningly possible future, Jeffery's work resounds with a universal truth."
– Lee Murray, multiple Bram Stoker Award winner.

DEMAIN PUBLISHING

Cover art by Roberto Segate / Design by Adrian Baldwin

A HEAD FULL OF PAUL TREMBLAY

Interview by Dave Jeffery

Paul Tremblay

With accolades from genre-giant Stephen King, and his books now courting Hollywood producers, Paul Tremblay is fast becoming one of horror's premier writers. His recent release The Pallbearers Club *is a new take on the concept of vampirism, and its narrative structure has a divided literary opinion of fans and critics alike. Here Paul talks about the book and some of the processes involved in developing his work.*

—Dave Jeffery

Dave Jeffery: Thank you for speaking to *Phantasmagoria*. I'm sure most of our readers are familiar with your work in the genre, but for those very few who are not, can you please tell us a little bit about yourself.

Paul Tremblay: Hi, my name is Paul. I like long walks on the beach. I've taught high school mathematics for a distressingly long time, and I write fiction. Mainly horror. Some of my novels include *A Head Full of Ghosts*, *The Cabin at the End of the World*, and most recently, *The Pallbearers Club*. I don't like pickles or coffee.

DJ: Both *A Head Full of Ghosts* and *Cabin at the End of the World* have been green lit for movie production. Was this something that you considered when originally writing your work?

PT: *A Head Full of Ghosts* is in development but they're not close to filming yet. *Cabin*, however, has already been filmed by M. Night Shyamalan, and the movie (*Knock at the Cabin*) is due to hit theatres in early February of 2023.

I've certainly daydreamed about one of my works being adapted for the screen, but it has always been a passive kind of daydreaming. Meaning, while writing the books, I never thought about film adaptation or what it would look like. I certainly don't write with a movie goal in mind. I write with the goal of making story "X" the best I think it can be in either the short or long fiction form, hopefully taking advantage of specific narrative opportunities those forms present. I guess what I'm saying is that a short story is a short story, and a novel is a novel, and neither are films or screenplays or treatments, nor should they be written that way.

DJ: Some of your works are known for the ambiguity of their endings, I'm thinking *Cabin at the End of the World* and *A Head Full of Ghosts* in particular. Is this something you consider when developing a project, or does it arise during the writing process? What is it about ambiguous endings that appeal to you as a writer?

PT: What we know and what we don't know make for great horror stories, or stories in general. I guess I'm somewhat (or a lot) obsessed with memory, identity, and reality being a lot more malleable and unknowable than we like to think they are. Most horror stories deal with death or the threat of it on some level, which mean those stories ultimately prod at life's final ambiguity; what happens when we die. We may believe we know what happens, but we really don't know, and that's an uncomfortable feeling/condition. Why not pick and poke at that as a horror writer? The thing I try to do when I employ ambiguity, is to make sure it's part and parcel of the theme of the story, of what's horrific about it, otherwise it would read like a cheap trick. (Not the band, who I enjoy). With *A Head Full of Ghosts*, my hope was that the most unsettling part of the story would be that we don't know and won't know what happened with Marjorie. In *Cabin*, I tried to build on that feeling with the added anxiety of not being in control of the situation while being offered the illusion of choice.

DJ: It could be said that your work explores the psychological impact of horrific incidents on the characters as opposed to being all-out horror. What is it about the human condition that fascinates you as a writer of genre fiction?

PT: "All-out horror" means something different to each reader, I think. Recently I had a conversation with Nadia Bulkin (Shirley Jackson Award nominee of *She Said Destroy* short story collection) about the difference between what she called aesthetic horror and the philosophy of horror (not a life/living philosophy, but the philosophy of a horror story). Lots of people who say they love horror, love the aesthetic. They like wearing black shirts with monsters and ghosts and they like their stories and movies with monsters and ghosts and body counts but they don't necessarily like when horror gets too grim/gritty/close to the bone/transgressive/real. All of which is fine. No moral or personal judgement here (mostly). The philosophy bit means (for me) that a horror story reveals (and maybe revels in) a terrible but essential truth and doesn't offer easy answers and happily-ever-after endings, which is not to say a horror story can't be optimistic (in fact I'd argue my ending to *Cabin* is optimistic). I'm probably not explaining myself very well, and for many of us there is no hard split. I enjoy both the aesthetic and philosophy of horror as described above. Monsters are cool and I own way too many t-shirts with monsters on them. So, I don't mean to fuss over word choice here, but I've been thinking about the horror genre question a lot lately and what it means and to whom. Work that "explores the psychological impact of horrific incidents on the characters" sounds like an all-out horror story to me, the kind that lifts my spirit precisely because it got stomped on first.

To link to the previous question, the human condition is fluid, is in flux, is in a constant ambiguous state as we interact with and are changed by evolving (or devolving) technology, the political state, the climate, etc. What we're capable of saying and doing, how we might answer existence's stickiest questions including "how do we live through this?" seems to me the perfect fodder for a horror story. When I come up with the horror "what-if" scenarios that eventually turn into my stories, the first questions I ask aren't plot-centred but are about the characters: Who are they? What will they decide to do? Can they live through it? The answers to those questions then drive the story and are usually (I hope) the source of horror.

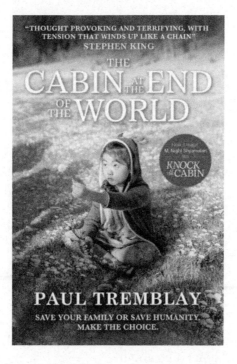

DJ: No doubt you've been asked before about your influences and inspirations in the genre, but what is it that inspires you to tell a particular tale over another?

What would be the driver for you to choose one idea to run with as opposed to an idea you would pretty much discard immediately?

PT: That's a great question and hard to answer. Typically, I don't have a lot of different story concepts to choose from, especially when we're talking novels. Once I finish a novel, I tend not to know what the next novel is going to be, and then I go on a mad and stressful search for the next book idea. That said, on the occasions I've had multiple concepts to choose from, the winning idea (or the idea that becomes a novel) is based on a concept that excites me more and I can more easily imagine the characters within that story. For example, the concept (and the title) for *The Pallbearers Club* fell into my lap and I was excited by the possibilities. However, if I didn't figure out who my main characters were, it would've remained a concept only. Concepts tend to be the new and shiny things to play with until either I'm not so excited or intrigued by them any more and I put it away in favour of the next new and shiny thing, or some characters finally show up, introduce themselves and they make the concept new and shiny all over again. In the case of *Pallbearers*, it wasn't until months later when I knew a little about who Art and Mercy were (or who they might be) that I fully committed to writing the book.

DJ*: You have also written detective-noir, is this a genre to which you plan to return? I mean, will there be another Detective Mark Genevich story?

PT: Never say never but I have no plans to. Maybe it would be fun to write a short story or novella with Mark, or something Mark adjacent.

DJ*: What is a typical day for Paul Tremblay, the writer?

PT: Well, I never used to have a typical day, particularly when I was teaching. On teaching days my day was teach, (depending on the time of year) coach, then come home, eat dinner, get an hour or so of writing in, reading, talk to the people and animal that live in my house, go to bed.

But for the next year or so I think my day will be: breakfast cereal with too much sugar. Dog walk. Writing/reading/maybe too much time spent on the Internet. Lunch. Back to the writing/reading/Internet bit. Exercises to keep my back from giving out. All of which takes me through late afternoon, and I'll wing the rest of the day/evening. Maybe I need to organize, make a planner or something.

DJ*: What would be your advice be to your younger self?

PT: Use face and eye cream and hand lotion. Drinking hot tea is a nice thing. Learn a second language. Tend to your back more often than you did. Writerly younger self? Be kind to yourself when necessary and when it's not.

DJ*: The Pallbearers Club is a slick and inventive coming-of-age story. How did the concept for this book come about?

PT: In November of 2019 I'd just finished copyedits on my novel *Survivor Song,* and I didn't know what I was going to write next. One Monday morning during one of our weekly all-school assemblies, I sat in the back row, not fully paying attention to the speeches and administrative announcements and such. Then a student went to the podium and announced he was starting a Pallbearers Club. Oh. He had my attention. Members would volunteer at funeral homes to serve elderly and homeless without any or many living relatives. I knew I had to use it somehow. Eventually I imagined my shy, awkward, teenage-self attempting to start this club back when I was in high school, which I never would've because I was too shy and awkward, and that conflict was the spark of the book. I knew it would be the found memoir of an alternate universe version of me, or the teen I keep huddled inside me. From there I discovered the story of Mercy Brown, which I won't detail here, but if you're curious, google the name. And viola, Art and Mercy, or Art versus Mercy, would carry the book.

DJ*: What are you working on at the moment?*

PT: I'm due to receive the edits for my next book any day now. It's a short story collection called *The Beast You Are.* It'll be out next summer. A good chunk of the stories are monster stories or feature characters doing monstrous things. It will include an original 30,000 word novella that is an anthropomorphic animal story featuring a giant monster and a slasher cat and written in free verse. Why? Because.

What I'm working on now is my next novel, due to my editor in May of 2024. I'm about a third of the way through, approximately. It'll be called *Horror Movie: a novel.*

DJ*: Given your achievements so far, what are your career hopes for the future?*

PT: I hope that people still want to read my future books. I hope that my future books don't ever feel like re-treads of my previous books. I hope that when I stop writing/publishing that it's my choice. I hope that someone makes cool t-shirts of/for my books and sends them to me.

DJ: Thanks again for chatting with us, Paul.

The Pallbearers Club *is available now from Titan Books, while Trevor Kennedy and Leanne Azzabi review* Knock at the Cabin *(2023) in the reviews section of this issue . . .*

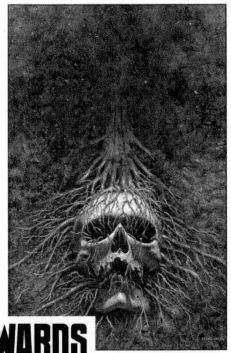

LES EDWARDS
www.lesedwards.com

"BE SEEING YOU!": *THE PRISONER* (1967–1968)

David Brilliance

Patrick McGoohan stars as "Number Six" in The Prisoner

He will not be pushed, filed, stamped, indexed, briefed, debriefed or numbered. His life is his own. 55 years on, David Brilliance takes a detailed look back at the classic British surrealist fantasy series, The Prisoner.

I'M GOING TO assume that folk reading this are familiar with the basic facts behind Patrick McGoohan's excellent and ground-breaking TV series from the 1960s; so, rather than go through all the background to the show being set up after being dreamt up by its star, this piece is going to go through all 17 episodes, and basically explain them. Back when the series was first shown, it was dismissed by many as a meaningless muddle, pretentious claptrap that, like a lot of modern art, didn't actually mean anything at all. This is patently untrue – the beauty of the show is that it can be enjoyed on at least two levels: the surface level spy story of ex-secret agent operatives imprisoned in the mysterious escape-proof Village, or a look at the struggles of an individual in a society he/she/they can't change and can't escape from. The series does have many symbolisms and double-meanings, some of which were intended, some of which are the result of viewers/fans like myself reading stuff into the stories; the joy of the show is that it easily lends itself to analyses like this.

Basically then . . . The show begins with a clap of thunder and the building up of a storm, as the main character prepares to follow through on a life-changing decision they've made. The main character works for the British Secret Service and has decided to resign. When they hurl down the envelope containing the letter of resignation, it's the release of the pent-up storm, which is an internal storm that has been building up inside the main character. As soon as they follow through on their life-changing decision, their way of looking at the world changes, and the way that world looks at and deals with them changes too – they are now a (for want of a better word) prisoner.

If you want to look at the show literally, of course, then what you see is what you get, and I could never understand the views of those critics who claimed the show was impossible to understand and follow: it's a complex series, yes, but fairly easy to follow the basic surface-level theme, and to see the various analogies in it. What follows are listings of the 17 episodes, with the literal storyline/plot, followed by the symbolic double-meanings. This being an article by myself, it also contains my usual personal touch, with reminiscences of when I first saw the eps and what I thought about them, with marks out of 10. I've also listed the episodes in an order that, if you *do* want to take the show literally, makes much more sense, as I explain.

'Arrival'

Writers: George Markstein and David Tomblin
Director: Don Chaffey
Guest stars: Virginia Maskell, Guy Doleman, George Baker

A secret agent resigns his job, and is subsequently knocked out and abducted to a small isolated Village where everyone has a number and nobody can leave.

Because this is the first episode, the symbolism basically explains the whole show – someone makes a life-changing decision (which, because the show isn't meant to be taken literally, can be anything you want it to be), acts on it and then their way of looking at the world alters, and people's attitudes to them alter too. The Village represents society, Number Six represents the individual (because the situation is not literal, it's possible to speculate that McGoohan is actually playing a completely different person/type in each story, each one of which has made a different life-changing decision), the sentient balloon represents the stifling forces of peer pressure and red tape, Number Two represents authority, and the citizens represent the majority who all follow one another blindly. Even the stock phrase in the Village, "Be seeing you" has several different meanings – as well as reinforcing the paranoia of who works for the Village (anyone could be seeing you later, via a monitor screen!) – and it reinforces the fact that life in the Village is inevitable, each person will always be seeing the others, because nobody can escape! I have to say my favourite part of the whole show is before the end credits, where we see McGoohan's face zoom forward from an aerial view of the Village, just before bars slam across the screen/his face, with a resounding clang. This seems to encapsulate the entire show and it's message in just three seconds!

I first saw this on a Channel 4 (UK) repeat run, starting in September 1983, on Mondays at 10 p.m. I loved it and always looked forward to it all day at work. This transmission was cut for some bizarre reason, the bars section outlined above being removed. Inexplicable, as it's only on screen for a few seconds.

10/10

'Dance of the Dead'

Duncan Macrae and Mary Morris in The Prisoner: *'Dance of the Dead'*

Writer: Anthony Skene
Director: Don Chaffey
Guest stars: Mary Morris, Norma West

Number Six is invited to a fancy dress ball being held in the Town Hall, and discovers a body washed up on the beach . . .

This episode is basically all about life – the "Dance of the Dead" the title refers to is basically people pretending to be full of happiness and joy in social situations but are really not enjoying them, and are only happy on a surface level: at the fancy dress party, the town crier declares, "There will be happiness and joy – by order!" It's like people visiting Disneyland and being told to "Smile – you're in Disneyland!"

Number Six dresses in his own suit, showing he's still himself; his female observer dresses as Little Bo-Peep ("who always knows where to find her sheep" as Number Six puts it), and the sinister-looking female Number Two goes as Peter Pan, ruler of Never-never Land. When Number Six is put on trial, his prosecutor and defender speak for causes they don't believe in, just because it's their assigned job – another comment on society again, perhaps? The series' somewhat misogynistic streak rears it's head, as Number Six flatly points out that you should "Never trust a woman".

This episode fits as the second because it makes it clear Number Six has recently arrived in the Village: he wonders where the food supplies come from; discovers the place has a curfew, and comments that he has never seen a night while he's been there. He also comments that "I'm new here!" So, this must be episode 2.

This ep isn't one of the best. It's rich with ideas and symbolism but doesn't have a strong, interesting story to contain them.

Typically, in that 1983/4 repeat run, this would be the one episode I chose to watch in front of my family, in order to show off to them what a brilliant series it was!

6/10

'Checkmate'

Writer: Gerald Kelsey
Director: Don Chaffey
Guest stars: Peter Wyngarde, Ronald Radd

Number Six gathers together an escape team, but their plan fails because none of the others trust him.

The obvious message of this one is that you cannot trust anyone, but without cooperation and help from others, you cannot achieve anything, all of which is true enough, I suppose.

The final line concerning the would-be escapees – "They'll be back on the chessboard tomorrow – as pawns" – perfectly sums up the nature of our lives, and how most of us have to work in jobs we don't like, just to make a living. This episode fits as the third, as there are again references to the fact that Number Six is new to the Village, and he's still obsessed with escaping at this point.

I thoroughly enjoyed this one when I first saw it in that 1983/4 re-run (it was shown sixth), and audio-taped the first 15 minutes until the tape ran out.

10/10

'Free for All'

Writer and director: Patrick McGoohan (using the writing pseudonym of "Paddy Fitz")
Guest stars: Eric Portman, Rachel Herbert

Number Six runs for office as the new Number Two. If he wins the election, he will be in charge of the Village and will be able to organise a mass escape . . .

The quintessential episode of the series, this is all about politics and politicians and how they are a sly and devious bunch who can't be trusted. The whole election is rigged from the start so that Number Six wins, but once the brainwashing he's been subjected to wears off, he is beaten up and carried back home on a stretcher. The electoral speeches Number Six makes make no sense at all, typical politicians' double-talk and bullshit ("Winter, spring, summer or fall, they can all be yours at any time!"). The villagers are shown to be mindless sheep – they enjoy the rigged spectacle but once the new Number Two has been declared, they lose any interest.

There are some great scenes with the newspaper reporters, who print what they want to, no matter what Number Six says; and once again, our hero is betrayed by a woman. The first thing he should have done upon becoming Number Two is throw that schemer out on her ear!

This episode nicely fits as the fourth one – the "so much time to give them what they want before they take it from you" is over, and the Village begins its attempts to break Number Six.

This was shown fourth in that Channel 4 re-run, and I loved it as usual. It was the first time it had been shown complete, as the previous screenings cut the scene of Number Six being beaten up at the end.

10/10

'The Chimes of Big Ben'

Writer: Vincent Tilsley
Director: Don Chaffey
Guest stars: Leo McKern, Nadia Gray

Number Six befriends a young woman recently arrived in the Village, and together they concoct an elaborate escape plan.

Don't trust anyone and don't readily accept situations for how they appear to be at first sight, are the messages here.

Once again, Number Six is betrayed by a woman (which illustrates how each episode has a different main character – if they were all the same man, wouldn't you think he was more than a tiny bit thick by this point?).

This is the first episode to ditch the actual location of Portmeirion and use studio sets and stock footage instead – even the beach is a set. Leo McKern's Number Two is one of the best, certainly my favourite, and has some great verbal jousts with Number Six.

The arts and crafts competition is once again entirely rigged from the start, and McGoohan makes some pointed criticisms of modern art – when he describes the "sculpture" he's made, he does so in pretentious and profound terms; but the real meaning behind the piece is obvious: he's built a boat! When Number Six's new female friend, Number Eight, starts to wander off in the woods and says "I must think", Number Six replies, "Keep to the paths." He isn't referring to the woods.

Another episode I loved when I first saw it.

10/10

Patrick McGoohan and Leo McKern in The Prisoner: *'The Chimes of Big Ben'*

'It's Your Funeral'

Writer: Michael Cramoy
Director: Robert Asher
Guest stars: Annette Andre, Mark Eden

Number Six discovers an assassination plot, directed at a retiring Number Two.

The theme of this one is the old favourite of politics. The Village authorities are shown to be ultra-devious in their plans to "save a pension" (sounds like our own government, who want people to work until they're 68 – and no doubt, as the years pass, higher than that!) and execute a retiring Number Two but blame it on the citizens. I love the part in the retirement ceremony where the MC lists all the remarkable accomplishments the old Number Two has made during his time in office, such as "the beautiful mural in the library!"

I place this episode as occurring directly after 'The Chimes of Big Ben' as Number Six here is very bad-tempered, suspicious and unwilling to trust anyone – after he was betrayed so badly in the previous episode, perhaps? Three of the guest stars here had previously appeared in the *Doctor Who* story 'Marco Polo' – maybe the casting director was a *Doctor Who* fan?

Behind the scenes, McGoohan was apparently getting very difficult to deal with; reportedly he sacked the director after only one morning, and took over himself, using a pseudonym, and later he became so worked up he almost strangled Mark Eden during the climactic fight scenes.

I wasn't that impressed when I first saw this one, and still don't rate it as one of the best.

7/10

'The Schizoid Man'

Writer: Terence Feely
Director: Pat Jackson
Guest stars: Jane Merrow, Anton Rodgers

Number Six becomes the victim of a plot to break him by making him doubt his identity.

This is a masterpiece, and one of the very best episodes. It's such a clever idea; to take the central character and brainwash him seemingly overnight, so that his tastes and reactions are different; then get a man who looks exactly like the hero, and pretend that the Number Six is the imposter, and the double is the genuine article!

Great performances from McGoohan and a great script.

The double of Number Six is given the number "Twelve". Number Six has a close female friend here – obviously this particular Six isn't so adverse to women – and she's given a name: Alison. This is the only episode where the balloon is called "Rover", and once again it takes place largely using studio sets and scenes not filmed in Portmeirion.

This was the first episode of the show that I audio-taped; it was shown fifth in that Channel 4 repeat run.

10/10

'Many Happy Returns'

Writer: Anthony Skene
Director: Patrick McGoohan
Guest stars: Patrick Cargill, Donald Sinden

Number Six awakes to find the Village is deserted, and there is nothing to stop him from escaping.

Another of the best episodes, this is a very clever story, one that illustrates just how horrific a situation the main character (if you want to take the show literally) is trapped in. The Village allows him to escape here, for two reasons: firstly, as an unusual birthday present (allowing him to briefly return home and see his former colleagues, his house and his KAR), and secondly, the far more sinister purpose is to discourage Number Six's escape attempts and get him to accept his life in the Village. Here, after a month away from the Village, they manage to get him back with no trouble or effort at all, and he's a prisoner once again at the conclusion.

The title of the story sums it all up: 'Many Happy Returns' – no matter how many times you escape, you will always be brought back; 'Many *Happy*

Returns' – Happy Birthday; 'Many Happy *Returns*' – Number Six returns to London and his old life.

The Number Two in this story is hidden until the end, when we see it's Mrs Butterworth – who else? It would have to be a woman. Out of the 8 stories so far, only one ('It's Your Funeral') *doesn't* have the main character betrayed by a woman.

The Village's plan seems to work – listing the episodes in the logical order that I have, Number Six never tries to escape again after this, until the finale. As a result, the emphasis of the show changes – rather than Number Six trying to escape, he focuses on remaining an individual in a community he can't change or escape from.

This episode was shown second in the Channel 4 re-run, which was rather bizarre. I enjoyed it but didn't fully understand what was going on until years later, re-watching it on VHS.

10/10

Patrick McGoohan and Georgina Cookson in
The Prisoner: 'Many Happy Returns'

'A. B. and C.'

Writer: Anthony Skene
Director: Pat Jackson
Guest stars: Colin Gordon, Peter Bowles

Number Six's dreams are invaded, as the new Number Two believes Six was selling out to the enemy after he resigned.

This fits nicely after the previous episode, as there is no attempt made by Number Six to escape. The hidden meaning of this one appears to be that you shouldn't let others interfere with your dreams – quite literally in this case!

The Number Two in this one reappears in the next story, but this is obviously the first time they've met as the dialogue makes clear. Number Six has two dressing gowns he wears – the usual one is dark blue, with white stripes (i.e. bars); the one he wears here is orange, with black stripes – what else can he be, but a caged tiger? Peter Bowles had worked with McGoohan before, but on this occasion apparently found him far less friendly and easy to work with.

I enjoyed this episode when it was shown (third) on Channel 4, complete with a photo from 'Free For All' in the *TV Times*. I wasn't aware at the time that it had been cut, with the scene involving "B" being trimmed. I just found the whole story rather confusing back then anyway!

9/10

Annette Carell in The Prisoner: *'A. B. and C.'*

'The General'

Writer: Joshua Adam (pen name for "Lewis Greifer")
Director: Peter Graham Scott
Guest stars: Colin Gordon, Peter Howell

The citizens of the Village are delighted by the new "Speedlearn" course they are ordered to participate in – except for Number Six who sees it for what it really is: brainwashing.

This episode had the education system as it's main theme – in the Village the numbers are taught facts about a subject (History) that is no use at all to them in the world they are trapped in, and they repeat the facts that have been subliminally beamed into them and delight in how "clever" they are. In real life, people in schools are taught facts about subjects that are no use to them in the real world, but if they memorise those facts and repeat them they are deemed "clever" and a "good scholar". The same Number Two appears here as previously, referring to Number Six as an "old friend". The computer behind it all is incredibly dated now, and takes up most of a wall, complete with the spinning reels that everyone thought looked futuristic and would still be in use in the 21st century!

This episode again was largely shot in studio sets, and it is the one story where Number Six is being helped by someone who doesn't betray him – a man! Why Patrick McGoohan had this apparent misogynistic streak, I've no idea but it is very prevalent throughout the show – yet another example takes place in 'Checkmate' where, upon coming up with his plan to separate the prisoners from the warders, Number Six boldly states, "Let's find our reliable *men!*"

I wasn't that impressed when I first saw this on Channel 4, as the symbolism of the educational theme went right over my head.

7/10

'Hammer Into Anvil'

Writer: Roger Woddis
Director: Pat Jackson
Guest star: Patrick Cargill

The new Number Two is a sadistic bully who drives a young woman to suicide; his next target is Number Six and he relishes the challenge.

The sub-theme of this one (which again, following on from 'Many Happy Returns' doesn't feature any attempt to escape) is that bullies are essentially cowards, and when their victim turns on them they crumble.

Patrick Cargill, who appeared in a different(?) role in 'Many Happy Returns' is excellent as the sadistic Number Two, and the story is one of the most easily accessible of the show.

There's quite a lot of Portmeirion footage here, too, though the overcast sky and lack of extras/villagers show that it's not tourist season as the place seems very quiet and deserted compared to the earlier episodes.

I enjoyed this one on first viewing – finally, a story I could properly follow and understand!

10/10

'The Girl Who Was Death'

Writer: Terence Feely
Director: David Tomblin
Guest stars: Justine Lord, Kenneth Griffith

To quote the Channel 4 continuity announcer (December 1983) – "The Prisoner is inexplicably at large in village England, complete with a handlebar moustache and a cricket bat."

This is a bizarre one. It presents the main character in a totally different setting/scenario, years before such shows as the various *Star Trek* series made it something of a familiar TV cliché (you know the sort of thing: Captain Picard awakens to find he's married with six kids and has an afro), but it stands out for that and is thoroughly entertaining and action-packed. It turns out to be a story told by Number Six to some kids in the Village nursery and Six realising he's being watched by Number Two says, "Goodnight children, everywhere" which sums up the whole thing – the parting line is really aimed at the audience, or at least that section of the audience who McGoohan identified as being mentally children – unable to cope with an adult, intelligent series. Clever, and quite daring to insult a segment of the viewing audience.

This is my favourite episode of the series, partly because it's so unusual and partly because it was the first episode I ever saw. Back in the summer of 1982, ITV had a strand called "Best of British". Over the course of several weeks, single episodes of old ITV shows would be randomly slotted into the schedules, and this particular episode was chosen to represent *The Prisoner* and was shown at 11.40 on a Friday night.

I'd read articles about the show, as well as one of the 3 novels published, and I was greatly looking forward to it. It turned out to be a crashing disappointment! Apart from the fact I considered the opening titles to be totally OTT (I knew they would show the main character driving through London to his headquarters and resigning – but driving a Grand Prix racing car down an airport runway, at 150 mph??!! That's what it looked like to me as a 15-year-old, anyway!) I didn't like the tongue-in-cheek feel of the story, not realising it was a one-off, and I was disappointed by the Village itself – I thought that the story was actually taking place in the Village, and it was nothing like I imagined! Still, I was only 15 . . . In later years, of course, I loved it.

10/10

'A Change of Mind'

Writer: Roger Parkes
Director: Patrick McGoohan
Guest stars: John Sharpe, Angela Browne

Number Six's antisocial stance will no longer be tolerated and he must prepare himself for "social conversion" – lobotomy – to make him fit in and be like everyone else.

Mental illness, the sufferers of it, and how they are treated by the community are the themes here. We can perhaps surmise that this particular Number Six is a diagnosed mentally-ill man or woman, and the episode goes about showing us the treatments that are given, as well as the lack of acceptance for those who suffer.

This could have been brilliant, but the episode is undermined by the eccentric direction (by McGoohan under his "Robert Asher" pseudonym), and the equally OTT performance of the show's star, who, on occasion, could rival William Shatner himself! Once again, a woman cannot be trusted, and the Village is represented by studio sets. Not one of the better episodes, I wasn't that enamoured with this one.

7/10

'Do Not Forsake Me Oh My Darling'

Writer: Vincent Tilsley
Director: Pat Jackson
Guest stars: Zena Walker, Nigel Stock

Number Six's mind is transferred to another man's head – not as part of a plan to break him, but in order to find a missing scientist.

This is a weird one. It was shot largely without Portmeirion/the Village, and largely without the star, as McGoohan was in Hollywood making *Ice Station Zebra*. Some shots that were filmed but never used for the titles are inserted – rather ineptly as it happens – into the action and it's obvious that it's McGoohan and not Nigel Stock in KAR. It's an intriguing mind/body transference tale, but it doesn't make complete sense: the Village authorities know how to swap minds, but they need Professor Seltzman to show them how to reverse the process. But there shouldn't be a "reversal" process as such – they just need to perform the procedure a second time to swap minds back to where they belong!

This episode perfectly illustrates the point about each episode having a different Number Six – in the rest of the show the main character has resigned, and is generally shown to be someone who doesn't have a high regard for women and is generally asexual. Here, Number Six has vanished while working on a case and is engaged to be married! Clearly then, not the same man.

This episode is very like the other ITC shows of the time, with various clichés including back-lots and stock footage used to represent a foreign country (Austria, in this instance), as well as gas being used as a weapon, plus fight scenes that always involve lots of gurning and face-pushing!

I didn't really like this one when I first saw it. It doesn't really have a subtext other than perhaps remaining true to yourself no matter what, and was written purely to accommodate McGoohan's absence.

7/10

'Living in Harmony'

Writers: David Tomblin, Ian Rakoff and Frank Maher
Director: David Tomblin
Guest stars: David Bauer, Valerie French, Alexis Kanner

Number Six is a sheriff in the Wild West in the town of Harmony. Harmony has a corrupt, all-powerful Judge, who uses his thugs to maintain order. Escape is impossible, as anyone who tries is lassoed and dragged back.

Another episode done because the production team had largely ran out of ideas for stories set in the Village. Another factor was Patrick McGoohan, who had always wanted to appear in a western but never had. This episode puts forward the idea that the concept of the show spans all ages and all places – Harmony is just a 19th-century American version of the '60s Village, and pressure is put to bear on the hero to not only become sheriff but also to wear a gun. It was the sheriff's refusal to carry arms for the good of the town that reportedly caused the episode to be unscreened during the initial US transmission, as the parallels to the then-current situation in Vietnam were uncomfortable.

The show's usual title sequence is redone in western fashion, but the title *The Prisoner* is curiously absent. This episode must have also confused the Channel 4 programme planners, as they almost missed it out during the 1983/4 repeats, and it had to be hurriedly inserted into the schedule.

10/10

Alexis Kanner in The Prisoner: *'Living in Harmony'*

'Once Upon a Time'

Writer and director: Patrick McGoohan
Guest star: Leo McKern

Number Six and a returnee Number Two are locked in a room for a week; Number Six is mentally regressed to childhood and is forced to relive his life, up to the fateful moment he resigned.

This has a good idea at it's core, but the static nature of the story combined with the fact that it's mainly just three actors (the mute Butler is also locked away for the week) in one set means it's a bit of a bore for the most part; McGoohan's trademark OTT direction and performance – perhaps done to show how the main character is starting to crack under the pressure – works against it, too. Leo McKern apparently had a breakdown whilst making this, and had to be persuaded to return months after for the finale (the show wasn't made in order and this episode had been filmed before 'The Schizoid Man'). The episode shows the central theme of rebellion against conformity very obviously and makes me wonder if all the critics and newspaper writers who dismissed the show as meaningless were either trying to create a cult of mystery around the show, or were genuinely thick.

I struggled to stay awake watching this one in early 1984, but reassured myself that the final episode would be better.

6/10

'Fall Out'

Writer and director: Patrick McGoohan
Guest stars: Leo McKern, Alexis Kanner

Number Six finally discovers the identity of the mysterious Number One and escapes.

I'd read an article about the show in December of 1980, long before I ever saw any of it, and that article had a lengthy synopsis of 'Fall Out'; I was therefore quite surprised when I saw it and it turned out to be nothing like I'd envisioned. McGoohan switches from symbolism to surrealism with this one, though there are plenty of parts that fit the symbolic pattern. When Number Six attempts to make a speech and is repeatedly drowned out by the assembled council – what else can that represent than the inability of the common man to make his voice heard? When Number Six, Number Two (Leo McKern, his character returned to life, complete with haircut), the Butler and the youthful rebel Number Forty-Eight wreak havoc on the place and escape, we see that the Village was somewhere in England – this shows how timeless the place is meant to be, covering all times and places. When Number One is revealed to be Number Six himself, McGoohan's intention was to show that man's worst enemy is himself – his evil nature the worst thing on earth.

At the end, to the accompaniment of an emotive score, Number Forty-Eight leaves the others and then tries to hitch a lift going back the way he's just come . . . aimless youth, drifting along with no real goal or destination; Number Two heads straight for the Houses of Parliament, showing that he was intended to symbolise authority/the Government all along; while Number Six and the Butler head to Six's London home, Six gets into KAR and drives off, while the Butler goes into the house, the door opening and closing by itself, just as in the Village. This all makes the show's "hidden" message all too obvious. The Village is basically society, Number Two is authority (the fact each episode has a different Number Two, a different form of authority, shows that, though society superficially changes as different men and women come to power, it remains essentially the same), Number Six is the individual who has made a life-altering decision, which causes the individual's way of looking at society to change too.

In closing, a brilliant series overall. Perhaps the view put forward by Six of One (the show's appreciation society) that there are literally thousands of interpretations of *The Prisoner* is rather exaggerated but the show always rewards repeated viewings and is never less than fascinating, ranking alongside such personal favourites as *Doctor Who*, *Star Trek*, *The Outer Limits* and *The Twilight Zone/Night Gallery* as one of the supreme achievements of "fantastic" television.

"Sphinxthulhu!" The Ziggurat t-shirt design and artwork by Dave Carson

THE MUSIC OF CTHULHU

Interview by Trevor Kennedy

Dwayne Boyd (left) with co-members of The Ziggurat,
Sterling Boyd, Steve Hamon and Matt Waldenville

*Trevor Kennedy speaks with American musician **Dwayne Boyd** about his*
*life, career and death metal, Lovecraft-inspired rock band, **The Ziggurat**.*

Trevor Kennedy: Hey, Dwayne! Thanks for chatting to us today. Are you or your band, The Ziggurat, working on anything as we speak?

Dwayne Boyd: Greetings and thank you for the opportunity to be here. Yes we are currently working on multiple things. Being that it is our 25 year anniversary, we are now in the studio recording some choice selections from our four previous albums to release throughout the year. I am aiming for each album to be released as an EP, with up-to-date, re-imagined artwork and productions, released each quarter of the year, starting with *Hymns of the Cthulhu Mythos*, followed by *Confrontation with the Disciples of the Shadow Walker*, *The Plague of the Pallid Mask* and *Beyond the Threshold of Reality*. Technology and cost has at last caught up to the independent artist and has made it possible for immensely better productions. While these classic songs are being released, we are also finishing some brand new songs along with unreleased material from the past 8 years for a release by December 2023. We are also playing our local region heavily in support of our anniversary.

TK: Could you tell us about the formation of the band, how it all came about, and something of your early days performing together please?

DB: Each incarnation of The Ziggurat has been through serendipity, a perfect alignment of stars and established recognition. Having others agree to join "your band" is a hard task. Everyone wants to do their own thing and be the creative fountain from which others drink. So I didn't expect anything in the beginning. I expected it to remain a solo project while I myself continued to join other local or established bands and acts. But sometime in late 1997, I took the chance to see if I could recruit others. I plastered the surrounding three towns with flyers and posters looking for a whole band from scratch, a seemingly impossible venture. But as life has it, when you take a chance, then you have a chance and I met bassist Brad Schoeneman. That first connection was immediately followed by my friend Nick Hileman on guitar, who brought with him an aspiring young guitarist named Scott Lawson. Once that began falling into place, my brother, Sterling "Sterthanas" Boyd, who I had played with four years earlier in a band called Abnegate, and who is the only other original member of The Ziggurat, filled the final spot. It came together surprisingly easily. The original plan was for The Ziggurat to be a five-piece band and I would be the vocalist, but the Ancient Ones had other plans for me. Those members changed and shuffled during the gestation cycle of the band, with some leaving and coming back. You know how it is, life happens and you have to roll with it.

Our first show was a house party in the college section of my home town. The home owner was a friend named Steve Gore, who was from a previous band I was also in called Pressure Group, a kind of alternative punk band in which I played bass during high school. We played in the basement, carrying gear down a questionable staircase that eventually gave way at a later show, and performed for 40 people, mostly friends. But they went nuts for us and by the end of the night we had another show scheduled for a few days later. It too was a house show, the early days were mostly house shows, but each crowd got larger and each response got better, so we kept the momentum going by playing out as much as possible. We all eventually turned 21 and that made it possible for us to finally perform at bars and age-restricted venues. Being able to play bars in two national college towns, Radford University and the internationally renowned Virginia Tech, was key in our ability to develop seriously as a band. It's the next best thing to living in a major city in terms of exposure, so we took advantage of that. The only thing we never got around to during the first incarnation of The Ziggurat was recording our music. We were always so caught up in playing out that our personal finances were totally consumed by it, though we did manage during that time to have two different shirt designs printed to sell at the shows. But those shirt printings were partly personal favours and cost was very low.

During that time members moved away and I took up whatever position needed to be filled. We kept that up until 2002 before life events forced us to sink beneath the sands, ending the first incarnation of The Ziggurat until the stars were right again, though at the time I didn't know if they ever would be.

Brad and I were the only ones who remained and when you're driven to create music, not many things can stop you. Brad was a major influence and had a heavy hand in the early years of songwriting, so having him and I be all that remained was a blessing. We completed unfinished material and set upon a path that would change the direction of the band forever – the recording of our first album, *Hymns of the Cthulhu Mythos*.

TK: Why did you choose "The Ziggurat" as the band name?

DB: The original idea for the band was for it to be strictly occult and mythology themes. My personal interest and path made this an easy choice for what I would do lyrically with my music. I was writing songs about The Lesser Key of Solomon, Odin, Siva, the seven days of creation, Sumerian battles between Marduk and Tiamat and the like. When I began thinking of a name that would convey these ideas and imagery, I started to look for something that would represent them all. But I felt that there were no words truly powerful or big enough to represent what I was going for. I always had a fascination with Egypt and desert temples and the imagery associated with it, but Egypt felt overdone and too easy. I turned then to the Sumerian and Babylonian side of things. Knowing lots of their mythology and history and the fact that I already had a song about the subject matter and was extremely familiar with the *Simon Necronomicon*, which gave Sumerian mythology an occult feel, I began digging for ideas and imagery associated with them. Ziggurats immediately stood out to me. Being a horror and history fanatic allows your mind to see things differently. I could see it in my head, a black sky, an endless desert, a massive Cyclopean structure in the middle of it, deserted and half destroyed, lit by torches that illuminate Stygian hallways where the echoes of those long since gone can be heard whispering unholy things from beyond. I was taken by it, fascinated by it, the picture my mind had painted was exactly what I was going for. It felt right, an ancient structure, one of the first temples constructed in the name of the gods. But "Ziggurat" alone wasn't enough, it needed to feel more important, more massive, singular, one of a kind. The band could never just be "Ziggurat", it had to be "The Ziggurat". There can be only one. And so it was.

The Ziggurat logo designed by Dwayne Boyd

TK: Aside from the aforementioned and obvious Lovecraftian influence to your music, what have been some of the other influences for the band collectively and yourself personally over the years?

DB: For me it's always been the occult, horror, sci-fi, religion and mythology when it comes to ideas and themes that inspire me. There's far too much to list. Musically my main inspirations are King Diamond, Judas Priest and Iron Maiden. But the death and black metal that emerged in the '90s really grabbed me. The intensity of it really influenced how I would eventually write my own music.

As for the band, I've always maintained that those who choose to bleed black and become fellow cultists of Cthulhu should have similar interests that also expand into further regions.

Matt Waldenville, of the second and third incarnation of The Ziggurat, is a devourer of horror movies which of course influenced and led him to heavy metal when musical interest kicked in. Through bands like Morbid Angel and others, he became aware of Lovecraft and occult themes and latched onto them. He was also a fan of the band before becoming a member, so The Ziggurat was also a huge inspiration for him.

Steve Hamon, bassist of the current third incarnation, is a long-time friend and fan and is influenced by bands I love, Judas Priest and Iron Maiden as well as Primus, Death and Cannibal Corpse. His interest in weird fiction, philosophy, horror and the occult are a perfect fit.

Sterling Boyd, drummer since before the stars were right, is inspired by '90s black metal in his approach to drums and is driven by personal strife which he channels and uses as a source of creativity. Using that energy he engages the drums as a conduit of suffering, anger and fear. Of course, being my brother, our other interests grew and developed side-by-side. At a young age we watched the same movies (*Evil Dead, The Thing, Alien, Pumpkinhead, The Stuff* . . .), we read Stephen King and watched MTV. Raised on '80s and '90s rock, it eventually changed when the show *Headbangers Ball* came on as we entered our teenage years. It threw open the doors to what else was out there and we immediately identified with it. All that eventually inspired us to become the musicians we are.

The Ziggurat perform

TK: Turning now to Lovecraft, when did you first discover the writer and his works and why have they become so special to you? What makes Lovecraft stand out from the rest?

The Ziggurat t-shirt design and artwork by Dave Carson

DB: Our first guitarist, Nick, suggested I read Lovecraft. He knew I read a lot of King and had just finished *Phantoms* by Koontz and *Demogorgon* by Lumley. He said I would love it. It was at least a year before I got around to it but I eventually bought a couple of smaller volumes that have the Michael Whelan cover art, the same art on the Obituary album, *Cause of Death*. I always thought that was cool.

I can't recall the first story I read by Lovecraft, somewhere in the beginning was 'At the Mountains of Madness', 'The Case of Charles Dexter Ward', 'The Thing in the Moonlight' and 'The Dream-Quest of Unknown Kadath'. They were unlike anything I had read before. Up until that point in my life, things I had read or watched were only spooky, scary or suspenseful. They were never actually terrifying or horrifying. The way Lovecraft wrote changed those emotions. When I read his work there was genuine dread and horror that spilled off the page. I found myself truly involved in the story and was fully there. It engaged me like no written word has since. Like Sutter Cane from the movie *In the Mouth of Madness*, he changed my reality through his books. There were gods, aliens, ancient temples, horror, space, occultism and so much more. It was a feast laid before me of all the things I was into and loved.

Once I started reading Lovecraft, I went out and bought everything and devoured it. I could feel the relation to my fascinations with *The Outer Limits, Twilight Zone, Night Gallery* and my film viewing history. But that wasn't enough. I went to other bookstores in search of similar authors but didn't know where to begin, eventually an employee at the local bookstore directed me to a copy of *Made in Goatswood* and suggested that I look into the Chaosium cycle books. I read it and was excited that there were potentially more. Hundreds of dollars and months later I had obtained and gone through almost all the cycle books. Through them I discovered a pantheon of mythos writers. Mark Rainey, Arthur Machen, Ramsey Campbell, Robert E. Howard, Lord Dunsany, Lin Carter and so many more. Then it was time to visit Lumley with Titus Crow and the "Hero of Dreams" series. I was drowning in amazing Mythos madness. I spent at least five years acquiring as much Lovecraftian literature as I could, reading it and rereading it time and time again. I've still kept up-to-date with new collections but always go back to the source.

One major thing that made Lovecraft change my life wasn't even Lovecraft. It was Algernon Blackwood and 'The Wendigo'. But not even him really – he is part of a chain. When I was very young there was a popular book called *Scary Stories to Tell in the Dark* with art by Stephen Gammell. The imagery in that book is without a doubt the most horrifying thing imaginable to a young mind and scared many children other than myself, I'm sure. The pictures gave me plenty of nightmares but the story 'The Wendigo' gave me the most vivid – shaking trembling night terrors of my roof being ripped off and being snatched from my bed and taken into the sky by some colossal being to die in some horrible way. I can't truly convey the intensity of those dreams. It left a deep imprint.

Years later, when I picked up a copy of *The Ithaqua* cycle as an adult and opened it to Blackwood's 'Wendigo' as the first tale, I thought nothing of it. I only read a few stories that first day but it was followed that night by the same dreams and terrors from childhood. I finished the book over the course of the week and the nightmares kept coming and coming.

Lovecraft created a way for me to experience real horror and fear. Through the web of stories and the influence of other writers I am now able to tap into actual nightmare fuel. Now when I read, watch or perform anything Lovecraftian, the horror is always there – not some fun spooky place, it's actually lurking in a hellish chamber locked inside me and that makes it real.

TK: Could you tell some more about some of The Ziggurat's Mythos-inspired songs and albums please?

DB: Our Mythos songs are in two different categories, one being nebulous but effective statements and descriptions about a particular part of Lovecraftian lore. Such as the song 'From Perfect Angles', which only details where and what they are. Or 'Nyarlathotep', which is an abridged history of moments he has appeared in various manifestations. 'Tendrils of Terror', 'The Dream Quest' and 'Windwalker' follow this pattern of writing. It's the unadulterated horror of Lovecraft you could say.

The second category is original Lovecraftian stories where I expand on existing tales or create new ones. Songs like 'The Hickman Cemetery Horror', 'The Plague of the Pallid Mask', 'The Road to Dunwich', 'Ghost of Yib'Ishnagarib' and 'Within the Central Void'.

'Chocolate Shoggoth Shake' is set in 1955 when an ice-cream shop with a pleasant owner pops up in a town during the hottest summer on record. He is secretly thousands of years old and dwells within a den of shoggoths hidden in catacombs far out in the countryside. He's been breeding shoggoths for a very long time. Always doing it a new way, breeding new shoggoths. This time, he's Eskimo Joe and he butchers some of the monsters, brings pieces of them to the shop, puts them in a blender along with the chocolate syrup and then feeds it to his patrons to start a new brood of shoggoths – the darkest sweetest chocolate you'll ever taste and as the locals say, it's to die for. If you've ever seen the movie *The Stuff*, then you can imagine what shoggoths being born looks like. It's an awful scene that I have a good time singing about.

Some of the original stories for Mythos material are derived directly from my nightmares. That is an important fact for me. When writing the new stories for lyrics I put in scenes from nightmares to make the song more potent, to put something real in it. If I'm going to sing about Cthulhu and horror and properly emote that, then my dreams are my path to tapping into fear and conveying it. It's an important ingredient in making the music powerful. People can feel when your music is real and you mean it. I would argue that it's easy to do that with love songs or party songs, but conveying the horror and fear of the Ancient Ones is a task suited for nightmares.

I took a new approach to one of our most recent songs, 'IA'. It is probably one of my favorite things to have been a part of. This song was written from the perspective of the cultists in the wooded swamps that Inspector Legrasse was watching in 'The Call of Cthulhu'. The song sounds like a death metal frenzied voodoo orgy, just as the story describes. It's written as a ritual for the awakening of Cthulhu. The opening minutes of the songs are in R'lyehian language, but at a certain point, after the chaos within the song climaxes, the words become frenzied sounds and new utterances of my design. It all turned out really well, the lyrics, the song and the delivery. Matt, Sterling, Chris Hoff and I really created something amazing. It became an immediate Zigg anthem. By the time the last notes are hit, crowds turn into insane cultists chanting "IA" to the stage like it's the idol of Cthulhu. It's glorious.

As for the albums, the rule of thumb is that every other album will be Mythos-related. *Hymns* was a Mythos album and then *Confrontation* was about mythology and occultism. *Plague* went back to Mythos and then we covered the *Night's Dawn* trilogy by Peter F. Hamilton for our fourth album, *Beyond the Threshold of Reality*. Our next album will be Mythos once again and contain the song 'IA'.

TK: The band also has an association with renowned Lovecraftian artist Dave Carson. How did this happen and could you tell us more about it?

The Ziggurat t-shirt design and artwork by Dave Carson
(The Ziggurat logo design by Dwayne Boyd)

DB: I was always very familiar with Dave's work. His art was there the moment I discovered Lovecraft. It was in the Chaosium books, in the pages of Lumley and in various collections I picked up. I used the Internet to find Lovecraftian art and images and saw some of Dave's work here and there. It always stood out. It was amazingly detailed, sick and truly Lovecraftian in a way that no one else does. He is his own Pickman for sure. Because it was the primary art I was exposed to, it became synonymous with Lovecraft. DC was the standard in my mind.

Sometime during the era of Myspace, back when you could put a song on your wall and force everyone to listen to it, I did my best to promote 'Plague of the Pallid Mask'. Plastering the Internet with it anywhere I could. One day, when I checked my Myspace wall, there was a post with a short message that said something like, "I like what you're doing. You're keeping it real. Nice one." The name on it was Dave Carson. I gave the name an apprehensive glare and then clicked it. When the page loaded and I looked at it, my jaw hit the floor. It was *the* Dave Carson page. I had a super fan moment before writing to him and said something about loving his art and always being a fan and that I was humbled that he dug what I was doing. This was a huge moment in my life. I finally felt like I was earning my place in the Lovecraft creative world.

We exchanged messages and I eventually commissioned a shirt design from him, an idea I'd had forever and that of a Cthulhu sphinx towering over a ziggurat. That shirt, which we also made into the drumhead we still use today, was the start of a new era for the band. Our Lovecraftian identity was now legitimate. It was real. Dave even wore our Sphinxthulhu shirt to a convention he was speaking at that year. Dave and I messaged each other frequently and shared a handful of phone conversations. We've got much in common, obviously, and friendship came easy and was there from the beginning. It's a shame we live on opposite sides of the ocean. In total Dave has worked on four separate pieces for The Ziggurat with hopefully more in the future.

TK: How would you describe the band's style of music and why?

DB: It's definitely death metal but it has an '80s and classic heavy metal sensibility and we prefer to call it "Mythos Metal Madness". It comes in many forms and each song varies artistically, sometimes drastically. As I've mentioned, I'm a huge fan of bands like Judas Priest, Mötley Crüe, Scorpions and the like. Their influence in my writing is massive. But my love for the early death and black metal explosion impacted how I wrote my songs as well. I found myself writing songs that bounced between the crushing heaviness of Suffocation, the catchy hooks of HammerFall, blistering riffs like Deicide and melodic passages that sound like Iron Maiden. Sometimes it's black metal, sometimes it's tech death, thrash or grandiose power ballad moments. It always varies. It's what comes out organically. The music I write simply writes itself that way. I think it's a big part of why we have such appeal anywhere we play. There's moments for everyone within each song. Something in each tune that fans can identify with. It also gives us the benefit of fitting in within any metal performance line-up.

Our sound has matured over the years due to how the line-up has evolved. By surrounding myself with musicians who listen to heavier music than I do, it brought a new ferocity to how I wrote. It also gave me the confidence to start leaving gaps in my writing and letting others have a hand in it. Matt knows exactly what I'm going for and can drop a fitting riff on command. Steve has taken existing riffs, torn them apart and reconstructed them and they're amazing. As for my brother Sterling, we don't even have to look at each other or think about it. We know what the other is feeling already and run with it. His black metal influence compliments the band in a unique way that makes the music faster, heavier and more intense.

We write whatever style of metal we want and let the writing attack the listener through the lens of death metal. It has become its own style for sure. It's all the metal genres, all the time.

Mythos Metal Madness.

Our fans sure seem to love it.

TK: With the advent of the Internet, the music and recording industries have obviously changed significantly over the years since The Ziggurat's formation. How much has this affected you and the band and have you embraced – or even rejected to a certain extent – these changes?

DB: Modern technology and the Internet have finally made everything accessible to everyone. You can have your own studio, record a well produced album and release your music through all the major streaming services with relative ease. Not to mention being able to market yourself to a world wide audience.

In the late-'90s, the Internet was new so marketing consisted of printed flyers and gas in the car. Recording was what you could afford and what was available in the immediate area. Living in a small town in Virginia, the best option was a country and bluegrass studio that a guy ran out his basement called Medicine Jar Studios where we eventually recorded *Hymns of the Cthulhu Mythos*.

A few years later computer technology advanced and I began learning to record at home. The result of that process became the second album, *Confrontation with the Disciples of the Shadow Walker*. The productions of each track were different and didn't have a cohesive feel. But I was learning and trying different approaches to recording. Finding my way through it. Promoting the album was easier with the introduction of endless message boards and groups online.

I recorded and produced *The Plague of the Pallid Mask* using all the knowledge gained while doing *Confrontation. Plague* is the album I am most proud of. I promoted the hell out of it online and it got us listed on HPLovecraft.com and many other sites. Home recording and the Internet put The Ziggurat on the map.

During the second incarnation of The Ziggurat, the Internet was finally the standard for show promotion. Word of mouth, buddies and endless flyers became fully packed bars and venues because of event pages and local live music sites. You have to embrace change and the Internet is no different. Of course the negative is that it's now full of countless artists screaming into the void, hoping to be heard. The amount of music on streaming services is staggering and impossible to navigate. Word of mouth, message boards, Reddit, Bandcamp, YouTube, Facebook and Instagram is how you get people to hear your music abroad, but it still starts with family, friends and the fans. Unless you start emptying your wallet for advertising, those are your core tactics as a group of working people who also just happen to be Mythos Metal Titans.

Today's recording technology is exciting and user-friendly. Great productions right out of your home and directly to your audience via the net. I've got a set-up that I've been recording with for the past several years, recording for various friends and my side project, Mesopotamia, with vocalist and keyboardist Paul Surratt. Because that band is a studio-only band, it relies on the Internet to exist.

It's an exciting time for an independent musician and band.

The Ziggurat: Dwayne Boyd, Steve Hamon,
Matt Waldenville and Sterling Boyd

TK: What future plans do you and the band have?

DB: The Ziggurat exists in the present moment. You never know how long the stars are going to be aligned before it sinks back beneath the sands like R'lyeh and dread lord Cthulhu beneath the waves. There's already been three incarnations of The Ziggurat. Our current third line-up is a result of the passing of our bassist of the second incarnation, Chris Hoff. We played a memorial show for him and then, lo and behold, we started getting show offers and it all fell into place effortlessly. I take every active moment of the band as a blessing and in turn take it very seriously. The immediate goal is recording. Capturing choice songs from the past 25 years and presenting them with better productions and releasing them on all the major platforms. Throughout this year we will be performing in Virginia and tapping the tri-state area, taking on larger and more worthwhile shows. Then it will be on to new and unreleased material being recorded for our fifth album, *Lovecraftian Sonnet Occultus*.

TK: And where can readers find out more about your music and listen to it?

DB: Go to our Facebook, Instagram, Spotify, YouTube and Bandcamp pages. Everything is there.

TK: Dwayne, it's been a pleasure. All the very best to you and The Ziggurat – here's to the next 25 years and beyond for you!

The Ziggurat t-shirt design and artwork by Dave Carson
(The Ziggurat logo design by Dwayne Boyd)

SWORDS & SORCERIES
TALES OF HEROIC FANTASY

Featuring some of the best writers in the fantasy genre today.

PARALLEL UNIVERSE PUBLICATIONS

A TRIBUTE TO CHARLES BLACK

Charles Black

David A. Riley

**with Stephen Bacon, Mike Chinn, Kevin Demant, Kate Farrell,
Paul Finch, Craig Herbertson, Paul Mudie, Thana Niveau,
Reggie Oliver, Marion Pitman, John Llewellyn Probert,
David A. Sutton, Anna Taborska and David Williamson**

*Friends and colleagues of the late writer and editor **Charles Black**
pay heartfelt tributes to him.*

I STILL VIVIDLY remember how shocked and saddened I was on March 16, 2019 when I was told on the phone by a nurse at St. Michael's Hospice in Hereford that my friend Charles Black had passed away earlier that day. At the time I was planning to drive to the hospice to visit him, knowing it would be for the last time as he had already been diagnosed with terminal cancer, but the end came sooner than anyone expected. The last friends from the horror genre to spend time with him were Kevin Demant and John and Kate Probert (Thana Niveau), who had the privilege of being with him the day before.

A writer, editor and publisher, and a big enthusiast for punk rock, Charles created Mortbury Press, which from 2007 to 2015 produced eleven volumes of his *Black Book of Horror* series, each with the unmistakable artwork of Paul Mudie on their covers. They included an incredible number of contemporary writers in the horror genre, mainly from the UK.

Though a talented writer himself, Charles was not prolific and there are only two collections of short stories by him. The first, published by Parallel Universe Publications in 2015, was *Black Ceremonies*. The second appeared three years later under Charles' Mortbury Press imprint, *A Taste for the Macabre*.

Charles's own stories appeared in a number of magazines and anthologies such as *Eldritch Blue: Love and Sex in the Cthulhu Mythos*, *Hell's Hangmen: Horror in the Old West*, *Late Late Show*, *Forgotten Worlds*, *Nemonymous 7: Zencore*, *Best New Zombie Tales*, *Cthulhu Cymraeg*, *Horrorscope*, *Whispers from the Abyss*, and *Kitchen Sink Gothic*.

For this tribute I have contacted many of the writers and artists who were involved with Charles over the years and asked them to share their memories of him.

Actor and author Kate Farrell fondly recalled that: "'Mea Culpa' was the first story I had accepted by anyone, anywhere, and Charlie revealed at a later date that occasionally he would have smiled, and when he read my story, that was one of those occasions. This was late November 2010, and our first collaboration was published in *The Eighth Black Book of Horror* the following year. I was also lucky enough to be featured in *The Ninth* and the anniversary edition, *The Tenth*. And *The Eleventh*. He was a complete joy to work with, his editing skills and observations were without equal. His eye was forensic, not a comma escaped him, and he cured me of my love affair with ellipses. Not before time. He *cared*. Throughout the collaboration we exchanged emails about all the crap of the day, and it was always good to see him at FantasyCon. The last time we met he was wearing a particularly natty pair of striped red and black tighter-than-tight jeans with giant boots, black t-shirt, black leather jacket. He looked simply fab, a bit like a troubadour.

"Those perfect little *Black Books of Horror*! No serious student of the macabre, the gothic, the conte cruel, the *other*, could resist them, nor would they want to. His anthologies were compared with *The Pan Book of Horror Stories* series, which were regarded as something of a benchmark in their day. Charlie Black's collections are right up there. He assembled a grand body of writers, drawing on the talents of Paul Finch, Reggie Oliver, Thana Niveau, Anna Taborska and many others, and found a willing accomplice in Paul Mudie with his artwork. I was, I *am*, so proud to be part of Charlie Black's stable."

Frequent contributor to *The Black Books*, Stephen Bacon wrote: "All I can say will no doubt be put more fittingly by others who knew him better, but to me he was a passionate and dedicated soul who managed to be both encouraging to new writers whilst at the same time having great respect for the mainstays of British horror and offering a distinct market which stood out against sometimes bland opposition. I feel incredibly proud to have been published in several of his anthologies and am deeply grateful to Charles' guidance and encouragement over the years. His passing leaves me with a regret that I'll never have the chance to chat with him over a beer at FantasyCon and to discuss which were our favourite editions of *The Pan Book of Horror Stories*.

"RIP Charles."

Paul Finch, perhaps better known for his crime novels these days, was a prolific contributor to *The Black Book of Horror* series. "Apart from being a fine editor and writer, Charlie Black had the most encyclopaedic knowledge of the horror genre, particularly the short story side of it, that I've ever encountered. As someone who's read anthologies most of my life, from my early teens right up until now, I've long been plagued by vague memories of stories I read long ago and loved but the authors and titles of which I could no longer recall. And then along would come Charlie. All you had to do was hit him with a rough approximation of the outline, or even just a stand-out moment from the tale, and without needing to go and look it up, he'd immediately reply with all the extra info you needed. Just one reason, among many, I suppose, why he was such a remarkable guy."

David A. Sutton and Charles Black on a panel at
the World Horror Convention, Brighton, 2010

Fellow editor, publisher and veteran horror writer, David A. Sutton remembers: "In 2010 I received in the post a copy of *The Seventh Black Book of Horror* . . . but I hadn't ordered it as I usually did with some of the previous volumes in Charles Black's excellent anthology series. To my delight Charlie had personally inscribed the copy, 'For David, some horrid, horrific and horrible stories – Charlie'. It was lovely to receive of course, and I thanked him for the copy. But I wasn't a contributor to that volume, and it was only sometime later that I noticed it also had a printed dedication to me on the acknowledgements page. I rather belatedly and shamefacedly emailed him again, to thank him for the esteem he had granted me. Needless to say, all *The Black Book of Horror* series had been dedicated to renowned anthologists: Herbert van Thal, Mary Danby, Hugh Lamb, Michel Parry, Clarence Paget, Peter Haining. The eighth volume noted Richard Davis, the ninth Christine Campbell Thomson; ten was Charles Birkin. Charlie's final volume was dedicated to the *Vault of Evil* forum, run by reviewer extraordinaire Kev Demant. I was certainly in very good company with those other editors, in fact much more able company than myself, and so I am eternally grateful that Charlie thought so well of my work as an anthologist. No doubt had he lived longer, future volumes would have embarrassed me further with more acknowledgements of superior collectors of horror yarns than myself!

"I met Charlie just a couple of times at conventions and he came across as very self-effacing, a decent man and a quietly accomplished anthologist. He accepted four of my yarns over the years that *The Black Book of Horror* published, and I wish I had been able to submit more work to him. Of the first volume, published in 2007, *Black Static* magazine commented, '*Black Book* stands squarely in the great literary tradition of horror and supernatural fiction . . .'

"It might have said great 'British' tradition, as most of the contributors hail from these nearer shores. And that the series has been compared elsewhere to *The Pan Books of Horror* is perhaps the highest testament to Charlie Black's dedication and prowess in the genre . . ."

Another regular contributor to *The Black Book* series was singer and writer Craig Herbertson who remembers Charles with fondness. "My first and only meeting with Charles Black was at the World Horror Convention in Brighton in 2010. Charles had published a couple of my stories in his celebrated *Black Books of Horror*. I saw him across a crowded room, a pale man with short black hair and a youthful punky look. Charles had all the enthusiasm of a reclusive hermit being forced to socialise. I was in a similar mood as I knew nobody, and I don't like crowds. But despite his shyness Charles' first action was to say, 'Would you like to meet Ellen Datlow?' This might sound strange for a man who was first published in a horror anthology in 1988 but I didn't know who she was. I'd returned to horror after a twenty-year gap, and I really didn't know anybody apart from a few names on the notorious horror forum *Vault of Evil*.

"One thing became clear later. Charles had thought it would be *good* for me to meet her. And that describes the man. Always wanting to help. Subsequently, he introduced me to the then budding author, Anna Taborska, and writers and editors, David and Linden Riley. I still have good memories and good feelings towards these people – all down to Charles and his desire to help everyone else make valuable contacts.

"I had long email correspondence with Charles, all about the stories I submitted to *The Black Book of Horror* series. He was a meticulous editor and an enthusiast who wanted to get it done properly. He only ever rejected one of my stories and when I looked again, I realised that I had broken his guidelines. That again was a measure of the man: No favouritism, no exceptions; just a desire to contribute to the genre and the satisfaction of doing a good job.

"I later discovered that, like me, Charles was an old punk rocker. If we had ever met again, we would have talked about those days but sadly it didn't come up.

"When he died, I was shocked. I simply had no idea he was ill, and I badly wanted to attend his funeral. I have never felt so frustrated that I couldn't get there to say goodbye. No car, no money. I checked buses, trains and phoned a few friends who stayed some 60 miles away from his last resting place on a lonely Welsh hill. It just wasn't possible.

"So, given that I couldn't pay my respects then I really appreciate this chance to say now, that Charles was a great person with a big heart, and I sincerely wish I could have met him more than once."

The writer Marion Pitman relates that, "Charles Black was a nice man. He wasn't a close friend, but we chatted at conventions, and he published three of my short stories; we were always amicable over changes to text, and he was encouraging. He is a great loss.

"He is the only person ever to have immortalised my likeness as a severed head, for the cover of *The Eighth Black Book of Horror*."

Mike Chinn had several stories in the *Black Book* series. He remembers that he "first met Charles Black at one of those sporadic and short-lived attempts by the British Fantasy Society to encourage Open Days/Nights outside London. This was Birmingham in 2007, in a pub (naturally) off the beaten track a little, so even though it was Saturday, it was fairly quiet and we had a sizeable corner to ourselves.

"At some point during the afternoon, David A. Sutton passed me and said he'd just been talking to this guy who was editing a new horror anthology. Maybe I should go and have a word with him. Now, I'm usually not all that relaxed about going up to someone out of the blue, but this time – no doubt spurred on by a real ale or two – I summoned up the nerve and approached Charles (not his real name of course, but I didn't find that out until I received a cheque for my first acceptance). Obviously he wouldn't have known me from Adam, but he was polite and gracious when I introduced myself and began to outline what *The Black Book of Horror* series was all about (a sort of modern day *Pan Book of Horror* series), and passing on his contact details. A short time later we were joined by Peter Coleborn (if memory serves) and somehow the conversation turned to Slash fiction – a sub-sub-genre which turned out to be a far cry from what I'd imagined. Shortly after that Charles left, needing to catch his train back to Wales (he'd come all the way to Birmingham just for a couple of hours).

"I had something which I thought might fit Charles's guidelines (in fact I had two, and like a cheeky bugger I sent him both, with a two-day interval between them). To my surprise (and delight) he accepted them. It would be another five years (and half a dozen rejections) before he took anything else. Charles might have been quiet and polite – but he knew what he liked and was never afraid to reject. Something I always appreciate in an editor.

"He was also a bloody good editor. He never asked for any major changes in my contributions, but the few things he did pick up on were incisive. A word here, a phrase there."

Kate (Thana Niveau) Probert recalls that: "Charlie was one of the very first people John introduced me to in the horror community. He was also one of the very first to publish a story of mine ('The Pier', *The Seventh Black Book of Horror*). Back then I was cripplingly shy and extremely insecure about my writing. It was overwhelming to go to conventions and meet so many established writers, some of them true legends of the genre. But Charlie was one of those people I immediately felt at ease with. In the madness and chaos of a convention, he was always a comforting presence. Perhaps he'd like that image: a silent ghost exerting a dark influence over his writers. Charlie went on to publish several more of my stories, and it was always an honour to be in one of his *Black Book* editions. I'm proud of all the stories I wrote for him, and I cherish those horrific little volumes. Who would ever guess what a lovely, soft-spoken man their creator was!

"One of my favourite memories of Charlie is from one late night in 2013 – at World Fantasy in Brighton. John and I had organised a show with readings from several authors. It was all over and everything was winding down. A few of us lingered with John and me: Reggie Oliver, Anna Taborska, and of course Charlie. It was lovely to get to spend time just hanging out and chatting with friends, away from the noise of the bar and the crush of crowds. It seemed like we were all ghosts that night, haunting the hotel. Perhaps we're still there now. *The Black Book* series lives on in all our hearts. There is nothing else like them, and nothing will ever replace them. Or Charlie."

One of the most prolific contributors to *The Black Book of Horror* series, John Llewellyn Probert wrote: "It's hard to believe it's now three years since we lost Charles Black. A story of mine appeared in every *Black Book* apart from volume 4 (solely because I didn't have time to write one) and Charlie was kind enough to put two of my stories into volume 5 instead. *The Black Book of Horror* was a series intended to emulate the old British horror anthologies of the 1960s and 1970s including those published by Tandem and Fontana, but especially *The Pan Book of Horror Stories* edited by Herbert van Thal, which was both adored by and an inspiration to Charlie and many of its contributors. Thana Niveau and I were with him at the hospice the night before he died, along with our good friend Kevin Demant of the *Vault of Evil* message board, a place where many of us like-minded pulp paperback fanatics first got to know each other. The *Vault of Evil* was also the springboard for Charlie's idea to create a series featuring the kind of stories that had so affected us when we were growing up. The three of us felt privileged to have been given the chance to have one last, lengthy conversation about the literature we loved before getting to say goodbye. Charlie was a tireless defender and advocate of a pulp horror writing style that sadly receives neither the recognition nor the respect it deserves nowadays. He loved the gleefully nasty tales of authors like Sir Charles Birkin and Robert Bloch, but most important of all he was a very nice man, gentle in nature, always supportive, and someone who despite being in a business that requires putting oneself out there, had no real wish to be in the limelight. We were unable to attend his funeral but we were able to send along a few words which were kindly read out at his graveside by our mutual friend Reggie Oliver and went as follows:

> 'Dear Charlie (because you'll always be Charlie to us)
>   It was a pleasure to know you, a pleasure to write stories for you, and a pleasure to read the books that you put together and brought out. Your tireless devotion and enthusiasm for seeing more of the

kind of literature you loved on our shelves remains an example to us all. You stayed out of the limelight because that wasn't important to you. You will always be remembered as an honest man, a genuine man and someone who we knew we could always trust. You were the 21st Century's Herbert van Thal and Mary Danby rolled into one and we were so glad we got the opportunity to tell you that. We hope you're having a chat with Charles Birkin now, sharing a glass of champagne with Dennis Wheatley or checking out Hugh Lamb's library. Whatever it is we hope you are having a horribly good time, because you deserve it.

RIP Charlie, our dear friend, you made the shadows a better place to visit."

One of the first people with whom Charles interacted with in the genre was Kevin Demant, 'demonik' of the *Vault of Evil*, which he runs or, in his words, "gets rid of the spam". "Charlie Black was a dear friend and a constant inspiration. We met online, drawn together by a shared fondness for ghost and horror anthologies and, significantly, those who compiled them. Charlie being Charlie, it was some months before he let slip that he'd been busy piecing together his own.

"We eventually hooked up at some suitably horrible function in London shortly after he'd published the first of *The Black Book* series. In hindsight, these improved with each new addition to the series, but it's hard to overstate the extraordinary impact of the original.

"For one thing, it seemed to come out of nowhere (in fact, he'd set out at an early age to revive the spirit of *The Pan Book of Horror Stories*.) For another, those of us who'd lost interest when dark-bloody-fantasy hit the fan, at last had something to get excited about, and several enduring friendships came about as a result. And then there were his own macabre tales, since collected over two paperbacks. As with the anthologies, Charlie's short, grisly contes cruels became more accomplished as his confidence grew.

"For what it's worth, my pick of them is 'The Con'.

"Via his Mortbury press imprint, Charlie also published another personal favourite, Anna Taborska's debut collection, *For Those Who Dream Monsters*, introduced and beautifully illustrated throughout by Reggie Oliver. This one bagged a Dracula Society Children of the Night trophy. Typically, he never made a big deal of publishing an award-winning collection, beyond admitting in private that he was thrilled.

"For me, an incident at the hospice on that last night pretty much sums him up. His first words were, 'You've got to give up smoking.' Yeah, right. He is concerned about *my* health? I quit in his memory, though sometimes I wonder if I did the right thing. After all, he'd promised to haunt me if I didn't.

"You do realise he'd probably have a moan at us for making all this fuss?"

Other than Charles himself the man most associated with *The Black Book of Horror* series is the artist Paul Mudie, who had this to say about him: "I never had the privilege of meeting Charles, as all our dealings were by email. Even so, I'd like to think we developed a mutually enjoyable working relationship pretty quickly. Charles would throw a very simple brief at me and he let my imagination run with it. And that's basically how we worked. He seemed happy with what I sent him, and I always looked forward to getting the next brief from him. It was always a thrill to hold the next *Black Book of Horror* in my hands.

"I think I expected him to turn to another illustrator at some point for the sake of variety, but to my surprise and delight, he kept entrusting me with the task of supplying the cover art. I'm very proud of the work I did for him and will always be grateful that he chose me to be the cover artist for the entire series.

"Even by email you can get a sense of a person, and Charles always struck me as an easy-going but determined man, honest and very humble. I could tell he was the sort of person who liked to work behind the scenes and shine the spotlight on the work of others, so I was very happy when I eventually got to provide the cover art for a collection of his own stories – *Black Ceremonies*.

"I was shocked and saddened when I heard of his passing, as he'd never mentioned to me that he was ill. That wouldn't have been his style. He was a rare man and working with him was one of the most fruitful and rewarding periods of my career."

David Williamson and Charles Black
at the World Horror Convention, Brighton, 2010

One of the few writers from the old *Pan Book of Horror* series to find a new home in *The Black Book of Horror* volumes was David Williamson. "I'll never forget the first time I met Charles Black. It was at the World Horror Convention in Brighton . . . l think it was 2010, as he was publishing my first story with him, 'The Chameleon Man' in *Black Book* 5. Anyway, l recall sitting there nervously with my plastic day-pass badge dangling from my neck, not knowing a solitary soul attending. It's funny how you get a mental picture of somebody you've never met before. In my mind, Charles Black was a tall, dark-haired man, full of confidence, wearing an expensive suit, as publishing moguls are apt to do. I nervously glanced once more at my watch as l awaited his imminent arrival in the bar area where I'd arranged to meet him.

"Then l heard a quiet voice ask, 'Dave?' somewhere behind me.

"I turned round to be greeted by a slight, nervous looking chap who wore a leather jacket and (though memory may be playing tricks here) a Sex Pistols t-shirt. He held out a slightly shaky hand, we shook and sat down to have a drink.

"It was then I discovered Charlie's great dry sense of humour and we both felt instantly at ease in each other's company.

"He was such a nice bloke. There was no 'side' to him and he was so laid back as to be almost horizontal!

"I used to laugh at the way he would leave his seller's stall unattended for most of the day. He was so popular that he always managed to find one of the other stallholders to look after his interest.

"Charlie created far more than a great anthology series. He created a family of horror writers who thought the world of him, as well as a good-sized fan-base for the *Black Book* series. And it has to be mentioned that Charlie himself was an excellent writer in his own right. Though as always, he wasn't the person to blow his own trumpet, always putting his guest authors before himself.

"He encouraged me, a writer who hadn't penned so much as a title in twenty-odd years, to start writing again and he wasn't shy about telling you if it wasn't good enough. I much preferred the Charles Black I met that day in Brighton to the one in my mind's eye. He put everyone at ease with his soft, gentle manner. His vast knowledge of horror, especially the *Pan Horror* series, his dry humour, love of punk and football made him what he was.

"His light was extinguished far too early.

"I really miss him."

Anna Taborska had a greater involvement with Charles and Mortbury Press than most of us: "The last time I saw Charles Black was in a hospital in Birmingham, where I visited him just before travelling abroad for a week. We arranged for me to visit again as soon as I got back, but the day before my return I got a message from Charlie's brother, telling me that I was too late. That day I lost not only my brilliant editor and publisher, but also one of my best friends. And I know I'm not alone in feeling his loss keenly. As well as being a visionary horror anthology creator, Charlie had a knack for bringing together some of the nicest and most talented people on the UK horror scene. I owe not only my horror writing beginnings to Charles Black, but also many of my dearest friends – whom I met through Charlie's *Black Book of Horror* series.

"I first heard of Charles Black thanks to my friend and fellow *Black Book of Horror* author Paul Finch, who very kindly put us in touch. Charles was the first to publish a short story of mine in print – in *The Fifth Black Book of Horror* in 2009, and I was very happy to finally meet him in person, at the 2010 World Horror Convention in Brighton, where he had organised a launch for the book and introduced me to the other authors.

"Charlie went on to publish several other stories of mine in subsequent *Black Book* volumes, and when I had trouble finding a publisher for my debut short story collection, he offered to publish the book himself, through his publishing house Mortbury Press. With an introduction and beautiful artwork by Reggie Oliver and Steve Upham, *For Those Who Dream Monsters* did well, and Charlie hoped to publish more books through Mortbury Press – particularly collections by other *Black Book* authors, but unfortunately his health started failing. Being the discreet and no-fuss person that he was, he didn't tell anyone just how ill he was. He never gave a thought to himself. Instead, he always worried about his friends and pondered what he could do to help them. A typical example of this, and one which moved me deeply, was related to me by Kevin Demant, who was with Charlie a few hours before his death. Kev told me that Charlie was preoccupied with the problems I'd been having getting *Bloody Britain* published. The two of them put their heads together and came up with the same name: David Sutton – legendary editor, creator of Shadow Publishing, and a *Black Book* author to boot. Charlie passed away that night, but Kev told me about their conversation, and the following year David Sutton published *Bloody Britain*, with artwork from my friends (and *Black Book* regulars) Reggie Oliver and Paul Mudie. Even in the last hours of his life Charlie was thinking of others.

"Charles Black was caring, generous, funny, smart and selfless. He was a talented writer, a superb editor and the kindest friend anyone could wish for. He always kept an eye on me to make sure I was okay, he read all my stories – whether he would be the one publishing them or not, and gave excellent advice. The time I got to hang out with Charlie at the World Horror Convention and FantasyCon was brief. Like many of his other friends (now my friends), we stayed in touch mostly online, but his support and encouragement could not have been greater. I like to think that Charlie is still watching over me and our extended *Black Book of Horror* family."

Actor, writer and artist Reggie Oliver completes this tribute: "I am proud to say that I was in Charlie's *Black Book* series – several times.

"In the course of his career as a publisher Charlie produced eleven volumes of the *Black Book of Horror*. They contained stories by established figures in the genre as well as introducing some bright new stars (like Anna Taborska and Kate Farrell) and they were a remarkable achievement, especially when you take into account that Charlie was something of a one-man band, living in a rather remote corner of Wales, and never sadly in the best of health. They were an astonishing achievement. I don't know where he got it from but Charlie was a natural at publishing and editing. Nobody, as far as I know, taught him. He just knew what to do and how to do it. The result is that those *Black Book* editions have already become collectors' items – so those of you lucky enough to have copies, hang on to them!

"What is it that makes a great publisher and editor? Well, it's not just a love of the craft, though Charlie had that. You have to know how to put a collection together and in what order. You also have to curate each individual story and offer guidance and suggestions. Charlie was amazingly good at all these things. Let me tell you that every writer, however good they think they are, needs an editor. You need them to tell you what doesn't work, and what might possibly work instead. On the other hand, what you don't want is for them to instruct you word for word what you should write. Just a gentle nudge in the right direction is what is required, and Charlie was expert at the gentle nudge. With me it was usually the endings. I won't tell you what exactly he suggested to me to improve my stories, mainly because I have conveniently forgotten: all I will say it was just enough and no more. Tactful, gentle, helpful, shrewd: that was Charlie. And that was not all: Charlie also produced a very fine collection of his own entitled *Black Ceremonies*, and under his own imprint Mortbury Press, a memorable collection by his friend, (and mine I am proud to say) Anna Taborska under the title *For Those Who Dream Monsters* for which I was lucky enough to contribute some illustrations.

"Yes, that was some achievement, but, as you can imagine, with Charlie it was not all easy going. I have to say that I have only one complaint against him, and it is a small one. He was almost impossible to take out to dinner. Whenever we met at some convention of fantasy and horror writers, we – his writers would want to give him dinner somewhere. He was always reluctant, mainly because he was such a genuinely modest person, that he couldn't quite believe anyone would want to treat him to a square meal. Then there was the question of what, because of his health, he could or couldn't eat. I remember on one occasion – I'm pretty sure it was Brighton – we did manage to persuade him to come out with us, but then arose the question of diet. He began to reel out a long list of foods that wouldn't suit him until someone sensible – I think it was Anna Taborska – asked him what he *would* eat. So Charlie had a think and eventually he came up with a simple answer: chicken and chips. I say simple, but you would be amazed how difficult it was to find a restaurant – in Brighton anyway – which would do you a decent plain dish of chicken and chips. Well, we did eventually find somewhere: believe it or not, it was a Chinese restaurant. So while the rest of us tucked into prawn balls and Peking duck or whatever, Charlie had his chicken and chips, and a good time was had by all, I'm happy to say.

"Charlie, all of us who knew you will remember you with love and admiration as long as we live. But even after we are gone, someone somewhere will pick up one of Charlie's books and revel in it and put it down and think, my word! This Charles Black: some publisher! Some writer! Some man!"

Charles Black, Reggie Oliver, Kate Farrell and Anna Taborska

The following illustrations by Reggie Oliver were originally for stories by Anna Taborska and which appeared in her collection For Those Who Dream Monsters, *published by Charles Black under his Mortbury Press imprint . . .*

'Schrodinger's Human' by Reggie Oliver

'Little Pig' by Reggie Oliver

Horror from Shadow Publishing

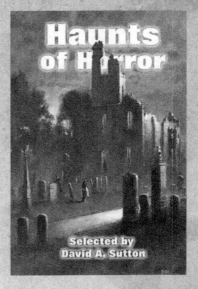

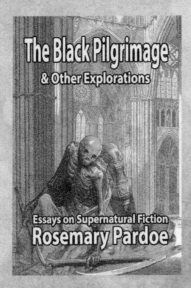

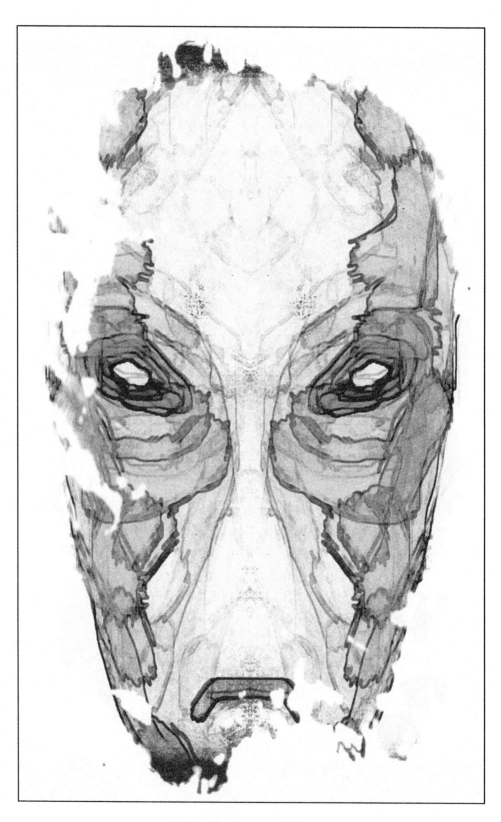

'Alien' by Peter Coleborn

WHO THE HELL IS NOEL K. HANNAN?

Interview/feature by Trevor Kennedy and Noel K. Hannan

Noel K. Hannan

After his fiction appeared in the last few of issues of Phantasmagoria, *Trevor Kennedy and* **Noel K. Hannan** *finally got chatting properly over a recent video call, discussing Noel's writing career so far. Here are some of the highlights in the following interview/article which they put together . . .*

NOEL K. HANNAN has been writing and publishing comics, short stories and novels since his early teens in the 1980s. Influenced by *2000 AD, Heavy Metal, Star Wars*, cyberpunk and the classic SF writers of the twentieth century, he has had a wide and varied part-time career which has encompassed dalliances with stage, radio and film, but which has always brought him back to his primary love of comic books and short stories. In parallel, he has forged a professional career in IT and subsequently cyber security, and has also been a long-serving Territorial Army/Army Reserve soldier and officer, serving worldwide including operations in Iraq and Afghanistan.

STRATOSFEAR (1983)

Published in 1983, it was the final example of teenage fanzine work and featured John Welding, who would become a lifelong collaborator, and it would be seven years before Noel needed to raid a photocopier again, with . . .

NIGHTFALL (1990-1994)

Nightfall magazine ran from 1990 to 1994 and morphed from an A5 photocopied 'zine into a printed A4 magazine over its five issue run, and also changed from predominantly illustrated fiction to all-comics in the final issue.

It was extremely well received at the time but the mix of comics and text – something which Noel loves – (early *Heavy Metal* and *Epic Illustrated* did this routinely) proved a bit divisive among readers and buyers at the time – the argument was a bit binary, and one which disappointed Noel, and still does. Time for a reboot, maybe?

Nightfall *issues #2 and #4*

NIGHT OF THE LIVING DEAD (1993-1995)

In the early 90s, in parallel with *Nightfall*, Noel and his team began to place short comics work in anthologies with some of the US independents such as Fantagraphics and Fantaco. Fantaco really liked their work and after some anthology appearances they were handed their primary license, the George Romero *Night of the Living Dead*, following on from a run by Clive Barker, no less. This proved to be quite a seminal run for Noel and Rik Rawling, with four issues including an "ashcan" edition, which was all the rage in those days. It also unlocked Fantaco's intent to allow some creator-owned titles, such as:

AIR WARRIORS (1994-1995)

Very much a departure for Fantaco compared to the rest of the stable, this was a Euro-inspired graphic novel, illustrated by Derek Gray with covers by US artist Tom Simonton. Not terribly successful, unfortunately nor was the attempt to republish it in US comics format in (roughly) 2000 or so, but it is about to be relaunched, with some new material, in a deluxe edition.

WEIRD WEST (1995)

Weird West ran for three issues and was in anthology format featuring several artists – Rik Rawling, Derek Gray, John Welding, Tom Simonton, David Gough, to name a few – within a "shared universe" of the SDZ – the Supernatural Disaster Zone – a sort of Cursed Earth encompassing the western states of the

USA and populated by vampires, ghosts, zombies, werewolves etc. Noel and Rik also wrote a few text stories set in this world which were released in what Noel has always termed "pirate photocopier" editions.

STREETMEAT (1995-1996)

Streetmeat *books one and two*

This became something of a signature production for Noel and Rik Rawling in the mid '90s. Originally destined for publication by Fantaco but promoted at a time when they had parted company from them, it eventually saw life as a self-published, two-book edition (plus a subsequent *Solo* special edition) which, as a printer, Noel virtually produced himself in terms of colour separations, plate making, binding and everything, bar operating the actual press! It was very well received and along with *Air Warriors*, was briefly optioned for film by Platinum Studios via the fantastically monickered agent Erwin Rustemagic, although unfortunately came to naught, as these often things do. They were very pleased to give it a twenty-first century makeover and in 2019 released a deluxe perfect bound edition via Lulu, collecting both books, *Solo*, plus some new work, also available from Lulu.

A new book of short illustrated text stories, *Blood Shadows*, is releasing soon.

NEW WORLDS (1997)

This was a very interesting development for Noel. He can't recall where he saw the request for stories to be submitted to a new *New Worlds* prose collection, but he did and submitted the story 'A Night On the Town', set in a future Nuevo Caracas where a young man tries to impress a girlfriend with his brother's supercar with the intent to take her to a mythical restaurant in the barrios. Inevitably, it doesn't go to plan (when does anything in any of Noel's stories?).

For those unfamiliar with *New Worlds*, it was a seminal publication in the '60s and '70s and the bedrock of the much-lauded British "New Wave" of SF (Moorcock, Ballard, Aldiss et al), however it can trace its routes back to 1936.

In this very nice 1997 edition, Noel shared the covers with Aldiss, William Gibson and Moorcock. He could have been forgiven for thinking he'd "made it", as he hadn't had much prose fiction published up to this point in time. However, despite good reviews, unfortunately editor David Garnett's message in his signed edition was eerily prophetic: "Thanks for a great first story – sorry it will also be the last!" We should point out that we believe this was his last editorial job after a long career!

NEGATIVE BURN (1996-1999)

The crew had a bit of a parting of the ways with Fantaco in the mid-'90s and started to broaden their horizons into the wider US independent market, most notably in Caliber's award-winning *Negative Burn*, where three strips were placed over a short period, including 'Big Mac and Frize' by Noel and Rik Rawling, 'Happenstance' by Noel and Alwyn Talbot (the amazingly talented son of the very famous Bryan), and 'Whatever Happened to Doc Donovan?' by Noel and Virgil Elvin.

WILD TUNDRA (1993/2005/2020)

Wild Tundra was Noel's very first novel, a dark fantasy set in a future Siberia and borrowing heavily from pre-Revolution era Imperial Russian, here having somewhat of a resurgence due to an icy apocalypse. Noel wrote it in 1993 in response to a competition challenge set by Commonword, a Manchester-based arts collective who had become his first professional publisher with stories in two of their anthologies. If Noel's memory serves him correctly, *Wild Tundra* was shortlisted for the prize but Commonword either cancelled the project or folded before it could be completed. The novel was hawked around the usual bazaars for the next decade until Noel discovered the joys of new-fangled print-on-demand via Cafepress.com, and laboriously scanned, OCR-d and corrected the original (typed) manuscript for publication through that route in 2004, having spent much of his downtime during a tour of Iraq as a military reservist, editing the book. It remains one of the author's personal favourite pieces of work and he recently gave it a makeover with two new editions via Lulu.com, available either directly from them or via Amazon.

SHENANIGANS (2000)

In 2000 independent publisher Pendragon Press approached Noel about putting together his very first short story collection, *Shenanigans*, which featured a striking cover by Frazer Irving (subsequently to become a very successful and popular comic book artist) and an introduction by the legendary SF writer Ian Watson, something of a hero of his who he had managed to cross paths with at an event in Nantwich near where he lived and kept in touch. This edition was also illustrated by many good friends of Noel's, such as Rik Rawling, Derek Gray, Nigel Dobbyn and many others, and was very much a collection of the "pirate photocopier" booklets he cranked out courtesy of many unsupervised photocopiers during that period!

Shenanigans *(2000)*

THE CHILDREN, BLOOD & VIRTUAL TREASURE
and *SATELLITE INFESTED HEAVENS* (2005, 2010 and 2015)

Cafepress.com, where Noel had published *Wild Tundra* in 2005, became his go-to for affordable self-publishing from this point forward, and he produced two more short collections and a further novel, *The Children*, a very dark supernatural horror/thriller set in a future Manchester where a cult leader holds sway over young people (very much inspired by the events of Waco and the Branch Davidians). *Blood & Virtual Treasure* (2010) is a collection of his SF war stories (of which there are many!) and *Satellite Infested Heavens* (2015), which was everything else, including some which would have been in the earlier volume. Short stories remain one of the writer's favoured mediums.

JOINT OPERATIONS ENTITY (2018)

An unusual one – a movie! In Noel's day job as a cyber security consultant, he has been involved with many conferences and events over the years and has had the opportunity on occasion to leverage his SF writer "chops" in some imaginative pieces for trade and event magazines, as the cyber community has been traditionally quite receptive to such approaches. In 2018, Professor Colin Williams, MD of SoftBox Ltd., commissioned Noel to come up with some way of dramatically presenting the potential downsides of Artificial Intelligence to the participants at the Cyber Security Practitioners 2018 event at York Racecourse in November of that year. After many potential iterations, the result was the short (thirteen minutes) animated movie which you can view from the link below, and which was also shown at the Comics Salopia event in Shrewsbury in June 2019. The second link takes you to Noel talking about it at the event prior to its screening.

https://1drv.ms/v/s!Apm2KTLTVyLnpUGKfHwK9HmRTCpP

https://1drv.ms/v/s!Apm2KTLTVyLn21louBOhLGec1YNg?e=SxgBMv

CAPTAIN CADWALLADER CHRISTMAS ANNUAL (2020)

The Captain – and later the Major – is a character which first took shape in the living room of artist David Gough on the Wirral in the early '90s. Bizarrely, despite the genesis of the character, Noel doesn't believe that Dave has ever drawn or painted him!

An unlucky – or lucky, depending on your perspective – Victorian army officer and adventurer, he is a unique hybrid of Flashman, Indiana Jones and a host of Monty Python characters. There are three prose stories; the first one was published in a photocopier edition with illustrations by Frazer Irving, and the second and third only in the 2020 Amazon print edition, with illustrations by Frazer, Chris Askham, Derek Gray and cover by Rik Rawling:

THINGS TO DO IN DERBY WHEN YOU'RE DEAD (2021)

Noel had decided to return to his "first love" (or at least, first professional gig) of zombie stories some time ago, and prevaricated about it until the Covid-19 pandemic gave him a hook on which to hang some ideas. Four stories set across a connected post-zombie pandemic world, there are three satires and one very doomy piece. It's a prose collection with illustrations by Rik Rawling (cover), Mister Hughes, Steve Kane, Derek Gray and Jaroslaw Ejsymont, and has gone down quite well on Amazon and at comic cons this year. Noel understands a copy may have ended up on Boris Johnson's desk . . .

THE 77 (2021), SHIFT (2021), PHANTASMAGORIA (2021) and SKUNK WORKS MANUAL (2022)

In addition to the self-publishing, this last couple of years has seen a very welcome increase in Noel's hit rate for submissions to professional magazines, and he has comic strip work upcoming in *The 77* and *Shift*, in addition to several acceptances by *Phantasmagoria*.

In *The 77*, 'Galactic Geographic' is a short sharp witty tale in the time-honoured "Future Shock" format, but like all good Future Shocks, has characters who refuse to go away (or at least a writer who bends to pressure from his friends). Illustrated by the incredible Warwick Fraser-Coombe, it was inspired by a story in *National Geographic* about panda handlers in China dressed in rubbish panda suits. Sometimes, you just have to take inspiration where you find it! There are two sequels and a spin-off series on the way.

In Shift, we have 'A Wakefield Winter's Tale' which introduces Yorkshire war robot and Martian basher Chuffin' Billy, hero of the 1899 war, reanimated into a (slightly) alternative Britain to face a new threat. Art is by Noel's long-standing friend and collaborator, John Welding. Further episodes are to come in *Shift* through 2022 and into 2023.

Again in *Shift*, we have coming up 'Unit 666', a World War II amalgam of *Commando* comics and vintage SF, horror and fantasy, with a special unit tasked to combat Hitler's undead legions, werewolves, zombies and captured alien tech. An ensemble artistic line up will include Warwick Fraser-Coombe,

Derek Gray, Bhuna, Azza, Matt Soffe, Rik Rawling and Chris Askham.

And finally from Rawhead we have *Skunk Works Manual* – a prose and comics collection amalgamating *Shenanigans, Blood & Virtual Treasure* and *Satellite Infested Heavens*, with some new unpublished stories, fully illustrated throughout. A quarter of a million words of fiction and some selected comics from over three decades of writing.

You can reach Noel K. Hannan by email and on Twitter and Facebook from the following:
    noel@ankhdigital.co.uk
    TW: @noelkh
    FB : www.facebook.com/strippedtothebone

'Galactic Geographic', episode 1, page 1, artwork by Warwick Fraser-Coombe

You can read Noel's 'The Selflings' in the fiction section of this issue . . .

THE RENAISSANCE:
A RESURGENCE IN GOTHIC HORROR AND VAMPIRES

William Bove

'Vampyre' by Jim Pitts

A passionate case for a new renaissance of Gothic Horror . . .

EVER SINCE I was a child I foresaw the Renaissance that was coming in society and with it a great raising of consciousness, energy, what it is to be human, and life. The Renaissance has been coming for 500 years and it is now here, bringing with it a great resurgence in literature, poetry, writing, theatre, the arts, and an understanding of human ability and capability – to create the world we are supposed to have, to bring us to where we need to be as beings.

Horror, terror, and romanticism have come back with it and with powerful immensity I feel it has not only come back but will be the biggest resurgence of it not seen since the Gothic romantic period in literature and the 1980s.

In fiery spirit and passion of the soul, Gothic Horror and vampires are alive again, resurrected from the imagination to satisfy the unquenchable taste, and undeniable hunger for all that we lovingly call spooky, scary, and terrifying. To hold dear all that we love most and live for. The very need of it drives us and I will tell you why:

Because we want to be chilled to the bone . . .

Because we want our blood to run cold . . .

We want to know what goes bump in the night but not let it get us . . .

And wonder what it would be like if it did get us.

We want our senses and our very beings to be seized by the mystique and whimsy of a craggy castle under the Moon.

Of mist in a graveyard, an unearthly howl of the wind in the middle of the night that shakes us with fear to our very core.

And we try to comfort ourselves with "rational" explanations as to why it's there in the first place.

Because these places and these things have such an inherit whimsy and mystique as to sway our souls with inspiration and enchantment as nothing else can.

Then there is the matter of the night itself.

We cherish the night because it is the soul of us – of who we are. The night gives us freedom, brings us comfort, never telling us we are bad or wrong, and it has never rejected us.

In the essence of the night we were reborn and given the means to create ourselves anew, and so find ourselves renewed. In darkness we find our purpose and freedom in imagination to create anything we want, making our lives anything we so choose – bringing our lives and ourselves into being.

The dark becomes sacred to us in finding all freedom and it is the soul of imagination granting us the freedom to breathe, to live, and truly be ourselves – who we are and what we are – forever youthful, wild, and free to live by our soul.

The soul of the creative burgeoning in us always.

This is why we hold the night as sacred – a cherished thing.

In the first Renaissance (14th–17th century), many painters featured art which showed a fondness for the horrific, the dark, and the macabre. Artists such as Caravaggio and Bosch showed imagery thick with rich and vivid colours, giving a grotesque texture to the scenes they created that could not but draw the eye. A head being sliced away from the neck and body while the one performing the murder looks on with a curious, but determined, stare. No fear, no shock at their own handiwork, but a satisfaction for the act they are committing.

Caravaggio gives us a taste of the dark to whet the appetite for horror and the grotesque. An act so savage and bloody, but one that reaches the onlooker with delight and entertainment. Each of us finding something new in the blood-soaked macabre every time.

Where we find brutality and massacre in Caravaggio, we find grotesque perversion and desolation in Bosch. Scenes of Hell depicting licentious acts of decadence so degrading and perverse that our minds recoil at the site of it, but our senses trace the curves of whole scenes that celebrate acts of hunger and desperate satisfaction. We wonder what it tastes like, how it feels, what would we do in their place – and the darkest parts of us rejoice in a hunger satisfied in a moment which leaves us hungry still for more. Savouring one juicy act after the next as we satisfy our love for horror, terror, and romanticism and experience all the artist has to offer in the mysterious, the grotesque, and the desolate. Celebrating love – true love – death, the supernatural, and the elements of nature – all things which are the soul essence of Gothic Horror.

Images soaked in blood and shed in raw passion (horror), scenes that depict murder and horrific acts both obscene and satisfying to those within the images and with whom the art is about (terror). Rich and vibrant colours heavy and thick that do not bog down the mind but set our senses free, inviting us to reach and touch what lies before us, as if these things were real and really happening (romanticism).

These are the three basic elements of Gothic Horror. With the first Renaissance these artists knew of these things and knew them well. They were intimate with them, held them close to themselves as one would a lover, because they found these things were to be cherished. These things gave them life and that is what they express to us in their art. Motivated by a raw and animal passion for life and hunger to be shown to us in their chosen media. Because these things are to be celebrated, loved, and lived for.

With the dawn of the 18th and 19th centuries we were given the Gothic Romantic period in literature. Again, a renaissance in science, philosophy, art, new thought, and a renewing of what is human and what it means. This age gave to us the mother of Gothic Horror, Mary Shelley. From the terrifying and monstrous womb of nightmares and thunderstorms she gave us *Frankenstein*, giving birth to a new soul in horror, terror, and romanticism. Her novel gave us new reason to fear the night and find ghoulish delight in every last scream, taunting our souls with wonder and curiosity as to what exactly is in the shadows. Leaving us to wonder if that shadow just moved and how long before it is coming for us.

Lord Byron and his physician, John Polidori, reached out in this time also, to fondle our fears of the dark, tempting us to love the night with a different kind of story in 1819 – 'The Vampyre'.

His vampire, Lord Ruthven, is, in my opinion, the most perfect figure to creep out from the crypt, the graveyard, and the catacombs, to teach us to embrace our love for the night with a delicious delight for blood. The vampire embodies not only the soul, but the spirit of Gothic Horror as well: love – true love – death, the supernatural, and the elements of nature. More so than any other monster, we are left in the rapture of constant seduction of this creature – and for it. All the danger, seduction, lust for life, and passion for living, all wrapped up in a hunger that beckons us to give ourselves over to it again with mind, body, and spirit – and every time we are all too eager to do it, age after age.

Vampires excite us with thoughts concerning the afterlife, nature, and the night. An uncontrollable wild, free passion that gives us a never-ending fuel for our imaginations like nothing else known – or unknown – can, satisfying both the known and unknown at the same time. In our wonder of this creature we are satisfied on every level, for the vampire is a thing that lets us glory and revel in answers to the questions we so long for about death, the afterlife, the night (does it have a soul?), and the nature of fear.

This is the essence that creates the fuel for our imagination and from this we have romanticism, and in turn then love of life, love for life, and for the living soul of life, a passion for living. The excitement of joy and wonder, the electric curiosity thriving in our blood, the constant and never-ending heartbeat that drives us to live no matter what. To be who we are no matter the cost or consequence:

"We don't read and write poetry because it's cute. We read and write poetry because we are members of the human race. And the human race is filled with passion. And medicine, law, business, engineering, these are noble pursuits and necessary to sustain life. But poetry, beauty, romance, love, these are what we stay alive for."

—Dead Poets Society (1989)

This is why Gothic Horror gives us life, this is why we live for the passion and beauty of the dark (horror and the macabre), of the glinted sky and the Moon (the night) and the human soul (romanticism):

"But first, on earth as vampire sent,
Thy corse shall from its tomb be rent,
Then ghastly haunt thy native place,
And suck the blood of all thy race."

—Lord Byron

From as far back as the ancient Greeks and before, the vampire has always been there waiting for us in the night, longing for us in the shadows, just as we long for it, howling and calling out to it under the Moon from inside of ourselves – from within our souls. Yearning for its touch once more, to grease the wheels of our imaginations. We offer it our throats – our blood – in the hope that all we are will be embraced by the night . . . forever.

Francisco Goya embraced a love for Gothic Horror in his painting *Saturn Devouring His Son*. A chilling scene of cannibalism depicting Saturn with a mouth full of torn and consumed flesh, eating his child with a wild look of madness and intense focus. One of Goya's most ghoulish scenes celebrating ravenous hunger, madness and the macabre, in a glorious scene that gives a heaping amount of texture to primal animal horror.

Henry Fuseli created a masterpiece that captures the soul of the Gothic Romantic period in all its glory of horror with a painting called *The Nightmare*. A darkened room, a bedroom embraced by a nightmare (a spectral and malevolent horse), joined by a sinister imp wearing a devilish grin and peering at a young woman held vulnerable and tormented by the images plaguing her mind, body, and soul. There is both an invitation and retreat in her prone form. She wants to escape but is arrested by the naked abandon of the evil that holds her captive. The dark enchantment of the moment is irresistible.

Henry Fuseli's The Nightmare

In 1897 another would step forward to bathe our imaginations in blood, teaching us to hunger for the night and be seduced by the vampire once more. Bram Stoker and his child of the night, *Dracula*, would show us how to love the dark and fall in love with horror and the night all over again. We have held the vampire in highest esteem ever since. *Dracula* built for all of us a new home for horror, terror, and romanticism, and a country made by the night to go with it, where we have all lived ever since. The very name "Dracula" rests on our lips dripping with blood and we gladly – very eagerly – drink every last drop, leaving us hungrier each time, licking our fingers, wanting more.

If Gothic Horror has a mother, then it certainly has a father in Edgar Allan Poe. It was Poe who showed me who I was and what I was to be through the story 'The Masque of the Red Death'. My soul was awakened as I sat back in spellbound wonderment at Poe's style and the passion of the written word. I was 6 years old and everything in my soul jumped up and said that this is who I am and what I am going to do with my life. I asked it how and it told me that it would show me. I have pieced myself together to be the Gothic Horror writer I was meant to be and will be for the rest of my life.

We started the Gothic Romantic period with Mary Shelley and we shall end it with her.

"Beware, for I am fearless and therefore powerful."
—Mary Wollstonecraft Shelley

Gothic Horror is also Gothic Romance, the two are intertwined. We are in love with the night, the shadow, the Moon, beasts associated with darkness and death (wolves, rats, ravens, crows, flies). Old castles and places believed to be haunted. In our excitement our senses are raised, our blood pumps, and our imaginations and souls are alive as never before. These things are romantic because they fill us with a courage for life which inspires us to do more, to be more, to explore places and become things that were thought far beyond our reach. Through these things we realize that we have had it in us the whole time and this makes the moment and life itself a truly wondrous things to behold, to live in, and live for. Leaving us with the knowledge that the moment is so important because it is filled with infinite hopes and possibilities.

"Gothic Literature is the catalyst of Modern Horror. Without the creation, there wouldn't be the amount of terror given to us in novels, movies, and media."

—Sierra Jackson

In this modern time we are experiencing a renewal once again for Gothic Horror and vampires. It is time again to taste fear as we once did when we were children. Not just the thrill of our first time on a Ferris wheel because of the height, or on a roller-coaster wondering if it will stay on the tracks at high speed going around a corner – the whole thing might just come toppling down from under us because the entire structure seems so rickety – but to have our blood chill in our veins, to know what lurks inside an abandoned building aged from the elements, and standing in just its frame the whole time feeling that it once had a soul (but what took it away and is it still in there waiting for us?), watching us as we decide whether or not we want to go in. By visiting a site where a massacre so gruesome occurred that only something supernatural could have claimed human lives in such an *inhuman* way. By going to a graveyard where a fog dwells under the Moon because we want to see if something hungry for blood will come crawling out after us – a deadly horror just for you and you alone.

Only horrors like these can reach the darkest parts of us like no other thing can, where we secretly ache to invite them in and wish them to stay. For only horrors like these can make us feel truly alive, inspiring our souls to what life can be just one more time, and we constantly hunger for this experience.

Gothic Horror has a soul and a will just like any living thing. It wants to live, it wants to be expressed, finding new ways to be reborn and enjoy another living century.

Gothic Horror's favourite, undying child reaches out for our blood and our lives once more, occupying the most favourite parts of our darkest selves and hiding in every shadowed part of our imaginations while we wait savouring the chance for the vampire to bring us into the night once more for another taste.

In movies, television shows, and books, it is the vampire which we find to be at the heart of our excitement. Vampires are the favourite horror that we want to share our blood with and our favourite creature of the night that we want to spill our blood – we spill it happily for the soul of horror and spirit of the night. The theatrical joy, the excitement, and the fun of a world that appeals to our darkest selves, served up to us every time with such ghoulish, delicious delight that we find it positively irresistible. The vampire can go anywhere and do anything.

There is one man alive today who knows the feel of the grave, one who ensures the castle does not go empty and that fresh blood still flows on a crisp autumn night under a bright full moon. Dacre Stoker, the great-grand-nephew of Bram Stoker, who follows in his great-uncle's footsteps, ensuring that the undead clawed hand of the vampire remains firmly around our throats. Like Mary Shelley, Bram Stoker's immortal work will live on as an iconic masterpiece of Gothic Horror. An eternal delight that not only reaches us on every level of being human, but a tale with a foundation and essential elements that satisfy deeply.

Dacre Stoker is the international bestselling co-author of *Dracula the Un-Dead* (Dutton, 2009), the official Stoker family-endorsed sequel to *Dracula*.

Travelling, touring, giving lectures and presentations, Dacre Stoker is keeping his family legacy alive one bloody footstep at a time, from the grave to our imaginations.

To speak with him in person was one of the most favoured experiences I have ever had as a Gothic Horror writer and one I will always cherish. His wealth of knowledge and presence are truly awe-inspiring and the most important thing to him is to keep the legacy of his great-grand-uncle alive, for his family, for Gothic Horror, and for the "resurgence", which he mentioned when I spoke to him in preparation for this article.

It is one of the greatest loves of my life to not only be a Gothic Horror writer, but to be part of the renaissance and resurgence of it.

So be sure to light a candle, wait for the dark, and go to a cemetery to pore over your most bone-chilling tales of Gothic Horror to celebrate your love and passion for the night.

> *"That o'er the floor and down the wall,*
> *Like ghosts the shadows rise and fall!"*
> **—Edgar Allan Poe**

'M.R. James' Rats' by Jim Pitts

SUPERNATURAL (2005–2020): THE FINALE

Owen Quinn

*Supernatural's Sam and Dean Winchester
(Jared Padalecki and Jensen Ackles)*

*A tribute to the Winchester brothers and the final episode of the long-running series in a feature that contains **major spoilers** for said finale.*

RIGHT UP FRONT, guys – I hate goodbyes! I'd be quite happy having my friends and great craic all around me for the rest of my life but all good things must come to an end, as they say (I bloody hate that phrase, too!).

Or things continue but in a new and different form. Friends move on and hopefully the friendship is strong enough to survive distance and the stuff life throws in our way.

Loved ones die or emigrate and the kaleidoscope of our lives bumps and impacts us in ripples we aren't even aware of.

Another true saying is that time flies and at a certain point you stop to look around and ask yourself, where the hell did that go?

That's exactly what happened when they announced the end of *Supernatural*. I stopped and thought, *fifteen years? Where the hell did that go?* More than that though, you suddenly realise how much these characters have been a part of your life and now they are only going to live on in repeats. After a certain point, I would never again see Sam and Dean in new adventures and follow their journeys alongside Bobby, Castiel and Jack. Covid drew it out slightly longer than originally planned but that was all right to me because it meant the end was not coming just yet. I really am terrible at coping with change and goodbyes and this one was going to be tough. But was it the right choice of an ending to the show? Did *Supernatural* end as it should have, or was it a missed opportunity?

Rumour had it that the main story of Winchesters versus God would be resolved in the penultimate episode leaving many to speculate what the final episode would be about. Would it be a trip down memory lane or a flashback celebratory story that would set the brothers on a new path, free from the writings of God? Could it be the brothers would finally get the chance at a normal life just as they tasted over the years, only to have it cruelly ripped away from them? Surely after all they had been through and lost, life would be kind and reward them for all their sacrifices.

The actors were doing promo, talking about a revival five years or so down the line which was to presumably throw fans off. Personally, I had a suspicion that one or both of them were going to die, and I was sadly right. I thought the answer lay in the lyrics of the Kansas song, 'Carry on Wayward Son':

"There'll be peace when you are done,
Lay your weary head to rest,
Don't you cry no more."

I also remembered Death's words to Dean that he was always destined to be the one to take God down, the slayer of God himself. If that was his destiny then what happens when God is defeated?

So God *was* defeated in the penultimate episode. Sam and Dean tricked him and his sons into walking into their trap. Jack was now a power void, pulling in every bit of God-energy displaced when Lucifer and Michael had fought and from God beating the brothers to a pulp. This allowed Jack to absorb God's powers, leaving the former Almighty mortal to age and die alone. Jack was now God, bringing all the people back to the world God erased and restoring harmony to Heaven and the world. Amara, God's sister, was now living in peace with the newly-promoted Jack. Sam and Dean had done it. They had stopped God in his tracks and fulfilled their destiny. But what happens to someone once destiny is sated?

Dean and Sam have died so many times before but always eluded it and come back through one form or another. Their eventual slamdown with God was always the reason why.

All bets were off as we see Sam and Dean visit a town where Dean gorges on a selection of pies. This was the brothers at their core: Sam mocking Dean about his love of pie and slapping him in the face with one. They had survived together. The world was still the same. There were still monsters to fight, but this time no God pulling the strings. This time there was a nest of vampires killing ritualistically. It was business as usual for the brothers as they took down yet another evil.

Almost.

In a fluke, Dean was impaled by a vampire on a spike while saving two children. It was just the two brothers alone in a barn in the middle of nowhere. We had seen huge finales in every season with spectacular effects, like Heaven falling or the battle of the Cage. Destiny had been satisfied, Dean had done what he was meant to do, so there was only one thing left for him now: to die. He had taught Sam well. They had come a long way together but now it was time to end. The show has always been about Sam and Dean Winchester, two brothers brought up to fight the darkness, the tantalising waft of a normal life always out of reach. They have always been each other's worlds.

Those worlds were now shattered though and Dean knew it was the end. Sam's first instinct was to find a way to bring him back but Dean refused. Dean made Sam promise that it's okay for him to die and tears streamed down his face. Sam then told his dying brother that it is okay for him to go.

That is *Supernatural* in a nutshell: Sam and Dean together against the world with only each other to rely on. This time, however, the journey would end and Sam was the one who had to end it so Dean could rest in peace. It was gut-wrenching and heart-breaking and exactly the right thing to do. Death was always going to come when they least expected it because no hunter gets to live a long, happy life. They've both always known it and seen it for themselves over the years but now it had come for one of them, the indestructible Winchester brothers. No matter what life had thrown at them they had always been there for each other. It was only fitting that Dean should be the one to go first. He had fulfilled his destiny and made Sam into the hunter with brains and brawn who would continue the fight because he is the one with the best instincts. With that, Dean Winchester died.

No one in real life is ever ready for death, even when it is expected, and when Dean died, it ripped the heart out of the audience. The boys have always found a way out, even when the world was burning. But not this time.

Jared Padalecki and Jensen Ackles in Supernatural

Sam must burn the body and carry on the legacy. He lives a full life with a son whom the last Winchester names after his late brother. Dean is left to drive through Heaven to the song 'Carry on Wayward Son', waiting on his brother to show up. In a beautiful symmetry, Sam's son tells him it is also okay for him to go. The camera pans back to show an array of photos above Sam's bed of those he loved over the years, including a family portrait with Dean, his father and mother. This was from the episode where John Winchester was brought to the present but his arrival disrupted the timeline so he had to go back to the past, but not before they had one last meal as a family. On a bridge, the brothers reunite to the tune of Neoni's beautiful cover version of 'Carry on Wayward Son'.

Yep, I'll admit I was in pieces at this point, as were millions of other fans. As I said before, I am useless at goodbyes. I'm even tearing up writing this piece. But it's not a goodbye, not really. It's a fifteen-year tale of family love, the bond between us that elevates friends and those we meet to be a part of our family circle.

Originally, the final scene was to feature all the characters the boys have met and been close to over the course of the show but Covid put paid to that completely. That's fine though because it's about the two brothers. The journey isn't really over, it just takes on a new direction.

Ironically, it is a throwaway reference to the fallen Castiel that gives us hope that the adventures of the Winchesters are not over yet. Castiel has sacrificed himself to the Empty to save Dean. He made a deal wherein he would be the Empty's prisoner for all eternity once he found happiness. Their surrogate father, Bobby, reveals that Jack restored Heaven along with a little help from Castiel, suggesting that somehow he escaped the Empty's clutches to come back to the world. This opens a future door for the Winchesters to go on more adventures, as anything is possible on *Supernatural*.

Things end, but some things are forged forever never to end. Who would have thought two characters we have stuck with for over fifteen years would be so ingrained in our psyche that the news they were going away struck as deep as losing a friend or family member? While we may not have any new adventures with the Winchesters on the way, we can take some comfort in the fact the brothers are still on the road in the Impala, watching over the world.

Bloody good job!

'Terror in the Grotto' by Allen Koszowski

PHANTASMAGORIA FICTION

Illustration by Dave Carson

"The water was in shadow now, so that it looked like a bottomless black hole to the world below."

MR. NOBODY

Graham Masterton and Karolina Mogielska

Artwork by Andrew Smith

IT WAS NOT until the prow of their rowing-boat bumped into the floating log that Marcin and Bogusław realised that it was not a log at all, but a man's dead body, lying face-down in the water.

"Holy Jesus," said Bogusław, winding in his fishing-line with a furious zizzing sound. Marcin lifted his oars out of the water and laid them down on the seats. Then he reached over, took hold of the man's sodden grey jacket, and rolled him over. He was so bloated that he bobbed up and down like a rubber dinghy.

The sight of the man's face made Bogusław retch, and press his hand over his mouth. The man's eye-sockets were hollow, and filled up with water, and the flesh that was left on his cheeks was puffed up like pie-crusts.

Even if he had been a friend of theirs, they would not have been able to recognise him. Most of his nose and his lips had been nibbled away by the pike and catfish which swarmed in the Bodzentyn fishing pond – his ears too – so that his face resembled a ghastly Hallowe'en mask.

"Who is he, do you think?" asked Bogusław. His throat was so constricted that he could barely speak.

Marcin slowly shook his head. "I have no idea, Bogusław. No idea at all. But he must be somebody."

"So who is this – this teenybopper?" Anna demanded, her voice shrill with disbelief. She wrenched the plug out of her husband's phone and tossed it with a clatter onto the table.

"Come on, tell me – who is this girl?" She dared to repeat her question even though her heart was beating painfully hard and she felt as if the floor was sliding sideways beneath her feet. "She looks about sixteen! You've sunk to such a low level that you're flirting with teenagers?"

Paweł had only just walked into the living-room, carrying a double-cheese and salami pizza which was still in its box and a can of Tyskie beer. He stopped, and set them down, looking from his phone to Anna and back again.

For a few seconds he said nothing. Over the past six months, his relationship with Anna had become increasingly frayed, and his usual reaction was to bark back at her, instantly and aggressively. But not this time. This time Anna could have sworn by his hesitation and the evasive look in his eyes that he was not only angry but also frightened, as if she had exposed a secret side of his personality and he was afraid of the consequences.

"Well?" she challenged him, although by now she was almost breathless.

"I'm only out of the room for five minutes and there you are, poking through my phone," Paweł retorted. "What the *hell* gives you the right to do that? But what you've seen there – it's not what you think it is. You're telling yourself the same bullshit again, aren't you? And then you're surprised that I haven't got a grain of respect for you! You don't *deserve* any respect, Anna! Because you're nobody! You hear that? You're nothing, darling! You're *nobody*!"

"Oh, it's not what I think it is?" snapped Anna "You wrote to her that she had a cute snub nose! And it really turned you on when you saw her twerking at her sister's party! My God, Paweł, you've even offered to take her out for a beer! You're thirty-eight years old! You're pervy and you're repulsive! You make me sick!"

Paweł looked down at the floor for a few more seconds as if he were trying to make up his mind about something and then without a word he stepped up to her and slapped her across the face, hard, almost knocking her over. Anna felt a fiery explosion on her left cheek and for a nightmarish moment she couldn't believe what had happened. In one instant she had been shouting at Paweł about his attempted seduction of a teenage girl and in the next she was standing in the middle of their living-room with her hand on her face, feeling a throbbing pain.

"Maybe that'll shut you up!" Paweł barked at her. "And from now on, keep out of my phone, okay? Unless we both start playing the same game, and I can poke through *your* phone and *your* email, too! Shall I? You haven't got what it takes to judge me, darling, believe me! So don't overrate yourself!"

Anna didn't answer him. She could see by the way that he was jiggling his feet around in a complicated little dance that he was ashamed that he had slapped her, not so much because he was sorry that he had hurt her, but because he didn't think that she had been worth it. Yet she had humiliated him by finding his text messages to that teenage girl, and she had deserved it.

She could feel a single tear sliding down her cheek even though she was trying hard not to cry. If she cried, that would make him believe that she was afraid of him hitting her again, and she wasn't. What she did feel was helpless, and suffocated, and humiliated.

She stood there, trembling, her hand pressed to her cheek. She watched in disbelief as Paweł sprawled out on the worn-out leatherette couch, one boot resting on the purple cushion that Anna had woven herself. He pointed the remote at the television to switch it on, and then he popped open his beer can, took a swallow, and started to tear with his teeth at his pizza as if he were a wolf.

After hitting her like that, Anna thought, how could any normal man be able to think about eating anything and watching TV, as if nothing had happened?

That and a hundred more bewildering thoughts were still whirling in her mind when the front door opened and Paweł's mother Halina came hobbling in – unannounced and without knocking, as usual.

"I brought ya some beer, Paweł!" she croaked out, holding up a four-pack of Żubr. "Hey – ya look angry, don't ya? Don't tell me ya fell out again! I can guess why! She didn't do the laundry again, did she? Didn't iron your shirts for work! I bet the stinky, lazy tramp spent her whole day scrolling on her phone like she always does!"

This short, stout woman looked up at Anna with a mocking grin, one eye closed, as if she were challenging her to defend herself. With her messy grey bun like a saucepan scourer and her tatty shawl, Anna thought that she resembled a witch from one of the fairy tales by the Brothers Grimm. Unlike the witch from Hansel and Gretel, though, she preferred vodka to chocolates and gingerbread cookies.

"Shut up, matka, you stupid cow, and get out!" snapped Paweł, with his mouth full. Usually, he would have invited his mother to sit down next to him and have a drink or three, but this evening he was clearly not in the mood.

For a moment, Anna felt a wave of relief, as if he had stood up for her, the way he used to, when they first got together. Halina gave a dismissive snort, tugged her shawl tightly around her shoulders, and hobbled back out of the front door, slamming it behind her. But after she had gone, Anna thought how low she had sunk, to be grateful that Paweł had not cursed her this time, but the old woman who insulted her almost daily.

Not for the first time, she thought that she should move out. But where would she go from here, on this early summer evening? To a hotel? Several nights in in a hotel would eat up almost all of the meagre savings she had left, after helping Paweł to pay off all his debts. To her friend Ola? Ola would expect her to confide all her secrets in her, and she was not yet ready to admit what a disastrous mistake she had made, marrying Paweł. And she couldn't bear the thought of rolling up her life in bubble-wrap and packing it into cardboard boxes and trying to forget the past as if it had never happened.

She had met Paweł less than two years ago. She had been nursing her broken heart after her twelve-year relationship with her first true love, Krzysztof, had come to a sudden and explosive end. In the early days, Krzysztof had seemed to be her ideal of a man. He was a lecturer, knowledgeable, urbane and witty. But he had always been short-tempered, and as time went by his outbursts of rage had become ever more frequent and ever more unreasonable.

He had once knocked an antique cuckoo clock off the wall because the cuckoo had dared to pop out when he was in a bad mood. He had shouted at a neighbour for smoking on the staircase and at a saleswoman who had short-changed him by only two zlotys. Anything had been enough to make him explode.

Krzysztof had never hit Anna, but Anna had always been spontaneous and a little chaotic, and anything she did that was scatty would set him off, too. His unpredictable rages and his constant scowling had led to her waking up suddenly at night, with her heart beating fast, as well as a chronic lack of appetite and stomach ulcers. At last she had packed their twelve years together into two cheap carpetbags, a military backpack and two rubbish bags, and left him.

Her friends had already noticed that during her time with Krzysztof the shine in her peridot-green eyes had been growing dull. She had become distracted and listless, and taken to biting her lip, and lost so much of her artistic spirit and her sense of humour and her self-esteem. She used to draw funny animal cartoons, Wojtek the Rabbit, but she hadn't drawn one in years. There had been nothing funny about never knowing when she was next going to be screamed at.

After leaving Krzysztof, Anna had moved into the spare bedroom in her parents' flat, and spent most of her evenings watching television or reading in her room. Sometimes she would sit and stare at her book and not turn the page over for half an hour. One weekend, though, her friends had cajoled her into joining them for an evening out. They had met in their favourite restaurant, Słoneczna Weranda, where they had ordered a giant-sized Hawaiian pizza and several bottles of the local wine, Emeryk XVI.

After three or four glasses of wine, Anna began to feel her good spirits coming back, especially in the company of her friends. She rarely drank in restaurants but this evening was such a relief after weeks of reading, TV and loneliness. She started to swap jokes with her friends and burst into laughter again and again and on her way to the toilet she even did a little dance.

Quite early in the evening, she had caught the attention of a man in a worn-out grey jacket drinking beer at the bar. He started to smile whenever she smiled, and he was obviously fascinated by the way she shook her tangly golden curls whenever she laughed. He watched her over the rim of his beer glass as she danced to the toilet and back again, but he made no attempt to join all these happy chirping girls. He was to tell her later that when he first saw her he thought that she looked like a naughty angel. He hadn't been able to believe that a woman like her would ever even glance at a scruffy-looking man like him.

That was why he had finished his beer and walked out of the restaurant without turning around.

Two days later, Anna was woken up by her phone jingling, telling her that she had a new Facebook message. She frowned at it sleepily, because it was from "Paweł Maciuszek", which was not a name she knew. It said, "Do you often come to Słoneczna Weranda? Maybe we could go there together one evening? It's a bit wistful to drink or eat alone, don't you think?"

Anna never usually answered chat-up lines like that, although she was sent them quite often. Her Facebook picture was quite provocative. It had been taken at sunset in a field in Wegryzn, with her curls blowing in the breeze and her sweater pulled down, so that one shoulder was bare, showing her bra strap.

Since leaving Krzysztof, though, she had been so lonely and bored and sorry for herself and this "Paweł's" invitation had an intriguing smell to it. The word "wistful" chimed so closely with the way she was feeling at the moment. So, she wrote back to him.

When they met at the restaurant for the first time, it was obvious to Anna as soon as they sat down that Paweł found her totally bewitching. He couldn't take his eyes off her, and he couldn't stop smiling, as if he had just won the lottery. But she was surprised how much she was attracted to him, too, and her luck in meeting such a man left her breathless.

He was good-looking, in a roughly rugged way – he was a builder, after all. More than that, though, he said everything that she wanted to hear. He could have been hiding in her bedroom and listening to her talking in her sleep, because he seemed to be her kindred spirit, a bird of her feather, a man of her kind, the best she could have ever dreamed of!

After that first meeting, they got together almost every day, and Paweł promised her an idyllic future. He would build them a new house, with a garden full of flowers, and he would give her children, a boy and a girl. He would buy her beautiful dresses and take her on exotic holidays. She would be the envy of all her friends.

As the summer passed, Anna realised that she was deeply in love with him, and his promises filled her with such excitement and anticipation that her friends told her that her shine had returned, and that they had never seen her so happy in years. She and Paweł moved into a third-floor flat on Armii Krajowej, and she decorated it with her own paintings and with some of the fairy figures that she had collected.

"Anna, for Christ's sake!" her mother snapped at her. "Paweł is an ordinary builder, a simple prole like a tosspot! What the hell has possessed you!? He wants to marry you? And you want to marry him? What are you talking about? What kind of a marriage could that possibly be? You barely know him! No, you don't know him at all! You are like chalk and cheese! It won't be long and you will be ashamed of him! You will be trying to discuss poems and psychology whereas your beloved Pawełek – I doubt if he could explain what happened in the last episode of *Life With Kiepscy*."

"But, mum, he *loves* me," Anna insisted. "He really loves me. He cares for me and he respects me. Nothing bad can happen to me when I have him by my side. Krysziek was educated – *e-d-u-c-a-t-e-d*," she repeated, in a sardonic, over-refined accent, "but after all those years together, look how *he* turned out! I would rather have a builder who cossets me than a lecturer who treats me like shit!"

Anna's mother pulled out the cutlery drawer so hard that a shower of knives and forks clattered onto the floor.

"Anna, he is an ordinary prole! You hardly know him, you do not know what kind of a man he is, and you do not know what kind of family he comes from! Why are you in such a rush? Are you pregnant or what?"

"Mum, I have known him long enough to know that he is a good person. I am a psychologist, for goodness' sake! How could he hide anything? We are living together! I would have noticed something alarming by now, if there were anything!"

"But you have only lived with him for two months, Anna! How can you be serious? He's an ordinary builder, that's what I'm trying to get through to you! He's a *builder*! A prole! A working-class prole!"

"Don't you dare to call him that!" Anna shrilled back at her mother. Her eyes filled up with tears and she stormed out of her parents' flat without even closing the front door behind her, and without even picking up her raincoat. It was the end of November now, and dark, and a cold drizzle was falling on the street outside, where she had parked her clapped-out Peugeot 406.

Before she crossed over to her car, though, she stood for a moment in the rain in her fuzzy grey jumper, and said, "At least he respects me, mum. And he wouldn't even hurt a fly." But she realised that she had only whispered those words, with the raindrops sliding down her cheeks. Or maybe they were tears.

"Anna – you need your head examined!" Krzysztof shouted at her, as he came trudging up the basement steps with a cardboard box filled with Christmas decorations. "I mean, what are you like? He's a builder who probably spends his lunch-hour guzzling vodka with his mates at work and swapping stories about screwing their wives!"

It was the morning after she had argued with her mother. Krzysztof had invited her over for a coffee so that she could collect the Christmas baubles and other "dust-gatherers" that she had spent years lovingly collecting, but which she had left behind when she walked out on him. He said that he was never going to decorate a Christmas tree ever again if she wasn't there. "I only did it for you, anyway."

After only five minutes they were already arguing like an old married couple.

"I can't believe that you destroyed our relationship for some dirtball from the construction site!"

"Krzysek, you and I were already over! And at least he doesn't explode like you! Paweł may be a builder but that doesn't make him any worse as a human being and a man! He promised me that I am going to be the happiest woman under the sun, if only I choose him!"

"Oh, really?"

"Yes, *really*! He's interested in everything I treasure the most, like these Christmas decorations! He loves my drawings, my music, even my collection of angels! He makes me breakfast every morning so that I can stay in bed longer and he always remembers that I sweeten my coffee with honey! He says that I'm his sunshine and that my rays warm him up!"

"It's your choice, Anna! But let's see if your Pawełek stays so warm and attentive after he's been having to put up with you and your ditsy childish behaviour for a year or so! It's going to be the best lesson that life ever taught you! One day you won't wash the dishes and he'll punch you in the face. Then you'll realise how much I protected you."

Anna picked up the box of decorations and said, "Do you know what, Kryszek? You can kiss my arse! Or rather, you can't! Not any longer!"

With that, she opened the front door and carried the box out, without closing the door behind her.

Education, she thought. *What good is education, if you can't be kind? I'd rather have a man who knows nothing and treats me like a princess, the way that Paweł does.*

"Good morning, sweetheart! Surprise!" Paweł had come home early from the building site, and now he marched into their flat, leaving footprints of mud and mortar in the corridor, and also on the new floral rug that Anna had bought only last week. "What are you cooking there? Pierogis? Leave them for now! I'm taking you out! No, I'm not telling you where!"

They drove out to the Bodzentyn fishing pond in Pawełs father's car. The sky was deep blue and billowing white clouds were moving slowly through it like Anna's memories, all wrapped up and sailing away. Paweł had brought a paper bag of stale bread so that they could feed the ducks and the swans.

"This is romantic, yes?" said Paweł, tossing the last scrap of bread to a limping duck, and then squeezing Anna possessively.

"You've had a drink already?" she asked him, because she could smell it on his breath.

"Oh, it's Marciek's birthday, so I couldn't say no, just one or two. And I'm surprised you can smell it! We usually only buy lemon vodka because the foreman would smell the pure stuff. Or any other flavour, apart from green apple! That tastes like toilet water after somebody's taken a piss!"

The wind began to rise, and Anna shivered. They climbed back into Paweł's father's car and he drove them to Słoneczna Weranda, where they ordered salmon steaks and salads. Paweł said "shit!" again when he saw the price of champagne on the wine list, but he ordered it anyway.

"We have to have champagne because this is a special day," he told her. He handed her a small red velvet box while the waitress looked on in amusement.

"I admit that it isn't a real diamond, because I can't afford it yet. But . . . will you marry me? It wasn't really Marciek's birthday . . . I had to take a few drinks to pluck up the courage to ask you."

Anna's heart was beating hard. Even though he might have had two or three drinks, she could see by the serious look on Paweł's face that he wasn't tipsy, and even though she couldn't help remembering what Krzysztof had warned her about – "He probably spends his lunch-hour guzzling vodka with his mates at work and swapping stories about screwing their wives" – she tried to tuck that thought into the deepest crevices at the back of her mind. It was jealous nonsense, that was all.

All the same, as she slid the silver and zirconia ring onto her finger, she couldn't help thinking about something else that Krzysztof had once said to her, that a man who truly loves a woman gives her a real diamond. But then Krzysztof had given her a real diamond to show his pure undying love, hadn't he? And look how that relationship turned out.

She was staring out of the window as she was thinking this. It was beginning to rain, and the raindrops were sparkling on the glass like diamonds.

"Anna – are you listening to me?" said Paweł. "I know sweetheart that you can hardly believe in your own happiness, but that is not the end of the surprises! We're going to build a house! It's still in the early stages yet! I've only drawn the plans by a pencil on my own, so far, but don't you worry darling, I'll take these soon to an architect and I'll do everything to make sure it happens! Our own brand-new house! You deserve the best, my sunshine! My lady must have everything she dreams of!"

"I, Paweł . . . take you Anna as you are . . . to love and to cherish . . . to have and to hold."

With tears in his eyes, Paweł slipped the wedding ring onto Anna's finger. They had chosen them together and they had decided for the ones made of white and yellow gold engraved with the quotation of Saint John Paul II: *"So far two, though not yet one. From now on, one, though still two."*

And now, less than a year afterwards, here she was standing in the middle of this musty room, still holding her cheek, watching Paweł chewing his pizza with his mouth open and focusing all his attention on Angelika, one of the characters in the *Lombard* TV series.

Only three months after they were married they had moved out of their flat and into this semi-detached bungalow next to Paweł's father and mother. It was partly because they could no longer afford the rent at Armii Krajowej but mostly because it was here in these grounds that Paweł boasted that he was going to build Anna her dream house. The bungalow was cramped and mouldy, and the garden outside was heaped with his parents' rubbish. And since she had gradually realised that Paweł would never have enough money to employ an architect, the dream house had remained a crumpled pencil drawing in the kitchen drawer.

They had not even been married for one year yet Anna already found it hard to remember when all those romantic evenings with a glass of sweet red wine had changed into nightly binges of vodka and smoking and television-watching with her mother-in-law Halina coming in uninvited from next door and taking her place on the sofa. Neither could she recall when Halina had stopped saying "Anna, dear, why don't you try these delicious pierogis with blackberries" and telling her in that croaky voice that she needed to have the starch taken out of her, and that "a real woman lets her husband drink and fuck her whenever he feels like it".

On top of that, she had found herself having to deal completely unexpectedly with Paweł's outstanding debts – loan instalment payments and final demands, even though she had no idea what most of them were for. He was always stony broke, and so she had paid them for him, even though her job as a psychologist at a children's home paid her only the minimum wage. But after she had paid an instalment for his mother's new television set, she had complained to him.

"Don't dramatise!" he had snapped at her. "So what? My mother needed a brand new goggle-box, and I couldn't buy her any old trash, could I? And you're not the only one who needs something pleasurable out of life! You buy yourself all those fucking books, don't you? How can you compare my fags and my vodka to your useless books? You have your own standards for life, and I have my own!"

At that moment, she had remembered her mother shaking her head and saying "chalk and cheese".

She had always had a slight awareness that Paweł was attracted to young attractive girls, but she could never have believed that he would cheat on her with the teenage daughter of their drunken neighbours up the lane. It was true that his "sweethearts" and "darlings" and "sugars" had changed over the months into "idiots" and "slags" and "nags" but even being called an idiot was better than being called a nobody. If you were a nobody, it was as if you had never existed.

She approached the sofa. "Paweł, you have just hit me! How could you sit here watching TV and eating this pizza as if nothing had happened? After all the things I have done for you! And after all the things you have promised me! It is not fair! Don't you care for me at all?"

Paweł took another swig of beer and wiped his mouth with the back of his hand. "You still don't understand that I don't give a God-damn what you're saying, do you?"

"How can you talk to me like that?"

"Because you can never let anything go, can you? All right, fair enough, I shouldn't have hit you. I'm sorry for that, but I couldn't help myself. You're guilty, too! You rummage through my phone, reading my messages, and taking them all the wrong way. I was only teasing with Kinga. Her old man told me she had serious behaviour and educational problems, so I chatted her up to help. You know, talk to her in teenage slang, just to reason with her in a way that she could understand. But as always you turned everything around. Not to mention the way you keep controlling me. I'm not your property, Anna! I'm not your fucking slave! You used to be completely different when I fell in love with you! You've changed so much!"

"Paweł . . ."

"Shut your mouth! I've finished this conversation. You're nobody."

He took another fierce bite of pizza. Anna stayed close beside the arm of the sofa but he didn't even turn his head to look at her.

"Paweł . . . I'm . . . I'm so sorry . . . I . . . I just was scared when I saw it . . . that's all! I've never wanted to control you, ever. Your phone was just lying on the table . . . and then . . . the message just came up and I took a look at it. Actually I wasn't going to, but when I saw her picture, I couldn't stop myself . . ."

Paweł continued to ignore her. She waited a few seconds more, her hands clasped together like a religious supplicant, but when he still refused to look around or say anything, she turned away and went into the kitchen.

She opened the fridge and took out a half-empty bottle of White Żubrówka vodka. To begin with, she pressed the chilled bottle against her cheek, to ease her throbbing pain. At the same time, she looked at the small angel magnet which she had brought back from Bieszczady Mountain, to protect Paweł, and her eyes filled with tears. She felt so guilty and remorseful, even though she knew that Paweł was lying. Perhaps everything that had gone wrong with their marriage *was* her fault, and that somehow she had turned into the accusing bitch that he and Halina said she was.

She enjoyed some fruit liqueurs, but she never usually drank white vodka because she didn't like the taste. All the same, she screwed the top off the bottle of Żubrówka and took eight small slugs. She had the impression that the angel was looking at her sadly, but while the ice-cold vodka burned her throat, it gradually began to give her a pleasant warmth in her stomach. More than that, it started to ease her feelings of pain, fear, anxiety and anger, almost like the wine at a holy communion.

Next to the angel was a photograph of the Great Bear constellation, which she had taken during her first holiday three years ago at her grandma Janka's house. It had been a magical time. In the evenings they had sat around a bonfire drinking blackberry liqueur and eating roasted sausages, while Grandma Janka told them scary stories.

Grandma Janka was nearly ninety, but she was full of hair-raising tales about rusalkas, the malicious water witches; and strigois, who were vampires;

and banshees. She told Anna about the mysterious tall man in black with a tall black hat who wandered through the surrounding cemeteries for no reason that anybody could understand. Or the devils who disguised themselves as small boys and misled local people into falling down wells or drowning in a marsh while they were out in the forest picking mushrooms.

Anna took one more sip of vodka, and then she screwed the top back on the nearly-empty bottle and returned it to the fridge.

I was so confident once, and I used to have such dreams. I used to shine so brightly and be the life and soul of every party. Here I feel as if I am worthless. Here I feel as if I am nothing at all. I know what I need to do. I need to visit Grandma Janka to rest in the countryside and tell her everything. Grandma Janka always has some recipe for people's illnesses. Perhaps she has a recipe that will bring my dreams back to life.

"Anna, eat something, please," Grandma Janka coaxed her. "Even if it's only a little bit. I'll make you a coffee. I know there is something wrong. Grandma's heart can always detect things like that!"

Anna had hardly touched the frikadelle and beetroot salad and mashed potatoes that Grandma Janka had served her on a pretty floral plate.

"Leave those cold potatoes, please. I can feed them to Gipsy. Why don't I whip you up some scrambled eggs with mushrooms – you want some? I picked some saffron milk cups in the forest this morning. Perfect for scrambled eggs!"

Anna couldn't answer. She dropped her fork onto her plate and started, silently, to weep. Grandma Janka came up to her and held her close, pressing her tearful face against her apron, which smelled as always of milk and butter.

She stroked Anna's wild blonde curls and whispered, "Let's drink some of my blackberry liqueur that you love so much. That will calm you down. But firstly, you must eat something, my child. You cannot drink anything on an empty stomach, but I feel the drink will do us good. I'll give your leftovers to the dog and, in the meantime, you wash your face. I'll be back in a minute and I'll make you those scrambled eggs—"

"Granny, Granny . . . he . . . *hurts* me . . .!" said Anna, wiping her tears with her fingers.

"—and then we can have a tot or two of my delicious liqueur, all right?" smiled Grandma Janka, winding one of Anna's curls around her finger, as if she had failed to hear what she had told her. But then it registered, and she stared at Anna in disbelief.

"Paweł, you mean? *Paweł* has hurt you? What did he do to you, Anna? Why didn't you tell me straight away?"

"Grandma, how could I have gone wrong so much? Not only did he hit me, but also cheated on me! With some teenager! He keeps on drinking, he runs up never-ending debts, his mother insults me all the time, his ex-girlfriend haunts me all the time, calling me a 'whore'! I cannot stand it anymore! I just can't!"

By the time she had finished, Anna was almost screaming. Her grand-mother kept her hand on her shoulder, not saying a word, but when Anna looked up at her, it was obvious that she was shocked, and angry too. She may have been wrinkled, and fragile, with frayed white hair, but there was a grim determination in her eyes, as if she were considering already how she was going to punish Paweł for what he had done to her.

"I won't be long," she said. "I'll just go out to the pantry at the back of the house and fetch us some plum liqueur. Dry your eyes, and don't worry. There are many forces in these forests that we women can call on to protect ourselves – forces that can make even the most brutal of men run away like frightened children."

With that, she walked out of the cottage, leaving Gipsy, her white Tatra sheepdog, staring at the kitchen door as if he thought she had disappeared by magic.

Anna stood up off her rickety stool and went through to the kitchen to pat Gipsy and tug reassuringly at his ears.

"Don't worry, boy, granny will be back soon. I know you think you should be guarding her every minute."

She looked around Grandma Janka's cottage. Grandma Janka was not short of money but she lived in the past. The cottage was divided into two large rooms, a kitchen and a living-room, and there were four beds altogether, two in each room, even though she had been living on her own since Grandpa Henryk had died ten years ago. The walls were whitewashed and then painted over pale blue, and fresh-washed snow-white lace curtains were hung at the windows.

Each windowsill was crowded with small pots of sweet-scented geraniums, which Grandma Janka grew not only for their fragrance, but because they eased her persistent earache, stuffing the leaves directly into her ears. Small posies of St. John's wort hung from the upper frames of the windows, and she used these to brew a tincture to settle her stomach.

The hornbeam floors were clean and polished and the chimney corner was neatly stacked with logs which Grandma Janka had chopped and carried into the cottage herself, even though she was so frail.

Anna opened the door of Grandma's pantry. Inside, it smelled strongly of tarragon and rosemary and mint. On each side the wooden stillages were crowded with jars of pickles and preserves and home-made jams, and at the back of the pantry was a collection of junk which grandma had always been too sentimental to throw away – worn-out wicker baskets and umbrellas with holes in and parts of a horse harness and blunted scythes that would never be sharpened and even the hatch from a World War II tank. Grandpa Henryk had been a gravedigger, and his shovel was still propped up in the corner.

Anna breathed in the fragrance of the pantry and then went back into the kitchen. Even Grandpa Henryk's bed was still there, with his black-and-white striped eiderdown on it, and on the windowsill next to it his safety-razor was still resting in its mug with a few of his stray hairs in it.

Next to Grandpa Henryk's bed, Grandma Janka's bed was covered with an eiderdown embroidered with puffy clouds and children flying on the backs of swans. Above the head of her bed hung a huge dark painting of the Mother of God in a heavy gilded frame. Mary was carrying a giant heart decorated with flowers and herbs, and a gromnic, or thunder candle. This was a blessed candle which was placed in the hands of people on their deathbed to ensure their acceptance into heaven, and which was also supposed to protect houses from storms and lightning strikes, and from wolves. All around Mary grew a profusion of wild roses and blackberry bushes and apple blossom and Saint John's wort and silvery artemisia.

Mary was staring out of the painting but not at Anna. She had a knowing secretive look like the Mona Lisa.

Anna had never examined the painting so closely before, but now she saw what appeared to be two yellow eyes. They were peering out from behind the wild roses, and unlike the Mother of God they seemed to be staring straight at her.

My God, she thought, *it's a wolf.* Its eyes were gleaming as if the artist had only just brushed on the yellow paint, even though the picture itself must have been at least seventy years old.

Anna's heart was beating fast. Why had she never seen this wolf before? She knelt up on her grandma's bulky pillows so that she could study the painting even more intently. It was then that she realised there was more than one wolf. What she had always taken to be dark blackberry bushes in the background were five or six more wolves, although two of them were looking up at the stars and the others had their heads bowed, and none of them were glaring at her with the same ferocity as the first wolf.

She gently touched the painted wolves with her fingertips, one after the other, and then she raised her eyes back up at the Mother of God with her gromnic candle, trying to see if there was any explanation in her face why all these wolves should be gathered around her. Mary's expression was sweet but it was remote, and it told her nothing.

Anna looked back at the first wolf. Even though she was now on the other side of the picture, it was still glaring at her directly, and there was something about the look in its eyes that made her feel that it could actually see her.

She felt a crawling sensation down her back and so she climbed slowly off the bed and backed away, just as Grandma Janka returned through the kitchen door, and she almost bumped into her. Grandma Janka was carrying two dusty glass flasks and she lifted them up so that Anna would not knock them out of her hands.

"Anna! Look where you're going!"

Anna's voice was tight with fear. "Wolves, granny! There are *wolves* in that painting! I've never seen them before and I'm sure that one of them is actually looking at me!"

Grandma Janka raised her eyebrows as if she couldn't understand why Anna was so terrified.

"Is that all? Of course, there are wolves! This is the picture of Mother of God Gromnic. We all know that she protects homesteads against evil, and against thunderstorms, but she also protects us against wolves."

Anna looked back at the painting. "Really? I didn't know that."

"Oh, yes. To begin with, wolves were the lackeys of Satan. They were demons in their own right. But Mary was clever and she was kind. She protected us from wolves by making them her servants. She didn't do this by threatening them, or killing them, but by taking care of them, and becoming their guardian. That is why they are so devoted to her. Take a look, sweetheart . . . the first wolf is hidden in the wild roses, which are the attributes of the Blessed Virgin. Here – let me just put these bottles down on the table."

She dusted the two flasks and then she filled two chipped crystal glasses with pale pink liqueur. She drained her own glass straight away, wiping her mouth with the back of her hand, and then immediately filled it up again.

"Plum home brew! I was keeping it in the pantry for a special occasion like this. It's delicious and it's healthy. I have some blackberry brew up in the loft but I'm not going up there in the dark. The floorboards are as old as me, and I don't want to fall down into the kitchen and land with my arse in the sink!"

She giggled, and then snorted, and at that moment Anna could see what a mischievous little girl she must have been.

"Before you have a drink, Anna, you must have something to eat. You're young, and you can't drink on an empty stomach. I'm going to reheat your potato soup zalewajka and I must say that I'm tempted to have another bowl myself."

She lifted the pot filled with potato soup back onto the top of the tiled stove, and handed Anna a ladle so that she could stir it while it warmed up again. Then she went to the cupboard and took out a freshly-baked loaf, cutting off two generous slices and slathering them thickly with home-made local butter. She brought out a poppyseed cake too, *makowiec,* and cut two slices out of that.

In the distance, they could hear a storm growling, so Grandma Janka took a gromnic candle out of the kitchen drawer, propped it at a wonky angle in a wide glass holder, and lit it. Then the two of them sat down at the table and for the next ten minutes they ate their zalewajka in silence, tearing off pieces of bread and dipping them into their soup-bowls.

After she had wiped up the last of her soup and sucked her fingers, Grandma Janka started to talk, quietly and a little sadly.

"You know . . . before I fell in love with your grandpa, sweetheart, I was healing from my very first romance, licking my wounds. I had fallen in love with a young man, although he was older than me. Tadeusz his name was. He promised to marry me, and he gave me a wonderful vision of a loving family with a house in the country and children. I was foolish and naïve and so lovesick so I surrendered to him. You know what I mean, don't you?"

Anna nodded. "You never told me this before, grandma."

"Well, it was something that I never wanted your grandpa to know about. I believed everything Tadeusz told me, so when we got together I went bald-headed, as young people used to call it. And I became pregnant. What I didn't know was that he was also having an affair with a young red-headed woman who was the daughter of a very rich family, Jadwiga. She knew about me, although she was a vicious young woman and she didn't care. But when her family found out her affair with Tadeusz, they forced him to marry her."

Grandma Janka poured herself another glass of plum liqueur and drank it all in one. Anna reached across the table and laid her hand sympathetically on the back of her crinkly hand.

"Tadeusz had given me an engagement ring. It was pure gold, which was rare at the time. But maybe he was more tempted by Jadwiga's money than he was by me, or her big bosom, or her flaming strands, who knows? Whatever it was, he had cheated on me with this ring, and here I was, left alone and pregnant, and convinced that I had lost my one true love.

"In reality, of course, the Blessed Virgin had removed the one festering ulcer from my life. Tadeusz was unworthy of my love. He had taken advantage of my innocence, and he had stolen my youth and my purity. I felt that I had lost my identity, too. Jadwiga told me to my face that I was dirty tramp, and that I would never become a lady. She said that sluts like me shouldn't even live, because I was a nobody. 'You hear that?' she said to me. 'You are a nobody!' And now the same thing has happened to you, Anna, and my heart bleeds for you. It bleeds."

"You were pregnant, and alone, so what did you do?" Anna asked her.

"Fortunately, nobody knew that I was expecting Tadeusz's child. But when he told me that he was going to marry Jadwiga, I wanted to die. Even though I was carrying our child under my heart, the vision of death seemed as sweet as a honeycomb."

"You really wanted to commit suicide?"

Grandma Janka looked Anna directly in the eyes for the first time since she had started telling her story.

"Yes. I walked all the way to that very deep lake in the forest – you know the one. Staw Umarlaka, they call it – Dead Man's Pond. I climbed up onto the highest bluff and I stood there for quite a long time. I don't know why, but in my mind I said that sentence that I have always loved, *'Blessed Virgin, come to save me even if only in your one court shoe'* and then *'Sub tuum praesidium –* under your protection.' Perhaps for a moment I had a grain of hope that Mary might save me. But then I thought of Tadeusz betraying me, and Jadwiga telling me I was nobody, and I jumped into the water. Did I tell you that I couldn't swim?"

Grandma Janka poured out the last of the plum liqueur, sharing it equally between their two glasses. She took a sip as if she needed another drink to tell Anna what had happened to her next.

"The cold water was such a shock that I was still holding my breath as I sank down. At first I had my eyes closed, but then I realised there was a bright light shining under the surface, so bright that I could see it even through my eyelids, and I opened them. I saw something completely unexpected and miraculous and even to this day I cannot tell you if it was real or just an illusion.

"I thought I saw a woman floating in front of me, with her arms open wide. She was smiling at me with such tenderness and such mercy, and she was surrounded by flowers and holding up a gromnic, which was lit, even under the water. I was sure that I could hear her voice whispering inside my head. *'Your love and your goodness has saved you.'*

"Perhaps I was hallucinating, but I sometimes wonder if it was the Blessed Mary herself, who had answered my prayer. It was then that I heard a sweet ringing sound, like a heavenly song, but sung from very far away. I didn't know if it was Mary singing to me or if it was the sound you hear when you are dying. The light was beginning to fade, but just before it grew completely dark, I swear I saw four beautiful young women, all of them naked, and they came swimming around me. I felt them take hold of my arms and hold me around my waist, and

138

they lifted me upwards, back up to the surface, and back up to life. I fainted. Everything went black."

"They were real, these young women?" Anna asked her.

"If they were not real, how else could I have been saved? When I woke up I found myself lying in the tall grass beside the lake. I was soaking wet, but I was alive, and I was thankful that I was alive, although I still found it hard to believe what had happened. I walked back home, and I was weeping all the way."

Outside, the storm was still prowling, but it sounded as if something was stopping it from coming closer. Perhaps the thunder candle was keeping it at bay.

Grandma Janka stood up, filled her kettle, and put it on the stove. She poured two heaped tablespoons of freshly ground coffee into two cast-iron mugs, although she spilled some of it onto the tabletop and bent down to blow it away. Then she went to the cupboard and came back with a biscuit tin, which she opened up and set down on the table.

"I tell you, Anna, I simply couldn't get over how I'd been rescued that day when I jumped into the lake. I went back there every day, sat on the shore and prayed to Mother of God Gromnic to thank her for saving me. At the same time my heart was still poisoned by the sorrow and bitterness I felt for Tadeusz, because I had truly loved and trusted him and I had nearly paid the ultimate price for it. Our unborn child had nearly paid the same price, too."

Anna watched her pouring boiling water into the coffee mugs, and it was then that it struck her that if those four young women had not saved Grandma Janka from drowning, then her mother Regina would never have been born, and she herself would not be sitting with her listening to this story. It made her feel as if the whole cottage were tilting. She never would have existed. It might be possible that this wonky old stool would still be here, but there would be nobody sitting on it. Not her, anyway.

Grandma Janka spooned sugar into the coffee mugs and stirred it. There was a distant look in her eyes, as if she could actually see the days that she was talking about.

"One afternoon, when I arrived at the lake, I could hardly believe my eyes. I saw them again, those four young women. They were at the opposite end of the lake, where the birches grew. Two of them were completely naked, standing in the shallow water up to their knees. They were washing clothes. The third seemed to be looking for something in the high grass. But the fourth one, she stood up, and she was looking straight at me. She was beautiful, with long blonde hair, and she was almost completely naked. She was covering her breasts with one arm, but the other arm was raised to shield her eyes from the sun."

"Weren't you embarrassed that none of them had any clothes on?"

"No, of course not. It was normal in those days. People had barely any money for clothes, so they wore the same thing every day, and their best clothes were kept for special occasions. They washed their clothes in the ponds, or the lakes, or the rivers, and they certainly didn't have such things as swimming-costumes. Girls used to swim naked."

"But if they were washing their clothes there, they must have lived somewhere near this pond. How was it that you had never seen them before that day when they saved you?"

"That is the turning point in this story, Anna. Because there were no houses anywhere near. It was all forest, the same as it is today."

"So what did you do next? Did you go and talk to them?"

Grandma Janka sipped her coffee, and then sipped it again. She frowned, and stirred two more spoonfuls of sugar into it.

"Yes," she said, when she was satisfied that her coffee was sweet enough. "I had to fight my way through the birches and the willow branches, and they caught in my hair. But my cheeks were burning with excitement, because I felt that this was going to be such an important moment in my life, although I didn't really understand why.

"In my left hand I was pinching the silver medal of the Holy Virgin that my grandmother had given me, and I said those words again, 'Sub tuum praesidium, I appeal for your protection, Mother of God.'

"I fought my way through the bushes, until I reached the clearing beside the lake where the women were washing their clothes – long white dresses, like nightgowns. The beautiful young blonde woman was staring at me as if she wondered what it was that I wanted. Although she was naked, her arms were hanging by her sides now, and I saw that her right hand was resting on the neck of a large brindled dog. The two women who were washing their clothes didn't even turn to look at me, and neither did the girl in the tall grass. I saw then that she was picking herbs and wildflowers, and was carrying a bundle of them over her arm.

"I came closer, although I still didn't know what I was expecting to happen. The blonde woman was looking at me in a very meaningful way, and smiling. There was something wolfish about her eyes. I don't know. They were starry and bright, but cunning, too, like a wolf."

"Weren't you frightened, grandma? Just a bit?"

"I think I was more hypnotised than frightened, to tell you the truth. I couldn't move and I couldn't speak. But then the blonde woman came up close to me, with the dog beside her, so close that I could smell her perfume, like musk. She said, 'Do you know why we saved you? We saved you because you are one of us. You are a daughter of our queen, and your heart is both clear and pure. Not only that, you have a power stronger than you think, and that is why you are safe.'

"I said, 'What power? I have nothing in myself but weakness.' I tell you, Anna – after the way that Tadeusz had treated me, I felt as if I had no strength at all. No character. I felt like nothing, and nobody. Even a ghost had more strength than me.

"But the blonde woman said, 'You have the gift of understanding of plants, both flowers and herbs. Because of that, you can make them your faithful servants. Everything in nature must remain in harmony. If there is evil, it must be balanced by good. You have been badly hurt, we knew that, which is why you were trying to end your own life. But you can use your gift to punish those who hurt you.'

"Of course, I didn't really understand what she meant, But then she said, 'In seven days, it will be Midsummer Night. On that night, pick Saint John's wort, as well as some mullein flowers, or Aaron's rod. Add some camomile flowers, grains of juniper, pumpkin seeds, the fruit of hawthorn, artemisia – the so-called "herb of oblivion" – yew-tree fruit and the juice of Saint John's wort, which some call the blood of Jesus Christ, and others call leporine blood.'

"'Lastly, and most importantly, you must add a single hair from your beloved who has hurt you. Then mix everything up with moonshine and leave it to steep. After three days, give it to your lover to drink it. I promise you that all your worries will disappear like the sun rising in winter, and you will have a brand new life, happy and quite different, and you will feel strong again.'"

Grandma Janka took a cookie from the tin and snapped it in half.

"I closed my eyes, Anna, and in my mind I repeated what this mysterious woman had told me, three times over, so that I would be sure not to forget any one of the herbs and spices that I was supposed to mix into this potion. You see? I can remember them, even today. For a moment, I wondered if the events of the past few days had driven me mad. I was even more shaken when I opened my eyes again and there was no sign of any of those women, or their dog. They had all vanished, and I hadn't even heard them walk away."

"You hadn't imagined them? You must have still been under so much stress at the time."

"I wondered that myself. But if I had imagined them, how had I known what herbs and spices to put into the potion? And I was able to start making it almost at once. Although some of the herbs were out of season, my mother had every herb and dried fruit you could think of in her larder."

Grandma Janka paused, and bit into her biscuit, and thoughtfully crunched it with her ill-fitting teeth.

"I asked my mother if she happened to know anybody who lived near the lake. Of course I didn't tell her what had really happened. I only said that when I was walking around there, I had heard girlish laughter and singing. My mother gave me a very strange look, almost as if she was frightened. She said that the only person she knew around there was a strange, lonely and weird young woman who lived in a run-down cottage way back among the trees, with only three or four greyish dogs as her companions. Many people thought she was a witch, so hardly anyone ever dared to venture out there. Not only because of her, but because of the wolves that had sometimes been seen around that part of the forest, even though this is not supposed to be wolf country. And not just witches and wolves, my mother told me! Once there was a fellow who went there picking mushrooms and he was supposed to have gone mad, because he believed he had met the Devil, in person!

"Anyway, I started to collect all the ingredients for my potion, even though I still wondered if I had been dreaming. I had to meet Tadeusz twice – the first time to pull out one of his hairs, and the second time to give him the potion to drink. He was not exactly delighted to meet me, in case his future father-in-law found out and gave him a hard time, but I told him I simply wanted to give him my ring back. I said that I fully accepted his choice, and I just wanted to mark out splitting up in peace.

"When we met, though, he balled the ring into my hand and said that I should keep it 'as a token of our love'."

Grandma Janka said this without any attempt to hide her bitterness, and took another sharp bite of biscuit.

"Anyway," she said, after chewing for a while, "I told him then that I would like to meet with him again, for one last time, so that I could give him a wedding gift, a drink to celebrate his new life. He would have to meet me on his own, before the ceremony, to avoid any embarrassment. He agreed to that, and so I put my arms around him, and I hugged him as if I was going to miss him. At the same time, though, I managed to yank out one of his hairs, without him feeling it.

"I collected everything for the potion, including the mullein leaves and Tadeusz's hair. I put them into one of my mother's carafes and filled it up with moonshine brewed by the fellow who lived next door. Last of all I picked Saint John's wort leaves which grew near the Bald Mountain, Łysa Gora, and added them. My mother had always told me that Saint John's wort would protect me from all kinds of evil, so I saved some of the leaves I picked that day, and dried them, and if you have ever wondered what is inside this little canvas bag I always wear around my neck, that is what it is.

"I knew that I was supposed to wait three days, but something told me that I had to meet Tadeusz that same night. I sensed when he arrived that he was rather sad. I was very pretty in those days, believe it or not, and I think he had been bribed by his father-in-law's fortune rather than Jadwiga's looks.

"I gave him the carafe and told him to try the drink which I'd mixed up for him. I was cheeky enough to quote his own words and say that it was 'a token of our love'. But I added that my love for him was stronger than my bitterness, and that is why I had wanted to give him a special gift for his happy life together with Jadwiga.

"Tadeusz uncorked the carafe and took a hearty sip of my potion. I gave him a quick kiss and then I walked away. He said, 'Janka,' but I didn't turn around, although I thought that I could hear him crying."

Grandma Janka took a deep breath. Anna saw that her eyelashes were sparkling with tears.

"What happened, grandma?"

"The next morning – the next morning I was woken up by mother screaming. 'Janka, Janka! Tadeusz . . . Tadeusz is dead!'

"One second I was in a deep sleep and the next my mother was flapping around and pulling open my bedroom curtains and I could hear some of our neighbours in the living-room. They must have come to tell her the news. 'For goodness' sake, how did he die?' I shouted at my mother, even though I had such a lump in my throat that I could hardly speak. Of course the first thing I thought was that my potion must have poisoned him.

"She said that our neighbours believed that Tadeusz must have mistaken the mushrooms that he had picked the day before, and eaten death caps. He was puking and hallucinating the whole night and he seemed to go completely mad, saying that he didn't know who he was.

"While it was still dark he got up and said he wanted to leave the house and go into the forest. None of his family could stop him. As soon as it was light they went looking for him and they found him beside the birches, on the edge of the lake, half in and half out of the water, and he was dead. They couldn't tell if he had drowned or if his heart had stopped."

Grandma Janka paused for a while, to dab her eyes with a tiny embroidered handkerchief. Anna waited in silence for her to regain her composure.

Eventually she said, "But I knew that it was because of me and my secret mixture given by the mysterious women that day by the lake."

"Why you have never told me about this, granny?" asked Anna, gently.

"What's to be proud of, sweetheart . . . killing the man that you used to love?"

"Grandma, you didn't poison Tadek, did you? At least you didn't poison him on purpose! You wouldn't do something like that, would you? You have a gentle heart, I know you enough to know that!"

"Don't be silly, Anka! Of course, I didn't kill him on purpose, but if I hadn't given him that potion he wouldn't have gone out that night and died. Maybe I look like an old witch like Baba Jaga these days, but I'm not a murderer, for God's sake! My potion wasn't deadly. I knew that it would upset his tummy and make himsee some things that weren't really there, but that was all. Of course I was bitter about the way he'd betrayed me, and yes, I'd wanted to punish him for it. But I hadn't wanted him dead."

She paused again, and outside the storm groaned loudly, as if it could feel her pain.

"I couldn't recover from my guilt for a long, long time. I tried to tuck it away in the back of my mind, especially since I was expecting a child. But the Mother of God Gromnic must have been smiling on me. Before too long, I met your grandpa at a party at my friend's house, and Henryk was the man of my dreams. He was always tender, and generous, and hard-working, and his heart was always full of warmth.

"Your mother was born in January. I remember how thick the snow was falling that day. Right to the end of his life, Henryk was never aware that Reginka wasn't his daughter. He adored her, as I do. She was always such a child of nature. Even from her earliest years she loved flowers and herbs and swimming in our ponds, and I always used to wonder if it had anything to do with those four young women – as if she was *their* child, as much as mine. After all, they had not only saved my life, but hers, too. But in my mind I could still see Tadeusz drinking my potion, and that vision went on haunting me, year after year. I could still hear him crying, too. I prayed every morning and every evening to my beloved Mother of God Gromnic but it seemed to have left a bleeding wound in my soul forever.

"One morning I met our new priest in the queue outside the village bakery, Father Antoni Pachucy. Our old priest Father Paul had been very severe and old-fashioned, but Father Antoni was always fatherly and friendly. He seemed to sense that something was troubling me, and he said that if ever I needed to talk I could visit him at home. It was almost like being talked to by God Himself. So two days later I decided to go to Father Antoni and confess what I had done. I went to his cottage and knocked at his door and when he answered it he didn't seem at all surprised to see me. He invited me into his living-room which was only tiny but crowded with so much furniture and with dozens of pictures hanging on the walls.

"He asked me if I would like a cup of coffee, and while he went into the kitchen to make it, I looked at his pictures. There was a profile of the Blessed Mary, with a garland of poppies and cornflowers and camomile in her hair. Next to it was a painting of a beautiful woman warrior, with a bow and arrows, and wolves resting at her feet. And then there was another picture of the Mother of God Gromnic, almost the same as my own, which made me shiver.

"When Father Antoni came back with two cups of coffee, I told him that I had almost the same painting at home, and again he didn't seem at all surprised. He told me that the Mother of God Gromnic was the protector of these lands of Świętokryszkie – from people who commit evil acts, from thunderstorms like that storm that's still raging outside, and from wolves.

"Anyway, I told him everything about Tadeusz and our unhappy love. I told him that I had tried to drown myself and how those strange women had saved me, and how they had given me the recipe for the potion. I told him that I still blamed myself for Tadeusz dying, although I had meant only to punish him, not to kill him.

"Father Antoni said that Tadeusz's death was not my fault and my feeling of guilt was completely unnecessary. He made the sign of the cross and he said, 'I absolve you of your sins, in the name of the Father, and of the Son, and of the Holy Spirit.' And I cannot tell you how much relief I felt at that moment."

"Didn't he think it was wrong for you to have tried to punish Tadeusz? Aren't we supposed to forgive those who trespass against us?"

"I asked him that, and he gave me a strange answer. He said that sometimes the Mother of God Gromnic will make sure that anybody who hurts her daughters will have to pay for it, and hadn't those mysterious women told me that they counted me as one of her daughters?"

Grandma Janka finished her tea, and brushed the biscuit crumbs from her dress, and then she stood up and said, "I think it would be a good idea for you to tell Father Antoni about your problem with Paweł, and how he has betrayed you with that teenie, and see what he thinks you should do."

"Really? How can he help?"

"Anna – *I* believe you should punish Paweł, the same way that I punished Tadeusz. Not by killing him, of course, but by making him feel sick for one night at least, and most of all that he is worth nothing, the same as he made you feel. But I don't want you to suffer the same guilt that I did. Perhaps Father Antoni will grant you absolution before you do it."

It was still thundering in the distance as they made their way to Father Antoni's cottage, and they could see flashes of lightning over the mountains, but it had not yet started to rain.

They knocked on Father Antoni's door and he opened it almost immediately, as if he had been waiting for them.

"Janecszka – Anna – come in! What a stormy night tonight!"

They entered his hallway, pushing past his raincoat which was hanging up like a dark grey phantom. The door of his tiny kitchen was open, and they could see that he had started to chop juniper kiełbasa into thick slices, and he had already peeled two onions and sliced three really huge garden tomatoes.

"We don't want to disturb you, reverend," said Grandma Janka. "We can always come back tomorrow morning."

"No, no, you're more than welcome. My supper can wait. I don't often have company in the evening, apart from Our Lord, and while I may worship Him, He is not a great conversationalist. Sit down, please. Can I offer you some lemon tea, or a glass of cherry liquor?"

"I think tea," said Grandma Janka. "At least until you have heard what Anna has to ask you."

While Father Antoni went into the kitchen to brew three mugs of lemon tea, Anna looked around at all the paintings that were clustered on the walls of his living-room. Jesus, Mary, and a whole variety of saints, all with a distant spiritual look in their eyes.

"That picture – that's almost the same as yours, granny. Mother of God Gromnic, with the wolves."

"Yes," said Grandma Janka, looking up at it. "As Father Antoni told me, she's the one who protects all of us in Świętokryszkie."

She nodded towards the large candle burning in the corner, its flame dipping occasionally in the draft. "And see, like me, he has lit a gromnic candle, so that she will protect us on a thundery night like this."

Father Antoni brought in their mugs of tea and sat down in his flowery armchair. When he tugged up his trousers they could see that he was wearing odd socks, one beige and one purple.

"I presume that this isn't just a social visit, Jacenzka. I imagine that you've come to see me because you're troubled about something. But never mind. That's my job."

"Anna, tell the reverend father about Paweł," said Grandma Janka. "Tell him what a pig he has been to you. No – that's an insult to pigs. A toad. A *warty* toad, at that."

Slowly, hesitantly, Anna explained how her marriage to Paweł had fallen apart, mostly because of his drunkenness, but also because she had come to believe that he had never really loved her in the first place, and had married her only because he fancied her sexually, and to show off to his workmates, and his former girlfriend.

Father Antoni listened, his hands clasped together, as if he were praying for Anna already. When she had finished, he said, "I don't know exactly what I can offer you, my child, apart from my sympathy."

"She wants to give Paweł the punishment he deserves," put in Grandma Janka. "She's hoping that if he sees for himself what it's like when your loved one treats you as nothing, he will mend his ways. Perhaps it will even save their marriage. And remember that it was you yourself, reverend, who married them, in the name of God. 'What therefore God hath joined together, let no man put asunder.'"

"I'm not sure I understand," said Father Antoni. "How does she propose to punish him?"

"In the same way I punished Tadeusz, with the drink that those women by the lake told me to give him – those women who saved me from killing myself and from killing Anna's mother, when she was still inside me. If it had not been for them, neither of us would be here today, sitting in front of you. I kept the recipe for that drink, all the herbs and spices that go into it."

Father Antoni sipped his tea, and for almost a minute he didn't speak.

Eventually, he said, "Do you know who those women were? I didn't tell you too much before, when you first explained to me what had happened to you. That was because they say that if anybody gives away her secrets, she flies into a furious rage, and makes them regret it, even if they do no more than trip over and break their ankle, or spill boiling water over themselves."

He shrugged. "Perhaps that's only a myth, but it's better to be safe than sorry. Or limping. Or scalded."

With that, he lifted his eyes towards the painting of the Mother of God Gromnic, with all the yellow-eyed wolves gathered around her. Both Anna and Grandma Janka had noticed that when he had talked about her becoming angry, he had not mentioned her by name.

"When I first came here to Bodzentyn, as young priest, I soon became aware that there was another spiritual influence around here, quite apart from the influence of God. And I mean I became *acutely* aware. For instance I noticed all the dozens of wooden crosses decorated with flowers – not only in churchyards, but also at the beginning and ending of every village, and on every crossroad. And I noticed that on every one of these graves, in the summer, mullein would grow.

"I expect you have heard stories yourselves about the unusually large number of people found lying dead in the local forests, even quite young people. Their deaths were usually attributed to them having weak hearts. But then there were all those who ended their lives in the local ponds, streams, and even in the fountains. *'You can drown in an inch of water,'* as the famous saying has it.

"As God's representative, I made it my priority to find out what this other spiritual influence actually was, because there was no doubt that it was real, and it was dangerous, and I would have to be competing with it. From many old books, I discovered that for thousands of years this part of Swietokryszie has been under the sway of one of the most powerful and primitive deities that this Earth has ever known."

He leaned forward, and lowered his voice to a husky whisper. "It was – and still is – Dziewonna, also known as the Lady of the Wild Creatures or the Hunt Lady. She is said to be a goddess of two faces, both life and death. It is a long story how she displeased God, and how God destroyed her magnificent white palace on the top of Łysa Góra. But even though He was angry with her, God understood that in this wilderness there is a fine line between good and evil, between what is right and what is rotten. He realised that Dziewonna was feared and respected by every human being and every creature in Świętokryszkie, from the wolves to the ants, and so He allowed her to go on controlling them, on His behalf.

"God's condition was that she should protect His people against evil, and against wolves, and against thunderstorms, which is why she became known as Mother of God Gromnic. She rebuilt a more modest palace on top of the mountain, where the monastery stands today, but she continued to command every wild animal and every plant and every tree, as far as the eye can see from the top of Łysa Góra.

"Not only that, she was the mistress of every spirit in Świętokryszkie, both good spirits and evil spirits, as well as every magical being, such as the witches who haunt the lakes and the ponds – the rusałki. And she remains their mistress, even today. Woe betide anyone who doesn't believe in her."

Father Antoni sat back, running his fingers through his wiry grey hair so that it stuck up as if he had been given an electric shock. He licked his lips which made Anna think that he was nervous about telling them all this.

"Janeczka, you told me that before you jumped into the lake you cried out *'sub tuum praesidium!'* because you thought you were appealing to the Virgin Mary to protect you. But there is plenty of evidence that this prayer had been used more than three and half centuries before the birth of Christ, and certainly before Mary was born.

"You didn't know it, but you were calling out to Dziewonna. I am sure of that, even though I am a Christian priest. It was not the Virgin Mary who saved you, but Dziewonna, who sent her rusałki to pull you out of the water. And it was Dziewonna, through her maidservants, who prompted you to get your revenge on Tadeusz, and told you how you could."

Father Antoni stood up. "May I offer you some more tea, Janecczka? Or perhaps it's time for some cherry liquor? There is quite a storm coming, by the sound of it."

Before Anna and Grandma Janka could answer him, there was a deafening bellow of thunder which shook the whole cottage. All the lights went out, and the front door burst open with a loud bang, and a blustering wind blew inside. The only illumination came from the gromnic candle, its flame dipping in the wind so that their shadows danced around the walls like demons.

Father Antoni went to close the front door, but before he could reach the hallway, he stopped, and took a step back, and then another, and crossed himself, and cried out, *"Jesus!"*

Very slowly, out of the darkness of the hallway, a massive wolf appeared, its grey fur bristling, its claws scraping on the wooden floor, its yellow eyes glaring at Father Antoni with utter malevolence.

Grandma Janka let out a hoarse scream and stood up, too. "Holy Mother of God!" she cried out. "Protect us! Protect us! *Sub tuum praesidium!*"

Anna was so frightened by the wolf's appearance that she felt as if every nerve in her body was shrinking, and she was unable to move.

The wolf snarled, its teeth dripping, and as it entered the living-room it never took its eyes off Father Antoni, who continued to back away until he bumped into his armchair.

"Janeczka," he croaked. "Your herb, Janeczka! Your Saint John's wort! And Anna – the gromnic!"

As soon as he had said that, the wolf leaped on him, so that he fell backwards into his chair and then tumbled sideways onto the floor with the wolf on top of him. He let out a strangled cry as it clawed at his shirt and started to tear with its teeth at his collar.

Grandma Janka lifted the little canvas sack from around her neck, wrenched it open and emptied the dried Saint John's wort into the palm of her hand. Then she lifted up the hem of her dress and knelt awkwardly down on the floor beside Father Antoni. He was struggling frantically to stop the wolf from biting his neck, but with her left hand she grabbed one of its ears, and twisted it hard.

"Its eyes, Janka!" gasped Father Antoni. "Throw it in its eyes!"

The wolf snarled again, and turned its head around to see who had twisted its ear. Without hesitation, Grandma Janka tossed the handful of herbs straight into its eyes.

The wolf yelped, a yelp that was almost a shriek. It shook its head, and jumped backwards off Father Antoni, trying frantically to brush the herbs out of its eyes with one of its paws.

Anna stood up now, and lifted the gromnic candle from the side table. Although she was trembling, she slowly approached the wolf, holding up the candle with her hand cupped around the flame to prevent the wind from the hallway blowing it out.

Father Antoni climbed to his feet, the front of his shirt in black tatters. He stood beside Anna and made the sign of the cross and shouted, *"In Dei nomine, quicquid es, abi et nunquam redi!* In the name of God, whatever you are, go and never return!"

There was another burst of thunder outside, and the wolf let out a tortured howl. It was shaking its head from side to side and it was shuddering with convulsions.

Anna took one more step closer towards it, so close that the gromnic candle was reflected in its yellow eyes. It suddenly turned around, bounded across the living-room floor, and leapt out through the window, smashing the glass into a thousand sparkling fragments. It raced off into the darkness, and thunder rumbled yet again, even more angrily, as if the sound of breaking glass had woken up the Devil.

For a few moments, Anna and Grandma Janka and Father Antoni stood staring out into the night in total shock. It started to rain, and raindrops pattered onto the windowsill.

"I should change," said Father Antoni, his hands trembling as he lifted up the black tatters of his shirt. "And I think I need a drink. In fact I think we all do. I can't thank you two enough for saving me. You and the Mother of God, between you."

He was so shaken that his voice sounded like a small child, and when Anna passed him to set the gromnic candle back on the table, she could see that two tears had slid down his cheeks.

"It's not at all natural for wolves to burst into houses and attack people, is it?" said Grandma Janka. She sounded as upset as him. "Maybe that one had rabies! Or maybe it was a werewolf!"

"I don't believe it was a werewolf, Janeczka, or even a wolf, for that matter. I'm almost certain that I was being given a warning by Dziewanna. Of course it wasn't Dziewanna in person, but her servant."

"Do you really mean that?" asked Anna. "But why?"

"Somehow she must have found out that you are here with me. And she must have suspected that I was explaining to you the mystery of how she and her rusałki saved your grandmother. Believe me, my child, there have been many times in the past when she has demonstrated how strong her influence is in this region, and how angry she can be when anyone gives away her secrets. She has demonstrated it again tonight."

He crossed himself twice, and then he said, "Let me change and fetch us a drink."

He went first into his bedroom and then into his kitchen. He came back into the living-room wearing a bobbly green cable-knit sweater, with a thick grey blanket draped over his arm. He was also carrying a carafe of vodka. Once had set the carafe down on the table, he went over to the window, climbed on a footstool, and hung the blanket from the curtain-rail.

"There! I don't know if that will keep any more of Dziewanna's demons out, but it will seal off the draught and keep out the worst of the rain."

He took three glasses out of his corner cupboard, tugged the stopper off the carafe and poured them each a large measure of vodka. He said *"naz drowie!"* and drained his own glass at once. He gave a shiver as if somebody had walked over his grave, and then poured himself another.

"Although this is God's land, every day-to-day occurrence in these villages and these forests is observed by Dziewanna and has to meet with her approval. Tonight we may have chased her servant away, but that doesn't mean for a moment that she has forgiven me, and that tomorrow I will be safe."

He swallowed more vodka, and coughed, and glanced uneasily at the curtain over the window, which was bulging in the wind.

"We will pray to her, reverend, that she takes you under her protection," said Grandma Janka.

"Well, thank you, Janeczka, I would be deeply grateful if you did. It's clear that you have a special bond with her, like a blood relationship, almost as if you were her own daughter. And around here she has the final decision over life or death."

He finished his second glass of vodka and poured himself a third, his hands still shaking. "Her rusałki gave you the formula, but it was Dziewanna who invested it with the power to punish Tadeusz for betraying you. You realise that if Anna wants to rap her husband on the knuckles, you will have to find some way of getting in touch with her again, either in person or through her witches.

"You have the recipe for the potion, but it needs Dziewanna's enchantment if it is going to work. Nobody gets punished without her backing. So if you can make contact with her in any way, then perhaps at the same time you could prevail upon her to forgive me for divulging her secrets."

Anna took no more than a sip of her vodka. Its taste reminded her too much of Paweł's breath, and it reminded her too painfully of why she had come here to Father Antoni's cottage, and how bitter she felt, and how cheated.

As she sat there, though, she wondered why Father Antoni seemed to be so ready to sanction her plan to punish Paweł. But then there was a sudden gust of wind, and the blanket bulged out again, with a whistling noise, as if some bulky creature were trying to push its way in through the window. Father Antoni gave a nervous little jump and spilled some of his drink, and Anna realised that it was not what happened to Paweł he was worried about. It was himself. He may have been the servant of God, but he was terrified of Dziewanna.

Anna spent the rest of night at Grandma Janka's cottage, huddled up under a blanket on the sofa, and fell into a deep dreamless sleep. She didn't even hear the cock crowing in the neighbour's yard as it began to grow light.

Just after seven o'clock, Grandma Janka shook her shoulder, and said, "Anna, sweetheart, wake up! I've made breakfast for us. Scrambled eggs with mushrooms, and fresh coffee."

Anna tied back her hair and sat down at the table.

Grandma Janka watched her for a while as she ate, and then she said, "Anna sweetheart, are you still sure that she want to punish Paweł? I was thinking about it a lot during the night. He's hurt you very much, hasn't he? And it's obvious that he never deserved you, any more than Tadeusz deserved me."

Anna nodded. "He promised me so much, granny. I thought we were going to have the most wonderful life you could imagine. A beautiful house, a boy and a girl, happy evenings together. Instead, what did I get? Drunkenness, and insults, and him cheating on me with a teenager. Worst of all, he told me over and over again that I am a nobody, worth nothing. He's ruined my whole life, granny. It's totally empty. *I'm* empty. I feel as if I don't have a soul anymore."

Grandma Janka poured her some more coffee. "If you still want me to, I can prepare Dziewanna's drink. Of course we will have to find some way of seeking her power to make it work. But I've been wondering if that woman is still living in that cottage amongst the trees – that woman who was supposed to be a witch. She'll be older now, much older, but if she really *is* a witch, then she should know how to get in touch with Dziewanna.

"I have most of the necessary herbs and spices already, in my larder, although we'll need to pick some fresh Saint John's wort, and you'll have to find a way of plucking out one of Paweł's hairs."

Anna put down her fork and reached over to the sofa to pick up her purse. She opened it up and produced a hairbrush, with hairs still clinging on to it. Most of them were hers, and blonde, but there were two or three dark brown hairs.

"The last time we were out together, at Rysiek's pub, it was really windy outside, and before we went inside Paweł borrowed my hairbrush. I've been meaning to clean it."

"In that case, sweetheart, we have everything we need. Finish your breakfast and we'll go out looking for the Lady of the Wild Creatures!"

They walked first to Dead Man's Pond, in case they might see the rusałki, but there was nobody there, and all they could see in the water were the reflections of the clouds, and the birch trees.

From there, they struggled their way through the ferns and the bramble bushes, and into the forest. It was gloomy and airless among the trees. No birds sang, and there was no sign of wolves, or squirrels, or any other creatures. Apart from the rustling firs, all that Anna could hear was Grandma Janka repeatedly muttering, "Under your protection, my Lady."

After nearly an hour Anna began to grow tired. "Granny," she said, "I think we're lost! We passed this same tree once before! I'm sure of it because it has a fungus growing on it that looks like a koala bear."

Grandma Janka smiled and tapped her forehead. "You're thinking that I've gone crackers in my old age, aren't you? You didn't see the signs. We've been straying because Dziewanna wants us to stray. She misleads everyone until she is sure of their intentions. But I believe she senses the bond between you and me, because we've been passing one by one the plants that signify her presence. There, you see – a juniper bush. Now we have only the mullein left."

She was right. They had to walk less than a hundred metres more before they arrived in a sunlit clearing. In the middle of the clearing stood a small wooden shack, surrounded by a nodding sea of mullein and mugwort leaves, with smoke running from its chimney.

"Why didn't we see that before?" asked Anna. She was bewildered, but strangely thrilled, too. The appearance of the shack was like something out a Grimm's fairytale. A massive grey dog was sleeping in the ramshackle porch. It looked like a wolf, but Anna recognised it as a Czechoslovakian wolfdog, a loyal breed which were rarely aggressive.

As they came closer, she saw another wolfdog sitting in the shade of a juniper bush by the side of the house, but this one was awake and alert and watching them intently.

They reached the steps in front of the porch. The sleeping wolfdog stirred, and at the same time the front door opened and a diminutive old lady appeared, carrying a basket filled with red apples, and again Anna was put in mind of a fairy tale.

The old lady's long grey hair was knotted into a bun, and she was wearing a white scarf around her neck with a pattern of nightingales and strawberries on it, and a long brown dress. But it was her eyes that caught Anna's attention. They were a wolf-grey colour, glimmering in the sunlight, and even though the old lady was smiling, there was something predatory about the way she was looking at them.

"Well, well!" she said. "We are seeing you again, Janeczka, after all this time! Have you come to visit us for any special reason? Not that we aren't delighted to see you, my dear, no matter why you have come to see us."

Anna found it almost impossible to shake off the feeling that she was in a fairy story. The old lady's face was constantly eddying and changing as if she were a hologram. One minute she looked like a kind-hearted old biddy who wouldn't step on a spider, but then she melted into a mischievous witch with hungry eyes, an elongated nose like a wolf's muzzle and a grin full of pointed teeth. She could have been the wolf from Red Riding Hood.

Grandma Janka mounted the first step up to the porch, but her voice sounded thin and dry, and Anna could tell that she was very nervous.

"I know that almighty Dziewanna has already granted me one favour, or I wouldn't be alive today. But now I need to ask for another."

'Then, my dear, why don't you?" said the old lady, still smiling in that wolfish way. As soon as she spoke, the wolfdog came trotting in from under the juniper bush and sat beside her, like a guard-dog, so that she could lay her hand on its neck.

"This is my grand-daughter, Anna," said Grandma Janka. "She has been hurt by the man she fell truly in love with, just as I was, all those years ago. He has misled her and lied to her and used her, right from the moment they first met. He has been unfaithful to her and he has struck her, too. And he still does it, and shows no remorse. He needs to be punished."

"And how would you punish him?" asked the old lady.

"I still have the recipe for the potion which Dziewanna gave me, to punish my own husband, Tadeusz. Most of the necessary herbs are stored in my larder, and Anna already has a stray hair from her husband, Paweł. All we lack now is Dziewanna's blessing, to give the potion its power."

"And this is what the priest said that you needed?"

Grandma Janka opened her mouth and closed it again, but said nothing. She looked around at Anna and took a step back down, clutching her shawl. There was only one way in which this old lady could possibly know what Father Antoni had told them.

Just then, both wolfdogs growled and stood up. Around the side of the cottage a young woman appeared – a beautiful young woman with curly blonde hair like Anna's, wearing a very short green dress, and sandals. As she came up to them, smiling like the old lady, Anna could see that she, too, had wolf-grey eyes, and white teeth that looked as if they had been sharpened.

"Viki!" said the old lady. "Don't you remember our Janeczka?"

"Of course!" smiled the young woman, and gave both Grandma Janka and Anna a friendly little nod of her curls.

Grandma Janka kept her shawl clutched tightly to her throat. "You look – you look *so* much like – but, no, you can't be. I'm sorry. It's only me being silly. That was all much too long ago."

The old lady said, "Come to visit me again, Janka, in five days' time. That will be the fifteenth day of August, the Assumption of Mary, when the sun's rays start to turn red. Bring your potion with you."

"Yes," said Grandma Janka. "Thank you. Thank you very much."

The old lady and the young girl said nothing more, but continued to smile at them. Grandma Janka took hold of Anna's arm and the two of them left the clearing and walked back through the forest, without turning around. Anna had a weird feeling that if she did, the old lady's cottage would no longer be there, vanished like a dream.

"Who did that girl remind you of, granny?" asked Anna, as they emerged from the forest and started back on the stony path that would take them to Grandma Janka's cottage.

"It doesn't matter, sweetheart. I think my brain has turned into a rotten mushroom."

Anna stayed with Grandma Janka for the next five days, borrowing some of the dresses that she found in the back of her wardrobe. She had obviously not worn them since Grandpa Henryk was alive, because they were far too young for her now, and they smelled of stale perfume.

Grandma Janka set a large iron pot on top of her stove and started to brew up Dziewanna's potion. The cottage was soon filled with a heady herbal aroma which made Anna feel quite light-headed. It persisted, this aroma, for the whole five days, and at night it gave Anna some of the strangest dreams she had ever had. In one of them, she was swimming in a dark lake with four naked girls, and she could hear quavering flute music.

When it was ready, Grandma Janka poured the potion into a one-litre glass bottle. Although it was brewed with herbs, it was a pale carmine colour. She carefully dropped in one of Paweł's hairs, corked it, and lifted it onto the shelf beneath the picture of Mother of God Gromnic, to steep.

Anna looked at the bottle from time to time and wondered if she were doing the right thing, taking revenge on Paweł. But then she thought of Paweł's lewd suggestions to that teenage girl next door, and how hard he had slapped her face, without feeling any remorse for it. He deserved to puke his guts up, she thought, and to lose his unbearable swagger, even if it was only for one night. Not that she would ever go back to him, even if he did learn his lesson.

On the morning of the fifteenth, after breakfast, Anna went out into Grandma Janka's overgrown garden, so that she could pick bluebells and oxeye daisies and cornflowers. The garden was crowded with dozens of butterflies, and she noticed that most of them were peacocks, dark red with spots on their wings that looked like human eyes. Peacock butterflies were rare, usually, but she knew that they were sometimes supposed to flutter over Dziewanna's head, like a living coronet, or a halo.

She held out her hand and one of the butterflies settled on her fingertip. Its eye-spots seemed to be staring at her, as if it knew who she was. Just then, Grandma Janka opened the kitchen window and called out, "Come on, Anna. Today is the day! We have to go!"

The butterfly flew off, and all the rest of them fluttered away, too, in a cloud. Anna stood there for a while, watching the last of them disappear. All she could hear now was the monotonous music of crickets. For some reason, she thought they sounded anxious, or perhaps the anxiety was hers.

Anna and Grandma Janka made their way through the forest again, and this time they were able to walk directly to the clearing. As they approached the cottage, though, Grandma Janka caught hold of Anna's sleeve and said, "Wait, sweetheart. Look. Those are not the same wolfdogs."

Standing in the porch were two brindled wolves, with gleaming yellow eyes. Their tongues were hanging out and they were panting in the midday heat.

The cottage door opened, and a third wolf came out to join them. It was immediately followed not by the old lady with her basket of apples, but by a tall young woman with braided blonde hair. She was strikingly beautiful, this young woman, with high cheekbones and slanted grey eyes, and she was wearing a short clinging dress of pale chamois leather, with fur around the collar and the hem.

"Dzeiwanna," breathed Grandma Janka, and she sank to her knees onto the ground. *"Sub tuum praesidium."*

Anna remained standing, with her hands laid protectively on her grandmother's shoulders, but she could hardly believe that what she was seeing was real.

Smiling, the young woman came down the cottage steps, and the three wolves came down after her, still panting. At the same time, the girl called Viki appeared around the side of the cottage, with two other young girls, both equally pretty, one red-haired and the other with wild wavy hair the colour of hazelnuts.

"Please, get up," said Dziewanna, holding out her hand to help Grandma Janka back up onto her feet. "You are one of my daughters, Janeczka. You and your daughters and your daughter's daughters can always rely on our protection."

"You remember us, Janeczka?" asked Viki.

Grandma Janka could only nod. Anna stared at the young women in disbelief. Were these really the same rusałki who had saved her granny from drowning? How could that be possible? Yes, inexplicably, she felt as if she knew them, as if they were long-lost cousins.

"You have brought the potion?" asked Dziewanna.

Grandma Janka lifted the bottle out of her canvas shopping-bag. She handed it to Dziewanna, and Dziewanna took it in both hands. She held it up so that the sun shone through it, and then she closed her eyes and pressed it against her forehead.

"Through drinking this potion, may Paweł learn the invincible power of womanhood," she intoned, as if she were saying a prayer. "May his arrogance desert him, as rats run off into the darkness. And may nobody recognise him, as he refused to recognise the woman he betrayed."

She handed the bottle back to Grandma Janka, and blew Anna a kiss with her fingertips, as gentle as that peacock butterfly. Anna wanted to ask her how in the world she had known Paweł's name, but before she could speak, Dziewanna turned around and climbed back up the steps to the porch, with her three wolves close behind her.

Viki and the other two girls smiled and waved and walked away, and in a few moments Anna and Grandma Janka were standing on their own.

"I think I might wake up soon," said Grandma Janka. She lifted the bottle of potion out of her bag, stared at it, and then put it back. "It doesn't *look* any different. But you know what you have to do now, don't you, Anna?"

Anna dialled Paweł's number. It was 11:30, but she knew that his break at work was not for another half an hour.

"Anka? I'm at work. I'm busy, for fuck's sake! Don't you remember that my lunch-hour is always at twelve? Is something wrong? What happened? Are you coming back?"

Anna found it unexpectedly hard to speak, but after a pause she managed to say, "Yes. Tomorrow morning."

"That's good. But listen – I can't talk now, don't you understand? I'll call you back when I've finished my lunch. I didn't write to you before because I wanted you to have a good time with your granny, and anyway I didn't want you picking fucking holes in me again. You always know better, don't you? I'll call you later. Well, maybe I'll call you later – so long as you promise to stop driving me fucking crazy."

With that, Paweł rang off, without saying goodbye.

He's never going to change, thought Anna. Her heart was beating fast, as if she had been running. Grandma Janka came up behind her and laid her hand gently on her shoulder. There was no need for words.

Anna waited, but it was nearly 2:00 pm before Paweł rang back. He sounded in a much better mood, but he was slurring his words, and she knew that he must have drunk his usual midday beers, never less than three cans of Tyskie, with lemon vodka chasers.

"Hello, my sweetie-pie! I'm so sorry I forgot to call you back. I'm happy you're coming home. I've been missing you, sweetie, do you know that? I've been missing your sweet pussy! I'll be back around twelve, okay? Think what you're going to cook for our lunch. Listen – I have to finish this call now. I'll see you tomorrow. Make sure you're ready – do you know what I mean?"

Anna put down her phone. Her hands were trembling. Any hesitation she might have felt about punishing Paweł had been completely dispelled by his blurry drunken voice, and by the way he still talked to her as if she were nothing, and nobody.

She returned to house early the following morning, before 8:00 a.m., and let herself in with the keys that were hidden under a stone. As soon as she walked in, she smelled the familiar fusty odour of dampness and mould. Since she had been away at Grandma Janka's, Paweł had done no cleaning or tidying up. He had left two greasy pizza boxes on the sofa and half-a-dozen dented beer cans on the coffee table.

He had started to sand the living-room walls and paint some undercoat on them, but he had failed to protect anything with sheets. Thick white plaster-dust covered her little desk, all over her laptop and her brand-new printer and the books she loved. The floor was crunchy with grit, and a half-empty bucket of pale yellow paint was standing in the fireplace, with a roller still in it.

In the kitchen Paweł had left his unwashed coffee mug in the sink, but there were no dirty plates, so while she was gone she guessed that he must have subsisted on nothing but pizzas and McDonald's take-aways. In the bathroom, the fluffy turquoise towels that her parents had given her for her last birthday were smeared in mud and oil, and one of them was scrunched up on the floor beside the toilet, and smelled of vomit.

Anna went into the kitchen, opened up her shopping bag, and started to prepare lunch – ham stew with mushroom sauce and puréed potatoes. She was tempted to start cleaning the house, but she resisted the temptation. After today, she was going to come back here only to collect her clothes and her belongings. All she did was pick up the pizza boxes from the sofa and throw the beer cans in the bin.

Just after noon, the front door banged open and Paweł came in, stumbling over the doormat.

"Hi, sweetie-pie!" he called out, and weaved his way through to the kitchen, where Anna was slicing up a cucumber. "What's for lunch? I'm starving!"

He came up behind her and squeezed the right cheek of her bottom, breathing alcohol and cigarette smoke into her neck.

"Paweł, don't tell me that you drove back here on your own! You're drunk! And you don't even have a license, anyway!"

"There you fucking are!" he blurted out, taking two unsteady steps back. "You always screw everything up, right from the start! The normal woman kisses her husband! And you say you love me? Why can't you be normal, like other women? Always bitching! Always picking holes! Anka the Almighty!"

Anna took a deep breath. She told herself that she needed to ease up on him, because she had come here with one purpose and one purpose only. She turned around and touched his shoulder, and gave him a conciliatory smile, although she couldn't bring herself to kiss him. His eyes were bloodshot and his lips were cracked and he was unshaven.

"Yes, Paweł, maybe you're right. Maybe I am too critical. I must have inherited it from my granny. But here, look, I've brought something else from my granny, something really delicious. It's her home-made liquor. You've tasted some of her liquor before, haven't you? You remember that blackberry vodka she gave us?"

"Great! We can start with some of that. But I've got a bottle of Soplica vodka and some red wine, and plenty of beer, so we won't go thirsty! Just let me go and water the horses!"

He staggered out of the kitchen and into the bathroom. He left the door open so that Anna could hear him noisily urinating.

While was out of the kitchen, she took out two glasses. One she filled with raspberry juice, which she diluted with water. The other she filled with Dziewanna's pale carmine potion.

"Here," she said, as Paweł came back in, struggling to zip up his trousers. "Let's drink a toast for us! Then, after lunch, why don't we go for a romantic walk by the river?"

"You, Anka – you're gorgeous!" said Paweł. "Let's drink to our love!" He raised his glass and bonked it against Anna's glass. *"Brzdęk! Ping!"* after which he chugged down his whole glassful in one.

After he had swallowed it, he licked his lips and frowned at his empty glass. "What flavour was that? I've never tasted a drink like that before. It's kind of bitter. You know what it reminds me of? When we used to smoke mugwort leaves at school, to get high."

Anna served out their lunch. Paweł hunched over his plate, shovelling his stew into his mouth so that it dripped down his chin. He said very little, as if everything between them was back to the way it was, before she had discovered that he had been unfaithful, and hit her.

He poured them each a large glass of red wine, although Anna only sipped hers. By the time he had spooned up the last of his puréed potatoes, Paweł had refilled his own glass twice.

He sat back and belched. "I feel weird. I don't know. Like the whole room's going up and down. Let's go out for that walk, shall we? I'll take the Soplica with us, if you're not too posh to drink out of the bottle."

They left the house and wandered through the fields, until they reached the path beside the river where Paweł sometimes went fishing, although he rarely caught anything. He stopped once or twice, swaying slightly, but then he shook his head and carried on.

"Are you all right?" Anna asked him.

"I'm not sure. Like I said, I feel weird." He took a swig of vodka out of the bottle and belched again.

As they reached the edge of the forest, though, he stopped and bent double, resting one hand against a birch. "Hold on a sec, babe. I feel sick. What did your granny put in that pink drink of hers? You had some, too, didn't you? Do you feel okay?"

Anna said nothing, waiting for him, but her heart was beating furiously, like a small bird caught by a cat.

After a while, though, Paweł stood up straight. "Okay, okay. I feel better now. I know what we should do. Instead of walking through the forest, let's go to Rysiek's and have a party. We hardly go anywhere these days. We can have drinks, and music, and dance, and maybe we can order a pizza later on."

Anna said, "Yes, let's go there. But look at me, Paweł, in these jeans and this scruffy old sweater. This will be kind of a celebration, won't it, so I want to look special. Why don't you go on ahead, and I'll just nip home and change into something more glamorous."

"Okay, sweetie-pie. Good idea. I'll go and heat up our seats and order some drinks, and I'll see you in a bit."

Anna left him and started to walk back along the birch alley by the river. After only few yards, though, she stopped, and turned around. She could see that he was still only halfway up the sloping field that led towards Rysiek's pub. Instead of walking any further, she made her way in through the wild rose bushes, and then the birches, brushing aside the branches as she went. She came to a fallen log, and sat down to wait.

Sub tuum praesidium,' she said, quietly, and a dunnock answered with a high-pitched chirrup.

As soon as he entered Rysiek's, Paweł crossed over to the bar and ordered a beer.

"Tyskie, but draught! I've got this really weird feeling in my belly." He winced, and pressed his hand over his mouth to stifle a belch. "My jill treated me to mushroom sauce today, and I reckon she must have made it with toadstools. I mean, Jesus."

"You poor man," said the young woman behind the bar, with theatrical concern. "Maybe you'd be better off with a cup of hot tea."

Paweł suppressed another belch. He had never seen this young woman in Rysiek's before. She was stunningly pretty, with curly blonde hair and mischievous grey eyes, and she was wearing a clinging green dress.

"Oh, babe," he grinned, climbing onto a barstool. "I didn't know that Rysiek hired such cuties! I need to visit more often, if only to goggle at you!"

Another young woman came up to Paweł and without hesitation she seductively straightened the upraised collar of his denim jacket. She had honey-coloured hair and a shiny bronze dress and was equally pretty. "Viki, why don't you give him some vodka with black pepper – that will eat through everything he has inside him. Toadstools and all."

She was joined almost at once by a red-headed young woman, with the same wolfish grey eyes and a smattering of freckles across her tilted-up nose. "Let's give him some Saint John's wort tincture," she giggled. "That should cure him for good and all!"

Paweł turned around and around, both bewitched and confused by the unbelievable beauty of these three young women. But just as he was trying to think if it might be possible to invite them all for a foursome, a man's voice called out, "Hey, you! Yes, *you*! This isn't a soup kitchen for the poor! This is a smart pub! You don't come in here looking like something the cat's puked up!"

Paweł looked to see who had shouted at him, and he was shocked to see that it was Marek, his next-door neighbour. He had been friends with Marek for at least five years, and they had often gone fishing together, but he was glaring at Paweł as if he didn't recognise him at all.

"Go on, get the hell out of here!" Marek shouted. "Sling your hook before Rysiek catches you in here!"

Paweł slid off his stool to go and speak to Marek, nearly bumping into a tall woman with exaggerated henna eyebrows. She flapped her hand at him and shrilled, "Don't you dare touch me, you filthy tramp! Don't even come near me! You stink! You absolutely stink!"

Three teenage lads at a nearby table were sticking out their tongues at Paweł and crossing their eyes. "Hey, muck-sucker!' one of them called out. "Look at the state of you! What a zero!"

Looking around, Paweł saw six or seven people in the pub that he knew really well, but every one of them was staring at him with undisguised revulsion, as if they had no idea who he was, and believed that he was nothing but an unwashed down-and-out. He couldn't understand it. Were they all playing some kind of hurtful practical joke on him? He turned back to ask the three pretty young women if they had any idea why nobody appeared to recognise him, but they had all retreated behind the bar, and were whispering in a conspiratorial way amongst themselves.

The door behind the bar opened and out came the owner of the pub, Ryszard Krzyczek, obviously alerted by all the shouting. Ryszard had also been a good friend of Paweł's, for even longer than Marek. Ever since Rysiek's had opened, Paweł had dropped in almost every evening on is way home, for one or two beers.

"What's going on here?" Ryszard asked. But then he saw Paweł standing by the bar.

He came up to him and said, very quietly, "Man, look at you. I'm afraid you're seriously spoiling the image of my pub. Now, because there are ladies in here, I'm going to ask you to leave in the nicest possible way. Do you understand me? If you need help, go to the homeless shelter, and make sure that the first thing you do when you get there is take a shower."

He beckoned to a bald, wide-shouldered man sitting at the opposite end of the bar. "Adi, help this gentleman to leave, will you?"

Adi heaved himself off his stool and approached Paweł with a slow loping swagger like an orang-utan. He gripped his left arm so ferociously that Paweł thought he might snap his bone in half.

"Come on, feller, I'll show you the way out."

"Adi, for the love of Jesus, it's *me*!"

"Of course it is. Everybody's called 'me'. Even me."

Adi started to pull Paweł towards the door, but then Viki came out from behind the bar and took hold of Paweł's other arm, and tugged it, gently but almost possessively. Her two young friends came out, too, and stood next to her.

"Leave him," Viki told Adi. She was smiling but there was a look in her wolf-grey eyes which showed that she was not going to brook any argument. "He belongs to us. We'll take care of him."

Adi looked across at Ryszard, who shrugged, and so he let go of Paweł's arm. The three young women ushered Paweł to the door, looking back only once to give Ryszard a strangely triumphant smile.

"Who the fuck were they?" asked Adi, when the door had swung shut behind them.

Rysazrd shook his head. "God knows. Never seen them before in my life."

Chattering happily, the young women escorted Paweł back down the field towards the river, and along the birch alley where he and Anna had been walking together. Two of them had to hold his arms to support him because he was becoming more and more unsteady, and as he reached the path he nearly collapsed.

"Maybe we should splash your face with some cool water?" Viki suggested.

Paweł nodded, his mouth tightly closed, but then, without warning, he sprayed out a thick cascade of vomit. He sank down onto the path on his knees, and then he vomited again, a glutinous tide of half-digested ham stew. He dropped sideways into the grass, curled himself up, and lay there with his eyes closed, shuddering as if he had a raging fever.

"Something really, *really* upset you, didn't it, sweetheart?" said Viki, and it was obvious now that she was taunting him. "Maybe it wasn't something you ate, after all. Why don't you lie down here for a while, darling man, until you feel better?"

She bent down to kiss his forehead, and then she stood up straight and looked directly towards the wild rose bushes where Anna was hiding. She stared in Anna's direction without blinking for almost a quarter of a minute, and then she beckoned to her two friends and the three of them walked off.

Anna beat her way out of the bushes. She had seen and heard everything. But when she looked along the path to see if Viki and her friends were still within earshot, so that she could call out and thank them, they had vanished.

She went across to Paweł, who was lying in the long grass, coiling and uncoiling with painful convulsions. His eyes were tightly closed, so he failed to see that she was standing right over him, or the look on her face. There was no hatred in her expression, nor triumph; only calm, and satisfaction, like a judge who has just handed down a fitting sentence to a felon who deserved it.

She dropped the half-empty vodka bottle beside him. Then she crossed herself and walked off, leaving him where he lay.

Throughout the whole night Paweł was vomiting and shivering and suffering from agonising stomach pains, and he was haunted by nightmarish visions – dark shadows that screamed at him and bristling spiders that scuttled across his face. He had no idea how long he had been lying in the grass, but when the sun rose behind the birches he managed to sit up. He was feeling dizzy and his mouth was dry like glasspaper and his clothes were stiff with dried vomit.

After a few minutes he climbed unsteadily onto his feet and start to shuffle along the path beside the river, although he still felt giddy and he had no clue where he was going. He couldn't even think who he was, let alone where he lived.

As he limped around a bend in the river, though, he saw five of his friends, including his best friend Rękas. They were out on one of their early-morning fishing expeditions, laughing and smoking and eating sandwiches. He felt a surge of relief and went up to them with both hands raised like a surrendering soldier.

"Hey, guys! Am I glad to see you! Could one of you give me a lift home, please? I feel really, really sick!"

Rękas stepped back in disgust, as if he was not only repelled by Paweł's appearance, but as if he didn't recognise him. "Fuck off, you woof-king! I'm not giving a lift to any stinking junkie! Don't even touch me!"

"Please, guys, I'm sick as a dog. I just need to get home."

"I said fuck off! Are you deaf, or what? There's a doss-house for derelicts like you!"

Another of his friends, Kevin, pinched his nose and said, "Jesus Christ! The smell on you, mate! You could knock a fucking elephant over!"

"Yes, get the hell out of here," Piotr chimed in. "You're scaring the fish away!"

Paweł kept stumbling on. He was heartbroken by his friends' rejection and when he looked back he could see they were still glaring at him, and Piotr gave him the finger. His stomach felt as if it were tightly knotted, and every muscle and bone in his body was aching. He couldn't understand what had happened to him and why nobody wanted to help him.

He had staggered only a short distance further when he was doubled up by another painful spasm. He knelt on the river bank and retched, again and again, but he had nothing left in his stomach to vomit.

Once he had stopped retching, he looked down and saw his face reflected in the surface of the water. He was startled, because he didn't recognise himself, and he turned around to see if there was someone standing behind him. Yet there was nobody there, and all his friends had returned to their fishing. He stared at his reflection again, harder. *Who is that? How can I see his face in the water?*

But then thought that he could hear a young woman's voice whispering inside his mind, even though he was kneeling on the river bank alone. She was blurry and indistinct at first, but then he clearly heard her say, "It's *nobody*."

Yes, he told himself, *that's right*, and he leaned over the reflection and repeated out loud, "You hear that? You're nobody! That's who you are! Mister Nobody!"

"You were born as nobody," the young woman's voice went on. It was soft and mysterious, and strangely liquid, yet he was sure that he recognised it, and it made his heart beat faster and faster, until it hurt. "You always had a chance to be somebody, but you wasted it, didn't you? Now you will *always* be nobody."

He still didn't realise that she was talking about him, and he was still staring scornfully at Mister Nobody when he noticed that the eyes in his reflection were subtly beginning to change shape, and become more slanted. Within a few seconds, they had become a woman's eyes, wolfish and grey and glimmering. Next, his whole face seemed to melt, and now he found himself looking at the young woman he had met in Rysziek's, with her tangled blonde hair floating all around her. It was that Viki, from behind the bar, and she was under the water, sneering at him. She grinned and bared her pointed white teeth, and in shock he tried to pick himself up off his knees.

He was too late. Viki surged up out of the water in a fountain of spray and seized him with both hands by the throat. Then she pitched backwards under the surface again, pulling him with her.

Paweł gargled, *'Nooo . . . blarghh!'* but Viki was too strong for him, and she dragged him deeper and deeper right down to the riverbed. He struggled, desperate for air, but after half a minute he could hold his breath no longer, and his lungs were flooded with cold cloudy river water.

Before long the surface of the river returned to a gentle rippling. The afternoon was sunny and the crickets were singing in the grass, while the dunnocks continued to chirrup as if the world had failed to notice that a human life had been lost. But then it was nobody's life, after all.

With a loud squeak, Anna opened the rusted gate outside the Maciuszek house. Paweł's mother was in her rubbish-strewn garden, taking down her washing.

"Anna! Where have you been, for fuck's sake? Finally I'll have someone to talk to again, apart from Grandpa!" For some reason she always called her husband Stefan "Grandpa".

She roughly folded up her damp sheets and crammed them into her basket. "So where's Paweł?" she asked him.

Anna followed Halina into her side of the bungalow. "He went to buy some wine and some bottles of vodka. I thought we could have a small barbecue tonight to celebrate our reconciliation. You were right, you know – I should have listened to you!"

"Ah, Anna, you seem to think you're so educated and so fucking clever, but most of the time you are goofy as a calf! No wonder everybody regards you as a nobody. I told you that Paweł was a good boy, didn't I? If you just let him drink you will have a life as happy as mine!"

She paused and then she screeched out, "Grandpa! Grandpa! Where the fuck is that old moron? Stefan! Fetch that vodka out of the freezer, we're going to celebrate!"

Anna smiled and said, "Don't bother, Halina. There's no need to bring out the vodka. I've brought a special drink for the both of you. It's very strong and very special – a special gift for two special people."

Stefan appeared in the kitchen doorway, sniffing and scratching his belly.

"Bring three glasses, grandpa," snapped Halina. "And don't fucking drop them like you did the last time."

Anna lifted the bottle of carmine liquor out of her suede bag and poured a glass for each of them.

"Na zdrowie!" she said, and watched Stefan and Halina empty their glasses in one.

"Bit sour, but tasty!" said Stefan, wiping his mouth on his sleeve.

Anna poured the two of them another glass each, but she didn't touch hers until Halina carried her washing basket into the kitchen and Stefan followed her, and then she carefully poured hers back into the bottle.

"I'm just going to start preparing the barbecue!" she called out. "I'll see you later!"

She felt a dark sense of satisfaction that Dziewanna was going to punish Paweł's parents for having insulted her and sworn at her and treated her like nobody, but the last thing she wanted was to stay and see them vomiting all over the floor. She left the house, closing the peeling front door behind her, and headed back to her own parents' flat.

It was three days later when two police officers, a man and a woman, came ringing the doorbell at her parents' apartment building. It was lunchtime and Anna was in the kitchen chopping cabbage.

"Anna," said her father. "They're asking for you."

"Pani Maciuszek?" said the woman officer. "May we come in? I'm afraid we have some bad news."

They took off their caps and Anna invited them into the living-room. They sat down and the male officer asked her, "Can I ask you when you last saw your husband?"

"Paweł? Three days ago. We were supposed to meet for a drink at Rysziek's but when I got there they told me he seemed to be drunk and that he had left with three young women. I haven't seen or heard from him since."

"I'm sorry to tell you that he has been found drowned in the Bodzentyn fishing pond. His body was identified by the ID card on his mobile phone. I'm afraid it's too early to say exactly what the cause of death was. But I'm sorry to tell you that the bad news doesn't end there."

Anna pressed her hand over her mouth in shock, and her eyes filled up with tears. The woman police officer reached across and laid a comforting hand on her knee.

"Before we came here, Pani Maciuszek, we tried to find you at the address that you and your husband shared with his parents. I regret to have to inform you that we found both of them deceased. Although we will have to wait for a forensic autopsy by a doctor, it appears that Stefan Maciuszek died after drowning in the bath. From the smell of him, he had consumed a considerable amount of alcohol.

"His wife Halina had called for an ambulance, but when the operator asked who she was and where she lived, she said that didn't know. By the time the call was traced and an ambulance was sent to that address we had already found her deceased. She gone into the garden and cut her own throat with a broken glass, and then she had drowned herself in their rain-butt."

"Are you serious? In their rain-butt?"

The officer pulled a face. "You know what they say. You can drown in an inch of water."

Long after the two police officers had left, Anna sat in the living-room with her mother sitting beside her, saying nothing, while outside it began to grow dark, and she heard an owl hooting.

Now she understood how Grandma Janka must have felt when Tadeusz's body was discovered by Dead Man's Pond. She knew that she was not directly responsible for the deaths of Paweł, nor his parents. She had set out to punish them, yes, but it was Dziewanna who had killed them. If only she had realised from what Grandma Janka had told her that Dziewanna's punishment for those who mistreated her daughters was more than sickness and turning them into a nonentity. She would send her rusałki after them, to drown them.

She was not to blame for what the rusałki had done, and yet she felt guilty, in a strange way, and that she was one of them.

That Saturday, Anna was having breakfast in her parents' kitchen when she saw on the local TV news that Father Antoni Pachucy had been found dead in the forest of Włoszczowa. A police spokesman said that his clothes had been ripped and his body had been clawed, which meant that it was almost certain that he had been attacked by wolves.

After breakfast, Anna went to see Grandma Janka. It was likely that she would know a lot more about what had happened to Father Antoni. She was friends with the local doctor, and he would have been called by the police when his body was found.

"She got her revenge on him in the end," said Grandma Janka, stirring her tea, without mentioning "she" by name.

Apparently Father Antoini had been playing chess with another elderly priest late in the evening when he had suddenly stood up and announced that he had to go out to the forest and pick some Saint John's wort. His companion had tried to dissuade him, but he had muttered something about witches and fending off the Devil, and disappeared into the darkness, even though he was wearing only a dressing-gown and pyjamas.

His body had been found by early-morning mushroom-pickers. Even though he had only been lying in the forest since midnight, he was surrounded by mullein leaves, and some of the stalks had even penetrated his pyjamas. In his hand they had found a silver pendant with a Latin prayer inscribed on it.

"*Sub tuum praesidium,*" said Grandma Janka, sadly.

Anna raised her eyes up to the picture of the Mother of God Gromnic and she knew now where her destiny lay.

Late that afternoon, as the sun had just sunk down to touch the top of the rustling firs, Anna came walking through the long grass to Dead Man's Pond. The water was in shadow now, so that it looked like a bottomless black hole to the world below.

She was wearing a simple white dress and she had let her hair fall loose over her shoulders. As she made her way through the birches at the side of the lake, she saw Viki and her two friends in the water. Viki was combing out her blonde hair and singing, while her two friends were washing their clothes. They were all naked.

Anna paused and peeled off her sandals, tossing them into the bushes. Then she lifted her dress over her head and dropped that aside too. All that she was wearing underneath was white knickers, and she stepped out of those, too, throwing them aside so that they were caught on the mullein leaves.

As she approached the three young women, they all stopped combing and washing and turned towards her, greeting her with almost beatific smiles.

They held out their arms and all three of them embraced her, and kissed her. Their skin was cool and slippery and Anna found the touch of their stiffened nipples very erotic. Viki started to sing again, and they stood like that as the sun was swallowed up by the surrounding trees, and the world grew dark.

Graham Masterton is mainly recognized for his horror novels but he has also been a prolific writer of thrillers, disaster novels and historical epics, as well as one of the world's most influential series of sex instruction books. He became a newspaper reporter at the age of 17 and was appointed editor of *Penthouse* magazine at only 24. His first horror novel, *The Manitou*, was filmed with Tony Curtis playing the lead, and three of his short horror stories were filmed by Tony Scott for *The Hunger* TV series. Ten years ago Graham turned his hand to crime novels and *White Bones*, set in Ireland, was a Kindle phenomenon, selling over 100,000 copies in a month. This has been followed by ten more best-selling crime novels featuring Detective Superintendent Katie Maguire, the latest of which is *The Last Drop of Blood*. In 2019 Graham was given a Lifetime Achievement Award by the Horror Writers Association. The Prix Graham Masterton for the best horror fiction in French has been awarded annually for the past ten years, and four years ago he established an award for short stories written by inmates in Polish prisons, Nagroda Grahama Mastertona W Więzieniu Pisane. He is currently working on new novels.

Karolina Mogielska is a psychologist who has been working for around ten years in a field where she tries to help people in various stages of life and environments to face and solve their problems. In her field, violence of every kind appears, especially domestic abuse. Currently, she is working for orphanages and kindergartens in south-west Poland, where she lives, where she has occasion not only to observe, but also bring some help to more and more younger victims of adult mistreatment, although she still feels that she is searching for her place on Earth and hopes that the publication of her first story will mean that her life's journey is finally going in the right direction.

When she met Graham Masterton in person by total accident, nearly two years ago, after many years of fascination by his artistic output and personality, the offer for co-working and encouraging her to try herself in the world of writing appeared quite quickly and she truly feels that it has brought a new light into her life, inspiring her in how she can help and entertain people in a completely different way. It is also motivation for her to train herself in being a better person. Now, her working with children and teenagers, helping them to cope with their problems, is a complement to her life's passion.

In Karolina's private life, she is bringing up a nearly 3-years-old little boy and trying to develop herself in the things she loves, like drawing. In her free time she plays harmonica, runs and spends as much time as she can with nature and animals, which she loves. She also loves learning about anything and everything, especially mythology, so she tries to do that all the time, too.

'Skull' by Peter Coleborn

THE COTTAGE OF DESTINY

Lionel and Patricia Fanthorpe

Artwork by Allen Koszowski

". . . the face as it turned was hideous, threatening and hostile."

THE WEATHER CHANGED suddenly as Jim and Elaine strolled back to Charter Cottage. It was a holiday cottage now, which they had rented for the first two weeks in July. It had been a fisherman's family cottage for many centuries and it still stood resolutely beside the coastal road not far from Blakeney on the North Norfolk coast.

Jim and Elaine ran a small business together, where they manufactured a wide range of domestic items and sold them in their small shop. The business was doing well, and they felt that it would be ideal if they could find someone to run the shop while they put more time into the manufacturing side.

They scampered the last fifty yards as the rain began to fall. Jim was searching his pockets for the keys as lightning flashed and a roll of thunder sounded. He found the keys, unlocked the door and stood back to let Elaine get safely inside. The storm was a heavy one, and they were glad to be in the warm and dry.

Elaine patted the nearest wall affectionately.

"You've sheltered dozens of people over the last few centuries," she murmured to the cottage. "Thank you for sheltering us now." There was nothing audible, but it seemed to Elaine that Charter Cottage appreciated what she had said. The storm outside eased into a regular pattern of prolonged heavy rain, and Jim turned on the TV. A film history programme was showing extracts from some classic horror films and as the set came on it was showing a clip from the 1931 version of *Dracula* starring Bela Lugosi.

Jim and Elaine watched for a few minutes as they dried their clothing on the radiator. The next extract was from the 1948 horror comedy involving Abbott and Costello and was Bela Lugosi's last appearance as Dracula.

"If we were making a horror film like these," said Elaine, "Charter Cottage would be an ideal setting." She paused and then chuckled. "We could think up a really new plot where a fisherman brings a mermaid home and she turns out to be a vampire!"

"That's certainly original," agreed Jim. "We could have her as a benign vampire who only attacks sharks."

"I'll play the vampire mermaid, and you can be the adventurous young fisherman who brings me home. What a film that would be!"

The rain eased and they walked down to the Charter Arms Inn which had an excellent restaurant as well as a wide range of beers, wines and spirits. After enjoying a delicious lunch they strolled back to Charter Cottage.

"We haven't really explored this place properly," said Elaine. "I've got the strangest suspicion that there's something hidden up in this old attic, something that's as old as the cottage – but a lot more sinister." She shivered.

They climbed the stairs together, passed their bedroom on the first floor and kept steadily on towards the attic.

"Look at that trapdoor," whispered Elaine. "It's been barred over."

"You hang on here," said Jim. "I've got a tool-kit in the car. I can soon get that undone."

Elaine waited carefully on the attic stairs until Jim came back with the tools. His engineering skills had the bars away in two minutes and he swung the trapdoor open. There was a strange smell coming from the attic: it was the stench of decay – and something more . . . the odour of something sinister and frightening.

Elaine had a handkerchief to her nose as they went up through the trapdoor together. The attic window was small, and the dark rain clouds meant that there was very little light outside even though it was still early afternoon. On the side of the tiny room that was farthest from the window, Jim and Elaine saw a sinister oblong box.

"That thing is coffin-shaped," said Elaine, and there was fear in her voice.

"I agree with you," said Jim. "Do you think that's the source of the foul smell up here?"

Elaine took the handkerchief away from her nose for an instant and nodded.

"Let's get back down," said Jim. "Then I'll put the trapdoor back and re-fasten the cover – like it was: but stronger!" He escorted Elaine safely back to their downstairs room, and then went back up and re-secured the attic entry trapdoor. When he had finished it was far more secure than it had been.

"What do you think was in that box where the smell was so bad?" asked Elaine.

"Something dead for ages: something that's taking an awful long time to rot away completely," said Jim. His voice was grim.

They were interrupted by a knock at the cottage door. Jim headed downstairs to open it and Elaine followed closely behind him. They opened the door and saw a tall broad-shouldered man wearing a clerical collar.

"May I come in?" he asked politely. His deep bass voice was powerful, but very pleasant and friendly.

"Yes, of course," said Jim. Their visitor stepped inside. "Come on in and we'll have a chat. We are just on holiday here for a couple of weeks."

"May I make you a cup of tea?" asked Elaine.

"That would be greatly appreciated," said their guest. "May I introduce myself? I'm Matthew Johnson, Rector of Blakeney."

Jim looked at him excitedly. "Are you *the* Matthew Johnson, the writer and psychic investigator?" Their visitor smiled and nodded.

"We've both read several of your books, which we greatly enjoyed," said Jim.

"It's a real honour to meet you," said Elaine, as she handed him a cup of tea and held out the sugar bowl. Johnson took a spoonful and stirred it in gently.

"I'm very happy to welcome you into my parish while you're staying here," he said quietly, "but I also needed to come to tell you about this cottage, Charter Cottage." He paused to let his words sink in.

"It's several centuries old," he went on, "and it's had what I would call a rather chequered history." He hesitated for a moment. "You tell me you've read several of my books, so you'll know about some of the psychic adventures I've had. This cottage has featured in one or two of them."

"Here in Charter Cottage?" asked Elaine.

"Right where we are now," said Johnson. "As far as I was able to ascertain from the parish records, it was originally built by the Cetarius family, who claimed that one of their earliest ancestors had originally been a Roman Legionnaire, when Caesar invaded Britain. He fell in love with a local girl, married her and left the army to become a fisherman, as his ancestors had been in Sicily." He paused thoughtfully. "Life went well for them for several generations, then in mediaeval times strange rumours began centring on the cottage." He paused again. "It was said that the Cetarius family took in a homeless girl who had been begging for food in the village and that after she arrived in Blakeney there were a number of strange deaths in the village. Several of the corpses looked very pale, as though their blood had been drained . . ."

"Was this beggar girl suspected of being a vampire?" asked Jim.

"That's a significant part of the Cetarius family history," agreed Matthew. "It was said that a party of angry villagers came looking for her, but the Cetarius family put up a fight to defend her, and when the villagers forced their way in and searched Charter Cottage they found no trace of her."

Jim and Elaine exchanged deeply meaningful glances.

"There's a trapdoor leading to the space above the attic bedroom," said Jim, "and there's a sinister-looking box up there. It's roughly coffin shaped."

"And it looks really old," added Elaine.

"It could certainly be mediaeval," said Jim.

They looked at each other again.

"There was a terrible smell in that attic space," said Elaine. "It made us think of death and decay – but it was somehow worse than that: as if it was something *worse* than death and decay."

"You've described it well," said Matthew. "Believe me there are things far worse than death." He looked intently at Elaine and Jim. "Will you let me up into that attic space so I can look in the box?"

"We would be honoured to help with anything you wanted to investigate," said Jim. "But we'll need my tool-kit to open that trapdoor. I made it as secure as I could after we'd seen and smelled that box."

Having secured the ceiling panel as thoroughly as he could, Jim took the bars away carefully and removed it.

"May I borrow your mallet and that big chisel?" asked Johnson. Jim passed them over and Matthew climbed up into the attic space. "Can you find a light anywhere?" he asked.

"I'll get the lantern we keep in the car," said Elaine and ran to fetch it. Jim carried it up into the attic.

"There is something very dangerous in that box where the stench is coming from," said Matthew grimly. He looked around the attic as Jim held the lantern for him, then strode across to the loft water tank and solemnly blessed the water within it.

"Holy water is one of the most effective weapons against evil entities," he said quietly as he looked at a group of small containers near the tank. He filled one from the tank that he had just blessed and handed it to Jim, who took it carefully in his left hand.

"Watch very carefully as I open that case and stand by to throw the Holy Water when I ask you to."

Jim nodded.

Matthew's immense strength made short work of the box lid and as it came away the foul stench from inside it grew stronger. Jim leant forward and brought the lantern closer. Two figures seemed to be struggling with each other inside the box. The first was what seemed to Jim to be a translucent demon; the face as it turned was hideous, threatening and hostile. The legs ended in hooves and the hands were claw-like. The other figure was a young, normal-looking human girl fighting with all her strength to break away from the demon.

"Throw the Holy Water!" ordered Matthew and Jim emptied the whole can over the demonic form grappling with the helpless girl.

Matthew drew a silver blade from his belt and plunged it into the demon with all his force. There was a terrifying scream as the fiend turned on Matthew.

Instinctively, Jim reached for the trembling girl and helped her to stand as Elaine came up through the trapdoor and stood beside him. Her strong, gentle hands led the girl away from the box where Matthew was wrestling with the demonic fiend. Then leaving the girl in Jim's care Elaine drew a long silver hatpin from her left lapel and moved behind the monster as Matthew wrestled with it. The pin was a dozen centimetres long, and its gleaming silver was reinforced with stainless steel. Elaine selected a target spot immediately below the base of the demon's skull and drove the pin in at an upward angle of forty-five degrees. The fiend gave another terrifying scream, but there was fear as well as demonic fury in this one. Jim left the girl they had rescued leaning safely against the loft wall, refilled his can with Holy Water and hurled the contents as hard as he could into the demon's open mouth. The scream that followed was pure fear and agony. Matthew plunged his silver knife into it again as Elaine withdrew her hatpin and stabbed up into the side of the demon's throat; then they both drew back from the monstrosity, which seemed to be imploding and falling to the floor as dust.

The girl they had rescued came slowly towards them, looking at the dust in a mixture of joy and disbelief.

"You have set me free," she whispered. "I cannot believe it – but I *know* I am free again." She looked gratefully and admiringly from one to another. "He has enslaved me for centuries, forcing me to do evil things I hated." She stirred the dust with her foot. "And now you have destroyed him."

"You are the homeless girl who was rescued by the Cetarius family," said Elaine gently.

The rescued girl nodded.

"They were wonderful people. It was centuries ago, but I can remember it like yesterday. They risked their lives to defend me." She shivered and stirred the dust again with her foot. "Then that evil thing appeared from nowhere – it just glided from its world to ours and took possession of me. I fought as hard as I could, but it was so strong that it controlled me, it made me drink blood . . . and then it drained all my strength from me . . ."

Elaine and Jim were exchanging glances.

"Let's go back to when all this started for you," said Elaine. "To begin with, what's your name?"

"Cecilia Cooper, my father was a barrel maker and my mother helped him." She hesitated. "We were so happy together and we lived well, then both my parents died of the plague. I couldn't bear to live alone, so I just left home . . . but nothing went right and I finished up as a beggar girl." She hesitated again. "The Cetarius family were good, kind, caring people. They took me in and things started to get so much better . . . They cared for me as if I was their own daughter – and then that demon destroyed my new life . . ." She stirred the dust again with her foot.

"We have a small shop with living space above it," said Elaine, "and we need someone to look after it while Jim and I make the things that we sell there. Would you consider joining our team?" She chuckled. "We're not old enough to be your parents, but you would be like a sister to us."

Cecilia's face glowed with happiness. "I would love to," she whispered.

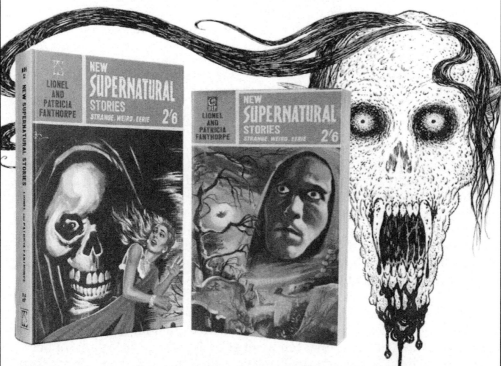

Seventy-one years ago, in 1952, **Lionel Fanthorpe** wrote his first sci-fi story. 'Worlds Without End' was published in *Futuristic Science Stories*, volume 6.

This was the start of a prolific writing career that last year celebrated its 70th anniversary – and Lionel is still writing new books and working on creative projects at the age of 87.

Not only has Lionel written hundreds of sci-fi stories, but together with his wife of 64 years, **Patricia**, has written books on an array of subjects including the paranormal, unexplained mysteries of the world, religion and poetry.

Indeed, Lionel can be likened to a modern day Indiana Jones as over the years he has travelled the world in search of the unexplained.

Lionel has presented many television series including the very popular Channel Four show, *Fortean TV*.

He has been described as the leather jacket-wearing, Harley-Davidson -riding, paranormal-investigating vicar! That's some accolade but there is so much more to this fascinating man.

He is a major contributor to paranormal research, a former journalist, teacher and head teacher, an army rock climbing instructor and a World Judo Association Black Belt Fifth Dan.

COMING IN 2023 BY LIONEL AND PATRICIA FANTHORPE . . .
THE QUEST FOR MEANING

The Quest for Meaning sets out to examine the meaning and purpose of life – and humanity's role within it – beginning with the mystery of individual self-awareness: the mind which does the actual exploring. It supports Socrates' concept that *the unexamined life is not worth living.*

The most significant and interactive parts of our environment are other human beings. There are some very close and special individuals who travel through life beside us. There are wider groups, communities and nations to which we belong and which have powerful effects on our lives. They are among the most vital signposts in our quest for meaning.

The Quest for Meaning goes on to explore the true nature of reality itself. Dreams can be so realistic that the worst nightmares seem like alternative realities into which we might fall. Avant-garde philosophers have suggested that there is *no* external environment: that everything we *think* is around us is only a projection from our own creative minds.

The Quest for Meaning also examines the *extent* of the Multiverse we live in – from its infinitely enormous external dimensions to the tiniest of its mysterious subatomic particles.

For more about Lionel and Patricia Fanthorpe you can find them on:
www.lionelfanthorpe.co.uk
www.youtube.com/@lionelfanthorpeofficial5752

Trevor Kennedy reviews Fortean TV: The Complete Series
in the reviews section of this issue . . .

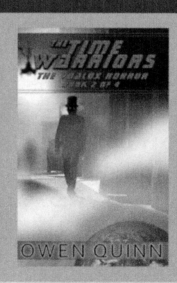

"The stark stars, cold and distant white, were wrong. They wound through the blackness in tangled, serpentine patterns."

THE MIDNIGHT MAKERS

Mark Howard Jones

Artwork by Dave Carson

"COME ON! JUST a little further." Mitch hoped that her coaxing tone would encourage the car to get her the final quarter mile to her destination. She was in no mood to walk the rest of the distance. This was her escape and she wanted it to get off to a good start. Car trouble just wasn't in her plans.

She couldn't stand the accusing stares of Angelique any longer – especially when they were wrapped in an hour's silence and served up with such relish – so she had decided that a break somewhere quiet was needed.

The little house near the beach that her aunt had left her was the first place she thought of. It had taken her nearly an hour on the phone to track down the letting agent and check that the place was empty. She'd expected it to be, now that autumn had arrived and the summer tourists had moved on. Once his oily voice had confirmed it, she'd packed a bag quickly and thrown it on the back seat of her ailing car.

As she pulled up the last stretch of rough road leading to the house, the car's engine was coughing and complaining. It had once been sleek and smooth, but she'd neglected it in her constant rush to get to places ahead of everyone else.

Mitch let out a huge sigh of relief as the cracked tarmac kissed the vehicle's weary tyres to a standstill outside the small house. "Thank you," she whispered to it, patting the steering wheel affectionately. She made a mental note to reward the the old Volvo by taking it in for a service as soon as she got back to town.

Meanwhile, she was looking forward to putting that life and all its problems behind her for a week or so. She glanced at the bags of groceries sitting on the back seat. They were her lifeline, as there were precious few shops nearby. It was over a mile back to the village, but she would be glad of the relative isolation.

The place made her think of a street that had been stillborn. There was just her aunt's old house and another on the other side of the road. She remembered her aunt laughing at her when she had asked as a child where all the other houses were.

A few dozen yards beyond the house, the road suddenly came to an end. In its place was a lane that led to a rickety line of marker posts. She'd had her first kiss in the dunes that lay just beyond the ruined wooden fence.

As she was loading her car, Mitch glanced across at the other house. She wondered who lived there. She remembered the woman who was there when she was a kid. But she had been old even then, so must be dead by now, surely? She'd keep an eye open for any residents. Then again, maybe it was empty and she really was all alone here.

The house was neat and small with two floors, but there was also something about it that puzzled her. Just below the eaves there was a small rectangular opening. It obviously led into the dark space under the wooden rafters, but she couldn't imagine why anyone would leave a hole open to the elements like that. She wasn't any good at judging sizes, but she imagined that if you could coax a small child to climb a ladder high enough, they might just be able to squeeze through it.

Shrugging off her momentary curiosity, she went inside, ready to prepare her nest for the coming week.

Later that day, Mitch began work in an upstairs room that had a view of her potential neighbour's house. Beyond the house, the grey and white sea stretched from horizon to horizon.

She was tempted to spend the whole day at the window, just watching the waves change, slowly and powerfully, from moment to moment, as she used to do as a child. But although this was a break, it wasn't meant to be a holiday. "No work, no eat," she reminded herself, turning back to her keyboard.

She glanced out of the window again later in the morning. The sky was greyer than before, any blue having been chased away. Down in the garden of the house across the way, she saw an old man tending to some flowers. She extinguished her cigarette and rushed downstairs.

The old man obviously didn't hear her approach. He almost jumped when she said "Hello". Lifting his head, he swept some white hair from his face, and peered at her curiously. Clearly he hadn't been expecting visitors. Maybe he hadn't even noticed her car, thought Mitch.

"Good morning," said the man, slowly. Mitch thought he seemed confused, and wondered unkindly if he had some form of dementia. She opened the gate and entered the flower-filled garden.

Seeming slightly startled by this, the old man took a step backward and stammered "W-who are you?" She stopped her confident advance, hoping that would put him at ease.

"They call me Mitch," she told him. He looked at her as if she had said something in another language – one that he clearly didn't speak. "It's short for Michelle – in a way," she added, attempting to rescue him from confusion.

He nodded. "So you are the new owner, are you?" he asked, waving a hand at Mitch's house.

"Yes. Well, I've owned it for a few years now – my aunt left it to me. I've been renting it out to holidaymakers."

The old man nodded again, seemingly lost in thought. "Such a shame about Sandrine. My wife and I knew her well. We went to her funeral. Not many people there . . ."

Feeling she had to defend her own absence, Mitch gabbled: "I was in Tokyo at the time. Too far to come, you see."

The old man's pale eyes held her attention. Perhaps he was expecting more of her, but Mitch was determined not to give it. Instead she changed the subject entirely. "What is your name, by the way?"

"My name is Noone. David Noone. We . . . I've lived here for a very long time."

Mitch nodded, although she didn't remember ever seeing him there before. She chuckled inwardly as she mused that perhaps his wife had kept him locked in the attic. She extended her hand to greet him and was met by a handshake that almost wasn't there.

"Pleased to meet you, Mr. Noone. You've got a lovely garden."

The old man nodded slowly. "It's what I spend most of my time doing. Of course, you're not seeing it at its best – not this time of year. So, are you down here for a holiday, then?"

Mitch shrugged. "Not exactly. I wanted a break from town but I've still got to keep working. I'm a freelance journalist, so I'm always busy!"

Mr. Noone nodded as if disappointed to hear of her occupation. "Oh. That must be interesting," he said softly.

"It can be," Mitch agreed as she glanced around at the various flowers and decorations in the small garden. Almost hidden behind a small shrub was a large stone, with something carved into it.

The stone reminded her of a Hollywood set designer's idea of an exotic altar from some film she'd seen long ago. One side had deep notches cut into it, and there was a narrow groove cut into the flat top and all down one side. Intricate spirals and scrolls covered much of the rest of it.

"What is this?" she asked Mr. Noone, taking a step closer and running her hand across the top. She noticed that moss was growing in the groove that bifurcated the upper surface.

"I don't really know. It's one of my late wife's sculptures. She had an odd name for it, but I can't remember what it was now."

The strange creatures carved into one side looked like fish or birds of some sort to Mitch. They were quite expertly done. She wondered if there might be a feature story waiting to be written here. A "lost" female sculptor tucked away all the way out here. Some of the editors she knew would eat that up. "Is there any more of her work around?" she enquired.

"There's a piece on the promenade. And I have one or two pieces inside, if you'd like to see . . . ?" The old man, assuming that Mitch did want to see, walked towards the door.

She followed him inside, expecting to be shown some small statuettes or similar pieces. What confronted her was quite different.

It stood nearly four feet high on a pair of sturdy metal legs. The whole thing was dark and showed patches of rust here and there. It seemed to depict some sort of deformed bird with no beak or face of any kind but possessing a pair of powerful-looking wings, folded at its sides. Then again, perhaps it wasn't a bird – it had arms, and there was a suggestion of claw-like hands, too.

Even with the little she knew, Mitch could tell this was the work of no amateur. She had seen worse – much worse – at the opening of a "hot" new art gallery she'd covered for this or that magazine. Mitch held aside a curtain to let more light fall on it. She'd hoped the light would reveal more details but the sculpture seemed to defy her attempts to see it more clearly. If anything, the light made things more obscure.

"My wife was especially fond of wildlife subjects." Mr. Noone clearly felt he should provide the illumination denied by the daylight.

Mitch nodded. "This is some pretty wild wildlife, too. What is it exactly?"

The old man looked at her blankly for a second or two, an odd noise coming from the back of his throat, before confessing: "I don't know . . . exactly."

Mitch chuckled slightly. "Right. Does it have a title?"

Again Mr. Noone didn't seem to know how to answer her question, taking his time as if there was a lag between his ears, his mind and his mouth. "No, I don't think so. If it has one, I can't remember it."

She berated herself for not noticing the sculptures on earlier visits. But then she remembered that, every time she'd been here since the house became hers four years ago, she'd been in a tearing hurry. In fact, the term "flying visit" didn't really do her velocity justice, she realised.

Well, she had some time now, so there was no excuse.

None of her other stories were going anywhere at the moment, so Mitch decided to see what she could find out about her neighbour's artistic wife.

An afternoon's diligent searching turned up next to nothing about a sculptor called Margaret Noone. There was an odd reference to a court fine for damage to property at a nearby cemetery nearly ten years ago. That, and a listing of a work in an obscure exhibition in Brussels over fifteen years ago, was all that Mitch could find.

Though she did come across images of the work of a Venetian sculptor called Francesco Scarno who was fairly prominent in the Italian art world about twenty-five years ago. As far as she could work out, the pieces looked almost identical to those the old man had shown her. *Maybe his wife had studied under Scarno*, thought Mitch. If that was the case, then Margaret Noone hadn't done very much to come out from under the shadow of her teacher.

Mitch lit a cigarette and wished she understood the twists and turns of the creative mind. She sometimes flattered herself that she was a writer but knew, deep down, that journalism was a different game altogether. One day, she promised herself. But not while Angelique was still around.

In the absence of any written information about Margaret Noone's work, Mitch decided that she'd better go and see the work for herself. Her husband had mentioned one of her works being situated on the promenade. She just about remembered where that was, so she set off down the sandy lane towards the sea.

There was less and less earth and more and more sand beneath her feet with every step. She kicked through it in her light canvas shoes as the grass grew sparser and the dunes grew up on either side. The path was so familiar to her from childhood expeditions and dozens of picnics.

Mitch's mother had always thought it funny that her sister lived so near the beach. "But where else could Sandy live?" she would chuckle. But as she got older, Mitch realised there was a sadness about her aunt that her mother always chose to ignore. It had become inextricably linked to this place in her imagination, though Mitch never saw or heard anything that might explain any such connection. Happy times were all she recalled.

Except that the dunes often felt lonely and desolate – a place to be left behind quickly, once the heat of the summer sun began to wane. There was a darkness in the deeper hollows that never seemed to dissipate, even on the sunniest days. It was the sort of darkness she used to imagine when she was a teenager growing up in the city – so deep that once you entered it you could never leave. Yet oddly she'd never found it on the familiar streets or in the alleys. She'd begun to believe that perhaps it could only be found inside people.

Her thoughts were interrupted by a sudden dazzle of sunlight as she rounded the edge of the dune, to be met by the wide sweep of sand, sea and sky.

The voices that the wind had stolen soughed across the sand, first calling out a welcome, then turning into a warning. Sudden gusts tugged uncomfortably at Mitch's jacket. She shivered, wishing she'd worn a heavier coat.

What the old man had referred to grandly as the promenade was, in reality, just a brick and concrete platform that ran a short distance along the dunes. It had been built towards the end of her childhood visits, Mitch remembered. As she rounded the curve of the highest dune she saw that it clearly hadn't been maintained. The shifting sands had retreated from the front of it, causing the brick wall to sag.

Mitch climbed the few cracked steps and stood looking out to sea. The grey and white beast heaved itself along the shore, breakers bravely mounting an endless invasion of the land that soon ran out of energy.

Turning her head, she saw the piece of sculpture that Mr. Noone had told her about. It stood at the end of the platform, just past a rotting bench that sat like a crouching sentinel guarding it. Mitch perched on the very end of the bench, afraid it might give way if she put her full weight on it. The sculpture was around four feet in height. It looked as if it had been placed so that it appeared to look over your shoulder as you sat gazing out to sea, close enough to whisper a suggestion or two in your ear.

Like everything else around, the sculpture had taken a pounding from the weather. She guessed it could only have been carved in the last decade or so, yet it looked as if it had been unearthed from a damp pit after thousands of years away from the light. It was still clearly a human figure, but if there had been a face, it had since been erased by the constant onslaught of the sea breezes. One leg of the wooden figure was raised off the ground, as if running or preparing to take flight. Mitch wondered if that was deliberate, or if it had simply rotted away in the salt wind.

She leaned forward to examine a small metal plaque that had been set into the brickwork by the figure. It too had been scoured almost clean. Only the letters "N" and "O" were still visible. Feeling oddly cheated, Mitch began making her way back to the house. The sculpture could tell her nothing about itself or its creator. She didn't truly know what she'd expected, but it was more than this.

She glanced back at the sculpture one last time. Its incompleteness reflected badly upon her, she felt, as if she was somehow to blame for its condition. The damaged figure felt like both a taunt and a threat to Mitch as she struggled to light a cigarette in the insistent wind. It was the sort of thing that would give a small child nightmares, she decided. She had to remind herself that she wasn't a small child.

Lying back in the antique bath, Mitch plugged the cold tap with her big toe to stop it dripping. As the hot water eased the aches of the day, she decided that she needed to refurbish the house. It was barely up to the standard needed for her to let it out to visitors. True, she'd neglected it – but she'd been busy.

Her mind was full of possible carpentry and painting projects as she dried herself off. She mused about redecorating the bathroom as she slipped into a large bath robe that she'd found in one of the closets.

As she opened the window to let out the steam from her bath, something on the house across the way caught her eye. She hadn't seen them arrive – they were just suddenly there – two enormous shapes crawling across the roof.

They were dark in colour, that much she could see, but the twilight hid any further details from her. Except for their wings, which they extended and drew back several times, allowing her to judge their size. They were far too big for bats but she couldn't think what breed of bird they could be, either. And they moved too slowly for birds, she thought. Birds were swift and sudden, but these creatures seemed slower and more deliberate in their movements.

The creatures seemed to hang beneath the eaves for a minute or two, crawling around and over each other, before squeezing themselves through the small opening. Mr. Noone couldn't be allowing them to nest there, surely?

But they must be birds, of course. The twilight was just hiding their true shape and size from her. Next time she saw the old man, she would ask him about his mysterious visitors.

Mitch sat in the front garden on the bench that couldn't decide whether to fall apart or not. She knew how it felt, as she sipped from a mug of coffee, hoping that her black mood would lift. It had been a frustrating day, filled with leads that led nowhere and evasive interviewees.

As she took another sip, she noticed Mr. Noone emerge from the path leading from the dunes and head towards his front gate. Mitch saw her opportunity and opened her front door just as Mr. Noone was reaching his. "Hello!" she shouted across. The old man turned and gave a small wave before turning to open his door.

Mitch covered the several yards to his front garden in record time. "I've been meaning to ask, Mr. Noone . . . about the birds you have nesting in your attic space?"

The old man turned his pale gaze upon her. "Oh, yes. Birds. What about them?" He seemed wary of her next question.

Mitch shrugged and tried to make it look nonchalant. "I was just wondering what sort they were?"

Mr. Noone looked at his shoes, as if remembering anything about the creatures was an effort. 'Umm . . . well, they're called the night lovers around here."

"Night lovers? But that's not a breed of bird, is it?"

"I don't think so. But my wife had her own way of expressing herself. She was a poet, as well as an artist, you see."

She gave a non-committal nod and prayed, to whatever gods she believed in that day, that the old man would not ask if she wanted to read his wife's poems. Because she definitely did not.

But the gods were merciful and he simply turned back to the matter of opening his front door. "Oh, I see," said Mitch. "She was a very talented woman, obviously."

Mr. Noone had gone inside and half closed the front door before he replied. "Yes. Well, have a good day. It might rain later if you're going for a walk. Take an umbrella with you." Then the door closed completely, and Mitch was left thinking how much the large birds opening and closing their wings reminded her of an umbrella.

Over the next few days, Mitch found herself unable to work on any stories. The dead woman's art seemed to exert an almost hypnotic influence on her. Even though she wasn't usually one to haunt art galleries in her spare time, they were unlike anything she'd seen before. Something about them brought to mind the feeling she got standing in front of some pieces of ritual art she'd seen in Mexico.

She saw the old man working in the garden each day. Sometimes she waved to him, but got little response beyond a curt nod. She resolved to ask him if she could photograph the sculptures. That way she'd be able to study them in detail.

Perhaps a still image might actually reveal more about the puzzling objects than their actual physical presence. Anything was worth a try, she thought.

It was a warm evening for that time of the year, so Mitch took her coffee and cigarette out into the front garden. Sitting on the bench that her aunt had placed there years ago, she had a perfect view of Mr. Noone's house. Picking idly at one of the sea shells decorating the bench, she wondered if the strange birds would make an appearance for her.

The light had faded and she was beginning to think about going inside when she realised she hadn't seen the old man in the garden that day. That was unusual. All the lights in his house were out, yet a strange bluish glow showed in the downstairs window from time-to-time.

She thought that perhaps she should go and check on Mr. Noone, to see if he was all right. Besides, it would give her a chance to quiz him on the mysterious absence of information about his wife and her work.

Mitch opened the garden gate and walked up to the front door. She couldn't see any movement inside, but the faint blue glow persisted. She knocked gently on the door and waited. There was no reply. After a few minutes she pushed it and it moved inwards.

The room was in darkness, as she'd expected, and it took her eyes a little while to adjust to the gloom. Then she saw Mr. Noone. He was unmoving, slumped in a chair like a puppet with no life of its own. In the gloom it looked like he didn't have any face, and Mitch thought she was looking at the faceless figure on the shore. She was sure that it was an illusion, but it appeared as if his face was knitting itself together the moment before she flicked the light switch on.

"Mr. Noone, are you all right? Why are you sitting in the dark?"

He turned his head to look at her and his face held an expression of unbearable sadness. "I didn't realise that the light had gone," he said, softly. In

181

his hands sat a small metal sculpture resembling a beakless bird with folded wings and a broken neck. It gave off a faint blue luminescence. Mitch guessed that it must be what she saw through the window, though she couldn't begin to imagine what sort of metal could do that.

"But you're okay? I mean, you're not feeling unwell at all?" Mitch heard herself speak and felt only slightly ashamed that her concern masked an ulterior motive.

Mr. Noone shook his head. "No. No more than usual. Thank you. In fact, I find the darkness quite restful."

Mitch nodded. "Yes, I suppose it is, in a way." Now was the time to strike, she decided. "By the way, have you ever heard of an Italian artist called Francesco Scarno?"

It was as if Mitch had stuck a needle in him. The old man seemed stricken in some way, and she was about to repeat her question about him being unwell when he spoke again. "Yes . . . him!"

If she'd been a cat, Mitch's ears would have perked up visibly. "Oh, you mean that you do know him?"

The old man rose from his chair slowly, placing the sculpture carefully on a side table, then turned to face Mitch. He was a good foot shorter than her, but Mitch suddenly felt intimidated by him for some reason. "Please, come out into the garden at the back. There's something that I'm sure will interest you there."

She followed him as instructed, and found herself in a garden even larger than the one at the front. It must have taken the old man hours each week to tend to a space so large.

The garden appeared to run off into the dunes with no fence to mark the boundary. Standing at the end of the garden stood two towering sculptures, acting like scarecrows to warn off unwary trespassers. Mitch couldn't make out any real details in the fading light, but they had a roughly similar shape and stance of the "bird" sculpture that stood inside the house. They were both much taller. Mitch guessed they must each be over six feet in height. She couldn't imagine why the old man hadn't mentioned these impressive pieces to her before.

When one of the figures moved, she almost exclaimed in delight. They were obviously kinetic sculptures, designed to move with the wind or gravity. Then the other figure took a step forward and Mitch's breath caught in her throat. They were alive!

"W-what . . . ?" she exclaimed, backing away. Then she realised that they also resembled the creatures that she'd assumed were birds. The ones nesting beneath Mr. Noone's roof. Except that, if they were the same creatures, they'd grown enormously.

Not daring to take her eyes off the things as they took another step towards her, she forced out the words "What are they?!"

Mr. Noone was at her elbow now. He gently put his hand on her back, as if to stop her retreating any further.

"You asked about Francesco Scarno just now. He's buried near here, you know. Or at least, what he used to be is. There's a grave marker with my wife's name on it, too. They both died during one of Signore Scarno's frequent visits to my wife. But . . ." His hand wavered in the air for a moment before indicating the nightmares that towered over Mitch.

". . . they had made other arrangements, you see." The old man lapsed into silence. His head sank between his shoulders as he lowered his gaze, unable to look Mitch in the eye.

"I'd like you to meet my wife and her lover. They don't have names any longer, because they don't speak. Not like you and I do, at least." He said the words as if making a formal announcement of some importance, then he sank to his knees in apparent defeat. Or perhaps in prayer. Mitch realised in horror that he might actually be worshipping these things.

"H-help me!" she yelled, hoping to reach any spark of humanity left in the old fool. Noone's head remained bowed as he slowly shook it from side-to-side. She wasn't sure or not if she heard him whisper "I'm sorry".

The two black things were either side of her now. She wanted to run, but her legs refused to listen. Silently the creatures raised their enormous wings above her, blocking what little light was coming from the house. The midnight black things began to make a low noise that sounded like a million insects scraping away at something, slowly.

Mr. Noone's voice reached her ears. The old man seemed to be in a state of near ecstasy. "How lucky you are – they're making midnight for you!"

Her skin felt as if it was crawling with electricity. Or as if she had become a living insect colony. It made her muscles ache, and she found herself pitching forward into an involuntary crouch.

"Stop!" she gasped. But she had no way of knowing if these creatures understood her, or even if they heard her. She wondered how many others before her had been forced to beg like this.

She squatted on the floor, hands moving up to cover her head. She tensed her back, waiting for the things to strike. Even though she knew they weren't birds, she imagined the sharp pain of beaks and claws tearing through her clothes and into her flesh. Her imagination couldn't supply any more appropriate image of suffering from these huge, dark creatures.

Instead, she felt a sudden sensation as if she was about to vomit. She tensed ready, but nothing came. Then the ground beneath her felt as if it had changed. The soft sandy soil of the garden had disappeared and she was forced to shift her feet to gain some grip on the loose, hard stones instead. For the first time in her life, Mitch felt unsteady on her feet. She had no idea where she was or how she'd arrived there. She wondered if this was some form of hypnosis.

The air was foul and it caught at her throat, making her cough. She covered her nose and mouth with her hand but it helped hardly at all. The darkness surrounded her far more closely than it should, clinging to her as if it was a garment. This felt like a place that she could never leave.

She peered around her but could see next to nothing. She had a vague impression of a vast, dark plain stretching away into the distance.

Mitch shivered and hugged her arms to her. She feared the cold would reach her bones, cracking them open for the unseen feasters that she knew surrounded her.

The stark stars, cold and distant white, were wrong. They wound through the blackness in tangled, serpentine patterns. There wasn't a single constellation that she recognised.

It was midnight, certainly. But midnight *where*?!

Mark Howard Jones was was born in a town in south Wales where it once rained fish. He has had dozens of short stories published around the world, some of which are collected in *Songs from Spider Street* (Screaming Dreams), *Brightest Black* (Screaming Dreams), *Dreamglass Days* (ISMs Press) and *Flowers of War* (Black Shuck). A regular contributor to *Weird Fiction Review* in the United States and to PS Publishing's *Black Wings* series, he is also the editor of both volumes of *Cthulhu Cymraeg*. His novella 'Still Life With Death' was published in the 2020 anthology *The Book Of Yig: Revelations Of The Serpent* (Macabre Ink).

'Portal of the Old Ones' by Dave Carson

REMEMBER LIZZIE?

Marion Pitman

I FOUND A photograph the other week, in an old folder, of the girls dancing – our Morris side, that is. Must be forty years ago; I remember it, as they say, as if it were yesterday. If I close my eyes, I'm there. I can smell the dope and taste the beer, hear the noise of the crowd, the clashing of sticks, the melodeons and fiddles and drums with different sides, all playing different tunes for different dances, the massive boom of a big drum with a North-West side, the yells of the Border dancers; and I can see our band and the other dancers around me – except Lizzie. I can't see Lizzie at all. I can't picture her, can't conjure up any idea of what she looked like. I know she was there. She must be the one just turning, furthest from the camera, all you can see is a blur of moving colour, a straw hat with flowers.

It started me reminiscing, and I left the paperwork and made coffee and sat looking at the photo. I worked out which festival it was at, and I eventually remembered the names of the other women there. One I only remembered vaguely, she left the side soon after I joined; three of them I'm still in touch with, and Sue lives nearby and we have coffee together every week or so.

But Lizzie's still a blank. Was she squire that year? She was always a leader, full of energy, good at organising people and making things happen.

I can't do that. I have ideas, and ask people to do things, but they don't do them.

When I finished the coffee I went to the spare room and rummaged among the boxes there, looking for more photographs. I know I lost a lot of stuff in the last move, and in the flood, there might not be anything.

I found a packet – a physical packet of photos and negatives from Boots! – seems really strange now, doesn't it. There were pictures from a tour, a bit later than the other one from the festival. Lizzie wasn't in most of them, not sure why. I remember the tour; I twisted my knee in the third dance, and spent the rest of the weekend sitting out and looking after the sticks and the coats. I know Lizzie was there, she organised it all, and she's in two of the photos, but once turning away from the camera and once disappearing off the edge of the picture. I don't think I took those, I was usually good at getting the right shot . . .

She was of medium height, with short fair hair, but that didn't summon up anything. She was still a blank. How did I know it was her? Well, it just was. I saw it, and thought, "There's Lizzie," and then tried to recall her face, and couldn't.

Mind you, I have forgotten a lot of things since the *annus horribilis*. It messes with your mind, when things go as spectacularly pear-shaped as that. Actually it was more like three years, but it was relentless. I had some sort of breakdown in the end, the doctor said it was a form of PTSD, and I should get treatment, but there's a two-year waiting list. I get flashbacks. I can't drive any more.

You shouldn't have to bury your children. It's all the wrong way round.

I had to get back to the paperwork then, and it took me the rest of the day to find all the letters and the copy death certificates, but all the time the thought of Lizzie was fretting at the back of my mind.

I lay in bed that night thinking about her, thinking how lively and cheerful she always was, how she made us all feel enthusiastic about things. I could even faintly recall the sound of her voice, but not her face. Even after looking at the photos, I had no mental picture of her. I couldn't even recall the look of her back that I'd seen in the picture that afternoon. I wondered what had happened to her – how had she managed to drop off the map so completely? Surely I would have done my best to keep in touch with her?

I remembered her so clearly. Except for the face.

That night I dreamed – as so often – I was back in the car, with someone screaming, and flashing lights dazzling me, and impossibly loud crashes and screeches of metal – but this time Lizzie was there, in the front seat, where Cory had been – why? Of course I still couldn't see her face, I was in the back seat, but I knew it was her. And I woke sweating, and gasping for breath, as usual. Of course that happens, you think about someone and your brain puts them into a dream where someone else should be . . .

The next day was taken up with phone calls and talking to lawyers and searching for yet more paperwork, and by the end of the day I was exhausted. I had a quick supper and went to bed, and slept. More dreams, fire and water this time, but still blinding light and roaring noise; I woke up shouting, my heart beating far too fast.

The day after was Saturday, and I had a bit of respite. Lizzie was still on my mind, and I felt I needed to talk to someone who remembered her. Sue was away, so I rang Debby, who lives in Huddersfield, and whom I don't see often.

We chatted and caught up a bit – her daughter got married again last month – and I said, "I was looking through some old photos the other day. Whatever happened to Lizzie?"

"Lizzie?" Debby sounded doubtful; I could picture her frowning.

"You know – you can't have forgotten her, she was squire for three years, she was from—" I stopped – where was she from?

"Lizzie – oh, yes. Yes, I think I remember. I don't know what happened to her – did she emigrate? Wasn't her husband Australian?"

I frowned; I couldn't remember her husband at all. "Maybe," I said. "I was thinking about everyone, and I wondered where they all were now."

"Well, Mags and Sue and Sarah and Jo were all at that reunion last year, weren't they? I heard from Claire at Christmas, she's in Inverness. Alison – I don't know about Alison."

"I don't remember Alison."

"Maybe not, she only stayed for one season, then she took up Appalachian clog dancing."

I thought of someone else. "What about Cathy?"

"Cathy . . . no, I don't remember her. It's a long time ago. Do you remember that woman with the incredibly gorgeous husband? What was her name?"

"Was that Jennifer?"

"Jennifer! That's it."

I said, "He wasn't really my type. Very pretty though."

Debby laughed, and said, "By the way, did you hear Judith's got another granddaughter?"

The conversation got on to grandchildren then, and I didn't want to sound obsessive about Lizzie, so I left it.

I was beginning to wonder if Lizzie was dead. But why did no one seem to remember her? Or were they pretending not to, because they didn't want to talk about it . . . suppose I'd murdered her, and they'd helped me get away with it? No, that was silly . . . Why couldn't I remember? The shock, the knock on the head – but why should it wipe out Lizzie? She hadn't been there. I remembered everyone else . . .

That night I dreamed the house was drifting inexorably away from me, and Luke and Cory were in it, and being swept out to sea; and Lizzie was being swept away too . . . I woke and found I was crying.

I spent Sunday at a meditation day, but Lizzie kept interrupting. *I am getting obsessed*, I thought; *this is silly*. When I got home I went online and searched for anything that might help; there were a few old pictures and references to the side, but frankly we hadn't been very notable. The fact that I couldn't remember Lizzie's last name didn't help.

That night's dream was almost calm, but desperately sad. I was at someone's funeral, and somehow I knew it was Lizzie's. I swear I've never been to her funeral in real life. It was a quiet old country churchyard, and the church looked derelict.

Monday was back to lawyers, and it all got a bit much. I had to have a lie down before dinner, and I tried consciously to think about other things.

It didn't work. I started thinking about what a great person Lizzie was, and how entirely unlike me. I should have liked to be more like her. Perhaps I should take her as a role model – or was it too late now? Probably. She was energetic, as I said, and outgoing, and good at organising. I have hardly any energy these days, and although I like socialising, it's always an effort.

I don't know what I dreamed that night, but I woke sweating and screaming again, and had to get up and make coffee, although it was three in the morning.

On Tuesday I rang Mags, we did the usual small talk – her brother-in-law was getting divorced – and I said about the photo, and wondering what had happened to people.

Mags laughed and said, "I have enough trouble keeping up with all the people I know now! Do you know I've got nine grandchildren?"

"Good grief!"

"Well, that includes Tony's three, of course. You still see Sue, don't you?"

"Oh yes. I was just wondering about the ones I've lost touch with. Lizzie, for example."

"Lizzie! Goodness, yes. Wasn't she a fireball?! And the red hair and everything, although I don't think it was really that colour. Do you remember when that chap tried to tell her it was blasphemous for women to dance the morris, and she emptied his pint over his head?"

"Um . . ."

"Or maybe you weren't there," she said, "no, I think you were ill that time. But she was a cracker!"

That wasn't quite what I remembered, but after all people's memories of the same things do differ. I vaguely remembered a redhead, but I thought her name was Tina.

Mags said, "Listen, I've got to go. Lovely to have had a catch up!"

And she was gone.

Then I had to go and see the solicitor, and swear an affidavit, and she was very solemn and portentous with me, greatly increasing my usual feeling of nameless dread, but I managed to hold myself together, and went home and had a large gin.

I got out the photographs again, and looked at them carefully. I tried to decide if Lizzie had red hair. I couldn't be sure. I found a group photo, but her face was hidden behind someone's hat. I could remember walking along the esplanade with her and a couple of others, but still I could not conjure up her face.

The whole thing was beginning to worry me. My memory is patchy, I know, and there are things I forget, but forgetting so completely one face when I remember so much of that time clearly, doesn't seem right. I began to wonder if Lizzie really existed. Was she an illusion? Were Debby and Mags humouring me? But on the other hand, perhaps their memories were patchy, and they had trouble remembering her too.

Then Sarah rang me up. She wanted to know if I was going to a festival in the summer. I made some vague promise to think about it, although I wasn't keen. Since I gave up dancing I have little appetite for watching other people dance. Sarah still dances – she's clearly got a portrait in the attic.

I told her I'd spoken to Mags, and passed on some of the gossip, and told her about finding the photograph. I said, "Whatever happened to Lizzie?"

"Lizzie? No idea. She doesn't come to festivals. I've lost touch with a lot of people since those days, you do, don't you. I've never seen her around. Did she move to Sweden?"

"Sweden? I don't know, I don't remember it."

"Mm. No, that was Joanne. Oh, do you remember Annie Taylor? I saw her the other day, she's dancing again – they've given her a new knee."

"It's wonderful what they can do."

And that night it was back to the car, and the screaming and yelling and rending of metal, and the blinding light. And I couldn't tell who was in the front seat.

I just lay and stared at the ceiling when I woke. Lizzie must be dead. That's what my subconscious was trying to tell me. We had been very close, and somehow I was involved in her death, and the shock, on top of everything else, had wiped the memory, and now it was trying to come back. But surely one of the other women would have said something when I asked? Surely . . .

I drifted off to sleep briefly, and started awake again at the sight of a mangled body, in Morris kit. Blood. Death. That was what my brain kept saying.

The next day Sue came back, and I went round with a bottle of wine. She told me all about the holiday, and I told her how it was going with the lawyers. Then we started reminiscing, and I asked her about Lizzie. And I said, "It's extraordinary, but I simply cannot remember what she looked like."

Sue frowned; "Lizzie. I don't recall the name. Are you sure you've got it right?"

That threw me slightly. Surely Sue wouldn't prevaricate, even if the others did. "Well," I said uncertainly, "that's the name in my mind, I'm sure . . ."

Sue shook her head. "Rings no bells. Some people just aren't that memorable though."

I said, "But Lizzie was very memorable! She was squire for three years, she organised all sorts of things . . . I can't have got the name wrong."

Sue gave me a slightly worried look, and changed the subject.

When I got home I sat for hours, staring at the photograph, willing Lizzie to turn round, to show me her face.

That night I dreamed Lizzie was walking ahead of me on a rather vague and cloudy street; she was in kit, and I knew for certain it was her; but I couldn't catch up with her, although I tried really hard, and she didn't seem to be walking very fast – you know how it is in dreams. I woke up feeling absolute despair. A voice in my head said, "Never, never again."

In the morning I was weepy and distracted. Thoughts came into my head, crazy thoughts.

When I was small I had an imaginary friend. Her name was Lizzie. I suddenly remembered this, and started to wonder – was Lizzie simply a fig-leaf of my imagination, as Luke would have said?

But that was crazy. Was I hallucinating? There she was in the photos. I recognized her – even if I couldn't remember her face . . .

I needed someone else to look at the photos. But . . . suppose I did. Suppose they looked at them and she wasn't there? That someone else, whom I knew very well, was dancing in her place, and there was no one to be Lizzie—?

Why does everyone pretend they don't remember her? What happened? Is she dead? She is dead, and I must have killed her. That's what they're hiding from me. They all know I killed her, but I haven't been arrested, so . . . they must have helped to cover it up. Did they make it look like an accident? Or did we bury the body? When I had the breakdown – was that why I killed her? Or was it because I killed her? Did I kill Luke too? No, that was his heart. He had a heart attack while we were clearing Mother's house. He was in the hospital. Wasn't he? I know the other things happened, they weren't my fault. Luke losing all that money, so we had to sell the house. The river bursting its banks, the flood. That couldn't be my fault at least. And the crash. The crash wasn't my fault, was it, was it . . . ?

Or maybe Lizzie never was real. Maybe she was a ghost – or else, a, you know, one of . . . the people of the hills. The Others. She came and danced with us for a while, and I'm the only one who can remember. Why can I remember? Is that why she wants to drive me mad, because I remember? So what about the photograph? If I showed someone the photograph . . . then they might remember, and she'd have to drive them mad too . . . Don't they have any photographs?

Perhaps she only appears in mine. Perhaps in their photographs she's somebody else . . .

How do I know the person in the photograph is Lizzie? Because she couldn't be anyone else. Besides, even if it isn't, I still remember Lizzie, her energy, her cheerfulness, her positivity about everything. She always sorted out problems, she made you feel that whatever you were doing would succeed. God, I need her now. I can't believe anything will succeed, ever.

I don't know how long it was before the circle of terror and despair was broken by the doorbell; rather to my surprise, it was Sue. She ignored whatever expression I had on my face.

"Hope you don't mind," she said, "seeing me twice in two days."

"Of course not. Coffee?"

"Thanks, yes."

We sat down with coffee and biscuits, and talked about the weather, and eventually Sue said, "Can you show me this photo? I'd be interested, and maybe it'll remind me who Lizzie was."

Well I was surprised, but of course I went and fetched the photo. I was half expecting it would have vanished, or Lizzie wouldn't be in the picture any more, but it was there, and just the same.

Sue took it with a word of thanks, and studied it for some time. She identified all the other dancers, and I agreed, and she said, "So which one is Lizzie?"

"That one, there."

She stared at it. "What's the dance?" she said.

I stared at the picture too. "Valentine's," I said

"Right. I agree. And so that's the position you danced, Beth. That's you."

And of course, it was. But it isn't now. And it never will be again.

Marion Pitman is Londoner who has been writing poetry and fiction all her life. She also sells second-hand books, and has worked as an editor, proof-reader, and artists' model. She has no car, no cats and no money; her hobbies include folk-singing, watching cricket, and theological argument. Her short story collection, *Music in the Bone*, is published by Alchemy Press. Her very occasional blog can be found at: www.marionpitman.co.uk

ROMERO'S CHILDREN

David A. Riley

"Senator Hardy launched an attack tonight against the widespread use of the age-retarding drug OM (Old Methuselah), in which he condemned black market sales: 'No one today knows what its long term results will be. It may halt aging in the short term, but it will be years, perhaps decades before anyone can say that its usage is safe or does not have possible side effects which no one at this time can predict. People take this drug with the hope of a longer, healthier life, but they do not know if this is all they will get.'"

**—One of the last newspaper reports
ever published in the United States**

THE OLD MAN could hear them scratching and clawing at the outside door two floors below, trying to get in. He'd been able to hear them for the last few nights as he lay in bed, trying to keep warm on the thin mattress of the old cast iron bedstead, with its well-worn blankets and hard pillow. But the door was strong. It would take months for them to wear it down and he felt secure enough to lie listening to them without any fear. Let them waste their energies. He was safe, if neither comfortable nor warm.

The next morning, his joints aching, Jack climbed out of bed and put on his clothes. Although the sun rose several hours ago, it was wintry and pale and gave off little heat, and the cold of the threadbare carpets, scattered like rugs on the bare floorboards, chilled his feet as he trod across them. He rooted out his boots from where he discarded them last night when he drunkenly made his way to bed, and tugged on the socks he'd stuffed inside them, then the boots themselves. He yawned, scratched for a minute or two, then padded across to the window. Its dusty panes looked down onto the street.

They'd gone. Romero's children nearly always disappeared when the sun came up. They preferred the night, with its darkness and shadows. In daylight they were easily seen and picked off. Even their dim minds were aware of this, self-preservation kicking in to make them hide.

Jack put on his padded outer jacket and slipped on his gloves. Snow was on its way, though he didn't need that to appreciate how cold it was. He reached for the rifle propped against the wall, safety catch on, one shell in the breach. Although he felt secure up here at night, there were always accidents – and enough survivors had been complacent in the safety of their homes that they ended up as meat.

Less than twenty years had passed since OM made its first appearance and still they were paying for it. And would till long after he turned into maggot food, Jack thought as he set about unlocking the series of doors that led down the stairwell to the street. He had installed them at the top of each flight, with spy holes through which he could see if any of *them* had gotten inside the building. That had only happened once so far. One night he had been too tired – or drunk, if truth were known – and left the door onto the street ajar. There

191

was a large piece of wood still screwed to the last door at the bottom of the stairs to cover the hole he'd blasted through it – and through the head of the thing mewling on the other side, its beautiful, youthful, dirt-stained face visible through the fish-eye lens.

OM. It was hard to remember it now as anything but a curse that had destroyed everything. Brought an end to all the calamitous fears of Global Warming too, since few cars, factories or anything else mechanical or electrical had functioned for years. Yes, we sure put a stop to that all right, Jack thought to himself ironically. Something to be proud of, at least.

He pushed an eye against the spy hole of the outside door and peered onto the street. It was a rarely needed precaution. And as usual there was nothing there. Just the permanently parked cars, their tyres long since flattened, while rust ate at their bodywork. There were streaks of ice along the road. And the inevitable debris.

With a sigh, Jack unlocked the door and pulled it open. It was heavy, and shut behind him with a resounding thud, before he locked it again. He swung the rifle from his shoulder and took a careful look in every direction.

In the distance three figures were running towards him. The nearest was a girl. He recognised Candice Roe at once, a hard-bitten seventeen-year-old from the settlement. And a damned good shot with a rifle. Which puzzled him. Why was her gun clenched in one hand when she was being pursued? It wouldn't be like Candice to have run out of ammo. Like most people these days she would carry at least a dozen rounds, stuffed in bags or in her pockets – anywhere they would fit. Ammo meant survival. Especially against stinkers.

Jack hurried towards her. He could see she was tiring, and it looked as if the creatures were gaining on her. They were a man and a woman, their unwrinkled faces grey with years of accumulated dirt, dried food and blood like flaking masks of mud.

Dropping to one knee, Jack aimed his rifle at the nearest, centring the cross-wires of the telescopic lens on one eye. He eased back the trigger. The shot took away most of the upper cranium in a spray of brains, bone and discoloured blood. He took out the other a few seconds later. Both lay twitching on the street when Candice reached him, gasping for breath.

"My rifle jammed otherwise I'd have taken them myself," she panted. "Must have run over a mile before I saw you. Gave me a second wind."

"Good job you did. Looked to me as if they were gaining ground."

"Persistent bastards. Comes from not having brains enough to know when you're exhausted."

Jack chuckled. "Stands to sense there must be some compensation for being brain dead psychos. That's just one of 'em."

Candice scowled. "Glad it amused you, Jack."

"It'll amuse you too as soon as you've got your breath back."

"And forgotten how close I came to becoming meat for those bastards."

"And that," Jack added, his humour dying a little. It was a danger all of them had to live with, and one that no one took lightly. They'd all seen the aftermath too often for that.

"How come you're out here by yourself?" Jack asked.

Candice regarded him edgily. "You're a fine one to ask that."

"That's my choice. One I've lived with for years. Wouldn't suit everyone, 'specially these days. But you're not a sad, dried-up old loner like me."

"No." Candice gazed down the empty street, with its stone-clad apartments, shops and offices, all of them derelict. "I just needed some time by myself for a while, that's all."

Deducing it was probably something to do with a boy and none of his business, Jack shrugged. "Okay by me. You can hunker down here for a while if you like. Leastways, I can help fix your rifle. And lend you a handgun. You should always have one as backup. Me, I have a Colt automatic. Stops 'em dead in their tracks every time. I'm not much of a shot with it, mind, but at close range I don't need to be."

"I usually have something. I just wasn't thinking today."

"Not thinking is what gets you killed." Jack gazed down the street, aware suddenly the cold had begun to sink into his bones. "I'm off after some fresh stores. D'you want to lend a hand?"

"Suppose that's the least I could do," she said, an uncertain smile twitching about her lips. "What's it today? Walmart?"

"As always. Canned section."

They walked down the street in silence for a while till they turned onto the car park at the nearest store, with its abandoned cars and the skeletal remains of several hundred bodies, a grim reminder of just how turbulent times had been when the after effects of OM showed themselves.

"How come you never took OM?" Candice asked as they passed the first of the bodies. "There aren't many people your age around these days. Almost everyone of your generation took it. Why didn't you? Religious reasons?"

Jack shook his head. "My wife. We were both in our fifties when OM hit the headlines. She'd already started with Alzheimer's by then. What good is a drug that'll retard ageing to someone with that? Putting off old age indefinitely isn't much of a lure for someone whose brains are turning to mush. Me, I couldn't take it while Rachel was like she was. Didn't seem hardly fair somehow. An extra forty or fifty years of life didn't appeal to me then. Hell, even suicide wasn't far from my mind when Rachel passed on, that's how bad I felt."

"You were lucky."

"You could say that, though I don't reckon as I would necessarily agree. This isn't exactly how I saw my Golden Years." Jack gazed across the car park. "It was bizarre how greedy folks were for it," he said a moment later. "It was never licensed by the government, you know. Most of it was sold on the black market – a black market that became huge quickly, the demand was so big. Things went insane. Everyone wanted it, especially those who'd passed their thirties. Made the profits during Prohibition small potatoes, believe you me. Made some criminal empires enormous. For a while, at least."

"Till its after effects destroyed them too."

"Destroyed everything – almost. There'd been warnings, of course. Some scientists spoke out against OM. But they were ignored. Immortality was too big an incentive for anyone to wait till all the tests had been completed – tests that would take years. Too many years for most folk. Hell, if OM had come along earlier, when Alzheimer's was something that happened to other people, not to us, I expect that me and Rachel would have taken it too. Why not? We'd have leapt at the chance of putting a stop to ageing and gaining all that extra time."

"And you'd have ended as stinkers too."

"Without a doubt. Never heard of anyone who took OM without that kicking in seven, eight years down the line. Made Alzheimer's look like a dose of flu. You think we've got it bad, girl, you should have seen what it was like when there were millions of the bastards going off the rails. Looking back, it's hard to imagine how any of us survived. If'n they hadn't been such dumb bastards I don't suppose we would. Luckily, they were more often as interested in tearing each other to pieces as attacking us. Cut their numbers down a lot in the first year till some of them started working together, those that were left. The *smart* ones."

"I can't remember any of that," Candice said. "I was only a baby then. Lucky for me, Mom was only eighteen when she had me and hadn't thought about taking OM then. Before she could, it all went to Hell."

"How is your mom?"

"Okay. Feeling her age these days."

"If she's feeling her age, imagine what I'm feeling." Jack gave her a sideways grimace, then tucked the rifle under his arm, ready to fire. They were only a few yards from the main entrance to the abandoned store. Its doors had long since been reduced to splinters. The dark interior was a vast array of tumbledown shelves and scattered produce, filled with shadows. "I don't expect to come across any stinkers here. They tend to prefer somewhere less well-trodden to hang out during the day, somewhere less likely to get them shot."

"They know that well enough," Candice said sourly.

"Those that've survived this long know it. There were a lot in the early days too dumb for that. I suppose it was survival of the fittest. The dumbest were culled early on."

"So, we've the brightest, eh?" Candice laughed. It was a sound that helped to lighten Jack's spirit somehow. He hated scavenging through derelict stores for the few undamaged cans of food still left in them. It depressed him. Candice's presence helped take away some of his gloominess. Perhaps he'd made too much of his preference for solitude. Now he was getting older perhaps it was time to enjoy some company for a change; maybe even join the settlement. They'd asked him often enough over the years.

You can't do penance for having outlived her forever, he told himself as he looked back on the last few days of Rachel's life. Ironically, her passing had coincided with the first of the stinkers. Romero's children.

If only they'd known how widespread it was going to be, all those politicians and scientists who had appeared on television, discussing the first cases of violence wreaked by the stinkers. The irony was that most of these people became stinkers too in the next few months.

Romero's children had sounded like a joke at first. Except these creatures weren't movie zombies. Not the shambling, ugly, walking corpses the great director had portrayed them as. They were neither shambling nor ugly. Nor dead. Far from it, Jack thought. But they were deadly all right. Just as deadly as anything ever dreamt up in Hollywood.

"Careful," Jack cautioned as they stepped inside the store. He eased some of the tension from his trigger finger as he scanned the poorly lit interior. He had been here often in the past. Knew almost every untidy pile of mouldering food that had been spilled onto the floor from burst bags and ruptured packets. In a few years there'd be nothing left worth scavenging. The alcohol went long ago. Fortunately, he had another source for that. One no one else had stumbled on yet.

Something scuffled deep inside the store, and Jack swore softly as he automatically fell into a crouch, gun at the ready, his eyes scanning the gloom.

"What was it? A rat?" Beside him, Candice held a knife in one hand.

Jack shook his head. "I don't know. There are enough vermin about. But that didn't sound like a rat to me." He passed her his Colt, then crept along the aisle, his head twitching from side to side. If there were stinkers present, he was confident of taking two or three of them easily enough. But there was always the chance a nest of them had decided to camp here. He had on occasion come across a dozen or more – though that was rare. The sensible thing would have been to get help. But that wasn't Jack's way. He'd been a loner too long to break old habits easily. And with Candice as back up, he felt sure they could handle up to four, maybe five between them without breaking into a sweat.

"Over there," Candice whispered. She jerked two fingers leftwards. "Behind the freezers. I saw something there. It's watching us."

Which was damnably odd behaviour for a stinker, Jack thought.

"You sure it's watching us?"

"Looked like it to me," Candice whispered back. He could tell she was disturbed. She had been brought up dealing with creatures like this and probably knew their behaviour as well as him. "Perhaps it isn't a stinker."

Jack didn't know. Could be someone else scavenging for supplies. But why hide? It would have been obvious who Candice and he were the moment they stepped inside the store. For a start off Stinkers didn't carry guns. Stinkers didn't talk either.

Coming to a decision, Jack stood up and advanced towards where Candice had pointed.

"If'n you're one of us step out," he said. "I'll hold my fire. We only shoot stinkers."

Even though the face had recently been washed, Jack could not mistake what hesitantly stepped out of the shadows in front, its hands above its head in an awkward gesture of surrender. It would take more than a few wipes with a wet rag to remove the years of ingrained grime from the creature's face.

For a moment Jack faltered. He knew he should aim and fire. He could have done that in a split second. Instinct tugged at nerve endings, urging him on. But he didn't. He couldn't.

He waved Candice's weapon down when she stepped up beside him.

"Why?" Her question was half bewilderment, half accusation.

Jack shook his head, uncertain. "Something odd about this thing," was all he could think to say as he stepped towards it, his finger still hooked about the trigger of his gun, aimed at waist level ahead of him.

"Who are you?" he asked.

Her clothes were tatters, held together by grease and dirt, which clung like a grimy, obscene skin to her scrawny body. The woman took a cautious step from where she had been hiding. Her fingers were black with crusts of blood and grease, the accumulated debris of a thousand meals eaten raw. She was a stinker all right. Jack was certain of that. But her face, especially her eyes, was wrong. There was fear in her eyes. And confusion.

"You hold it right there," he told her. "One more step and, like it or not, I'll fire."

The woman came to an unsteady halt. She was trying to speak. Jack was certain about that. But her tongue and jaw muscles moved awkwardly as if from lack of practice.

"What the fuck is it doing?" Candice asked.

"Damned if I know." Jack squinted through the gloom. Like every stinker he had ever seen she looked youthful. However old she may have been when she first took OM it had stopped the years from gaining on her, even though nearly two decades had passed since she took it. The drug may have messed up her brain, but beneath all the accumulated filth her body was as perfect as the day she took it.

"Awake . . ." The woman spoke in a stutter, her voice thick, as if her tongue was too large – or unaccustomed to the motions it was being forced to make. "Night . . . mares . . . gone . . ."

"You're the fucking nightmare," Candice grumbled, her eyes venomous as she stared at the woman. "We should cap that thing."

Gently, Jack touched the girl's arm. "Easy now," he said. "Stinkers don't talk."

"Then what is she if she isn't a fucking stinker?"

"That I don't know," he said. "But stinkers don't talk. I know that, if I know nothing else."

The woman swayed. She looked as if she hadn't eaten in days.

"Awake . . ." she repeated.

While Jack heaved a sack of canned goods on his shoulder, most of their labels unreadable, Candice led the woman back to his place. The stinker's hands had been tied together in front of her. Jack had relented on this precaution. If he hadn't, he suspected Candice would have used the slightest excuse – an unsteady step or an odd movement – to open fire and kill the thing.

"You're taking one hell of a risk taking this thing back to your place," Candice grumbled.

"We'll see," Jack said, unsure why he trusted the woman. But somehow, though, he did. Perhaps it was the pain, the confusion and the look of horror in her eyes that convinced him. He didn't know. Less than an hour after discovering her, though, she was sitting in a bath of warm water in Jack's apartment. Apathetically, she let Jack, and then Candice set to work scrubbing decades of grime from her thin body. For the most part the woman was placid, either through exhaustion or fear or both. After a short time, she looked almost human again. Or would have except for the fact she was unnaturally youthful and too mature at the same time despite the tiredness and fear on her face. The woman's hands, especially her fingers, had blackened lines of grease and blood that would take more than soap to remove. Like Lady Macbeth, Jack thought to himself, her sins would haunt her in her hands for years to come.

He gave her a pair of trousers and a jumper to replace the shreds of clothing they had peeled like layers of diseased flesh from her body. The mess had reeked so much Jack had been forced to open one of the windows and toss them out into the street, though the apartment still had the unmistakable stench of Romero's children. They weren't called stinkers for nothing, he thought.

"What next?" Candice asked after the woman had been led into one of the bedrooms to rest.

Jack shrugged. "See if she'll eat some of our food. That's the ultimate test. Stinkers aren't interested in normal food."

"Just off the bone with the pulse still pumping," Candice said, more than a trace of bitterness in her voice.

"Never seen one eat cooked food, even when it was available."

"So if she does, she's cured? Is that what you think?"

"Maybe."

"Would you trust her then?" Candice glanced at the closed door to the bedroom the woman was in.

"I don't know," he said. "I'd have to hear her talk. Hear her story. See what she's got to say for herself. Weigh it up."

It was dark by the time they were sat about the table. Jack had prepared a thick stew from some tinned potatoes, beans and meat they'd brought back from the store. He placed a bowl of it before the woman, along with a spoon. There was a feeling of tension as she stared at it for several moments, and Jack saw Candice's hand stray towards the Colt still tucked inside the belt of her jeans. Uncertain, the woman grasped the spoon. It shook in her fingers as she awkwardly held it between her them, then dipped it in the bowl, before slowly lifting it towards her mouth, spilling half its contents. She stopped as the edge of the spoon touched her lips, as if she was struggling to remember what came next. Then she pushed the spoon into her mouth. Some of the stew spilled down her chin but she barely seemed to notice that. For a moment what was left of the food rested inside her mouth, and it looked to Jack as if she was tasting – or testing – the oddity of it. Or trying to recall when she last had food like this. Cooked food. Seventeen, maybe eighteen years was a long time to remember. Could he remember what the food he ate back then was like?

After gulping what remained on her spoon, the woman surprised him by going on to clear her bowl with an appetite that made Jack wonder how long it was since the last time she ate, though he tried not to think what that meal might have been. That was her past. This was her present. Her different present, he hoped.

When they'd finished eating, Jack eased his chair back from the table and regarded the woman. Her complexion looked better now – more normal, he thought. Almost.

"Do you recall your name?" he said.

Though physically she looked no more than thirty, Jack knew she had to be fifty at least. Nearly twenty lost years of madness lay between the last time she'd used her name and now. It was easy to forget this when looking at her youthfulness.

"They – they called me – Lucy – once."

It was painful to hear that voice. It jarred with her face. A fractured, husky whisper, it made Jack's hair rise on the nape of his neck. He could see the same reaction in Candice. Which was worrying, he thought. Maybe practice would ease a more acceptable sound into the woman's voice.

Jack nodded to Candice. He introduced her to the woman. "My name is Jack."

Lucy repeated their names as if to memorise them.

"How long have you been back with us?" Jack asked. "Since the nightmares ended, I mean."

"Days – nights. I was – frightened. I hid."

"What do you remember?"

She closed her eyes and shuddered. "Nightmares. On and on . . . endless . . . nightmares."

"Before then, before the nightmares started?"

For a moment Lucy opened her eyes. She stared at him as if struggling to search back through the decades, then burst into tears. They streamed down her face unchecked. Even Candice looked concerned.

"Easy now," Jack said, quietly. "No need to struggle. If you can't remember, it doesn't matter. If those memories are there they'll come back with time."

"If you want them to," Candice said.

That night, while they lay in separate rooms, Jack heard the scratching outside again. Lucy might have come through whatever Hell she had been to, but others were still living it.

Eventually, though, he slept.

It was three, perhaps four in the morning when he awoke, aware the sounds outside had stopped. Realised they were wasting their time, he thought, though those bastards had time enough to waste, he thought to himself, aware of the irony.

He felt a chill in the air, and he wondered if the window had slipped open. But he was reluctant to leave the warmth of his bed and walk to it, knowing how bitterly cold the air would be. He opened one eye and was surprised to see how light it was. It had snowed overnight, and the building across the street was coated with piles on every ridge and window ledge, reflecting moonlight into his room. It was then he heard something move. Instantly he was wide-awake. He reached for the rifle he had left against his bed. It had gone. Prickles of alarm shivered through his body as his hand reached into emptiness. He moved his head and scanned the room. He saw a figure by the doorway, staring at him. It was Lucy. He recognised her even in the gloom. She was holding something in one hand. It was dark and round. In her other hand he saw the glint of a blade. It was broad like one of the high-tech butcher's knives from his kitchen. His breath caught in his throat as his eyes adjusted to the gloom. Beyond her he could see two other figures in the open doorway. At the same time, he recognised the smell that wafted from them. Had she gone downstairs and opened the bottommost door to let them in? Her fellow "children". Down the front of her clothes Jack saw the vomit that had begun to dry, of the stew she must have thrown up as she lay in bed as the nightmares came and took her again.

Jack swung out of bed, though he had little hope without his rifle. But in the top drawer by the window he kept a handgun. If he reached it he would have a chance. But the thing, that had briefly been Lucy again, flung the object she held in her hand across the floor at his unshod feet, tripping him. Sprawled helplessly on his back, Jack cried out as he recognised Candice's face staring up at him from between his feet.

Lucy moved towards him; her grease-stained fingers hooked like claws.

David A. Riley is a writer specialising mainly in horror, fantasy and SF stories. In 1995, along with his wife, Linden, he edited and published a fantasy/SF magazine, *Beyond*. His first professionally published story was in the *11th Pan Book of Horror* in 1970. This was reprinted in 2012 in *The Century's Best Horror Fiction* edited by John Pelan of *Cemetery Dance*. He has had numerous stories published by Doubleday, DAW, Corgi, Sphere, Roc, Playboy Paperbacks, Robinsons, etc., and in magazines such as *Aboriginal Science Fiction*, *Dark Discoveries*, *Fear*, *Whispers*, and *Fantasy Tales*.

His first collection of stories (four long stories and a novelette) was published by Hazardous Press in 2012, *His Own Mad Demons*.

A Lovecraftian novel, *The Return*, was published by Blood Bound Books in the USA in 2013.

A second collection of his stories, all of which were professionally published prior to 2000, *The Lurkers in the Abyss & Other Tales of Terror*, was launched at the World Fantasy Convention in 2013 by Shadow Publishing. Hazardous Press published his third short story collection, *Their Cramped Dark World and Other Tales*, in 2015. Both Hazardous Press collections have now been reprinted, with brand new covers, by Parallel Universe Publications.

A fantasy novel, *Goblin Mire*, and a horror novel, *Moloch's Children*, were both published in 2015. He and his wife recently relaunched Parallel Universe Publications, which originally published *Beyond*. Parallel Universe published twelve books in 2015, including an anthology of new stories, *Kitchen Sink Gothic*, edited by David A. Riley and Linden Riley.

David Riley's stories have been translated into Italian, German, Spanish and Russian.

TWILIGHT ON A DYING WORLD

Mike Chinn

HIS REPTILIAN MOUNT'S walk had become a slow, painful plod. Its hind legs, normally capable of striding across long unwavering distances, struck the cooling sands irregularly. It staggered. The armoured figure strapped into the high saddle across the creature's ridged back knew if they could find no shelter soon, his equaar's metabolism would slow to the point where it was little more than a barely breathing, scaley statue.

Night had caught them too far from Burnharnh, alone in the vast, stony wastes of Tlantykh. Once the furnace sun had dipped below a jagged horizon, the thin grey sands cooled with alarming speed. Even the warm blooded humans of the Cities found it difficult to survive a night unprotected, far from food and hearth.

A low ridge thrust up from the sands before them. The armoured figure thought he saw, in the last thin gleams of day, a darker blot where the toothed ridge met the ground. A cave? Shelter? Urging his limping mount up a scree slope, goading it on with a drawn sword, they came at last to the cave's twisted mouth. A silent scream in the upthrust rockface.

Suppressing a shudder he blamed on the cooling air, the rider guided his mount inside.

Inside the dark cavern he felt the equaar's muscles relax fractionally. There was no draught, and the still air retained some of the daytime's dry heat. Staying mounted, the rider pulled a brand from the gear hanging off his saddle and lit it with a glowing flame-pot. Limestone walls and pillars leapt into abrupt clarity in the dancing flames. Beyond the sphere of light however, the cavern was engulfed in black shadow. It was deep, penetrating far into the mountainside, far deeper than the rider had expected. Did that mean the temperature would remain constant throughout the day and night? Cool, but not fatally cold? The rider hoped so.

Shrugging within his all-encompassing, baroque armour, he dismounted and pushed the brand's end into the thick layer of loose shale which covered the floor.

Quickly, he removed saddle and half-armour from the wheezing equaar, taking a handful of resin-impregnated sticks from a waxed bag. Firing one with the brand he made a frugal blaze – careful not to waste any of the rare and precious fuel. He pulled off grimy, articulated gauntlets and flexed raw fingers, luxuriating in the sense of freedom – but he left his grotesquely-horned sallet helm in place, merely dropping the bevor to expose his mouth. Like all Knights of Xanine – and every knight of the Five Cities was required to be a devotee of Xanine the Invariable – he would never willingly allow his face to be uncovered. Even in private. The comfortable leather cowl he wore when out of armour was back in Burnharnh. Keeping on his sallet was a penance for allowing himself to be stranded out in the unforgiving desert.

He ate sparely: heating a can of water to boiling point, then stirring in a handful of coarse grains. Once he had finished the crude porridge, he cut a lump of dried meat from a chunk wrapped in old cloth, tossing it to his grumbling equaar. The reptile nosed the food with disinterest, then took it anyway. It was too cold for its digestive system to begin work – but once the creature was warmed by the morning sun the meat would nourish it long enough to return home.

The knight relaxed slightly. He unbuckled his heavy studded belt, removing basket-hilted broadsword and dagger from their sheaths, keeping both close to hand. He remained dressed in his jointed armour, despite the sweat-clotted sand chafing his skin. He wiped hands on an already stained green tabard that bore the silver mask of Burnharnh, then took up the torch and sword, deciding it was time he explored his temporary shelter.

The cave went deep underground, far deeper than he intended to venture. Besides, he imagined it would be no different a hundred yards on: the same dried stalactites and stalagmites – speaking of the fabled days when water flowed freely – the same pale, bone coloured walls and ceiling.

A trickle of shale by the entrance alerted him. Turning, he levelled his broadsword, dropping the torch and stamping it out. Its light was too revealing. He drew back into the dark, away from the dancing shadows thrown by his fire.

A figure stood in the entrance, highlighted by the flames. Its long, iguana head swung back and forth as it searched the cavern, black eyes emotionless. After a moment, the creature stepped towards the fire on inhumanly-jointed back legs, its long tail thrust out stiffly behind, a tall crest erect along its head and neck. It paused by the fire, glancing at the torpid equaar, and leaned on the head of the long hafted axe it carried.

The knight held his breath. He recognised the creature as a member of an intelligent lizard-race, despite the human-like affectation of clothing – one of many things strange which had appeared on Earth since the Fall. He did not like to consider where it had come by its clothes: they fitted it badly, clearly meant for a completely different body shape. What was it doing in the lowlands? No lizards came down from the arid, inhospitable mountains of Merykh.

"Come forth, mammal. Why hide when your presence is so obvious?" The lizard spoke the human tongue with surprising ease; although the reptilian throat distorted the vowels and gave the speech a sibilance that washed coldly over the knight. He stepped into the light. The lizard appraised him carefully.

"What do you want?" he demanded.

The other yawned and flicked a thick tongue. "The night is cold and your fire warm. Could I not share?"

The knight bit back a laugh. "A lizard? Share? You'd cut my throat the moment I turned my back."

"Possibly. Or you might do the same for me. But we both need heat to live through the night, and are far from our homes . . ." It let the huge battle-axe fall, holding up empty claws in a universal gesture. "I propose a treaty. If you prefer, we can stack our weapons over there, beyond easy reach." It indicated a shadowy cleft in the cavern wall.

"Thank you, no," said the knight. "I will sleep all the more soundly with my sword in easy reach. But you may stay—" he pointed at the far side of the cavern "—over there. I have no food except for myself and equaar, however."

"I ate four days ago." The lizard sat down and hissed with pleasure as the heat from the flames soaked through the ill-fitting jerkin it wore. The knight had heard that these creatures, after gorging themselves, could last days before needing to eat again. No wonder they managed to survive in barren Merykh, he thought. No human could survive those arid highlands: instead they huddled in the Five Cities, around the salty puddles that were all that remained of a great ocean.

"I am Aubeq-Senn," said the lizard, breaking the knight's reverie. "From the design on your armour I see you are from Burnharnh."

The knight touched the silver insignia unconsciously. "Yes. My name is Sivym-Dar, of King Jerhet the Third's personal guard."

Aubeq-Senn nodded his long skull in imitation of a human bow. "I am honoured. You strayed too far, I take it?"

Sivym-Dar ignored the question. "And you? I had thought lizards found the winds of Tlantykh too chill."

"I was searching Khan-Da – but found that for which I sought had already gone."

"Down to the plains?"

"Just so."

A silence descended, an uneasy one. Sivym-Dar fidgeted uncomfortably as he watched the lizard's immobility. Despite the unreadable eyes and expressionless face, he knew the creature was observing him just as closely. That inscrutability unnerved the knight more than anything.

A keening howl split the cavern's still air, dropping to a low drone which trembled the limestone pillars before fading altogether. The echoes seemed to go on forever. Both human and lizard were on their feet instantly, sword and axe held ready in hand and claw. The desolate sound had emanated from the shadows deep within the cave.

Another noise shook them – this time a metallic shriek – and Sivym-Dar could see the faintest glow spreading in the darkness, deep within the cavern. Pulsing, glowing stronger with the rhythm's echoes. The light intensified, resolving itself into a glowing tunnel beyond their cave. It continued even further into the cliff than Sivym-Dar had imagined.

He looked at the lizard, Aubeq-Senn. "Do we investigate?"

"If you wish, mammal." It hissed a bubbling laugh. "I imagine you would be unable to sleep otherwise."

Sivym-Dar did not miss the faint stress on the word *you*. Sword and dagger in hand, he paced cautiously towards the light. With Aubeq-Senn at his back, he felt trapped between two unknown, potentially lethal forces.

Several more bursts resounded up through the glowing tunnel, jarring the knight to his teeth. The Baragan? he wondered. No – that vast and rare creature was far too large to even squeeze through the cavern's twisted entrance. Unless there was another way in.

Within his helm, Sivym-Dar licked dry lips and clutched his sword hilt the tighter.

They entered the rhythmically glowing tunnel, their footsteps slow and measured. After a moment the knight felt as though he was drowning under waves of advancing and receding light, spinning and dancing around him. The pounding was deafening, relentless. Every sense was under assault. He could hear nothing but the crushing rhythm, see nothing beyond the encircling glare. A cloying, sweet stench clogged the air, so dense he could taste it. He gagged. He was sure he was screaming.

There was a final, deafening shriek which threatened to burst Sivym-Dar's eardrums, then silence – save for the ringing in his ears. There were no echoes. Even the light died to a muted glow.

Ahead was another, smaller cavern, lit by fiery sprites which soared and spun among the smooth rocky walls. They cast a spectrum of dancing shadows. Both man and lizard stood at the cavern's entrance, dumbstruck. A jumble of strange machines was scattered before them in varying stages of dissolution, littering the cavern. Some were great square blocks, as solid as a boulder, others were thin, ephemeral things that seemed to have no more substance than smoke. They squatted, or reared, or spun towards the roof like deformed crystals. One or two pulsed with faint lights which died even as they watched; others puffed thick, oily smoke, or burned fitfully. Fussing over them, cursing in its own tongue, was another lizard, dressed in loose, shabby robes like a discredited priest. Its tail thrashed angrily from under their skirts, scattering pieces of broken machinery across a floor thick with powdered rust.

Aubeq-Senn snapped something in the lizard tongue, and the other spun around. It was like no other lizard Sivym-Dar had encountered, or heard described. A short horn grew up from the tip of its muzzle, with two more thrusting forward above eyes that flashed with a rainbow scintillance. An angular frill of bone grew straight back from its head, giving the whole skull a wedge-like appearance. The creature hissed in surprise, then spoke in the human tongue – even more fluently than Aubeq-Senn.

"Ah – visitors. You are welcome, both, but I'm afraid you find me presently embarrassed."

Sivym-Dar heard a dry rattle. Behind him Aubeq-Senn was indicating the confusion of machinery with its axe. The crest upon its head stood erect, quivering. An angry display. "What were you doing with those abominations?"

Sivym-Dar recalled idle tavern gossip he had once overheard, claiming lizards loathed the science and machines of pre-Fall humanity. Perhaps it was true.

The horned lizard tilted its angular head. "At present, nothing. They are too degenerate for my purposes. I believe these caves were once much damper than you see. Their materials have not survived the many centuries of waiting. Regrettable. I shall have to look elsewhere."

Aubeq-Senn lowered its sword. "Salin Thur," it said. There was something in its tone suggestive of satisfaction among the earlier outrage. "Finally."

The other looked surprised. "You know me?" Its scintillating eyes squinted, as though searching for something in the other lizard's expressionless face. One of its scaled claws performed a peculiar gesture. Sivym-Dar was sure he saw a momentary flicker of phosphorescence.

"Ah – you are Aubeq-Senn," said Salin Thur. "The dreamer who nurtures a peculiar vision of lizard unity. Yes?"

"While you tinker with obscenities most of us have the good sense to leave untroubled."

The horned lizard shrugged. It was an odd gesture in a creature that had barely any shoulders. "We are both heretics, then."

Aubeq-Senn shook its long head. "My visions will become reality. Your meddling—" It glanced at Sivym-Dar. "No good can come of it. This world's history is eloquent proof of that."

"And yet you have been seeking me. Why, I wonder? Is it because your dreams – for that is what they are – and my *meddling* overlay each other in ways only the Boundless can know?"

Aubeq-Senn looked uncomfortable.

Salin Thur hissed, flicking a long tongue around rigid lips. The creature radiated a smug air. "I left Khan-Da quickly when my researches revealed the location of this cache." It glanced back at the smoking, decaying pile of machinery. "No matter; there are other caches. One day—"

A machine of clear yellow crystal fused into a shapeless metal casing began to emit low, odd noises. For a moment Sivym-Dar imagined they were words in some unrecognisable language.

Salin Thur's strange eyes widened in alarm. "Come. The centuries have done more than corrode these constructions' physical frameworks." It moved towards the tunnel entrance, robes billowing. "I believe they have also gone quite insane." It disappeared into a shaft that was now dull and unlit.

Aubeq-Senn cast a suspicious glance at the muttering crystal and metal shape before following the other lizard.

Sivym-Dar did not move. Something itched at the back of his mind. A memory? An unconscious recollection awakened by the alien sounds? He moved towards the machine as a sequence of lights began to flash. There was a pattern there. A meaning. He dropped his sword and leaned upon the pulsing console. If he could just concentrate . . .

His left hand moved of its own accord to a mauve light flickering within the crystal. His bare skin stroked the cold surface. It warmed instantly. The muttering ceased. Sivym-Dar sensed the silent, rusty cavern was poised, waiting.

He had heard Salin Thur's words: *lizard unity.* Images skated through his mind like taunting nymphs, accompanying the words. The forces of humanity locked in battle with Aubeq-Senn's lizards. The Five Cities razed. The survivors imprisoned forever . . .

He could change that! Stop it before it had even happened.

If only he could think straight . . .

Within his horned helmet, Sivym-Dar began to laugh. It was so obvious. His fingers slid across machine's twisted form like a lover's caress.

"Of course," he sighed. "Of course."

Aubeq-Senn emerged into the larger cavern just behind Salin-Thur. The fire had dropped low, so the robed figure carefully added more of the human's resinous fuel to it. The equaar drowsed heedlessly – glad of the warmth and shelter.

"They are an inquisitive species, these mammals," said Aubeq-Senn in their own tongue.

"Like hatchlings," agreed Salin-Thur.

There was a sudden metallic shout – filled with triumphant loathing – and an odd, smacking sound which made the cavern quiver. Again there were no echoes. Light blazed from the tunnel – of a colour neither lizard nor human had a word for – followed by a grey pall of dust. A shroud of shattered rock and metal. There was also the stench of something which had been long dead.

The horned lizard brushed at its robes. "It was their undoing once. I have no doubt it will be again."

As the grey dust settled, a fragment of console blinked sullenly through the red stickiness bathing it. A twist of crystal dripped. After a moment it began to mutter contentedly to itself.

Mike Chinn has edited three volumes of *The Alchemy Press Book of Pulp Heroes* and *Swords Against the Millennium* for The Alchemy Press. His first Damian Paladin collection, *The Paladin Mandates*, was short-listed for the British Fantasy Award in 1999; and an expanded edition is due out from Pro Se Press in 2020. Pro Se published a second Paladin collection, *Walkers In Shadow*, in 2017. He sent Sherlock Holmes to the Moon in *Vallis Timoris* (2015, Fringeworks), and has two short story collections in print: *Give Me These Moments Back* (The Alchemy Press, 2015) and *Radix Omnium Malum* (Parallel Universe Publications, 2017). In 2018 Pro Se published his first Western: *Revenge is a Cold Pistol*.

Illustration by Jonny Boyle

MYDARKSIDE(DOT)COM

C.M. Saunders

IT WAS JUST after midnight when Freddy Myers fell down the rabbit hole. It wasn't ideal, as he had work at the deli in the morning.

This wasn't an actual rabbit hole, obviously. That would be pretty weird seeing as he was cooped up in his flat where the only wildlife to be seen was the occasional cockroach. It was worse than an actual rabbit hole.

It was the fucking Internet.

He'd just been surfing, checking out some upcoming horror movies and making a mental list of the ones he wanted to see. It had to be a mental list, he was too stoned to write a physical one, when somehow, some way, he stumbled across this freaky website called *My Dark Side.*

Something about it made him stop and pay attention. Maybe it was the gaudy font, the cartoonish severed hand, the blood-spatter effect, or the general creepiness. That must have been it. The home page looked like the front cover of an '80s video nasty.

"The fuck is this shit?" he muttered to himself. "Must be some kind of pastiche."

He was about to click off the site when a drop-down menu appeared. Curious, he scanned the sections. The top one was entitled "Trophies". Absently, Freddy clicked on it.

The screen instantly changed to show an arty collage of overlapping pictures. Dozens of them. They appeared to show random articles of clothing and jewellery. Ripped t-shirts, rings, bracelets, bras, panties. Even some boxer shorts. Leaning closer, Freddy could see they were soiled, the crotch discoloured by piss or some other bodily fluid. "Lovely," he said.

What kind of website was this, anyway? God, the Internet was a cesspool.

He clicked on the next section. This one was called "Body Parts".

And that was exactly what it showed. Body parts. Limbs, mostly. Hands and feet, a few forearms, a thigh, and some fingers and toes. Lots of fingers and toes. In little piles. They'd all been separated, dismembered, cut from the body they were once a part of.

Freddy couldn't help but admire the craftsmanship. If these things were prosthetic, they were incredibly realistic. If he looked closely enough he could count the individual hairs peppering the outer layer of puckered, waxy skin covering flesh and sinew, and even make out the glint of stark white bone beneath it all.

What was this? Was the whole site just an interactive ad for a movie or a book? That would explain a lot. But if that were the case, as impressive as the site was, it was doing a piss poor job of promoting anything as there were no taglines, release dates, or even titles, to be found. Anywhere.

But you're still looking at it, dumbass, said an annoying little voice inside his head.

Marketing these days was more sophisticated. You couldn't just drop a few names and expect people to give a shit. If he was interested enough to actually spend time hunting for information on this thing, whatever it was, you could bet he wouldn't forget it in a hurry. He might even Tweet about it, or tell his Facebook friends. Smart.

The next section Freddy clicked on was called "Snuff". It was a video clip. A trailer? Maybe this would tell him what he wanted to know.

A little hesitantly, he pressed play.

The video looked to have been taken at night, probably on a smartphone. The absence of specialist equipment was obvious. The shaky, grainy footage seemed to show a dimly-lit underground car park. Most of the bays were empty.

A door opened, and a man in a dark suit carrying a briefcase emerged, his footsteps echoing around the concrete chamber. The camera jerked, and for a few moments all that could be seen was the side of a car. It was almost as if the person holding the camera had suddenly ducked down out of sight.

Why were they hiding?

The camera poked out over the bonnet of the car. Freddy could see Briefcase Dude fumbling in his pockets for some keys as he approached another car. It looked like a Lexus. A big white one. His back was to the camera.

For the first time, Freddy became aware of the video's soundtrack. Not that it was much of a soundtrack. It was just the sound of a man breathing. Panting. As Freddy listened, the breathing became louder and more pronounced, taking on almost sexual overtones.

Then, the camera panned around. Apart from Briefcase Dude and whoever held the camera, the car park appeared to be deserted.

Next, it focused on the cameraman's other hand, slowly and deliberately. By this point, Freddy was positive it *was* a man. The thick, muscular forearm and wrist matted with thick, black hair was a dead give-away.

The hand held a meat cleaver. Freddy gasped as a streak of fluorescent light reflected off the wicked-looking silver blade. It looked insanely sharp.

The camera was moving. The user apparently intent on sneaking up behind Briefcase Dude before he got into the Lexus.

"Hurry up!" Freddy said in spite of himself. He was almost positive this was some kind of staged promo video. And even if it wasn't, it had been pre-recorded. Whatever he was about to watch had already happened.

Still, he couldn't help himself. He was becoming emotionally invested in the whole experience. If this was indeed a piece of marketing, it was genius.

Then, Freddy's hand went to his mouth as he watched the man making the video swing the meat cleaver at the back of Briefcase Dude's head, where it lodged in his skull with a sickening *thunk*.

Still holding the phone in one hand, the attacker struggled to free the weapon with the other. It wouldn't come loose.

Briefcase Dude dropped his precious briefcase and began to turn around, his eyes wide with shock as if silently asking what the fuck had just happened. He winced, and raised both his hands half way to his injured head where they stopped, as if he was unsure what to do next.

There was remarkably little blood. That gave the game away slightly. There should be more, shouldn't there? I mean, if you take a cleaver in the back of the head there should be gore galore.

Not if the blade stayed in, the annoying little voice in Freddy's head explained. *Then it would kinda plug the wound.*

Suddenly, the arm gave an extra hard yank on the handle and the cleaver came free, closely followed by the blood. It spurted out of Briefcase Dude's head in a crimson torrent, dousing him, the side of the Lexus, and covering the camera lens in a murky red film. The man sank to his knees, his mouth opening and closing. The only sounds coming out were a faint gurgling.

The cleaver-wielding arm swung again. This time, he aimed high, and sliced off the top of Briefcase Dude's skull, which landed somewhere out of shot.

Briefcase Dude slumped forward onto his hands and knees as if trying to crawl away, one of his extended legs jerking and kicking spasmodically.

Fucking hell. Not only were the special effects amazing, but this guy was one hell of an actor.

The attacker, perhaps belatedly wary of being splashed with blood, retreated a few steps. He was breathing hard now. Between gasps, he zoomed in on the victim, as if desperate to capture the moment his life ebbed away.

Apparently satisfied with his efforts, he then lifted the cleaver one more time, bringing it down on Briefcase Dude's extended fingers as they lay splayed on the floor with a hoarse grunt. Sparks flew as the cold metal sliced through flesh and bone and impacted on the concrete.

The attacker stooped, momentarily laid the cleaver down next to the still-bleeding body, and picked up one of the severed fingers. It was still twitching. Freddy noticed that there was a gold band around it. A wedding ring?

"For the trophy section," slurred a low, guttural voice. The finger disappeared from shot for the briefest moment and the heavy breathing interrupted, the implication being that the attacker was using his teeth to remove the ring.

Freddy felt his stomach lurch. If this was CGI or some other kind of special effects, it was extraordinarily well done. In fact, the whole production, though obviously low-budget, was very well done.

Then, he remembered the title of the section of the website he'd found this video.

Snuff.

Weren't snuff films the kind where people were actually killed? That, combined with the name of the website.

My Dark Side.

No, it couldn't be. Freddy was still leaning toward some kind of elaborate marketing campaign, or maybe even someone's idea of a joke. If it was real, how could this stuff even be allowed online?

The Internet is a pretty lawless place.

That fucking inner voice again.

Perhaps the authorities haven't found it yet. It could have been uploaded just a few minutes ago. Or maybe everyone just assumes it's not real. Like you . . .

As Freddy was considering his options, a notification window popped up in the corner of his computer screen.

New email, sender unknown.

"Probably more spam," he sighed. Quickly switching tabs to his Gmail account, he navigated to his inbox, and opened the new email. It was simple, and to the point.

Hello, Freddy.

I hope you enjoyed looking at my site. Isn't technology wonderful?

I'm on my way over.

And I can't wait to show you my dark side.

Chris Saunders, who writes fiction as **C.M. Saunders**, is a writer and editor from south Wales. His fiction has appeared in almost 100 magazines, ezines and anthologies worldwide and his books have been both traditionally and independently published, the latest release being *X5*, his fifth volume of short fiction.

cmsaunders.wordpress.com

twitter.com/CMSaunders01

www.facebook.com/CMSaunders01

'Branch Thing' by Allen Koszowski

MR. PERFECT

Josh Strnad

"SO WHAT DO you think?"

Lynn swirled her Martini as she watched Marsha's expression. She had expected a reaction, any reaction, but Marsha's face remained an inscrutable mask. She seemed to be grasping for things to say. "He's certainly . . . good looking."

Lynn snorted. "Good looking, nothing. He's totally hot, and you know it."

Marsha smirked a little and cocked an eyebrow. "All right, so he's a hottie. Hottie McStudmuffin from planet Ooh-Lah-Lah, as delectable a piece of man-candy as I've ever seen. That better?"

Lynn chuckled and sipped her drink. "Now that's the Marsha I know. You had me worried for a moment. It's not like you to hold back." She looked over the balcony at where Antonio was working in the yard below, carrying loads of mulch from the back of a pick-up truck and spreading them around freshly-planted rose bushes. He was shirtless in a pair of tight blue jeans, and the afternoon sun shone on his rippling, bronze muscles. "He's more than that, you know. He's handy around the house; he cooks and cleans and can fix anything. He speaks seven languages and his head contains as much knowledge as a digitized encyclopedia. He can play any musical instrument, gives the most incredible back rubs, and is the best salsa dancer I've ever—"

"And when he farts," Marsha cut in, "I'll bet it smells like daffodils and lollypops."

Lynn spewed a mouthful of gin and vermouth across the table with a sudden burst of laughter. "I don't know," she said, coughing. "I haven't tested that function yet."

"Still," Marsha said, wiping her bespattered hands and face with a cocktail napkin, "I'm surprised you went ahead and got one. I mean, you've been talking for months about buying yourself a Mr. Perfect, but I always thought you were, like, joking."

Lynn frowned. "Why would I joke about it?"

Marsha shrugged. "I just thought it was the sort of thing women talked about but never really did. Don't you find the whole thing just a little bit . . . I don't know . . . creepy?"

Lynn swished with her hand as if to brush away any objections. "Antonio is absolutely safe, if that's what you mean. Just to get approved for consumer markets, the Mr. Perfect design had to be subjected to hundreds of tests and re-tests. Surely you're not about to start telling me I should be scared of automata."

"Of course not." Marsha ran a hand through her hair and sighed. "Maybe 'creepy' wasn't the right word. There's just something weird about the whole robotic lover thing to me. I can't get used to the idea."

Lynn's frown deepened, and she poured herself another drink. "I don't see what's so wrong about it. After all, men have had those fembots for nearly the past decade now to satisfy their whims. You don't think *that's* weird?"

Marsha shrugged. "Of course it is, but you're not being totally fair. Not every man out there wants to own a robimbo he can, like, order around all the time. Whatever you say, there are still good guys in the world who are capable of treating real women with respect. Besides, this isn't about them. This is about you."

"Since when do you start defending men? Whose side are you on here?"

Marsha winked at her. "Yours, of course. As your sassy BFF, it's my job to call 'em like I see 'em." She paused, as if searching for the right words. "Does he love you?"

"Of course! I'd take him back to the store in a heartbeat if he didn't."

Now it was Marsha's turn to chuckle. "Sure you would. But that's exactly what I'm getting at. He's not a person, really. He's, like, a machine. He has no choice but to be and act exactly the way you want. One-hundred-percent satisfaction guarantee. That's not love. That's . . . programming."

"Listen to who's the romance expert all of a sudden," Lynn scoffed.

"You know I don't pretend to be any such thing. I just think you can do better for yourself, that's all. Seems to me that you're settling for what's easy rather than what's best."

"If I didn't know better, I'd say you were jealous."

"And if I didn't know better, I'd say you were afraid."

Lynn stood up and leaned over the balcony to watch Antonio, turning her face away from Marsha. She sipped her drink and spilled a few drops, which made dark, wet spots where they landed on the patio below. "You're ridiculous, you know that, dear?" she said, squeezing a burst of phony laughter from her lungs. "One moment you're acting like you're suddenly scared of new technology, and the next you accuse *me* of being the one with emotional hang-ups. What in the world do I have to be afraid of?"

"Only you can answer that," Marsha said. Her tone was not accusatory, but the simple frankness of it set Lynn's teeth on edge. "You are afraid, though."

Lynn whirled on her. The world seemed to wobble a bit as she did so, and she had to catch herself on the edge of the railing to maintain her balance. "I'm not afraid of anything."

"Oh yeah? Isn't that what this is all about? You're afraid to take any risks — to get hurt. I'm your best friend, Lynn! Don't pretend you can hide it from me. You, like, work so hard to keep your world perfect and tidy by putting up all these walls and blocking other people out. Then you cope with the loneliness by surrounding yourself with comforts and cheap imitations of relationships rather than risking pain in the real thing. It's not healthy."

Returning to the table, Lynn scrambled for her purse.

"Don't shut me out, Lynn," Marsha continued. "Real life is messy, and in order to get the best out of it, you sometimes need to be willing to get your hands dirty and your feelings hurt. That's your problem. You want it all, but you want it all on only your terms. Real life doesn't work that way. I'm sorry the truth in hard to hear, but sometimes—"

Marsha stopped mid-sentence and slumped forward onto the table, her face blank, her eyes staring straight ahead. Breathing hard, Lynn returned the remote control to her purse. "That's quite enough out of you for today," she said with a snarl.

She collapsed into her chair and poured herself another drink, which she drained in three gulps. She glanced down into the yard where Antonio, her Mr. Perfect, had just finished spreading the last bag of mulch.

He waved up at her, his face lit up by his gorgeous crooked grin. "Want to come have a look, Darling?"

"I'll be down in a minute," she called back. She rose a trifle unsteadily, taking slow, careful steps toward the door. Reaching it, she turned to glare once more at the inert figure of her sassy BFF. "For your information," she whispered, slurring her words ever so slightly, "I am *perfectly* happy."

Marsha, of course, made no response, and Lynn stumbled into the house alone.

Josh Strnad is a writer, educator, and seemingly perpetual student from Southwest Florida. When not guzzling tea and typing out stories on his trusty desktop computer, he dabbles in video production, writing music, and drawing cartoons. Check him out at: www.joshstrnad.com

Image created by Stephen Clarke

FINAL SUNSET OVER EDEN

Neal Sayatovich

"ORDER THIRTY-NINE." A deep voice boomed through The Cast Iron's dining room.

A bulbous man in a grease-stained apron stood at the ticket window. He scanned the 1950s-style diner in search of a waitress. Some of the Beach Boys greatest hits bellowed from the reproduction jukebox in the far corner of the dining area. The music wasn't from the '50s, but no one cared.

"Samantha!" the man yelled.

"I'm here, Marco, calm down," a woman in a pink '50s style dress said as she hurried from the restroom.

"Do you plan on serving the food to my customers sometime before the polar ice caps melt? Or will I need to comp yet another order today."

"No, I got it," she huffed.

Marco walked back into the kitchen swearing in a muffled grumble. Samantha Riggs moved an errant strain of strawberry blonde hair behind her ear and plastered a fake smile on. She carried a tray of two cheeseburger meals over to an elderly couple who stared out the front window. The cherry red upholstery squeaked and groaned with every movement they made.

"Here you folks go, I am so sorry it took so long," Samantha apologized.

"About damn time," the old man growled.

"Oh, hush, Leonard. She is doing the best she can," the woman said.

"Well, she's terrible, Margaret."

"Don't mind my husband. He's grouchy without his coffee. May we get some syrup, please?"

Margaret's face was avionic in nature, down to the elongated nose and slightly angled face. Gray streaks penetrated her most recent brown hair treatment. Glasses with attached chains were seated high on the bridge of her nose. Her appearance reminded Samantha of Ms. Montgomery, her sixth-grade biology teacher.

Leonard took on the appearance of a Russian peasant. His wrinkled face was partially hidden behind a scarf striped in various shades of grays and browns. A tight-fitting ash cap was pulled over most of his eyes. Shivers danced through him despite his navy blue wool coat.

"Yes ma'am, I will be right back," Samantha said as she grabbed a small bottle of maple syrup from behind the counter and brought it over.

"God bless you," Margaret said. "We're from Florida and not used to your type of winter."

"What brought you to Eden, if I may ask?"

"There is a minister we adore who is having a tent-style revival. We wanted to wait until he came to Florida, but we learned he was only doing one here in West Virginia. I told Leonard to pack a suitcase and we made reservations over in Norwood."

"Why across the river in Norwood?"

"I like Ohio," Leonard said between bites of cheeseburgers. "This state would be better off burnt to the ground."

Margaret put her cheeseburger down. "You stop that right now. These people have been kind to us."

Marco yelled another ticket number and Samantha excused herself. After twenty more minutes the lunch rush died down to a trickle. Debbie, the chronic texting teenager who worked the evening shift came in early to grab some extra hours for a new iPhone. Excited to get off work early, Samantha clocked out and tossed her apron in the dirty basket near the dishwasher.

She strolled over to her beat-up Chevy Cavalier. The once ocean blue paint had begun to lose its battle against the wave of rust. While it wasn't pretty, it ran just fine other than issues with the heater. Samantha watched her breath for the entire twelve-minute drive to Eden Elementary. Chad Burkosky, her daughter's history teacher, glared at her from the front door. Chad disliked Samantha and had called her "White Trash Sammy" to other teachers in the building. Even at The Cast Iron, she has heard that nickname whispered.

Marissa popped out of the front doors and sprinted toward the Cavalier. A wide smile spread across her pale, freckled face. Dirty blonde pigtails bounced in the chilly breeze. Today she wore a simple black shirt with matching skirt. She climbed in the back seat and fastened her seatbelt. Chad shook his head with disgust and spit on the ground.

The short drive across Eden to her apartment was filled with her excited daughter talking about everything she learned at school. Samantha noticed the traffic on Dayton Road, the main road in Eden, was heavier than normal. It took ten minutes longer to turn right on Devola Boulevard and into a small apartment complex. Both buildings were covered in nicotine yellow siding. Four faded brown doors were equally spaced across the front of each building. She pulled the Cavalier into her parking spot. Marissa jumped out and nearly tripped over the cracked, uneven sidewalk.

Alan Hindel sat outside his door on his green plastic chair. A USA Gold cigarette clinched between what few teeth remained ingrained in his diseased gums. Ashes fell on a stained and ratty West Virginia University t-shirt and jacket. A gold "B" hung haphazardly on the door behind him.

"Evening," Alan said scratching his blond chin stubble.

"Hi Alan, how are you today?" Samantha said, unlocking her door and shepherding Marissa inside.

"I'm doin' all right I guess; another day not pushin' up daisies."

"Always a good thing, I suppose."

"Hear about the preacher comin' to town?"

Samantha stared at him in confusion. "What preacher? Someone mentioned it earlier, but didn't say who."

Alan extinguished his cigarette on the concrete porch.

"I dunno. Some big city minister from Charleston or Memphis, I think. Can't 'member his name for the life o'me, though."

"That explains why I had some people from Florida and New Jersey come into work today."

"Yeah, they're settin' up a big tent and everything. Real old school, if you know whatta mean?"

Before she could ask any more questions, he excused himself to run errands. His sister drove up in a beat-up silver Ford Taurus and beeped the horn. Samantha wished him a good evening and walked inside to make sure Marissa wasn't raiding the cookies. Every cookie was left intact, as the television had distracted her. Reruns of *The Wiggles* played on the one channel they had. Nevertheless, Marissa sang along and danced all the same. Samantha had enough time to set her keys on the kitchen counter before a soft series of knocks interrupted her.

"Who is it?" she yelled.

There was no answer.

Samantha picked up a baseball bat she kept near the entryway. She set it on her shoulder and crept toward the door. A sigh left her as she reached out and quickly twisted the knob and pulled the door open. A small man in a pastel green buttoned shirt and khaki slacks stood at the door with a small paper bag of groceries.

"You scared the crap out of me, Reverend," she said.

The Reverend cast his eyes toward his dull leather shoes in apology.

"I didn't hear anything. If you yelled, I'm sorry."

Reverend Nathan Walls was a very small and socially awkward man. He preached at Eden United Methodist, the only church in the eastern half of the county. Nathan tried to avoid eye contact with everyone so as to not set off his crippling stage fright. Each year the congregations had been getting smaller due to ground being broke on a Pentecostal church in nearby Ellenboro.

"I'm sorry, I'm just on edge. Please come in."

She brushed some toys from the threadbare floral couch and ushered him to have a seat. Marissa took the bag from her and stumbled into the kitchen. A few seconds later she reappeared with a cookie in each hand. When Samantha made eye contact with her daughter, the cookie thief bolted to her room and quickly closed the door.

"I wish she would use that energy for her school work."

"Kids being kids," Nathan said softly.

Samantha let out an exhausted sigh.

"Reverend . . ."

"Please, just Nathan," he interrupted.

"Sorry. Nathan, what do you know about a preacher coming to town?"

Nathan flushed crimson.

"He is a fanatical man named Herb Moses. He is a televangelist from Memphis who preaches fire and brimstone on a weekly basis. He decided to come here to hold a special sermon. I don't know why, though."

"I'm going to go see it, will you please watch Marissa tonight? No offense Nathan, but God hasn't been helping me, no matter how much I pray. In just over a year my husband cheated on me and divorced me, I got laid off as an accountant and I've been on food stamps. God hasn't exactly done me any favors recently. Maybe this tent revival will have answers."

Nathan paused and made eye contact for a few moments. She saw fear in them. Not a stage fright type of fear, something more primal.

"I sincerely hope you don't go, but I won't stop you. I will watch Marissa until you come back, just please don't stay too long. I don't want to see you get corrupted by his hate speech."

Samantha nodded soberly. She reached to her neck and fiddled with a silver crucifix pendant. She excused herself to change into clean clothes. Once out of her waitress uniform, she was in a black shirt, form fitting jeans and black flats. The occasion called for very little make-up, unless she wanted people to call her a whore non-stop. Fifteen minutes later, she was psyched up and driving back down Dayton Road, toward the center of town.

A pristine white tent was erected at the intersection of Dayton and Oakwood. People were huddled in a crooked line outside the entrance. The tent covered every one of the eight lanes worth of road between Dayton and Oakwood roads. Crisp white pinnacles waved gently nearly three stories above. Every parking space in a three-block radius was taken with a rainbow of state plates. She finally found a spot near Marquette Street and parked. Orange rays from the setting sun filled the city streets.

Inside the massive canvas structure there was standing room only. A wooden stage was raised in the center of the room. Onlookers filled in the remaining space to form a ring around the main spectacle. Three people were placed in medieval-style stockades that forced them to remain on their hands and knees. Next to each prisoner was a man in a white suit with an axe in hand. Each guard had a white bandana covering the bottom half of their face. A crimson red cross, situated perfectly in line with their nose and mouth, was stitched on the bandana.

Herb Moses walked around the disc-shaped stage. His pot belly protruded through his crisp white button-up shirt that showed small sweat stains near the armpits. Charcoal pants held it in place with the help of matching suspenders. Snow hair was trimmed in a conservative style and highlighted by steel gray eyes. A battered, leather-bound bible was gripped tightly in his sweaty hand.

Samantha found a small gap near the entrance. A middle-aged couple entered and battled toward the middle of the mob. Music erupted through speakers littered throughout the tent. Hymns were led by Herb for nearly half an hour. Upon conclusion, the mob applauded and shouted until Herb gave them the motion to settle down. Claps and voices abruptly ceased to an eerie quiet.

"Good evening, thank you all for making the drive to this wonderful town." A crooked grin grew across his face. "Now, I'm sure you are all wondering why I chose Eden of all places. Quite simply, it is the epitome of all the Godlessness sweeping this once Christian nation."

A mixture of confused and somber looks met him. It was announced nearly a month ago that Eden United Methodist was slated for demolition. Village council members determined the church was unnecessary and that the residents would be better served with something that created jobs to help the impoverished citizens.

"That's right, how evil we have become to lay waste to the house of the Lord, even if it was just a Methodist church."

Laugh and grumbles worked their way through the crowd. The few individuals left who remained Methodist were not happy with the snide remark.

Herb appeared oblivious to the disgruntled murmurs isolated near the back of the mob.

"I have prayed for guidance on how to help the people of Eden. It took a few days, but God has provided me the answer. We have to make an Old Testament sacrifice to prove that we will cleanse the evil ones."

Whispered conversations sparked all over the mob. Many people were asking if this was actually Christian or not. A handful of people walked outside. Samantha could not hear much of the grumbled protests other than a handful of sentences referring to Herb as a charlatan. The preacher watched them leave without any expression of regret.

"Those of you who stayed, understand that God's will is sometimes bloody, but must be done." He glanced around the room. "Residents of Eden, I have gathered these people from other locations. To atone for your sins, you must offer one of your own."

A loud protest broke out as various people rebuffed the idea.

"White Trash Sammy is here. Somebody grab her!" Chad Burkosky yelled.

Two large men appeared from the crowd and subdued her before she could react. They dragged her onto the stage and forced her to her knees next to a petite woman with lavender hair. Samantha saw many concerned faces in the crowd, but no one spoke in her defense. She tried to escape, but both held her tightly in place.

"Servants of Eden, let's begin with a prayer." Herb prayed as if it was a normal Sunday service, instead of a macabre ritual. "Folks, I have brought you things that are not only sub-human, but have caused the moral collapse of this country."

He casually walked over to a tall, dark man in a threadbare shirt and jeans. The man pleaded and begged as Herb approached him. Herb didn't acknowledge the man. Instead, he just nodded to the executioner adjacent to him. The executioner nodded in response and raised his axe, as did the other two. Samantha counted her blessings that there wasn't one next to her.

"I present your penance for your sins." He motioned toward the dark man, "The negro." Herb continued past a flamboyantly dressed man and slapped him on the head. "The faggot." Finally, he stopped at the lavender-haired woman. "The whore."

Herb paused for a moment. Not one voice could be heard in the crowd. The minister raised both of his hands as if he expected to touch Heaven itself. Another long prayer left his lips and after the crowd murmured a unison "Amen" he dropped his hands. All three executioners dropped their axes. There were horrified screams from the audience as three heads rolled toward the front of the stage. Both men tightened their grip on Samantha as the closest executioner approached them.

A loud shriek tore through Samantha's – and everyone else in the tent's – mind. Five beings tore through the roof and slowly descended onto the stage. Four of the five were about six and a half feet tall, with two metallic wings. Each being was silver and metallic in nature. Samantha couldn't see any seams, gears or anything showing that the beings were actually mechanical. Most disturbing were their faceless heads and four metal claws on each hand.

Between the four angelic aberrations was a gold angel, that stood nearly eight feet tall with six gem-encrusted wings.

The men holding Samantha down loosened their grip and she took the opportunity to run off the stage. She turned to watch the angels while she backed toward the entrance. Herb approached the gold angel with a wry smile.

"Were you sent by God to bless this town?" he asked.

Each silver angel walked toward the audience with feminine grace. The gold angel looked down at Herb. Herb never flinched as he stared at his reflection in the faceless metal. With unnatural quickness the being wrapped its claws around Herb's face. An unearthly groan echoed through everyone's mind as the gold angel snapped its claws closed. Herb's skull was shattered, the front of his face ripped off when the claws pulled forward. Brain matter and blood poured onto the stage. People screamed and stampeded outside as the silver angels began to kill anyone within reach.

One of the angels descended on Chad Burkosky. Before he could scream a clawed hand ripped his vocal cords from his throat. Samantha swore she heard a grinding laughter from the angel as it threw Chad's corpse away in disinterest. It crouched and scanned the retreating mob. A boy of about nine years of age was bumped out of the mob and right into the line of sight of the angel. It took less than a second for the angel to pounce on the unsuspecting child and drive its claws deep into the boy's stomach. Loud, weeping sobs left the boy's lips until the being spread its clawed hands and split the boy in half.

Gore sprayed across the crowd and snapped Samantha out of her macabre trance. Horror finally seeped into her body. She sprinted headlong into the mob and prayed to God that she could sneak through without getting murdered. As she worked through the crowd, she grasped her cross while she muttered silent prayers.

Her breath caught when she made it outside. A legion of silver angels unleashed a wave of death and destruction on the streets of Eden. Corpses littered the streets. Pools of blood painted a gruesome Rorschach three blocks wide. More screams erupted as an angel launched itself through the canvas side of the tent. Margaret, the older woman from The Cast Iron, was left in a dismembered heap near the entrance. Her body was separated at the waist and her left hand was torn off and forced into her intestines. Five feet from Margaret, Leonard sat propped against a late model Ford pick-up. Leonard's shirt was removed to reveal splintered ribs and an open chest cavity.

Angels picked off people at a disturbingly quick rate. Samantha ran inside the Valley Grocery store to hide from the carnage. Valley Grocery was four isles wide with two old cash registers at the front. Samantha swore that most of the equipment had been there since the '80s. About six other people had taken cover in the store. Samantha took cover by a display tower made from cans of sweet corn. A young woman of about twenty was huddled behind register one. Three large windows framed the ensuing chaos outside. After a couple of long minutes there was silence. Nobody was brave enough to even let out a breath for fear of being found out.

The girl behind register one let out a high-pitched sneeze. A wave of horror washed over everyone in the store. Silence lingered for another few minutes. The girl grew a relieved smile and let out a long sigh. An angel crashed through the front window and landed on the girl behind register one. As soon as they hit the ground, the angel dug its claws into her stomach. Bile and intestines rained over the front of the store as the angel ripped and pulled everything it could grasp from the girl's stomach. When the angel was done, it threw her corpse down the frozen food isle.

Adrenaline filled Samantha as she sprinted toward the fire escape. The angel pursued her until a bulbous man in his Sunday best waddled into the angel's line of sight. After a second of consideration, it ran up behind the bulbous man. The angel reared up and dug both claws into the man's shoulder blades. With a quick motion it pulled the man's torso down. A sickening snap echoed over the screams of the remaining people as the man was bent into a horseshoe.

Samantha slammed through the fire escape into an alley. Alarms brayed inside Valley Grocery. An occasional muffled scream could still be heard over the loud ringing. Mechanical screeches and laughter tore through her mind. Blackness encroached the edges of her vision. She pushed the faintness back and ran toward Marquette Street. Violence hadn't reached this far away from the tent yet. She fumbled with her keys, regained control and got in the Cavalier. The Cavalier choked to life and she floored the gas. She reached for her cell phone before she realized it wasn't there. It took a few seconds before it dawned on her.

"Shit, I left it at work again."

She turned the car north toward The Cast Iron. Five minutes later, the store front came into view. A mangled corpse lay smashed under the skillet logo of the sign. Samantha couldn't make out who it was, only that she hoped they died on impact. Bones jutted from their right arm and thigh. Body fluids streamed down into the nearby storm drain.

Samantha sidestepped the twisted figure and stepped inside. Glass littered the floor and front row of booths from the shattered windows. Debbie was impaled on a broken bar stool. A brightly decorated phone was jammed through her teeth. Samantha couldn't hold her lunch any more and vomited. Marco kept most of the cell phones in a phone basket in the back. She made her way into the kitchen toward Marco's office. Scents of burnt meat wafted past her and caused more retching.

Marco's face was seared to the flat top grill. Blackened, crusty skin crept up his left cheek. Sclera leaked from his eye sockets and sizzled on the grill. A metal burger press was forced into the top of his skull. Samantha vomited again. It took a few minutes of her crying into the pool of shit-colored vomit before she regained her wits. She crept past the frying corpse and found the bright blue plastic basket that contained multiple cell phones. On top of three smart phones was a beat-up Motorola Razor flip phone.

She took the phone and wept as she ran out of The Cast Iron. Three angels strolled seductively down the street. Metallic chattering and groaning rattled around her skull. Samantha quietly got in the car, watching them through the rear view mirror. All three of them stopped for a moment. Samantha turned the key and the engine turned over three times before clanking to life. Screams bellowed through her body and mind. What little bit of focus remained was used to drive and steer the car. Pop music resonated through the tiny phone speaker. *Nathan* appeared on caller ID.

"Oh my God, are you and Marissa okay?" Samantha asked before she even got the phone to her ear.

"Yes, we're both hiding in your house. What's going on out there?" His voice quaked.

"I know you won't believe me, but angels are murdering everyone in Eden. Please, take Marissa and leave. Her father lives in Norwood and can at least provide her three meals and a bed."

"What are you going to do?"

Samantha paused to choke down a sob. "I'm going to go and pray for forgiveness."

"Are you sure you don't want to come with us? You can escape and be in your daughter's life."

"I'm sure, I need to set things right with God."

"Okay, I will get some of her things packed and we will head to Norwood. Please, reconsider."

Before she could respond, the line crackled and died. She tossed the phone into the back and pressed harder on the accelerator. Two angels appeared at the intersection of Marshall and Mountaineer roads. Both watched her blow past but did not pursue her. A few minutes later she was at Eden United Methodist. Dirt and mold stained the once pristine white siding. Two of the windows were boarded up after the church couldn't afford to fix them when some kids had thrown bricks through them.

Samantha burst through the door and headed for the large statue of Jesus nailed to the cross at the back of the sanctuary. When she reached the shadow of the cross she dropped to her knees and began to pray. Tears streamed as she remembered every nightmarish sight she had witnessed. Halfway through her prayer she started to sob hard enough that most of the words were unintelligible. Tears crashed against the crucifix around her neck.

A crashing noise caught her attention. She stood and turned to see the gold angel had burst through the doorway to the church. It moved less gracefully, but with more of a purpose. Samantha pressed her back to the wall in hope it wouldn't see her. The logic was weak, and she damn well knew it. The angel came two feet from her and abruptly stopped. Seconds passed with no movement. Samantha let out a breath to calm herself. The angel reached out and wrapped its claws around her throat and lifted her up.

"Why are you doing this?" Samantha gasped. "I love God and we all believe in him here."

The angel faced her. In her mind she could hear its voice painfully clear.

"Stupid woman. Your God does not exist. We are what created you." Then the angel's grip started to tighten.

Neal Sayatovich is is a freelance writer who has published some short stories and self published a novel. He also likes to spend time with his wife, German Shepherd, and four cats in Ohio. An avid cigar smoker and coffee drinker, he will come out of his hoval to talk with you if you can offer either of those things.

THE SELFLINGS

Noel K. Hannan

For John Wyndham, with respect

IT WAS, IN retrospect, the highlight of my career, but one is rarely so cognizant of such events as they unfold in real time. It is only later, under the scrutiny of High Command and the After Action Reports, reviewing the bodycam footage and the subsequent international media frenzy, and the promotions and the awards, that you can truly appreciate the magnitude of what we achieved that day. We literally saved Mankind.

The reports state factually that my team deployed to the small fishing port of Lubec, Maine on the evening of Saturday 10th January, 2042. This far north, there was snow on the ground and the good people of Lubec had yet to take down their Christmas decorations,which looked sad and faded in the dull lights from the port. Further south, this would have earned them a reprimand from the Protocol Patrols, but here right up against the Canadian border, there was less visibility, and much less governance. These people had been smugglers since Europeans first landed here. Fish, tobacco, alcohol, drugs, weapons – whatever needed to cross the border, they would carry it, for a price. It had always includedthat most common yet sought-after commodity – people – and now it included dangerous, heretical technology.

Even in its heyday there were only ever a handful of hotels or motels in Lubec. This place is a dead end, the US Interstate-189 morphing into the Canadian Interstate-774 and then dropping neatly into the Bay of Fundy off Campobello Island. The target had been identified in the cheaper motel, so my team booked into the more expensive one, and let the US Government pick up the tab.

The team was very small – just myself in command and operating as the intelligence collection officer, and three door-kickers; The Duke, Dutch and Connor. I had worked withthem before and I had hand-picked them for this mission. None were under 40, and they were all dependable, resourceful, veteran special forces operators with enormous experience of this kind of discrete operation. Ghosts, my Grey Ghosts. I had hoped that their more kinetic skills would not be required on this occasion.

It is hard for men like this to blend in, they have a physicality and confidence most men lack. Here in Northern Maine, in January, its was a little easier, as we could bury ourselves under layers of damp flannel plaid, work boots and duvet jackets, and look to all the world like four weary fishermen heading for the bar after a long trip in the Bay. And that is exactly what we did, occupying a window snug in a tavern overlooking the motel, and watched the wide flat frontage until the target emerged from one of the doors, looked furtively left and right, then made her way down to the motel reception, returning a few minutes later with a carton of milk and a pack of sodas. She disappeared into her room. *We were on.*

The target was female – *of course*. Dr. Lindy Neumann, aged 45. Degrees in Biochemistry and Genetics, commissioned military service in the US Marine Corps Reserve, active duty tours in Belarus and Taiwan, a Senior Corpsman. Once a Marine, always a Marine. I doubted she would come quietly, hence my small but perfectly formed team of Ghosts. I figured three of those bad boys were worth one Marine, and a female one at that.

They were worthy – but only just. The Duke – the biggest and most aggressive of myoperators – didn't bother with the usual discreet knock device and just shouldered the door in – he was intimately acquainted with the poor structural integrity of Comfort Inn motel rooms. He stamped on the falling door and stepped to the left as it fell, clearing the entrance and allowing Dutch and Connor to enter quickly behind him. All had Glock pistols drawn and up in the aim. Dr. Neumann was sat on the bed, her own Glock an arm's length from her on the bedside cabinet to her right, and her left arm around a young girl of no more than 8 who had her hair and colouring – pale and Nordic.

We had bagged ourselves a selfling. Bingo.

There was a second or two while Dr. Neumann considered reaching for the gun, but a quick appraisal of the situation made her think twice and that was enough. I was in the room immediately after Connor, lifting the door back into its place behind me and jamming it upright, as Dutch and the Duke seized the two females on the bed, separating them, flipping them on to their fronts and plasticuffing their hands behind their backs. Neither made a sound.

Dutch and Connor did a quick cursory sweep of the apartment – one room and a bathroom – then both exited via the shattered doorway, sealing it behind them as best they could. They would run security, leaving myself and The Duke to conduct the tactical assessment.

We left the girl face down and focussed on Dr. Neumann to start with. I turned her over, pulled her into a sitting position on the edge of the bed. She stared at me, eyes full of barely contained rage, but her face impassive. She was an attractive woman in a slightly weathered, outdoor kind of way. Not really my type. It didn't surprise me that she was an insurgent, and a senior one at that. This was really shaping up to be a significant bag for us.

"How did you find us?" she asked, voice calm with just the hint of a tremor. There was a certain resignation in her now, a flicker of the flame in her eyes, as if it was preparingto be extinguished. Often a calm like that can mask an intent, a sudden outburst of violent action. She was certainly capable of that, and I would need to be very careful. I pulled a chair over from the dressing table and sat in front of her, straddling the chair back, out of arm's reach. I sensed The Duke's presence at my shoulder, like a wardrobe about to fall.

"Loose lips sink ships," I said. "It was too much to resist, wasn't it? Mom and Dad inthe neighbourhood. Wanted them to meet little . . . what's-her-name? For the first time?"

Dr. Neumann closed her eyes and dropped her chin.

"What is her name Dr. Neumann? Your . . . *daughter*?"

Dr. Neumann lifted her head and a nerve visibly twitched in her neck. Precursor to violence. I felt The Duke shift in his stance and gravity a little, just a vague disturbance in the airflow and displacement in the room.

"Laura."

"Laura. Hey Laura, don't worry, we won't hurt you. We just need to ask your Momsome questions. We'll be right with you, baby."

The girl didn't stir. She had her eyes open and was staring at Dr. Neumann, unblinking.

"But the thing is, Dr. Neumann, she isn't really your daughter, is she? Not really."

Dr. Neumann did not respond to this. She just stared me out with a "Fuck You Marine" look. I stood up and began to move around the room, moving in and out of her personal space, daring her.

"Unfortunately, Dr. Neumann, you couldn't resist showing her off to Mom and Dad. A *granddaughter* for them at last. Of a sort. Mom was over the moon, wasn't she? Thought she looked just like you. *So much like you.* Dad. Well, Dad wasn't so convinced, was he? A good man, your dad. Career Marine. Loyal citizen. The kind that notes and reports things to the appropriate authorities. Oh, I'm sure it pained him, giving up his only daughter like that. But he did the right thing. Don't judge him too harshly. He is, after all, just a man."

A fat tear rolled down Dr. Neumann's left cheek. Her shoulders shook slightly."You bastards. You bastards, making him do that."

"He did it all by himself, Dr. Neumann, didn't need any encouragement from us. Like I said, good citizen. What say we take a look at our little selfling here?"

She made her move as I crossed in front of her to place my hand on the girl. Dr. Neumann came off the bed, head and shoulders low, intending to butt me into The Duke, but he was very fast for such a big unit and he intercepted her easily with one meaty paw, swooping up and under her head to grip her throat and lift her back on to the bed in one swift and apparently effortless movement. I saw him take a moment to pinch her neck and cut off blood and oxygen to the brain, just enough to make her gasp, then pushed her back down, standing over her and trapping her with his body weight against her legs.

"Now, that was a stupid move, Dr. Neumann. Moves like that will only end in tears. The Duke here graduated top of his class at the Specialist Applied Rapist School in GNTNMO-2, didn't you, big guy? Let's not allow him the privilege of showing you just how good he is today – that is not what we are here for, oh no."

The threat could not have come as a surprise to her, but it quietened her all the same. The Duke released his weight from her legs and assumed a guard position close by, thumbs in his belt.

"Well, you have what you need. What else do you want from me?"

"The girl? Oh, we didn't come for the girl. The little selfling was a bonus. We're taking her, oh yes, but that isn't what we came for. Duke, take little Laura out to Connor and Dutch, will you?"

Dr. Neumann didn't move while The Duke lifted the girl effortlessly and took her outside.

"Don't worry, she won't be hurt."

She snorted at this. "You're going to dissect her like a frog. It won't give you what you want, no one can give you what you want. Darwin should have listened closer to his barnacles."

I did not know what she meant by that. "And what is it that I want?"

"The formulas and algorithms for creating selflings. Male selflings. To clone men. Men who can breed."

"That is correct, Dr. Neumann. If that information was shared with our government then our respective communities can pool resources and solve this problem. But your community has chosen to hide itself away on Grand Manan Island, just inside Canadian waters, and perfect the art of female cloning. Your intent is the ultimate destruction of the male gender, is it not?"

She shook her head so vehemently I almost believed her. "No, that is not true. Male chromosomes do not react to the cloning process in the same way that female chromosomes do. We have spent years trying to solve this, our intent was to create a genetically sound process which could create fertile males and females to redress the balance. But that has failed. The female selfling process is the only success we have had. And besides—"

She paused and looked down at the bed again.

"You need a womb to carry a selfling to full term. Look at our country. What we have become, a totalitarian religious dictatorship. We have no wish to become a race of breeding cows for you."

I almost hit her at this point, but I didn't. Instead, I smiled. "But Dr. Neumann, without *Man*, there can be no *Mankind*."

It was her turn to smile. " We could just be . . . *Kind*?"

I hit her then, a backhand across the face, just as The Duke re-entered the motel room, alone. Dr. Neumann spat blood on the bed-sheet and turned to face me again.

"Raptor inbound figures ten," said The Duke in his flat Texan drawl. I nodded. "Time for a firework show, Dr. Neumann. Come, to the window."

The Duke lifted her from the bed by her upper arm and guided her to the rear window of the motel, looking out over the sound to Grand Manan Island, just a smudge of lights now in the dark. As he did so, Connor burst into the room, hyperventilating from exertion.

"Boss. She's gone. We lost her."

At that point I didn't know if he meant she'd escaped or they'd accidentally killed her. I could only clarify that later. But it didn't matter, either way. She was a bonus, and if we'd lost the bonus, we still had the prize.

"You should know that she's mute," said Dr. Neumann. "An unfortunate and as yet unquantifiable side effect of the selfling process. If we cannot fix this, our sisterhood will be a silent one—"

She was interrupted by a low, distant crump and the entire skyline of Grand Manan Island lit up with a blazing orange glow. Somewhere in the sky, visible only as a brief void of stars, a Lockheed Martin F-22 Raptor had dropped a payload of incendiary JDAMs (Joint Direct Attack Munitions) on the scientific facility within Canadian territory. There would be hell to pay, no doubt, but then, there always was. And we rarely gave a shit.

She turned then and smiled. This confused me – how could she smile at this time, so many of her friends and colleagues having just died, their laboratory and work destroyed, and she could not have possibly known, as I did not, if her selfling, her clone, was dead or alive.

"Oh, there is something else you should know. We didn't work in isolation. There are labs all around the globe. Kyoto, Dublin, Birmingham, Johannesburg,

Cape Verde – stop me when you've heard enough. We share our research, continually, iteratively, remotely. You destroyed a node, that is all. You will never shut us all down, never. Sorry to *piss on your parade.*"

We left the target area with our collateral soon after. The motel was torched as a precaution. No evidence of our operation was left behind.

This is not over. The struggle continues. Mankind must survive. We had the parade. She didn't get to piss on it. Not yet, at any rate.

Noel K. Hannan has been writing and publishing for over four decades. His comic and graphic novel work includes *Night of the Living Dead, Streetmeat* and *Air Warriors* and he has appeared in many US independent anthologies from Fantaco, Fantagraphics and Caliber. With Rik Rawling he publishes comics, novels and short story collections via their imprint Rawhead. You can find his books on Amazon by searching for "Noel K Hannan". He is also a professional cyber security consultant and military veteran with over three decades service including operational service in Iraq and Afghanistan.

Image created by Stephen Clarke

THE COVE

Eugene Johnson and Paul Moore

DESPITE THE BREEZE, the surface of the cove remain undisturbed. Flanked by trees and separated from the lake by a thin channel, the small body of water was as serene as it was isolated. In fact, movement of any kind was rare around the secluded pocket of nature. Most animals tended to avoid the woodlands around the cove. It occurred to Martin that in the four years he had been frequenting the area, the only signs of life he had observed were the occasional *plop* that sounded when one of the fish decided to break the glassy surface and swallow an insect or two.

The cove was always quiet.

Perhaps that was what Louise had found so compelling about the remote location. Martin had always found the detached inlet eerie and unsettling. For three years, he had dreaded the last Sunday of each month. Those Sundays had entailed a two hour drive, a four hour picnic and two hours for the return trip. The time had not been the issue for him. Nor was it the travel. He had loved Louise from the day he found her and ten times that amount the day he lost her. He would have done anything for her and he did.

The thing that had caused the insidious, expanding knot in his stomach one weekend a month had been the *silence.*

Not the unnatural silence created by the natural barriers surrounding the cove. Not the silence of being completed removed from society. As far as Martin knew, he and Louise had been the only people to visit the odd pocket of nature.

It was the silence the place instilled in Louise that had bothered him.

For the entirety of seventy-two years, Louise had been full of life. She never spoke needlessly, but she talked endlessly. She was a born storyteller. Louise never engaged in gossip, mundane conversations about the weather or the local politics and she refused to tolerate witless banter. Each word was precious to her and she used them for maximum effect. In their fifty-two years of marriage, Martin had never heard her repeat a story or recycle an idea. It was one of the main reasons Martin fell in love with her and subsequently married her. They had never run out of things to talk about.

Except when they visited the cove.

Louise would begin the day her usual animated self. However as their drive brought them closer to the cove, the conversations dwindled. By the time they had parked the car and hiked to the waterfront, her responses had become monosyllabic, at best. After that, it was four hours of quiet reflection as he watched her walk the shoreline or sit on the dock and stare into the water. Martin understood why she had done this and his heart shattered each time it happened.

As vociferous as Louise had been, there was one subject they never discussed. The death of their grandson, Joshua.

His death had been a tragedy. A senseless accident. An innocuous family trip to the beach that had ended in death and sorrow.

Martin and Louise's daughter had married a good man and that union had produced a healthy, bright son. A grandson that Louise had adored above all other things. Martin had, too, for that matter. For Joshua's tenth birthday, Martin and Louise had planned and financed a beach vacation for the entire family.

They had rented a beach house at a popular tourist trap destination. A place where overpriced, inferior carnival rides led to overpriced, near inedible meals in restaurants that seemed more concerned about how much kitsch they could cram on the walls than how much flavor they could extract from a frozen cod. The adults were all aware of the cynical nature of such establishments, but . . .

Joshua had loved them.

The faux pirate décor, the worn and tattered miniature golf courses and the dilapidated fun houses all held a special appeal to the imaginative child. He could transform even the most rudimentary of experiences into an adventure. Laura, Martin and Louise's daughter, took after her father. Pragmatic, introverted and contemplative. Her son, however, took after his grandmother. Vocal, fanciful and bubbling over with zest and curiosity.

Ironically, it was the similarity between grandmother and grandson that Martin and Louise were discussing just minutes before Joshua died.

The three of them had been strolling the beach. Joshua wanted to play in the surf one final time before dinner. It had been a popular stretch of beach on a calm day and neither Martin nor Louise saw any harm in granting his request. As Joshua splashed in the water, they sat in the sand discussing the night's agenda and engaged in polite conversation with other couples walking the beach. It was Martin who noticed that a half hour had passed.

He had excused himself and walked to the edge of the surf. Joshua had worked his way far from the shore. Too far.

Martin had shouted to the boy to return, but the child was too far away. Panic had seized Martin.

Partly because he knew that waters beyond the surf were dangerous, but mostly because Martin could not swim. Martin had wasted no more time on the shore. He had sprinted to Louise and the younger couple with which she was conversing with. Moments later, they were all racing toward the surf.

Joshua was nowhere to be seen. The younger man charged into the water as his wife called 911. Martin had to restrain Louise as she struggled to join the younger man. Eventually, the emergency personnel arrived and for hours people searched the darkening depths as the sun sank behind the horizon.

No one was to blame. It had been an accident. A similar accident to the countless others that befell curious children. Martin and Louise's relationship became strained for awhile as did their relationship with their daughter. But the axiom "time heals all wounds" proved to be true and after a few cautious years, the family's wounds mended and Martin had finally allowed himself a measure of forgiveness.

Louise never found that peace. Instead . . . she found the cove.

It was the glassy surface that had entranced her. The winds broke against the tree line and no tide affected the isolated pool. It was the definition of tranquility. Far away from the roiling currents and random rip tides of the ocean, Louise could quietly commune with or remember Joshua. At least, that had been Martin's suspicion. He had never asked his wife about the allure of the cove. He had simply accepted it. If that was what she needed to do to find contentment, then so be it.

For three years, Martin had indulged her. He had prepared the lunches. He had driven in silence.

He had worked his way through an astonishing amount of paperback novels as Louise had sat and . . . *communed* with the water. That was best way Martin could describe it. Whatever Louise received from those visits, Martin had not been a part of it. He had taken no offense at that.

In a weird way, he was not surprised the day she drowned.

Martin had been reading another in an endless line of pulp novels that had advertised themselves as a "taut and twisted journey through the mind of a killer and the one woman who could stop him" while Louise had sat on the dock and smiled mutely as she stared into the placid waters. It was routine fiction he used to pass the time on a routine Sunday. A Sunday the two of them had experienced countless times before. No reason for concern. No reason to worry.

No reason for Martin to watch the water. No reason at all.

The police had ruled Louise's death "accidental". Despite Martin's objections, they had concluded that she had, whether in a fit of dementia or nostalgia, decided to disrobe and swim. They had also concluded that due to her advanced age, in conjunction with her diminished mental faculties, she had overestimated her abilities and drowned. Martin did not believe their absurd theories for a moment, but he signed the reports anyway.

He knew the truth. Louise had never found her forgiveness. She had simply bided her time until she had found the perfect place and the perfect moment. He did not try to explain the truth that he knew. He simply allowed the police to quietly close the case and file it away. Even if he did convince them, what would it have accomplished? Louise would still be gone and he would still be alone.

Instead, Martin took up fishing.

Martin opened his tackle box as he settled on the dock. A seasoned fisherman would have been appalled by the contents, or lack thereof. However for Martin's purposes, they were more than adequate. He had a sandwich, chips, two bottled waters and an assortment of lures and spinners that the salesmen had assured him were perfect for catching freshwater fish.

In the year he had been returning to the cove, Martin had never caught a fish.

Martin once asked his wife how she had found the cove and what compelled her to keep returning to the spot. Was it the silence? The privacy?

She responded to both questions with a single answer. She said that it "called to her". When he had pressed for details, she had simply stared at the horizon with unfocused eyes. Whatever Louise's connection to the cove had been, it was personal and spiritual. Perhaps even supernatural, although Martin was not a man prone to such explanations. He often found that most people were too eager to embrace a metaphysical explanation under unpleasant situations because the logical, earthbound answers were less exciting and usually involved some level of culpability on their behalf.

Regardless of Louise's reasons, the cove was where she chose to end her life. A headstone had been erected over an empty grave in a family plot, but the grave was just that . . . empty. The cove was where Louise *wanted*. It was her final resting place and though Martin did not understand her rationale, he respected it.

In honor of Louise's unspoken wishes, Martin had opted to take up fishing so he could sit at the water's edge and keep her company. He had come to realize that, even in death, his wife was far better company the most of the living people that surrounded him.

Having threaded and baited the hook, Martin cast his line in the first of many attempts to drag something from the depths.

It was well past noon when Martin decided to break for lunch. He had been carefully casting and recasting his line and the results were nothing if not consistent. Of course, this was typical of his days at the cove. The fishing was what actors called "business". A non-essential, frivolous activity to perform on stage as they waited to say their lines.

Something to make me seem less pathetic, he thought as he chewed his sandwich.

Something to make me seem less alone.

A loud *plop* sounded in the cove and Martin's head snapped to attention just in time to see ripples dissipating on the water's otherwise placid surface. Curious, he hauled himself to his feet and wandered to the end of the dock.

In the water below, nothing moved.

Martin had not expected to see anything. Just the sound of something. Other than himself, moving around the cove was headline-worthy news. If Martin had actually *seen* a fish, he probably would have passed out from the excitement. He made a mental note . . .

I should start bringing beer up here.

He was not a who imbibed regularly, but he did enjoy an occasional—

PLOP!

The sound was alarmingly loud and Martin's eyes went wide with surprise. He scanned the surface and once again saw diminishing ripples. However, now the ripples were larger and closer. Once again, he stared into the murky water.

This time, he did see something.

What is that?

He knelt at the dock's edge and leaned forward. He stopped short of endangering his balance, but he had a feeling he would regret all of the stretching and extending when he woke in the morning. However, those were distant concerns. At that moment, he was mesmerized by whatever was flitting back and forth beneath the water's glassy surface.

It's not a fish. At least, I don't think it's a fish.

Martin was certain he was not seeing a fish, but whatever it was, it felt *familiar*. Perhaps it was another form of marine life? Or one of the many optical illusions that are created when water and light meet? Maybe it was something as simple as litter caught on a sunken branch?

It's not anything like that. It's something else. Something that doesn't belong.

The *thing* made another pass. This time it was closer to both the surface and the dock. It was almost as if the *thing* was daring Martin to chase it. Or catch it.

He watched it as it fluttered by the dock yet again. Despite not being able to discern any details, Martin saw enough to advance his mood from *unsettled* to *anxious*. He was now certain it was not a fish. The *thing* was not covered in glittering scales and its movements were not the jerky and darting patterns of a fish. Instead, it appeared to be covered in something akin to *flesh* and its movements were fluid. Almost hypnotic.

Martin felt an overwhelming need to touch it welling inside of him. It was more than an urge; it was an imperative.

As if sensing Martin's resolve, the *thing* slowed as it neared the dock. It began to lazily trace diminishing concentric circles as Martin leaned further forward over the edge. The *thing* responded by closing the distance between them.

Martin's outstretched hand was trembling as his fingers touched the surface. A few more inches and he would—

"Don't do that. Don't touch it."

Martin's hand and blood froze simultaneously. His veins became icy as his breath caught in his throat. For a moment, he thought he was going to suffer a heart attack while suffocating. He withdrew his hand as he stood and looked toward the source of the voice.

Louise's voice.

Martin's jaw went slack as he stared at the naked visage of his wife. Her skin was livid and waterlogged as she floated on her back. Louise was about twenty feet from the dock and the one eye that had not been devoured by the fish was trained on Martin.

"Louise . . .?" Martin quietly stammered. "This . . . This isn't . . . This is not happening."

The thing in the lake that looked like Louise responded, however Martin did notice that its ruined jaw was not moving.

"You should touch nothing here. Nothing save me."

"Why?" Martin asked aloud. It was a ridiculous question considering the myriad of other questions he could have asked.

"The things here are not to be trusted. Ignore them. Join me."

Once again, a flood of questions crashed across Martin's mind, but he felt obliged to pursue the voice's wishes. *Louise's* wishes.

"I can't," Martin replied as he took an involuntary steps forward, "I can't swim."

"I know. You don't have to. I will swim for the both of us."

Another step.

"This isn't real. You're not real."

"Does it matter? I'm what you want. What you need."

Tears began to spill over Martin's cheeks. "I don't know who you are."

The flesh of Louise's distended stomach *pulsed* as *something* moved beneath the skin.

"I am who you need me to be. Just as I was who she needed me to be."

Martin had stepped to the edge of the dock. His reflection on the still waters was pristine. "And who was that?"

"You know. You've always known. Join me and I will show you all. I will take you to them."

"Do you promise?"

"Yes."

Martin turned his face skyward and took a final look at the sun. So much light. So much life. He smiled through his tears as he stepped off of the dock.

The world beneath the surface was dim and populated with shifting shadows. Pale, decaying hands coiled around Martin's legs as his chest tightened. He felt himself being pulled downward as his lungs began to burn.

Martin shook his head from side-to-side as he struggled to break free of his restraints. The hands become tendrils of weeds. The more he struggled, the more constrictive they became.

This was a mistake. A deception. All of the fury and rage over Joshua's death collided with the guilt and helplessness he felt over Louise's passing and erupted inside him.

Bubbles poured from his mouth as he thrashed and flailed. Around him the flowing lengths of weeds had transformed again. Now, Martin was surrounded by tentacles. Oily, slithering monstrosities covered in suckers and bony teeth. They curled around him and shredded his flesh as they dragged him deeper into the darkness.

Martin looked toward the surface, but it was gone. He was surrounded by inky darkness and membranous, pulsating flesh. Throbbing tentacles swirled at the edges of his vision.

As the last of the air exploded from his lungs, Martin had a final, cogent thought . . .

How far down does this go?

Bram Stoker Award-winner **Eugene Johnson** is a bestselling author, editor, filmmaker and columnist. He has written, as well as edited, in various genres, and created many anthologies. His anthology projects include *Fantastic Tales of Terror* from Crystal Lake Publishing, *Appalachia Undead* with Jason Sizemore, *Attack from the '80s* from Raw Dog Screaming Press, *Drive in Creature Feature* with Charles Day, the Bram Stoker Award-nominated non-fiction anthology *Where Nightmares Come From: The Art of Storytelling in the Horror Genre*, *Dark Tides* with John Questore, the *Tales of the Lost* series, and many more. He has written articles for various sites and publications including *Ginger Nuts of Horror*, *The Zombie Feed* and more. He lives in Appalachia with his family.

Paul Moore is a filmmaker and author who has written and directed four feature films and multiple short films. Among them, *Keepsake, Requiem, Leftovers* and *Paper Wasps*. His first short story, 'Spoiled', was published in the well received anthology *Appalachian Undead*. He followed that with the story 'Things' published in *Drive-In Creature Feature*. In addition, he has contributed to such anthologies as *Dread State* and more.

SAFE HAVEN

(Parts IV and V)

Evangelia Papanikou

A continuation of the author's serialised story

IV: IN THE MIND

I COULD ONLY imagine the terror these babies would bring to mankind if I waited any longer. What great power would they have and what would they be capable of doing if they grew up? Who in their right mind would blame me for "taking care" of all three of them already? Certainly not Father George, and he knew best. He led me to them, after all, and he explained everything to me.

I couldn't wait for five more years in order for the three sisters to become six years old, at which point the signs of their possession would be clearer, as the demon would mark each one of them with the unholy "6", in order to form the Number of The Beast. And how would I ever be certain that the demon wasn't shifting from one girl to the next until then, growing stronger? I had to take care of all three.

Father George mentioned clearly that the final revelation would take place on their sixth birthday, at which point, each one of the sisters would be marked and appointed as a servant to one of the triple hypostases of the demon: Satan, Lucifer, Baphomet.

And then, literally with the demon's soul and power inside each one of them, who would be able to stop them from gaining world power? It would be too late for all . . .

I didn't mean to harm the parents, though. I don't blame them for their ill fate. No one would want to bring into this world a cursed-from-birth baby, let alone three of them at the same time, let alone all girls. What are the odds of having triplets, anyway?

The parents, indeed, tried to give me a scientific explanation at the time – at the demon's will and command, no wonder. They argued that statistically, the likelihood of having triplets is increased with in vitro fertilization, and mentioned about a hundred times that their doctor had already predicted it from the beginning of the pregnancy. As if I would fall for that excuse. Scientists are the most ignorant and pathetic of human beings. I would let them be sacrificed too if I had the chance. They are the right hand of the demon throughout history – no morals, no ethics, and they look down on religion too. They know nothing about God's will and they go against it.

And even after Father George's expert insight, they still went through with it.

"We do not know any Father George!" they were both screaming at the top of their lungs.

"Liars! Father George told you all about it!" I kept screaming back at them.

The fact that they went through with their cursed pregnancy, makes them already guilty – they obeyed the demon's orders, they fell in the death of the dark lord instead of joining God in a life of pure light. They should have fought the demon off any way they could instead – and if that meant having no children at all, that would have been the will of God. And if that meant taking their own lives, then that would have been the will of God, too. And the correct thing to do.

I do blame them for not cooperating with me, however. Even after all my arguments,they strongly disagreed and they weren't willing to help me achieve the higher purpose I strove for, not for myself or my sake, not for my salvation, but for humanity and God's sake.

"Would you happen to know which of your three babies is the one that was cursed first?" I asked them politely. They screamed and catapulted vulgar insults, "crazy lunatic" being one of the mildest. They even threatened me with calling the police.

"Please, leave all three of them with me and save yourselves at least." I even gave them a choice. They insisted that they wouldn't abandon their – already screaming like hell – children at the mercy of a "demented psycho-path".

That's when I held them at gunpoint and forced them all into their own car. I had no time for this.

My gun wasn't even loaded – who was a "demented psychopath" then? Certainly not me . . .

I still remember seeing the cursed family through the rear-view mirror, as I started the car with all five of them packed in the back seat.

The expression on their faces was a mixture of outrage and terror, a combination of pleading and guilt – who was a "psycho" then? Certainly not me . . .

I have to admit, I drove away like a madman in their vintage car. But that was only because I didn't want to give the two adults of that damned family a chance to stop me.

And because I hadn't driven a stick-shift in years. Okay, and because I didn't have a driver's licence . . .

The looks on both of their faces turned to blank as the car engine revved and the tires screeched. Shortly after, all five of them were screaming and bouncing around the back seat, trying to hold on to themselves and each other and survive my driving.

I tried to enlighten them and motivate them. "You should just try to see it as an epic road trip . . . Seek expiation! Seek redemption! Find peace! Save the world! See yourselves as Ulysses returning home to Ithaca."

Actually, I was thinking "Ulysses visiting the Underworld", but I didn't want to scare them any more.

Instead of the parents calming down even a little and stopping screaming, they both became angrier. They cursed in unison, aiming at what they thought were aspects of my personality. I forgave them, although that scene has been playing continuously in my head since then: "Damn you, you're twisted and distorted!" the mother yelled at me.

"Hell, dude! What's wrong with your head? You're the devil himself!" the father shouted.

"Where is your mother to talk some sense into you?" the mother continued crying.

"If you kill us, they will lock you up for ever and you will not see your family again, not even your mother," the father added without losing his temper this time.

"Such rudeness, cacophony and blasphemy at the same time and you patronise me too. You two were made for each other. Don't you think it's wrong using such language in front of your children? It seems after all that the demon chose these children because they're yours," I couldn't help but answer. "Like I care for my family!" I added emotionlessly. "How many Hail Marys would Father George give for penance to you?" I finally asked them.

I talked calmly, crossing myself with my right hand and holding the steering wheel with my left. I recited in silence the prayer my grandmother taught me while they started screaming again:

"Who the hell is this Father George you keep on mentioning? Why hasn't anyone locked you both up in a mental institution yet?"

I stopped paying attention to them and continued with my prayers . . . *"Wash away all my iniquity and cleanse me from my sin."*

And that's exactly what was about to happen to them . . . These satanic triplets would get washed and cleansed from sin for good. Right then and there. Before they actually formed the triple number six, the number of the Beast, at six years of age.

"The triplets who you share a birthday with should be obliterated during your thirty-third year," I heard God's voice repeating in my head.

"Would you be so kind to cooperate and tell me which one of the triplets is the already possessed one?" I asked the parents, calmly and politely with a sweet and honest smile, one last time.

"You're delusional!" the mother screamed.

"You're a schizo!" the father exclaimed.

"It could be that we can still save the other two with baptism, toil and exorcism before the dark power is attached to them for long and the possession spreads deeply into their souls like a nasty flesh-eating irreversible virus. We only need to kill one at this point in order to break the triple number they would form," I explained again, hoping for a quicker solution. I even mentioned Father George and his bloodline and how I was the Chosen One to whom God revealed His prophecy through visions and through Father George.

It took me a while to locate the family's home, but my excellent social engineering skills led me to them finally – with His grace: *"You need to locate the triplets that share the same birthday as you."*

I simply couldn't wait for the demon to become stronger through them. These seeds, watered by demonic forces that love to toy with humans, could take deep root within them. I couldn't risk the demon gaining strength and forming in full glory into this world through these babies.

"That's why I need to kill at least one of them!" I concluded.

Trying to explain all this to the two blinded-from-unconditional-love parents was futile, however . . .

Father George had predicted this when he warned me about the fate of the

Chosen One, which is "to speak the truth but not be believed by any" by the works of the demon always.

"Cassandra possessed the gift of prophecy but she was cursed so none would ever believe what she prophesied," I told them in order to persuade them. They did not respect the morale of the ancient Greek myth, nor its symbolism or the knowledge it offers. Their obscene language show was followed by offers of increasing amounts of money, as if they were at a bargain game at a slave auction.

"What is money good for if the demon devours us all and this world as we know it falls into oblivion?"

I rejected all of their financial offers. And the ones after those and all that followed. I decided to continue my quest in silence. I drove the car towards the river bank as fast as I could, constantly reciting my prayer: "*Wash away all my iniquity and cleanse me from my sin.*"

God helped me jump out of the car when it plunged into the river, carrying its five human passengers and the demon towards their final destination at the bottom of the freezing cold water.

"The servants of God are baptised in the Name of the Father and of the Son and of the Holy Spirit," I chanted as they were falling in.

Amen.

I only heard their muffled, terrified screams for a few seconds before their bodies were embalmed with the dirty river water.

V: IN THE REALITY GAP

I stayed lying down on the wet grass. I felt warm and fuzzy inside. I was very pleased with myself and the final outcome.

After all, if I had made a mistake, God almighty would save them, wouldn't He?

I imagined all five of them underwater: their wide-open glassy eyes mirrored death, similar to those of demonic dolls, all subjects of an otherworldly dark refraction.

In their final attempt for oxygen, they must have inhaled water, to not exhale ever again. A serene smile appeared on my tired face. I couldn't remember when I had last smiled so happily – it must have been many years ago when as a kid I sought out my parents' approval, which never came . . .

Look, Mom! I'm a holy superhero! Almost a Saint! I saved the world! I almost cried out by the river, as I thought of the family's wet, heavy, lifeless bodies, their frozen-in-time souls and their soon to be deformed faces – oh, especially the dead bodies of those babies would puff up in the water in no time.

They wouldn't be that useful to the demon any more, would they?

I couldn't wait to tell Father George about my success. I was pleased that the parents and their children were together, in a better place where pain was no longer felt, with their minds at peace in the infinite afterlife. All clean, no blood was shed. The demon didn't manage to turn them into his puppets. And they owed that to me.

What an unsettling grimace their faces must be wearing . . . but who would see that underwater, anyway? Soon, they will be packed away in a casket, underground forever.

I performed a quick funeral service for them. Father George would approve. "You shall sprinkle me with hyssop and I shall be clean. You shall wash me and I shall be whiter than snow."

Amen.

The inflicted sharp pain in their lungs as they drowned was the ideal way to scourge themselves, to achieve the state of grace many wished for. I sympathised with the sense of panic the two adults must have felt.

Did the grimness of their situation take over their will to live even one second longer? Would they now exchange their babies for their lives? Their despair and distress was surely enormous.

We would never know. It was too late. And too bad they didn't honour their sacrifice. It was, after all, for a higher purpose. It was a small price to pay in order to reach oneness with the Lord, to renounce Satan. As their bodies toiled – "the more painful the better", as Father George said – they achieved the ultimate baptism. Their minds cleared as they reached a zone of inner serenity, on their last second on Earth, before they went to meet Him.

I continued their funeral service. "Like a blossom that wastes away, and like a dream that passes and is gone, so is every mortal into dust resolved; but again, when the trumpet sounds its call, as though at a quaking of the earth, all the dead shall arise and go forth to meet You."

I imagined momentarily their hands and hair, moving in strange slow motion, around their heads and bodies, adrift to the whirling motion of the current. Waving left and right, like their hands belonged to a haunted puppet that had demonic life of its own. Hopping up and down, like their bodies belonged to a paranoid puppeteer who was pulling their strings violently, without love, transferring through them his soul's darkness. Swinging back and forth, as the river current dragged their souls into the world of the dead, like Acheron, the stream of woe, led the dead directly into the kingdom of Hades. This surreal and grotesque show would go on until the moment they would be taken out of the water and placed safely in black body bags.

Finally! What an impressive farewell to the demon!

I sighed in relief. My lips whispered my prayer again: *"Wash away all my iniquity and cleanse me from my sin."*

The serene thoughts and smile didn't last long. I suddenly became worried. I observed the surface of the water to ensure that something resembling Father George's descriptions of a monster-like, scale-covered demon didn't jump out of it. I wanted to see if escaping the drowned children's bodies would disturb the river's surface at all or if the demon would return defeated to its dark, impure kingdom, forever, without any further signs.

The police sirens soon dissolved my thoughts.

'Safe Haven' will be concluded in the next issue of Phantasmagoria . . .

Author's note: This story is dedicated to "'95', Rare Alliance Greece" (https://rarealliance.gr/), which is a Greek non-profit organization advocating for all who live with a rare and undiagnosed disease, in order to raise awareness about rare diseases and their impact. The number "95" in the distinctive title of the organization symbolizes the percentage of rare diseases that do not have an approved treatment, while the name "Greek Alliance" highlights the need for cooperation in order to improve the quality of life of people with rare diseases. Timely diagnosis and early access to care can save rare disease patients' lives and improve their own mental health and psychological well-being, as well as that of their families and society's as a whole, in effect, too. The stigma and the associated isolation of rare disease patients along with the issues of a non-inclusive culture can lead to a personal tragedy for each and every one of us.

—**Evangelia Papanikou**

Evangelia Papanikou lives in Greece. She is a published author with her books, articles, poems and short stories receiving praise and recognition, including a first prize award for her first book. Unlike her studies (B.Sc. Computing for Industry & M.Sc. Information Systems Management in the University of Northumbria at Newcastle upon Tyne), her writing interests and inspiration lie in Greek mythology and Ancient Greek literature which she tries to give prominence to through her stories. She was the president of the organisation committee of a Greek fantasy festival for a series of years.

You can connect with her on:
facebook.com/mythalogia and youtube.com/evangeliapapanikou

'Fiend Without a Face' by Allen Koszowski

237

SPECTRAL ZONES
(a Rondel Supreme)

Frank Coffman

There be weird spectral zones well-hidden,
Yet there be some who choose to go.
Of arcane wisdom they would know—
The eldritch spells that are forbidden!

These I have sought, although long chidden
By foes and fellow alchemist enow.
There be weird spectral zones well-hidden,
Yet I was one who chose to go.

And now my nights are horror-ridden,
My conjurings a source of endless woe!
Since I dared pass that human middan,
Bones of the damned—dead long ago!
There be weird spectral zones forbidden,
Alas! I was one who dared to go.

Frank Coffman is a retired professor of college English and creative writing. He has published speculative poetry, fiction, and scholarly essays in a variety of journals, magazines, and anthologies. His poetic magnum opus, *The Coven's Hornbook & Other Poems* (January 2019), has been followed by his rendition into English Verse of 327 quatrains in *Khayyám's Rubáiyát* (May 2019). Both books are available from Bold Venture Press and on Amazon.

He is a member of the Horror Writers Association and the Science Fiction & Fantasy Poetry Association. He established and moderates the Weird Poets Society Facebook group and he selected, edited, introduced, and did commentary for his *Robert E. Howard: Selected Poems*.

See his Writer's Blog at: www.frankcoffman-writer.com

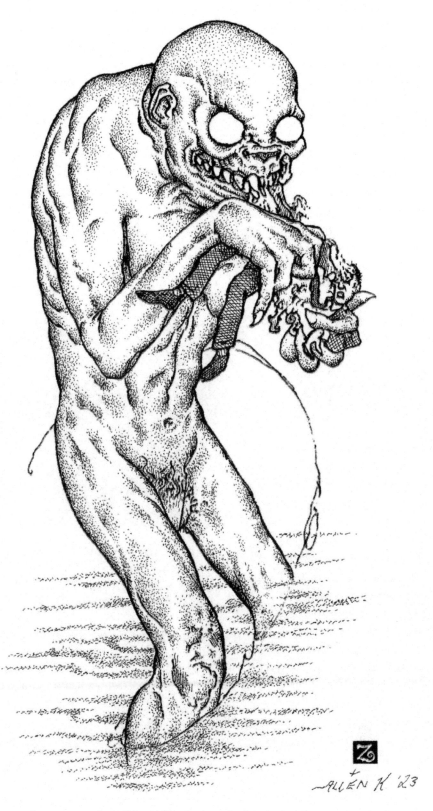

'Hungry Ghoul' by Allen Koszowski and "The joey Zone"

PHANTASMAGORIA REVIEWS

LITERATURE

THE HOUSE AT PHANTOM PARK by Graham Masterton

Contains spoilers

LILIAN CHESTERFIELD WORKS for a property development company and her latest project is to turn the now abandoned Jacobean St. Philomena's military hospital building in Surrey into a block of luxury apartments. Problems begin to arise, however, when two quantity surveyors employed by her – Alex and Charlie – fall victim to inexplicable ailments when out inspecting the former hospital. Alex can't stop screaming in apparent extreme pain, despite not having been injured in any way, while Charlie falls into a mysterious coma. Other odd occurrences are also happening in the building – ghostly figures seen standing at windows, possible poltergeist activity in the kitchen, and the discovery of a partial human skeleton on the grounds.

Along with the help of her assistant David, a former military medic, Moses, doctors at the nearby hospital, and eventually the police, the cynical, career-focused Lilian soon finds herself embroiled in the mystery of St. Philomena's, one that is connected to former servicemen who were injured in

Afghanistan, ancient south-central Asian legends, spontaneous human *explosion*, and an enigmatic gardener who still tends to the grounds of the hospital.

As with his recent *The House of a Hundred Whispers*, this brand new title by Graham Masterton, sees the author put yet another unique spin on the "haunted house" (or in this case a haunted hospital) trope. The concept of "Spirits of Pain"/the dead being punished to suffer eternal pain is a fascinating one and a neat take on the various forms of religious Hell, as is the Afghanistan-based folklore which is used to great effect here in what is, at its very core, an anti-war novel – what gives us the right to go poking our noses into other people's cultures, even if we do abhor them? – taken from the point-of-view of both the young British soldiers on the front line ("cannon fodder"/"lions led by lambs") and the beliefs of old of the people of Afghanistan. Indeed, this certainly ain't no regular haunted house tale!

Fans of Masterton's work can also expect plenty of the author's regular visceral gore and violence – characters literally explode in graphic detail at times, although in the context of the story at hand it makes complete sense – while his dual-career (along with horror) as a crime author also serves well in the realisation of the police procedural investigation side of the story.

The House at Phantom Park is a compelling read overall – slick, stylish, well-paced and characterised with a particular gut-punch of an ending for the main character – and one that just goes to prove that with someone like the prolific Masterton in charge, horror can indeed still explore and address very real-life and hard-hitting topics.

The House at Phantom Park is published by Head of Zeus and is available to purchase from Amazon and many other outlets and bookstores.

—**Trevor Kennedy**

FAIRY TALE by Stephen King

WHEN YOU'VE BEEN around and highly influential on the writing circuit, it's only natural that other mediums and writers take their influence from you.

And when you've been around as long as Stephen King, it may be that you need to take influence from those you've influenced.

Told from the viewpoint of a 17-year-old, *Fairy Tale* arrives like a "Point Horror" novel from the early-'90s. Likeable Charlie Reade's life has contained tragedy, yet his time at high school is going well for him. One day, Charlie is able to help Howard Bowditch, a grumpy and reclusive neighbour who has suffered an accident. Howard soon becomes somewhat of the former's benefactor.

Bowditch also has a German Shepherd by the name of Radar, an animal that Charlie takes an instant liking to. The two mimic an Ash-and-Pikachu relationship of love and protection. But it's not long before Bowditch's age catches up with him. And Charlie is the surprise inheritor of all he owns. The house. The money. The dog.

And something else; a secret entrance to another world. One where Charlie feels it necessary to visit in order to save the rapidly ageing Radar. A world reeling in despair due to the takeover of an entity known as Flight Killer.

Whilst King may have been able to expand, rather than distance, himself from the "Master of Horror" title after decades, his attention or love for gory and frightening moments hasn't left him. Even when he was writing thrillers that contained no supernatural elements, horrible acts of violence were never far away.

Fairy Tale sits at a disadvantage with these moments. Due to most readers being aware that original fairy tales are grotesque, King doesn't seem to be doing anything daring with the genre. The format and elements of fairy tales are referenced throughout, but King doesn't satirise them.

Once the small-town American, high-school narrative dissolves into the new fantasy world, King is pretty much making it up as he goes along. Although I have to admit my excitement when the aesthetic and goings-on take that of an '80s Saturday morning cartoon. And whether King is a fan of *Stranger Things* may come into question as Lovecraftian vines and large beastly creatures start to creep into the surroundings.

Fairy Tale plays out like *The Dark Tower* for teenagers. The third act contains exhaustive tropes which a younger audience may still be thriving for; but after nearly over twenty years of YA fiction and popular films using the familiar "prophesised" character, I was yearning for the return of the real world and how the strange looks against it.

King has brought back his transportive and imaginative talent; if more for himself than anyone. Whilst long-time fans may not be overly-impressed; he has done that rare thing and written a novel that is accessible for newcomers. By building his world with familiar building blocks, this is a door older teenagers can step through. And if part of the plan was to get them hooked while they're young, there's enough treasure here for them to feel rich upon.

Fairy Tale is published Hodder & Stoughton in multiple formats and is available to purchase from Amazon and many other outlets and bookstores.

—**Christopher Gray**

ALL OUR HEARTS ARE GHOSTS & OTHER STORIES
by Peter Atkins

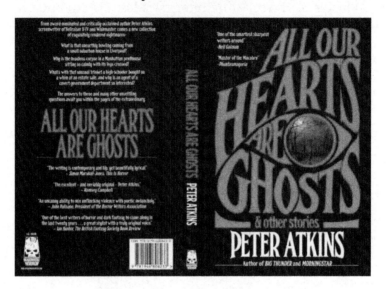

I'VE NEVER MET Peter Atkins in person, however I'd like to one day. He comes across as a really fun and cool guy to be around, and this is also very much apparent in his writing, too.

All Our Hearts are Ghosts & Other Stories is Atkins' poetically-titled new collection, but don't let that fool you. The author's literary style is indeed rhythmic and lyrical (perhaps due to his background as a musician as well as screenwriter [1997's *Wishmaster*, the first few *Hellraiser* sequels] and various other forms of the written word), but there's still plenty of good old-fashioned, pulp-style, fast-paced action, gore and humour in there at the same time. It's a great – and unique – mix of styles.

The stories collected here never really leave the reader with a chance to catch their breath, very much in the manner that many of us – myself included – enjoy their fiction. Readers such as us can very much tell when writers like Atkins are having a ball in the creation of their tales – here, Atkins' enthusiasm leaks onto the page, backed up by an obvious depth of intellect and natural storytelling skills, resulting in a wonderful combination.

The main stories are bookended by two Lovecraftian tales that originally appeared in the Stephen Jones-helmed anthology series, *The Lovecraft Squad* – 'The Stuff that Dreams are Made of' and 'The Thing About Cats' – while the Jones connection doesn't end there with two more entries – 'Z.O.A' and 'You Are What You Eat' – having also been published in the editor's related *Zombie Apocalypse* series. All four of these are pleasurable takes on their respective sub-genres.

The title story is a profound, thought-provoking one concerning an ageing television stuntman/bit-part actor in Hollywood who must settle an old score with a former rival – all our hearts our ghosts indeed, perhaps always trapped in, and haunted by, our pasts.

Of the others printed here, and while each certainly have their own merits, my personal favourites would have to be 'Eternal Delight', an early novella by Atkins, set in his native Liverpool and featuring a young man whose body is invaded by a parasite and which goes to some really bonkers and darkly humorous places (the finale set in a council estate social club is insanely good!), and 'The Return of Boy Justice', about a former small-time TV star who finally gets the opportunity to relive the adventures of his fictional alter-ego, and one that also ends on a rather heart-warming, life-affirming note.

There's no shortage of bonus material included either, with a comic book script featured alongside background stories for the three characters who were transformed into Cenobites in the Atkins-penned *Hellraiser III: Hell on Earth* (1992), so definitely worth looking into for fans of the *Hellraiser* universe and Atkins overall.

If books are reflective of the personality of those who have written them, then this one is most definitely a rather cool and fun one to behold (including that retro 1980s-esque cover!), just like its author. Why not buy it and find out for yourselves?

All Our Hearts are Ghosts & Other Stories is published by Shadowridge Press and is available to purchase from Amazon and other outlets.

—**Trevor Kennedy**

CLOSE TO MIDNIGHT edited by Mark Morris

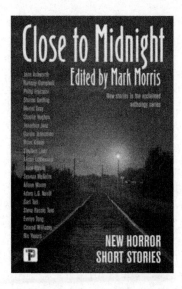

THEMED ANTHOLOGIES HAVE dominated the market to such extent in recent years that it is refreshing to see a collection of stories from new and established writers that doesn't require conformity to subject or style.

Mark Morris continues his series of collections of the miscellaneous best in contemporary horror (*Beyond the Veil* and *After Sundown* are the other titles) and demonstrates a discerning eye in selecting material from both established and emerging genre writers, as well as four stories from newcomers gathered from a Flame Tree Press open submissions exercise.

Of course, the lack of a stated theme doesn't mean that the stories don't mirror the zeitgeist and there are certain motifs that range across this collection and overlap (sometimes within the same story). Modern folk and fairy tales of new rituals that echo older mythos get an airing in the sombre opener 'Wolves' by Rio Youers, as well as in stories by Philip Fracassi, Stephen Laws, Alison Littlewood, Laura Mauro and Adam L.G. Nevill's strong closer 'Rise Up Together'. Traditional staples like incubi (Janz), werewolves (Youers) demons (Gray) and ghosts (Hughes, Williams, Rasnic Tem) feature but in new forms and from fresh perspectives.

Body horror hasn't gone away, as tales by Campbell, Keene, Gosling, Tait, Mcguire and Moore demonstrate but most of these leave the reader wondering whether it is the mind or the body that has mutated or fallen apart.

There will always be a market for clever and well-crafted variants of 'The Monkey's Paw' tale of *caveat emptor* and Gray's 'Best Safe Life for You', Ashworth's 'Flat 19', Tait's 'The Forbidden Sandwich' and Carole Johnstone's 'The Nine of Diamonds' are all flawlessly executed and guiltily satisfying.

In his introduction, Morris comments on how loss was the pervading emotion he saw as flowing through most of these tales, which he sees as connected to emerging from the common experience of living through Covid; and personal loss and grieving does indeed link several tales, as do warnings that refusing to let go and move on can prove harmful also.

Many of these tales are narrated from positions of powerlessness, helplessness and lack of agency, a possible reflection of the lockdown experience.

Overall, there is a muted and stoic tone that more than a few share and anyone looking for the gleeful gore of Splatterpunk might need to look elsewhere; not that the overall mood of the collection is depressing, rather that the lingering effect is one of rueful reflection and mournful resignation, rather than the cleansing sense of catharsis some horror tales can affect.

This is a solid and substantial collection and, akin to one of the old Pan horror anthologies, presents well written quality tales that don't require writer or reader to strain themselves to be innovative or cutting edge (not that more than one story here isn't both). Like with every anthology, I'd have a few minor quibbles at some of the selections (the Keane story comes across as an unfinished fragment, albeit a terrifying one and thematically, for me, Seanan Mcguire's 'Collagen' doesn't quite hang together (a bad pun you'll get if you read the story!) but all are worth reading and personal preferences and tastes are likely to dictate which tales will find favour with the reader.

Special mention to Mark Morris, a genre giant who looks set to assemble an anthology series to rival the Pan classics, and to Flame Tree Press, who continue to encourage new talent and repackage existing ones in their innovative and beautifully designed editions.

Close to Midnight is published by Flame Tree Press and is available to purchase from their website, Amazon and other outlets. For more information please go to: www.flametreepublishing.com

—**Con Connolly**

CELTIC WEIRD: TALES OF WICKED FOLKLORE AND DARK MYTHOLOGY edited by Johnny Mains

EDITED BY JOHNNY Mains for The British Library, *Celtic Weird* is an impressive anthology that brings together tales of folklore, legends and hauntings from the historical regions of its title – Scotland, Ireland, Brittany, Isle of Man, Wales, Cornwall and Gaelic respectively.

Impressive, not just because of many of the stories included, but also due to the editor's skills as a researcher and "horror historian" coming to the forefront once more – painstaking perhaps, in his continuing efforts to seek out old, obscure and long-forgotten about genre-related works from across the British Isles and beyond. *Celtic Weird* is very possibly Mains' finest work in this regard, or at least of those I have read anyway.

Of the writers included that I was already familiar with, some of the highlights would have to be Nigel "Quatermass" Kneale's humorous 'The Tarroo-Ushtey', about a local Manx conman who claims to have "second sight" and knowledge of the sea monster of the title, Arthur Machen's 'The Gift of Tongues', featuring a Welsh Christmas Day church service with a difference, while Robert Aickman's 'The Fetch' is a sheer masterclass in atmosphere, tension and deeply unsettling, briefly glimpsed at imagery, and one that lingers for long afterwards.

My pick of the others included would probably go to 'The Cure' by Dorothy K. Haynes, a darkly realised cracker of a coming-of-age tale, Jasper John's 'The Seeker of Souls', an atmospheric one concerning a haunted Irish castle, 'Kerfol' by Edith Wharton, involving ghost dogs in Brittany, and the Wales-set 'Mermaid Beach' by Leslie Vardre.

'The Other Side: A Breton Legend' by Count Eric Stanislaus Stenbock and the closing two entries – Eachann MacPhaidein's 'The Butterfly's Wedding' and 'The Loch at the Back of the World' by Reverend Lauchlan MacLean Watt – are additional stand-outs and hauntingly dark fairy tales, a category that the opener – 'The Milk-White Doo' by Elizabeth W. Grierson would also fall into, incidentally.

To somewhat echo Mains in his Introduction, these types of Celtic myths are indeed ancient, very often beginning, and passed on, through word-of-mouth, but, sadly, also regularly falling out of popularity and being neglected over the decades and centuries. However, with *Celtic Weird*, the editor and The British Library have done a great service in keeping these types of tales alive in the public consciousness of the current and future generations. For this fact alone, I salute them, and as a Gothic/historical anthology of horror and ghost stories in and of itself, it is certainly a very strong one into the bargain.

Celtic Weird: Tales of Wicked Folklore and Dark Mythology is published by The British Library and is available to purchase from Amazon, Waterstones and other outlets.

—**Trevor Kennedy**

PENNIES FROM HEAVEN by James P. Blaylock

ACTIONS HAVE CONSEQUENCES, and often those consequences aren't visited upon those who perform the actions. This is called history. Nations feel the impact of history every day, and families gather over the impact of their own history.

It goes to an even smaller microcosm, affecting individual people.

Jane and Jerry Larkin find this out in *Pennies from Heaven*, by James P. Baylock.

This one is set in California, and boy, is it ever Californian.

Jane and Jerry have moved to the City of Orange, which is in the County of Orange. It's only lacking an orange grove which supplies an orange juice factory.

Jane is the benefactor of a grant that she used to start a Co-op, which is going poorly due to the recent bout of heavy rain. The enormous amount of pressure she has on herself to achieve makes her a highly strung and anxious kind of person. On the opposite end, Jerry is a carefree and calm kind of person.

He knocks about, doing this and that, currently as externally aimless as Jane is focused. What he's mostly concerned about at the beginning of the story is fixing up the house they've moved into.

The house itself is very Californian, too. It's an old Spanish-style home, with a few immigrant Chinese touches. It's that mix of Spanish and Chinese immigrant history which formed the consequences that Jane and Jerry have to deal with.

At the beginning of the story there's an earthquake (California, see?) This causes a crack in an odd brick wall in the basement, in which Jerry finds what he believes is an old coin.

But it isn't an old coin. Lettie Phibbs, local historian and independently wealthy, helps Jerry find out that the "coin" is actually a Chinese funeral charm, buried with the dead. Phibbs is the kind of person that one wouldn't want to interact with unless they had to, being an unpleasant, brisk, haughty, and casually cruel person. Unfortunately for Jane she is one of the people who has to interact with her, as Phibbs is a potential investor in the Co-op, one that could single-handedly keep it from failing.

Phibbs forms a curiosity about the charm, and what it could mean regarding a local legend, developing an ever-growing obsession which consumes her.

Pennies from Heaven is a great example in a revelation of character. We see the characters behave in ways we don't expect, but which are believable given the increasingly bizarre and horrific situations they find themselves in. Who they are as people are revealed through the actions and consequences on a personal level.

In *Pennies from Heaven*, the past rises from the depths and sinks its teeth into the present, in more ways than one. Like a funeral charm gripped between a corpse's teeth.

Pennies from Heaven is published by PS Publishing and is available to purchase from their website and other outlets. For more details please go to: www.pspublishing.co.uk

—**Carl R. Jennings**

THE MAN WITH KALEIDOSCOPE EYES by Tim Lucas

THE AUTHOR'S NOTE at the beginning of *The Man with Kaleidoscope Eyes* states that, while the book is a work of fiction, it ". . . deals with the hallucinogenic drug LSD and the man who dared to make the first dramatic motion picture about this controversial subject." It also says that the book is ". . . a most unusual reading experience."

The author's note is so important because it's a completely factual statement.

The Man with Kaleidoscope Eyes is set in 1960s Hollywood. One of the protagonists, Peter, is the son of the Golden Age movie star, Henry Fonda. Peter was given a script to read, *The Trip*. He was discovered by his wife Susan, lying in the bed, completely focused, as he usually does when he's reading a new script. But this one is different: Peter finished reading it. The reader can see, through Susan's knowledge of her husband, that this one is different.

The Trip concerns the experience of using LSD. It's highly artistic, unconventional, and more like a stream of conscious than a structured framework that gives it a genuineness.

Oh, and one other thing: the script was written by Jack Nicholson. *That* Jack Nicholson, before he was *that* Jack Nicholson.

This leads into what I want to emphasize the most about this book: Lucas, the author, has not only a deep knowledge of the nuts and bolts of Hollywood – he's spent some time "behind the curtain", as it were – but also a strong love for Hollywood as well. It's as much about that is it is LSD.

The story may be fiction based on true elements, but there is such a casual *detail* of what Hollywood *is*: the area, the people, the thoughts, the ideas, and the real and unreal sandwiched together like a PB&J sandwich.

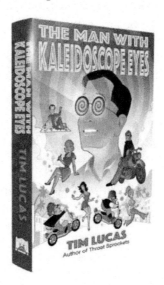

I could summarize in these few paragraphs but it would take something away I have no right to: it's art, more so than many other books I've reviewed. This is something that needs to be experienced. I could warp it into something academic, taking away what is the point, like pulling a Slinky toy out into a straight, flat wire. Sure, the totality is there on display, but is missing the point.

One does need a level of interest in Hollywood's past to get the most out of this book. Not quite to the level of Quentin Tarantino or a YouTube video essayist, but there will be a wasted element if at least a little soft spot for a previous Tinseltown isn't there in the reader. Back before the era of "content" and movies as homogeneous as a Home Owner's Association, when passion had more sway in decision making. Because, in the end, that's what this book is: a passion.

The Man with Kaleidoscope Eyes is published by PS Publishing and is available to purchase from their website and other outlets. For more details please go to: www.pspublishing.co.uk

—Carl R. Jennings

CHILDE ROLANDE by Samantha Lee

WHEN I FIRST reviewed *Childe Rolande* in 1989, talk of gender identity was as rare as literature discussing it and books featuring hermaphroditic central characters were even rarer. Storm Constantine had begun her series of Wraeththu novels in 1987 with *The Enchantments of Flesh and Spirit*, but the androgynous beings in her books were genetically altered and more akin to the "emo" and "goth" characters portrayed on screen and in the musical culture of those times.

Two years later in 1989, Samantha Lee's *Childe Rolande* was published with little fanfare by New English Library in the UK but became a slow burn cult classic amongst fantasy and science fiction critics and devotees.

Described as a "hermaphrodite" and "freak", Childe Rolande is born into the fiercely matriarchal nation of Alba at a time when its fabric is crumbling.

A prophecy says that one day a "Redeemer" will appear who will be "both one and the same", and who will sweep away the age-old tyranny of Alba's female rulers and bind the nation together in peace. Rolande fulfils all those qualifications.

This mystical being holds the wisdom of the ages in its eyes and reputedly transforms into an eagle at will, which is the hope and dream of Alba's downtrodden males.

At the Dark Tower, Rolande must defeat the evil sorceress, Fergael, and unite the polarized kingdom if they are to fulfil their destiny.

The book is written cleverly in the first person so Lee doesn't have to compare the main character to his/her gender. This allows Lee to step out of the political themes of the book and explore Alba, a kingdom ruled by any one part of its population. *Childe Rolande* also draws on poetic influences, particularly on Byron's poem 'Childe Roland to the Dark Tower Came' which has drawn more than one contemporary author to its portentous portals.

Samantha Lee's classic is for all fantasy fans who want to understand human politics – and perhaps, those who maybe questioning their own sexuality – through the freedom of fantasy with enough allusions to play Umberto Eco's game of hunt the reference.

A courageous, compassionate, innovative and intriguing novel when it was first published, it marks a milestone moment in the history of science fiction and fantasy and is today an example of what can be achieved in the genre fiction.

Childe Rolande is published by Parallel Universe Publications and is available to purchase from Amazon and other outlets. For more details please go to: paralleluniversepublications.blogspot.com

—**John Gilbert**

TERROR TALES OF THE WEST COUNTRY
edited by Paul Finch

THE TITLE OF this anthology is one of the most helpful kind: the kind that doesn't waste time in getting into what it's actually about. *Terror Tales from the West Country,* edited by Paul Finch, is half-fiction, half-folklore, all centred on the region in England known as the West Country. See how helpful the title is?

Don't mistake that with frivolous, however. It is a wonderful repository of both local history, ghost stories, and short stories inspired by the region.

'The Horror at Littlecote'

This is a true story, as much as a legend that comes from the 16th century can be true. That is, it goes from historic account, to something hazy, to outright rumour, just like good ghost stories should.

A midwife is whisked away in the night by hooded figures. She is blindfolded and taken to the home of a noble person. We soon see that he is anything but noble, as there is a servant girl in labour. She has the baby with the midwife's help, and the gentleman takes the newborn and tosses it into the burning fire in the hearth. The midwife is deposited back home, guiled by her inadvertent role in the gruesome affair.

As time passed, people began having sightings of spectral beings and experiencing eerie events related to this murky event.

'The Hangman's Pleasure'

I'm featuring another local legend because I'm a sucker for both folklore and the profession of executioners.

As beautiful as the West Country is, it has played host to some of the more notably horrific revolts in English history. The worst of all the uprisings was the Pitchfork Rebellion of 1685. After a disastrous series of battles, the rebels were soundly defeated. Those that didn't die in battle or at the firing squads of the soldiers had to face being hanged, drawn, and quartered.

Such a gruesome event leaves a scar on the collective psyche, which manifests itself in ghost stories. People tell of sounds of soldiers marching prisoners off to execution, a tragically doomed celebration, and ragged figures of wounded men seen in the fog.

'The Woden Jug'

A short story by John Linwood Grant, the narrator is an antiques appraiser. He's quick to point out he doesn't have a life of interest, which is as good as a promise that the events of the story are going to be very interesting indeed. A promise which is fulfilled.

The narrator meets with an Irish mason friend of his for coffee, during which she tells him of a strange event at a tea house she stopped by the day previously. The proprietress was in an uproar about recent events, events which apparently spawned by the opening of a witch-bottle, a superstition from centuries past to ward off curses and misfortune. A superstition that the narrator finds, in this case, is horribly misinformed.

Terror Tales of the West Country is published by Telos Publishing and is available to purchase from their website, Amazon and other outlets. For more information please go to: www.telos.co.uk

—**Carl R. Jennings**

REVELATIONS: HORROR WRITERS FOR CLIMATE ACTION
edited by Seán O'Connor

CONSIDERING THE PERCEIVED worthiness of most climate action initiatives and the general apathy with which they tend to be greeted, anyone would be forgiven for approaching a collection of stories on the subject with some trepidation, weary and wary as many have become to yet another well-intentioned lecture: However, horror isn't the most didactic of genres and there isn't a single green sermon to be found here, just a remarkable gathering of musings from genre writers on what we stand to lose and how we might mourn the loss.

As he explains in his introduction, during the common loss of freedoms we took for granted during the Covid lockdowns, Dublin writer Seán O'Connor assembled this anthology by reaching out to twenty-two of the masters of the field and selecting previously published stories linked to the overarching theme of climate change. In the case of some of these tales, the link isn't immediately apparent, and Sadie Hartmann deserves special mention for her secondary introduction which takes a relevant sentence from each story and weaves a tapestry of unease that is more than the sum of its parts.

Some stories can be bundled thematically; for instance, those by Laird Barron, Richard Chizmar, T.E. Grau, John Langan and Adam L.G. Nevill all have some element of Lovecraftian influence, something that might seem unusual in the context of climate action until one considers that lack of awareness of hidden connections, a failure to perceive the true nature of reality. Meddling with forces best left alone are common causes of catastrophe in Lovecraft and greater powers than our own are, at best, indifferent to our fate, as is terrifyingly displayed in Nevill's 'Call the Name' and Langan's 'Inundation' in particular

From *Soylent Green* to *Interstellar*, movies about climate change tend to focus on the dystopian effects and Paul Tremblay, Sarah Langan, Gemma Amor and Tananarive Due all give us glimpses of societies barely hanging on (literally in the Amor story 'Fields of Ice'!) and scavenging the remnants of ravaged worlds in doomed quests for more than survival. Of these, Due's 'Carriers' – which topically adds drought and an incurable virus as harbingers of the death of trust, community and family ties – feels disturbingly real and uncomfortably familiar.

Ranging from the Flood to the Gaia Earth Mother hypothesis, cautionary fables have been a long-established common means of warning us of the consequences of our misbehaviour towards the planet we live on, as a well-wrought symbol can often carry a message better than a mass of statistics. Clive Barker, Philip Fracassi, Joe Hill, Priya Sharma, Nuzo Onuh and Gwendolyn Kiste give us (respectively) tales of enchanted and enraged woods, beaches, trees, islands and rivers, while Kiste's 'The Maid from the Ashes' is a haunting allegorical reminder that not every phoenix rises.

For anyone who may think the theme of this collection lends itself only to gloom, Laird Barron, Sarah Langan, Joe R. Lansdale and Josh Malerman all manage to find varying degrees of humour in it, even if most is of the gallows variety: The overriding tone, however, is undeniably elegiac, with Tim Lebbon and Sarah Pinborough both contributing reveries of regret, wistful reminiscences of lost promise and dashed hopes.

Two of the acknowledged grandmasters of the field, Ramsey Campbell and Stephen King add their own elegies with 'No Story in It', which, like its title, can be read as a metaphor for quiet calamities and the noble futility of delayed action to protect those you love, and King's masterful 'Summer Thunder', is pure *On the Beach* territory, a meditation on grief for an extinguished future, as the remnants of humanity cling to love and companionship as they painfully await an inexorable extinction.

Seán O'Connor shows great potential as an anthologist and has produced a collection well worth owning, even for those familiar with some of the tales contained herein, and buyers are advised that they are also buying into a better future for the planet, with all proceeds going to Climate Outreach (https://climateoutreach.org).

Revelations: Horror Writers for Climate Action is published by Stygian Sky Media as is available to purchase from Amazon and other outlets.

—**Con Connolly**

MUSIC IN THE BONE AND OTHER STORIES
by Marion Pitman

I FIRST READ Marion Pitman's writing in *The Alchemy Press Book Of Horrors*, which contained her story 'Apple Tree'. I remember enjoying it and when I was asked to review *Music in the Bone*, I returned and re-read it. Her writing is not just one style and she very much writes what she likes, which means you never get the same voice. For me, this is a real treat as I like different. Throughout *Music in the Bone*, her adaptability in storytelling is proficient and robust. I would compare this to *Tales of the Unexpected* – it really has that quality of no story being like any other but each one is enjoyable and stands on its own merits.

The title story of this anthology sets the bar high, in terms of the quality of writing. Lena is a folk musician who regularly attends open mic nights in a club. One night she meets Ed. After being captivated by his music on stage, she can see his talent has not only enchanted her but the rest of the audience too. Lena also feels a physical attraction and one thing leads to another but as much as she is enamoured by his talent, his lovemaking is often rough, like he's testing her somehow. Still, she finds herself going back for more and can't fathom why, when it hurts. Maybe it's the music he plays whilst they have sex, or maybe, there's something more.

Another story that I really feel is worth mentioning is 'Out of Season'. Two sisters, Dorothy and Mabel, are inseparable. They spend their summers together holidaying in Coombe, Devon. As they're such regular faces, they become friends with some of the locals and Mabel gets close to Jack. One night the group tells the girls they can't meet up because they have something to do and Mabel and Dorothy aren't locals, so can't be there. But they see a procession carrying a horse skull, late at night.

Years later and Mabel is terminally ill and asks Dorothy to take her back to Coombe, so she does. This time the procession has become a tourist attraction and as Dorothy watches from the window, she can't believe what she sees.

I liked the pagan influence in this story. Pitman has used the West Country's pagan history to craft her story without it being occult.

'Looking Glass' is a short story about death and lost love and at the end – there's a brilliant twist delivered in one line. What Pitman does here in such few pages, takes skill.

Finally, I recommend you read 'Dead Men's Company'. My favourite story in the collection, not least because it's about pirates.

Lec and Lee have escaped slavery by killing Manero. They've buried his body, taken his money and fled. Lee decides they will use some of the money to buy clothes and stay in a swanky hotel. However, Lee has a bad feeling about it all, not least because he is convinced that Manero will rise from the dead and look for them. But they have bigger problems when the female crew of a ghost ship raid the hotel and they are taken to Captain Swan for her harem.

At the end of this collection, Pitman cites her influences as M.R. James, Arthur Conan Doyle, folk music and old movies. You really get a taste of these influences in her writing. Pitman's homage to these influences is no bad thing, it enhances her writing. After all, shouldn't a writer write what they know?

Music in the Bone and Other Stories is published by The Alchemy Press and is available to purchase from Amazon and other outlets. For more information please go to: alchemypress.wordpress.com

—Helen Scott

SWORDS & SORCERIES: TALES OF HEROIC FANTASY VOLUME 5 presented by David A. Riley and Jim Pitts

FRITZ LEIBER COINED the term "sword and sorcery" in 1961 after British author Michael Moorcock requested a name for the type of fantasy-adventure stories he had written. Originally, Moorcock proposed the term "epic fantasy", but, in early 1961, Leiber replied in the journal *Ancalagon*, suggesting "sword and sorcery" as a good popular catchphrase for the field.

A consensus of literary opinion describes the S&S sub-genre as comprising fast-paced, action-rich, fantasy stories set in quasi-mythical or fantastical worlds. As opposed to high fantasy, sword and sorcery tales tend to be more personal, with danger confined to the moment of telling. Sword and sorcery stories are more often than not set in exotic locales, and protagonists are inclined to be morally compromised.

Whilst sales of high fantasy have soared in recent years, support for sword and sorcery has declined amongst the big publishing corporations and imprints. It has fallen to independent publishers, such as Parallel Universe Publications, to keep it alive with reprints of classics and new tales with anthologies such as the *Swords & Sorceries* series, which contains this very mix. It is, as always, expertly edited by fantasy champion David Riley and illustrated by genre maestro Jim Pitts.

Volume 5 of this series – published towards the end of 2022 – is dedicated to Charles Black who inspired the series, and commences with a fulsome introduction by the editor which introduces the authors and provides background to some of the tales.

The anthology kicks off with a newcomer to the series but a veteran American author, editor and poet, Charles Gramlich, whose works include *Swords of Talera, Wings Over Talera* and *Witch of Talera,* novels inspired by Edgar Rice Burroughs' John Carter of Mars series. His contribution to this anthology, 'The Rotted Land', a fast paced, atmospheric tale, is the third instalment in a series featuring the the legendary warrior Krieg, who this time becomes entangled in a conflict between a witch and a sorceress whilst travelling through a gloomy, reptile-infested swamp.

British SF&F author Harry Elliott, largely known for his military fiction, showcases his prodigious genre-hopping talents with 'Skulls for Silver', featuring Mann and Hel, creature-hunting sell-swords who hitch up with a caravan of travellers with a monstrous, slave trading, secret.

Gustavo Bondoni's 'For the Light' has the feel of ancient Rome, with bloody sport for the glory of the gods and a high stakes chariot race, while 'People of the Lake' by Lorenzo D. Lopez takes us back to the swamps as Morwenna runs from an army of skeletons sent after her by Skeloric, a sorcerer who will conjure anything to make her his bride.

Dutch writer Tais Teng's silkily narrated 'Free Diving for Leviathan Eggs' stands out amongst cut and thrust of most heroic fantasy fare due to its ethereal style. It is more of an Arabian fable – somewhat in the mould of fiction by Ursula Le Guin or Tanith Lee – than a sword swinging action romp and unlike the previous entries in this anthology, it is a first-person narrative. His "heroine" is the third wife of a 300-year-old magician who keeps his spouses young with magic – his first wife is 90 years old and still looks young and voluptuous. Her aunts pity her plight, chained, as they see it, to such a decrepit old man. She is sanguine about the arrangement but when he turns her into a sea creature and uses her to further his own magical ends, she begins to understand the cost of the love she so desperately wants from him.

Dungeons and caves are the focus of the next two, much more traditional S&S stories. 'The Black Well', by Darin Hlavaz, tells the story of an expedition into the gloomy depths of the Well of Oanjuntoo in a quest to recover a sorcerous staff. It is very much a story in the tradition of H. Rider Haggard, a fast-paced adventure with natural and supernatural hazards along the way. 'Degg and the Undead' by Susan Murrie Macdonald, is similarly subterranean, but there the similarities end as Degg is a lone adventurer who incurs the ire of a necromancer when he steals an enchanted sword.

The next two stories have a historical twist to them and again read more like legends than straight S&S. Fantasy mixes with history in David Dubrow's 'The Mistress of the Marsh' when a legion of Roman soldiers, sent to occupy the town of Parma and keep the peace, are suddenly afflicted with a deadly illness that turns man against man and which may have been inflicted by the Thucers, a mysterious tribe of swamp people.

'Silver and Gold', by Earl W. Parrish, begins on a Roman road where Pierre, a Holy Knight, rescues Jeannette, a woman, impaled by an arrow and hanging from a tree, who is about to be burned alive. As they journey on together, and she refuses to leave his side, he begins to wonder whether she was ever truly a maiden in distress.

'Bridge of Sorrows', by Dev Agarwal, is part three of the legend of Lord Commander Simeon, also called the Stone Snake – the first two tales, 'Stone Snake' and 'The Iron Woods' having been included in earlier volumes of the anthology series. Accompanied by Princess Irene, and guided by ben Kim as they journey towards The Bridge of Sorrows, they are not prepared for another confrontation with Silver Mask and the evil brood of Dagonists – yes, a nod towards Lovecraft's Mythos – awaiting them there.

No contemporary sword and sorcery anthology would be complete without an entry by "Dream Lords" and "Star Requiem" author Adrian Cole. In the final entry in this anthology, Adrian takes us to the world of Elak of Atlantis, originally the creation of American pulp author Henry Kuttner, with 'Prisoners of Devil Dog City'. King Elak has unified the Atlantean continent and his people are enjoying a time of prosperity and peace. And yet, in this tale set at sea and wrought with supernatural dangers, the gods and monsters will continue to have their battles.

Of the eleven tales laid out in this fifth volume of *Swords & Sorceries*, those that stand from the pack are the ones that exhibit a freshness, style and sophistication all of their own. They are 'Free Diving for Leviathan Eggs', which bears the form of a silkily written fable, 'Silver and Gold', which defies the more traditional, Conan-esque, tropes of the sword and sorcery sub-genre, and the gripping 'Prisoners of Devil Dog City', which demonstrates the versatility of a true master of the fantasy/SF genre. That said, each story in the anthology earns its inclusion and stretches the boundaries of what would normally be considered under the banner of sword and sorcery. This volume may be the fifth instalment of this anthology series but it ably demonstrates that the sub-genre continues to survive and to draw a lively audience.

Swords & Sorceries: Tales of Heroic Fantasy Volume 5 is published by Parallel Universe Publications and is available to purchase from Amazon and other outlets. For more details please go to:
paralleluniversepublications.blogspot.com

—**John Gilbert**

CASTING THE RUNES: THE LETTERS OF M.R. JAMES
edited by Jane Mainley-Piddock

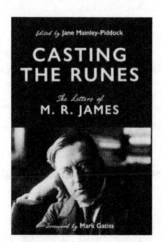

ANYONE EXPECTING THESE letters to be in any way similar to those of H.P. Lovecraft or the recent Hippocampus collection of Clark Ashton Smith's correspondence with August Derleth, in which, besides discussing subjects of particular interest to the writers, they write about their stories, may be disappointed that there is no mention within any of James' letters about his ghost stories.

But, I hasten to add, don't let this put you off, as they are an illuminating glimpse into the everyday life of the author, particularly helped by the notes added after every letter by Jane Mainley-Piddock, which, if anything, are even more interesting than the letters themselves, adding many much-needed background details and facts.

The letters are an easy read, usually written in a chatty, laid-back style. They start with his earliest letters in 1873 and go on to 1927, when he was Provost of Eton.

One of the longest notes goes on to discuss James' fascination with Charles Dickens' final, uncompleted novel, *The Mystery of Edwin Drood*, and his attempts to find a solution to it, as well as his fondness for detective stories, in particular Conan Doyle's, which had an influence on the structure of his own ghost stories. Jane Mainley-Piddock's notes, in fact, are worth the price of the book in themselves, with great insights into James and his stories.

Contrary to what I expected, I read the entire volume of over 200 pages within just a few days and was never bored. Definitely something for anyone who loves the ghost stories of M.R. James and would like to read more by and about him.

It comes with a foreword by James enthusiast Mark Gatiss, and an introduction by the editor.

Casting the Runes: The Letters of M.R. James is published by Unbound and is available to purchase from Amazon and other outlets.

—David A. Riley

MISERY AND OTHER LINES by C.C. Adams

C.C. ADAMS, A LONDON native and horror/dark fiction author, is the creator of such pieces as *But Worse Will Come, Forfeit Tissue* and *Downwind, Alice*. *Misery and Other Lines*, published by Sinister Horror Company, is a cleverly written collection of short stories with a charming foreword by Kit Power and a brilliant cover by the author and J.R. Park. Adams can be found at www.ccadams.com or on Twitter as @Mr.AdamsWrites.

First of all, Adams is an extremely talented writer, with a true gift when it comes to the macabre. In *Misery and Other Lines*, one finds themselves injected deep into the veins of the London capital's Underground. Here interwoven stories transpire as the reader walks shoulder-to-shoulder with people masquerading as both monsters and men. Part of Adams' magnetism is the way he expertly depicts details, ones that magnify normalcy while revealing a deeper complexity linked to fear as certain masks begin to slip.

Halloween night is thirsty and the dot matrix is pulsating with final destinations. The collection unfolds with 'Someone is Late', the story of a man named Samuel who is no stranger to the unspoken rules of the rails. Adams incorporates interesting facts about the lines, introducing history into the present. As for myself, one who has never had the opportunity to experience this form of transportation, I was completely captivated by the world beneath. It felt as if I were experiencing these sights first hand and it awakened my curiosity. Adams' writes not to his audience, but allows them inside his mind to absorb every sensation.

As we follow Samuel in his attempt to reach his date Hanadi, one soon takes notice that something is amiss in this land of ups and downs. Did he read that clock correctly, how is it suddenly the middle of the night, and where did all the other passengers disappear to? Adams' constructs a Twilight Zone in which motion is the only thing perpetual – unless one counts the terror that follows.

This collection is flawless, each story building upon the next until it reaches that final exit. From cannibalism, to beings that buzz and beg, a traveler must always take caution when locking gazes with that of a stranger. Especially those who carry carved smiles.

Life on the lines tends to take on different morals, as seen in the story 'Uneasy Prey'. Charlie soon learns that hunger has its own rulebook – you either ride or you rot.

There are so many pieces within this work that deserve praise, but my personal favorite was 'Dancers Like Nishka'. Adams' tempts his audience through clever persuasion and hypnotic dialogue. Nishka, an exotic dancer at The Who Zoo is truly someone that all readers must experience at least once in their lives. Darkness at its delicious pulse.

Misery and Other Lines is beautifully constructed with an ending just as compelling as the writing within. From its title, to the author's distinct voice and knowledge of the London Tube, this collection has it all. C.C. Adams has quickly become one of my absolute favorites.

Misery and Other Lines is published by Sinister Horror Company and is available to purchase from Amazon and other outlets.

—**Jessica Stevens**

THE RESURRECTION CHILDREN by Frank Duffy

THE RESURRECTION CHILDREN is the first of Frank Duffy's books I have read. With a front cover that displays the art of Roberto Segate and the skills of Adrian Baldwin, it certainly draws you to pick up this book and read it.

Duffy sets the scene by taking us to a dark place, centuries ago. A child, Malvern, is running through the woods, pursued by men. She flees to the sea but can't escape the zealots because she is trapped on the edge of a cliff.

Fast-forward to 1975 and Bron, a young girl, is the fatal victim of a tragic accident when a dune collapses.

Accelerate again to the present, the home of James and Myra Constable. A book launch party for James' latest novel and an evening of frayed edges hidden behind smiles. Not least because their son Ethan is at another party in the pursuit of drugs and their daughter Katie leaves somewhat spontaneously.

But when Katie goes missing, this dysfunctional family must join together to find her. Ethan must face his own demons along the way and a girl in a purple dress affects them all in leading the way to Katie.

Duffy's story is set in snowy Liverpool at Christmastime, a time when it's joy to the world. However, the tragedy the Constables experience and the truths they learn about each other along the way are the antithesis of joy. In fact, Duffy skilfully uses Ethan's drug dependency to show his reader that hope comes in many forms and not always what we expect. Duffy bounces his characters off of each other with dialogue and this creates palpable tension for his reader. You, the reader, can see every flaw of every character but also why they are the way they are. By using alcohol, drugs and adultery as transgressions for his characters, Duffy builds believable people that you can understand, if not always sympathise with.

In addition, the way the story plays out to the final denouement and joins the threads of Malvern, Bron and the Constables together is well executed.

There was definitely an "a-ha" moment as the storylines come together, which is difficult to do. Duffy has produced a fine piece of writing, that I enjoyed and would recommend.

The Resurrection Children is Frank Duffy's third publication with Demain, who, as a side note, have quite the bibliography of talented writers. He has also written *Distant Frequencies* and co-authored *Night Voices* with Paul Edwards. Duffy also has a Facebook author page and some content on YouTube. Go check it out.

The Resurrection Children is published by Demain Publishing as is available to purchase from Amazon.

—**Helen Scott**

A BLACKNESS ABSOLUTE: A COLLECTION OF SHORT HORROR by Caitlin Marceau

CAITLIN MARCEAU IS a Canadian author and editor. She holds a B.A. in Creative Writing and is an active member of the Horror Writers Association. Her works include *Palimpsest*, *This is Where We Talk Things Out*, and *Femina: A Collection of Dark Fiction,* to name a few.

A Blackness Absolute is a stunning collection of short horror published by Ghost Orchid Press with cover design and illustration by the creator herself.

Marceau's writing is a house forever haunted, walls papered in the stories that ghosts leave behind. I cannot praise this collection enough or her distinctive ability to satisfy through both curiosity and fear. *A Blackness Absolute* accomplishes just that.

The collection opens with 'Zoey', a reluctant girlfriend who finds herself buried beneath a town long since abandoned. Despite her trepidation, Liam is determined to retrace his father's youth deep into the belly of the mine, a world in which even light cannot travel. Marceau builds up the tension, then unleashes every horror. Beautifully written and gripping to the very end.

'Sarah' is the story of a deformed girl who struggles within the shadow of her abusive religious father. Vanity is a sin, or at least that is the message she has always been taught. When Sarah requests a small birthday party in order to help her image at school, she discovers that the truth of beauty is far uglier than the reflection it once cast. An absolute favourite of mine.

'The Broomsay' is another powerful story with a classic horror feel. Edgar hadn't planned on returning to Foulness Island but there are some things you can't leave behind no matter how hard you try. A cautionary tale, one that generates both sympathy and bloodlust. Marceau at her best.

'The Blue' is the tale of a mysterious copper mermaid that sits upon a pillar in the middle of Lake Tulrid. A statue that never tarnishes despite the rising blue that surrounds her. Reid, haunted by her irresistible pull, finds himself on the fringes of obsession, a craftsmanship just begging to be touched.

Marceau's strength lies in her skill to weave stories that blend effortlessly, yet each remains a masterpiece within its own right. Caitlin Marceau is a true talent with ink in her bones. *A Blackness Absolute* is a genuine testament to the versatility of horror.

A Blackness Absolute: A Collection of Short Horror is published by Ghost Orchid Press and is available to purchase from Amazon and other outlets.

—Jessica Stevens

THE SWARM by Seán O'Connor

SEÁN O'CONNOR IS a contributor to *Phantasmagoria* and the editor of the anthology *Revelations: Horror Writers for Climate Action* (Stygian Sky Media), which contains a host of big genre names, with proceeds going to Climate Outreach. He is also the author of the novels *The Mongrel, Weeping Season* and *The Blackening*, as well as the short story collection *Keening Country* (all available via Idolum Publishing).

This novella is certainly dark and, if the basic set up of a widowed father trying to protect his young son in a hostile and frightening post-apocalypse world brings Cormac McCarthy to mind, this is hardly coincidental, as the author of *The Road* is cited as one of O'Connor's personal favourites on Goodreads. Unlike that book, however, we are given a very plausible and cautionary explanation of the causes that have led to civilisation falling apart and the reasons why the handful of surviving humans need to shelter indoors in silence when darkness falls. While the implacable threat of the Reavers is reminiscent of *Pitch Black*, this world has no equivalent of a heroic night-sighted Riddick and only luck, intelligence and determination can keep Daniel and his son Remy alive, even while he considers the possibility that his efforts are doomed to merely postpone the inevitable.

The story opens in the aftermath of a plane crash in the Arctic, with the injured father and his son the sole survivors and with descriptions of the harsh and frozen landscape and the privations it visits upon both of them reminiscent of the environmental endurance horror tales of John Langan or Adam Nevill, authors cited by O'Connor in interviews and, like Nevill's *The Ritual*, the reader senses from the start that this will be no heart-warming tale of man's triumph over nature. The threat posed by a polar bear to the pair's access to the meagre fishing opportunities is countered only by summoning an even worse menace and Daniel's discovery of a badly injured woman, Matilda, only increases his desperation at the insurmountable odds the party face in trying to reach the scientist's outpost where, she insists, they will find sanctuary and aid.

When they eventually reach the outpost, the presence of a military unit, food and home comforts feels reassuring but, as anyone who has seen *28 Days Later* will know, army discipline can be fragile in the face of the apocalypse and, to quote Alfred Henry Lewis's dictum, "there are only nine meals between mankind and anarchy", and the base's supplies are nearly exhausted and no one seems willing to tell Matilda what has become of her scientist husband.

To give away any more would spoil what is a taut but graphic read, as O'Connor expertly reveals just how dark the remaining days of the remainder of humanity will become. Experience and knowledge prove inadequate in the face of an implacable threat and dwindling resources, while endurance soon reaches breaking point and actions unthinkable to the civilised mind are embraced by the brute will to survive.

There are no heroes or villains in O'Connor's tale, just those who suffer in order to survive and those who perish; dreadful circumstances lead to dreadful choices and the question of whether preserving one's life at the cost of one's humanity is ever valid looms large over the narrative.

There is a sense of shock and loss that persists throughout this story that elevates it from the typical survivalist fantasy and, while nothing can compare to the existentialist angst of McCarthy's aforementioned *The Road*, it struck me that the ending here is similarly ambiguous, either a paeon to the persistence of hope in the face of desperation or a naïve longing for a *deus ex machina* from a machine broken beyond repair.

The Swarm is published by Idolum Publishing and is available to purchase from Amazon and other outlets.

—**Con Connolly**

A HANDFUL OF ZOMBIES: TALES OF THE RESTLESS DEAD (CHAPBOOK NO. 1) by David A. Riley

IF HORROR STORIES of the zombie variety are your thing – and it's pretty obvious that David A. Riley rather enjoys them, too – then I would imagine that you would quite like this neat little near-60-page chapbook from the author, containing reprints of four of his undead tales, each one a different take on the sub-genre, and each with their own merits, the illustrations contained by regular collaborator and friend of Riley's, Jim Pitts.

The opening tale, 'Dead Ronnie and I', possibly my favourite of the four, sees two men attempt to escape the ensuing madness of the apocalypse in the UK by plane, but things naturally don't go as planned.

'His Pale Blue Eyes' sees a young girl attempt to locate her parents and survive the wasteland, while 'Right For You Now' is a gritty one set in Britain and which also features Haitian voodoo practices.

The chapbook is wrapped up with 'Romero's Children', an obvious allusion to zombie maestro George (and which is also reprinted in the pages of this current issue of *Phantasmagoria*, by the way). It's an interesting one which sees the populace infected by the "OM" virus, as opposed to the traditional zombie fare.

The zombie sub-genre on film has seen something of a strong resurgence in the twenty-first century, from Danny Boyle's *28 Days Later* though to several varying-in-quality Romero remakes, the *Resident Evil* series, and *The Walking Dead*, however in terms of literature I don't believe it is a field that has ever really left us. David A. Riley is one of those authors who, it appears, is certainly attempting to ensure that it continues to stay around for a while to come.

A Handful of Zombies: Tales of the Restless Dead (Chapbook No. 1) is published by Parallel Universe Publications and is available to purchase from Amazon and other outlets. For more details please go to: paralleluniversepublications.blogspot.com

—**Trevor Kennedy**

LIVE PERFORMANCE

GARTH MARENGHI'S TERRORTOME: BOOK TOUR
(The Auditorium Liverpool at M&S Bank Arena
performance, 17th February, 2023)

The stage is set for Garth Marenghi's TerrorTome,
The Auditorium Liverpool at M&S Bank Arena, 17th February, 2023

Starring Matthew Holness.

Garth Marenghi's TerrorTome; *or* The Liver Birds *vs.* Bread

STANDING IN THE queue to see Garth Marenghi, I saw a sign that clearly stated: *If you have anything metal in your pockets, please put it in the tray before you pass through the security scan . . .* So, I placed my wallet – which had my front door key in the zipper – on the tray. Instead of the security man inquiring why I'd placed it there, he made a crap attempt at comedy; about trying to bribe him with money. However, I decided to let it go, as it was my first time out in over three years – so, I wasn't feeling at my most confident; and because if I'd pulled him up on it, the people behind would have been held up and there were only ten minutes or so for everyone to get to their seats. But, of course, I regret it now, because when Trevor and I were sat in our seats, a good half of the audience didn't stumble in until a good ten minutes or more after the curtain up time. (Typical Liverpool; that sort of slack time-keeping just wouldn't be allowed to happen in the West End.) So, there would have been time after all to tounge-lash the Scouse prat.

When I said they "stumbled in", I wasn't kidding. Piss-coloured beer in crappy plastic cups was the mass choice beverage of the night. So, it didn't come as much of a surprise when a fight broke out amongst a loud-mouthed, pissed-out-of-her-brains young "lady" and several only slightly better behaved members of the audience. It was like Carla Lane's *Liver Birds* versus the Boswell family. I thank the Lord, that when I was a wee nipper, my family moved down south to Bracknell, Berkshire – to Home Counties Horror and day excursions to the London Dungeon and Tower of London. I prefer my open-mouthed, toothless hags, and small-brained, rude security men to be made of wax, or wearing a silly daft yeoman uniform. The beating of raven wings, please, and the creepy winking of dummies, not the flappin' 'n' cacklin' 'n' burpin' of a mass group of Carla Lane comedy extras.

So, where did that leave Trevor and I? Well, not sitting too comfortably, to be honest with you. But at least we had Matthew Holness as Garth Marenghi to look forward to. He'd be great, right? Well, yeah, that's what we thought. But, on the whole, we were wrong. The first part of his talk was unoriginal and overly silly.

The second part – the Q&A section – was better; genuinely funny as Matt/Garth riffed his way through the surprisingly adroit queries. Things were looking up; but then Holness let us and himself down by only letting it be known he wasn't going to be doing the signing *after* he'd sold as many copies of the book as possible in the lobby. An accidentally, but oh-so-done-on-purpose, cynical cash grab manoeuvre worthy of any *Darkplace* or *TerrorTome*.

As for Trevor and I . . . We partied until dawn in Room 237 of The Adelphi Hotel. The dead old wrinkly gal in the bathtub is a right good laugh when you get to know her over a Diet Coke or two. Tony is an idiot, though. Sadly, Matthew Holness is, too.

—Marc Damian Lawler

Illustration by Jonny Boyle

FILM

The End is nigh! Promotional image for Knock at the Cabin *(2023)*

KNOCK AT THE CABIN (2023)

Directed by M. Night Shyamalan.

Written by M. Night Shyamalan, Steve Desmond, Michael Sherman and Paul Tremblay (based on his novel The Cabin at the End of the World).

Starring Dave Bautista, Jonathan Groff, Rupert Grint, Nikki Amuka-Bird, Ben Aldridge, Abby Quinn and more.

Mild spoilers ahead . . .

IT'S THE END of the world as we know it in this latest M. Night Shyamalan supernatural thriller, this time based on a novel by Paul Tremblay.

Andrew and Eric are a gay couple who, along with their seven-year-old daughter Wen, are enjoying a relaxing break away in a remote cabin in the woods (even mild fans of horror/supernatural shenanigans will immediately know that this choice of locale never ends well!). When out collecting grasshoppers in the surrounding woods, Wen is approached by a hulking, intimidating, apparently conflicted man named Leonard with unknown intentions.

After Wen flees to the safety of the cabin, Leonard soon arrives at the front door with three companions – Redmond, Sabrina and Adriane – who demand to be let in as they have information of the utmost importance to relay to the family – *so* important, in fact, that it will be the difference between Armageddon either happening or not. When these Four Horsemen (and women) of the Apocalypse force their way into the holiday home, Andrew and Eric find themselves with an impossible decision to make.

To begin with, it was nice to see a film where the trailers have not revealed the best parts, as so many seem to sadly do these days, however, perhaps the ones that were released have been a little *too* sparse, not really enticing or selling it that well, therefore resulting in – again, for a modern day change – the final product actually being a lot better than what was expected.

Shyamalan has had his critics over the years, ever since his arrival proper in 1999 with the very well received *The Sixth Sense*, although many of us have also always had a soft spot for his generally enjoyable, *Twilight Zone*-esque brand of storytelling (as a side note, the writer/director would most surely have been a more ideal candidate to helm the recent reboot of the above classic series, as opposed to the one we did get with Jordan Peele). *Knock at the Cabin* also bears a few similarities to the Shyamalan-produced and written *Devil* from 2010.

From a technical point of view, Shyamalan is an accomplished film-maker who knows what he is doing when behind a camera, certainly in terms of building tension and pacing, but what really saves *Knock at the Cabin* (which at times can feel a little padded, predictable [no trademark Shyamalan twist this time sadly!], and lightweight and unoriginal as an overall concept) is the strong performances by the cast who really do sell the dilemma they find themselves in. Particularly impressive are Jonathan Groff and Ben Aldridge as the couple, and former wrestler-turned-actor Dave Bautista who conveys well the conflicted emotions of Leonard – a caring, good man at heart who is forced to commit terrible acts.

Despite some flaws, *Knock at the Cabin* is a pretty entertaining hour and forty minutes which results in quite an emotional ending, albeit one that hardly came as a shock. Worth recommending, for sure, but just don't go into it expecting anything too daring or original.

—**Trevor Kennedy and Leanne Azzabi**

AVATAR: THE WAY OF WATER (2022)

Directed by James Cameron.

Written by James Cameron, Rick Jaffa, Amanda Silver, Josh Friedman and Shane Salerno.

Starring Sam Worthington, Zoe Saldana, Sigourney Weaver, Stephen Lang, Kate Winslet, Cliff Curtis and more.

IT FEELS LIKE a millennia since I watched the first in the *Avatar* series – realistically only fourteen years ago. Only! I remember being blown away by the CGI and special effects upon viewing the 2009 flick.

In going to see its successor recently, there was the good Christmas vibe – pre-excitement and cinematic atmosphere – but it was the three-hour slog that would put me off going back to Pandora.

Avatar: The Way of Water: *The Smurfs, all grown up*

I always go into a film with a balanced mindset – always. I stick my fingers in my ears and resist the contrasting banter between my friends as we enter the cinema.

Let's not forget either . . . it is the first film to be created and shot solely in 3D for its entirety and well, take it or leave it but the effects of 3D are *still* to be marvelled at these days – they ultimately give the viewer that closer proximity to the characters' world. On viewing it, Pandora seemed more alive compared to the first movie, filled with visually stunning landscapes throughout, both under and above water this time.

I really enjoyed the ocean and aquatic scenes, and you can also see Cameron's affinity for the water almost immediately in this film – a lot of his previous work has carried through here, with the likes of *Titanic* and *The Abyss*, not just visually but I also drew comparisons with the musical score and sound effects of the machinery and transportation utilised throughout the film.

Now the plot itself is not much different from the first. It's another revenge story, largely, this time with Jake Sulley (a paralysed marine) protecting his Na'vi family against his former race who are (surprise, surprise) greedily chasing a life-changing product that halts human maturity – on this occasion, it's a golden chemical goo called Amrita, produced by the Tulkun, a hyper-intelligent species of whale with telepathic capabilities. The antagonist of the first film makes his reprise (Colonel Miles Quaritch, the leader of the human military force on Pandora) and ultimately he wants Sulley's non-avatar blood.

I feel there are some pitfalls across the dialogue at times. You would hear a plethora of instances of the Sulley children addressing each other with "bro" and "dude" which on reflection, would be odd in a tribal world such as Pandora. Yes, on planet Earth, in our 21st century (or even in Bill and Ted's realm!) it sounds purely natural among young folk, however it does not quite fit the premise for the traditions and ways of an alien planet population . . . Totally, *not*!

This film is a great watch if you are a massive fan of the original. The 3D is faultless, nevertheless, it *is* solely down to the special glasses that make the magic happen for this drawn-out sequel. In a nutshell, *Avatar: The Way of Water* is a low-brow plot which is shrouded in the pizzazz and glamour of a high-brow sci-fi movie. But do view it for yourself, of course.

—Allison Weir

PEARL (2022)

Axe marks the spot: Mia Goth takes on the title role in Pearl *(2022)*

Directed by Ti West.

Written by Ti West and Mia Goth.

Starring Mia Goth, David Corenswet, Tandi Wright, Matthew Sunderland, Emma Jenkins-Purro, Alistair Sewell and more.

IN THE LAST regular issue, I wrote a review for a new slasher film from director Ti West called *X*. That film has characters you really enjoyed meeting and getting to know, despite how naive they all are while making a porno. The villain especially was a violent psychopath, but we were given flashes of helplessness from her at the same time, her name being Pearl.

Pearl is the title character in *X*'s prequel. Fans are placed into the world of Pearl and see what makes her become the evil woman we got to know in *X*. Pearl is hell-bent on killing anything that corrupts her environment and is played by Mia Goth who gives a pretty chilling performance, I have to say. She plays vulnerable and evil quite well and certainly adds a certain charm to the merciless killer.

However, that's it. The film on all other aspects falls flat. It's boring, boring – did I mention boring? We are supposed to feel for Pearl throughout the film as she transitions into the monster we know. However, it just falls flat, and her performance is wasted with nothing but unnecessarily long shots and scenes that should have been cut and/or edited down, giving it a David Lynch-type of filming. Sorry, that's not a compliment. Less is more.

Unlike the first film, this has no real fun or cringe-worthy moments that we can all chat about when it is over. The characters are few and far between and when they are on the screen they are unlikeable, besides a few, and they are peppered in just for the body count. There are some family moments that really could have worked, but the director felt it necessary to walk away from those moments of potential chaos and focus on the outside characters.

Home is where the heart is and that should have been the film's main focus. It offers up some good scares and does have some fun with misdirections that come from those family moments but they are lost by the time we get to them and I had sadly already checked out by then.

Pearl has had quite a few welcoming reviews and maybe I am missing something and the series is now going to be a trilogy with *XXX* upcoming, a sequel to the first film. Perhaps it will go back to what worked for the original. *Pearl* tries too hard to be smarter than the original and maybe it is, however, smarter is not necessarily better for a slasher film, especially when *X* was such a pleasant surprise and a wonderful homage to those films we all grew up with, loved and still love today. This just felt like an episode of *Little House on the Prairie* meets Lizzie Borden.

Shame.

—Ciaran Woods

CHRISTMAS BLOODY CHRISTMAS (2022)

Riley Dandy does battle with a robotic Santa in
Christmas Bloody Christmas *(2022)*

Directed by Joe Begos.

Written by Joe Begos.

Starring Riley Dandy, Sam Delich, Jonah Ray, Dora Madison, Jeff Daniel Phillips, Abraham Benrubi and more.

BY MY RECKONING there are around 700 "fucks" – the word – in *Christmas Bloody Christmas*, or one roughly every seven seconds on average. At first it's annoying (who are they trying to impress? you wonder) but after a while the pouring-forth of expletives comes to have its own demented charm, like much else in this merrily daft antidote to seasonal mushiness.

The scene is a small town somewhere in the USA, or maybe a parallel universe where Tinder and video cassettes coexist. It is Christmas Eve, and the film opens on a series of numbingly mundane TV ads promoting Santa live in concert, festive cannabis edibles, a show called *Killed at Christmas* . . . and the new RoboSanta, now available at the town's T.W. Bonkers toy store.

This robotic Saint Nick is based on re-purposed defence technology which "fully replaces your local degenerate mall Santa". We don't meet RoboSanta just yet, though; first there's a lengthy flirtation between local record store owner Tori (Riley Dandy) and her employee Robbie (Sam Delich), after which they head off from a bar to the toy store. Meanwhile a TV newscast reporting that the RoboSantas are being withdrawn, because some have started reverting to their old military programming, goes unnoticed.

Needless to add, though, the RoboSanta at T.W. Bonkers is soon on the move, and the visit he pays to a local family is not to deliver presents. Nor is the cop (Elliott Gilbert) at the scene of slaughter, who shoots RoboSanta and confidently pronounces "he's not getting up", going to last much longer.

Yes, everything plays out exactly as you'd expect, because there's nothing like tradition at this special time of year; this Santa may look like the Terminator but he's a slasher at heart, and indeed *Christmas Bloody Christmas* supposedly has its origins in a project to remake *Silent Night, Deadly Night* (1984). His first victims are a couple having sex, and Tori will of course be the Final Girl after guns, taser and sword all fail to shut down the robot.

The story itself is intentionally dumb and predictable, then, and doesn't bear very close examination (RoboSanta initially seems implausibly programmed for indiscriminate slaughter but then turns to specifically hunting Tori). And *Christmas Bloody Christmas* does also suffer from a rather pedestrian ending – you might have been expecting some spectacular ingenuity, or an ironic twist, but instead it just *stops*.

Still, there is an engaging energy and sarcastic humour to much of the film, particularly in the scenes between Robbie and Tori, both of them amusingly and convincingly acted. Their long repartee gets in a dig at Blumhouse, much discussion of Motörhead and other music, and a commentary on the virtues of *Book of Shadows: Blair Witch 2* (2000), known here as *Book of Motherfucking Shadows*.

Abraham Benrubi is a chillingly expressionless RoboSanta, Jeff Daniel Phillips contributes good support as a local sheriff, and Steve Moore's electronic score helps to provide some real tension at times. Director Joe Begos and cinematographer Brian Sowell also manage to give this low-budget outing a distinctive visual flavour by shooting in 16mm and heavily emphasising the Christmas colours of green and red, both within the action (Santa's mouth and later his eyes flash green, Tori's bloodied face is red) and more impressionistically (the police station washroom is bathed in green, for example).

The word of mouth for seasonal silliness last Christmas was favouring *Violent Night*. But for those who prefer to get their festive dose of ill-will toward all men via streaming, this much lower-budget exercise is one for the shortlist.

The concept may not sustain the two sequels Begos reportedly has in mind, but the big joke of the premise is nicely balanced by some droll smaller-scale humour, the two central performances are strong, and the writer-director keeps things moving along well. It's fun while it lasts.

—Barnaby Page

TELEVISION

STAR TREK: PICARD (season 3, episodes 1 and 2)

Patrick Stewart, Jonathan Frakes and Jeri Ryan in Star Trek: Picard *season 3*

Showrunners: Terry Matalas, Akiva Goldsman, Michael Chabon, Kirsten Beyer and Alex Kurtzman (series based on Star Trek: The Next Generation *created by Gene Roddenberry).*

Starring: Patrick Stewart, Jeri Ryan, Michelle Hurd, Jonathan Frakes, Gates McFadden, Ed Speleers and more.

IT'S FAIR TO say that the first two seasons of *Star Trek: Picard* sent the titular character boldly going where no classic Trek had gone before: maximum warp up the slipstream of new Trek's weepy, foul-mouthed, corruption-laced Starfleet, akin to the divisive Kelvin timeline. And while both seasons fared well with critics, many fans were a little less enthused.

For season 3, *Picard* and *Star Trek: Discovery* showrunner Alex Kurtzman has handed the bridge to *Star Trek: Voyager/Enterprise* veteran, Terry Matalas. So, does this change of helm fundamentally alter the show, and is it any good now?

The answers are: Instantly and yes.

First and foremost, this does not feel like *Star Trek: Picard* season 3, this feels like "Star Trek: The Next Generation – The Motion Picture", with influences from *The Wrath of Khan*, *The Search for Spock* and, cautiously, *Nemesis* sprinkled throughout. This is evident during a rousing orbital spacedock sequence, brought to life by a soaring score reminiscent of James

Horner's iconic *Star Trek* themes. Not only does this feel cinematic in scope for *Picard*; it feels epic for a sci-fi TV series in general, deserving a decent home cinema to truly enhance the moment.

What's it about? After fending off a hostile alien attack, Beverly Crusher sends an encrypted distress call to Jean-Luc Picard, advising him to trust no one. This brings us to the first of many surprises. Gone is the weepy, apologetic Picard from before. In his place stands the reserved, fortified and commanding version of Jean-Luc Picard from *The Next Generation* series, albeit older and more reflective. This is evident when he meets former First Officer William Riker and they share a respectable quip rather than a tearful embrace. It should be noted that Jonathan Frakes's Riker is a return to form, too, oozing warmth, trust and a boldness that solidifies his place beside Picard. Here, the duo plot to locate Crusher by boarding Riker's former starship, the USS Titan-A, under the pretence of an inspection. Their plans, however, hit a snag when the ship's hard-nosed Captain Shaw sees beyond their legendary status and denies their request. Amidst it all, Amanda Plummer delivers a delightful, if theatrical, villainous turn. Meanwhile, Raffi, now an intelligence agent, investigates a tip-off that soon escalates into a terrifying spectacle.

Overall, the first two episodes of season 3 offer a glimpse into a self-respecting, mature sci-fi adventure ahead. Sure, the lights are still dim, the odd naughty word slips out, and it's another overarching story, but it's a clear course-correction that effectively shifts the tone of the first two seasons. Most of the former *Picard* cast have been ditched, which rumour suggests is for the entirety of the season, replaced by *The Next Generation* crew. In fact, you can go into season 3 like a blind four-year-old Geordi La Forge and still miss nothing. It's a strong opening reboot that promises to give *TGN* crew the send off that *Star Trek: Nemesis* never could. Set phasers to stun. 4/5

—**Phil Young**

CHAPELWAITE (season 1)

Developed for television by Jason Filardi and Peter Filardi, based on the short story 'Jerusalem's Lot' by Stephen King.

Starring Adrien Brody, Emily Hampshire, Jennifer Ens, Sirena Gulamgaus, Ian Ho, Hugh Thompson and more.

IN THIS AGE of multi-platform streaming services and a seemingly never-ending barrage of horror, fantasy and science fiction content, you would think we would be spoilt for choice with our entertainment these days, but alas, what we are *actually* given instead, for the most part anyway it appears, is mere quantity over quality. There is some real quality out there, for sure, but we really do have to go searching for it. It therefore gives me great pleasure to report that the recent 10-part series *Chapelwaite* is one of those quality shows that may very well have slipped under many people's radars.

Based on the superb short by Stephen King, the story is set in 1850s Maine and sees widower and former whaler Charles Boone and his three children inherit the family home of the title from his cousin Stephen, believed dead in tragic circumstances along with his daughter, Marcella, and father, Phillip. When Charles and his family arrive in Chapelwaite they begin hearing what they believe to be rats in the walls of the house and they are soon shunned and abused by the residents of the nearby town, Preacher's Corner, who despise the Boone family name and hold Stephen and Phillip responsible for a strange sickness that has swept through the area. Charles maintains his innocence and attempts to disassociate himself from his dead relatives by bringing work to Preacher's Corner, but when people begin to go missing he finds himself questioning his own sanity and facing up to his family curse, a forbidden book, and a dark secret residing in the neighbouring town of Jerusalem's Lot.

Adrien Brody in Chapelwaite, *a series to really sink your teeth into*

I have to be honest here and state that the first couple of episodes of *Chapelwaite* irritated me slightly – it's a slow burn and contains some modern TV and film tropes which always bug me, such as people in historically-set dramas speaking like they've just time-travelled there from the twenty-first century. It's not actually particularly "woke" though and, in reality, Charles' half-Asian children would have probably received much worse racial abuse than they do here, but I just found myself struggling to become invested in it. However, once it gets into its stride and the Gothic horror starts to kick in properly, it really is of an extremely high standard and some of the best Lovecraftian/Poe-esque horror drama I have seen on screen for quite some time – dark, grim, foreboding and bloody excellent! Episode 9 is a particular stand-out with considerable pay-off and set-up for the finale, although the final episode does have its issues, in that everything seems to be resolved too quickly, it feels like more of an epilogue, and contains some pretty illogical factors, given what has come before. It is a *very* emotional ending, to be fair, and a rather bitter-sweet one for some of the main characters.

Chapelwaite is finely produced and written and aesthetically it captures a Gothic look and feel well, while the performances on display are generally very strong, especially from Adrien Brody in the lead who is surrounded by a quality supporting cast, particularly Gord Rand and Hugh Thompson as the tormented Minister Burroughs and Constable Dennison, respectively. The culmination of the Minister's storyline is a hard-hitter and one of the overall highlights. I also quite enjoyed the commentaries on organised religion.

It's not perfect, but *Chapelwaite* is most definitely a breath of fresh air in today's entertainment climate and one in which I would personally give a strong recommendation to.

—Trevor Kennedy

DISC

FORTEAN TV: THE COMPLETE SERIES

Front cover for Fortean TV: The Complete Series

Presented by Reverend Lionel Fanthorpe.

"Join Reverend Lionel Fanthorpe for a skate on that thin crust known as reality . . ."

WHENEVER *FORTEAN TV* was originally broadcast on Channel 4 (UK), back when it was still edgy and non-mainstream, from 1997 to '98, it was during the height of a public love and fascination with all things "out there" and *X-Files*-related. Perfect timing, and more than likely no coincidence either, the writers of *The X-Files* reportedly also regularly poring over the pages of *Fortean Times* (itself inspired by the work of writer Charles Fort), of which *Fortean TV* was spawned from. Perhaps, then, *Fortean TV* could be best described as the "Real-life British X-Files".

There are two things that really separate *Fortean TV* from the many other "factual supernatural phenomena" shows that we've seen over the years, however:

1. It never takes itself too seriously, its tongue firmly planted in its cheek, and is a huge amount of fun because of this.

2. It is presented by arguably one of the best presenters in British television history – the Reverend Lionel Fanthorpe, prolific author, weight-lifting and judo champion, preacher, biker, singer, paranormal investigator and so much more! Fanthorpe is extremely likeable, while at same time entertaining, knowledgeable, humorous and an eloquent, fascinating speaker – in short, a complete one-off! His comedy songs at the end of each episode of this new complete series boxed set issued by Network are worth the asking price alone!

The basic premise of each episode sees Father Fanthorpe touring Britain and various other parts of the world investigating strange anomalies and supernatural mysteries, such as reports of ghosts, sea monsters, aliens, vampires, the South American "chupacabra" goat-sucker, mummification, the Missing Link, the Holy Grail (with the rather controversial "Bishop" Seán Manchester – he of "Highgate Vampire" tall tales!), a lady who can speak "cat", medical, animal and foodstuff freaks of nature, an "electric" woman, a haunted old Ford Cortina in Eastbourne, and a mysterious Asda shopping centre check-out till that causes the young women who work behind it to become pregnant!

It's all as barmy and eccentric as it sounds and all the better for it – massively entertaining and a pure cult classic!

Television these days, for the most part, seems to consist mainly of increasingly ridiculous soap operas, moronic, cheap-to-make "reality" drivel, dull dramas, unfunny "comedies", and deeply irritating, idiotic presenters like Ant and Dec and Michael McIntyre. However, I would genuinely rather sit down and watch the good Reverend Fanthorpe read from a telephone directory than have to suffer through any of that dross and would additionally also absolutely *love* for *Fortean TV* to make a return to our small screens, even for a one-off special!

So, if you just so happen to enjoy the wackier side of life and missed *Fortean TV* during its original airing, then give this boxed set a whirl – and even if you did manage to catch it back in the late-'90s, it is most definitely worth revisiting!

A brilliantly bizarre classic.

—**Trevor Kennedy**

GAMES

HALO INFINITE (2021)

Promotional image for Halo Infinite *(2021)*

Writing credits: Dan Chosich, Joe McDonagh, Aaron Linde, Paul Crocker, Jeff Easterling.

Starring Steve Downes, Jen Taylor, Nicolas Roye, Bruce Thomas, Darin De Paul, Ike Amadi and more.

THE LONG AWAITED *Halo Infinite* video game, produced by 343 Industries for the Xbox Series X/S consoles finally made its debut in 2021. And let me add that it has not been a disappointment, unlike its predecessor *Halo: Guardians* (2015). Perhaps there were so many complaints by fans such as myself that just for once someone in the 343 Studio hierarchy listened and delivered a polished product. The moment I pressed start, this science fiction, first person shooter, smacked me right in the face. The opening sequence is simply fantastic. Just here alone I saw improvements that were on the equivalent of the first *Halo: Combat Evolved* (2001).

    Halo, like most first person shooters, has at least two modes: campaign and multiplayer. Campaign being the part where the player can engage deeply into the story right away or partake in side missions. This is my preferred choice. I have little interest in going online and participating in a multiplayer deathmatch, or some capture the flag round. Don't get me wrong, *Halo* in all of its iterations produces a solid product there as well. I'm just more of a story person than someone who likes to rack up the kills or boost his rankings for bragging rights. For me the story mode connects to the overall lore of the Haloverse and that's what I feel as being most important. Without the campaign mode *Halo* might just be an elaborate *Pac-Man*, going around in repetitive maps and doing the same thing over and over again. Thank the Covenant *Halo* knows no such folly.

Here in *Infinite* the saga goes even further. It is so detailed that if you had a problem going on in your life before you began playing it could quite possibly make you forget it. It is literally the closest thing to an Oculus without the headset. It's engrossing and you believe that you are somewhere in the vastness of the cosmos on a Halo ring, created by advanced beings known as the Forerunners. The gameplay is tight. There were no glitches or lag in the multiplayer when I decided to participate in a match. In addition to that, the level of difficulty against bosses is fair this time. You can adjust it to your liking, or rather patience, at any time. I know I did a couple of bosses, maybe three, that were just ridiculous. I wanted those jokers dead so I could proceed further into the game. Doing it this way made it possible to have multiple save points at any difficulty setting to keep players such as myself from getting frustrated.

I play *Halo*, as I indicated earlier, to interact with the story being told. I have no interest in seeing how many times and ways a boss can take me out until I finally figure out the best formula to produce the quickest win. That's so meaningless to me and definitely not worth my $60.00. In the end, I can see that for many the game will provide tons of replay value. I more than likely will play it again when, and if, I have the time to do so.

This is the longest of all *Halo* games and it was very satisfactory. I felt like I got my money's worth and then some. However, it still kind of left me wanting more considering the way it ended. Obviously, there's more on the way, but how much longer will it be for the next game?

I give this game a high old-school rating of 12 quarters.

—Abdul-Qaadir Taariq Bakari-Muhammad

PHANTASMAGORIA FANS' EUPHORIA
(Readers' Comments and Feedback)

Thank you for your flattering introduction in the Special Issue of Phantasmagoria *No.6. First and most importantly: if I've failed to say so already, it
was/is as handsome as any edition which, following Karl Wagner's most exceptional No.5, honored my fiction as warmly and honestly as any other
literary tribute to man or genre ever could have. In short, I found it as much
and more praise than I have ever deserved; so genuinely earnest praise that I
couldn't put it down until each meaningful word had been taken to heart.*

*But then again, whose feelings would fail to be touched on reading these
comments of so many exceptional co-existing or bygone colleagues and
contemporaries? And who would fail to feel so humbled by so much acknow-
ledgement and honest praise – not least from you yourself, Trevor?*

*You are doing a truly terrific job for fantasy fandom, and for me
personally the return – if partial – of so many great memories.*

—Brian Lumley

*A great volume on a true master. Arrived in perfect condition. A great and
thick special issue devoted to a true modern master of horror, Ramsey
Campbell. Some great articles and reviews. Fiction including a real classic
from the man himself. Add to this some truly great artwork, including pieces
by Dave Carson who captures Lovecraftian horrors like no other, and you
have a splendid tome.*

—Stephen G, 5 star Amazon review of
Phantasmagoria Special Edition Series #4: Ramsey Campbell

*"Superb volume. Arrived in perfect condition. I have only recently discovered
this publication. It has it all. Great fiction, informed articles and reviews.
Added to that splendid artwork."*

—Stephen G, 5 star Amazon review of
Phantasmagoria Special Edition Series #3: M.R. James

ACKNOWLEDGEMENTS

Illustration by Allen Koszowski

THE PUBLISHER HAS made every effort to source and credit the copyright details of all the photographic material, artworks and other material used in this publication, and adhering to the "fair use" policy of using film images for critiquing purposes. The publisher would be pleased to correct any errors or omissions, if contacted: tkboss@hotmail.com.

All book/film cover/poster/advertisement images used within *Phantasmagoria Magazine* issue 21 copyright © the relevant artists/publishers/studios etc.
Page 1: 'Can Such Things Be' frontispiece artwork copyright © Randy Broecker 2001, originally for *Can Such Things Be?* by Keith Fleming (Sarob Press).
Pages 3, 4, 8, 17, 22, 53, 120, 121, 166, 209, 237, 238, 239 (with "The joey Zone"), 268, 282, 284, 287 and 288: Artworks copyright © Allen Koszowski.
Pages 5, 7, 109, 115, 116, 190, 199, 241, 277, 285 and 290: Artworks copyright © Jim Pitts.
Pages 10, 12, 70, 75, 78, 82, 123, 174 and 184: Artworks copyright © Dave Carson.
Page 11: 'Editorial Notes: Introducing Our New Website' copyright © Trevor Kennedy 2023.
Page 14: Artwork   copyright © Andrew Smith, originally for the story 'Berryhill' by R. A. Lafferty, published in *Whispers* #9.

Illustration by Allen Koszowski

'H.P. Lovecraft's The Strange High House in the Mist' by Jim Pitts

Printed in Great Britain
by Amazon

19333563R00167